TOO FAST

Developmental Editing by Melanie Yu, Made Me Blush Books
Line Editing, Copyediting, and Proofreading by VB Edits
Cover Design © Silver at Bitter Sage Designs

Contents

To the readers who read Too Safe, considered three hot-as-hell football players, then decided they wanted the Stats Daddy instead: This one is for you.

Content Warning

Too Fast contains content some may find triggering, including on page panic attacks, kidnapping, hospitalization, mentions of past abuse/child neglect, detailed description of past sexual assault of FMC (chapters 20-25), discussion of death of a parent and grief, violence by way of revenge, and chronic illness.

Boys will be boys

Whispers of what happened;
Truths I'll never know.
"Boys will be boys," they say.
A thin, hollow echo.

The sky didn't take me then.
The water won't help me now.
Treading,
Slipping,
Sinking.

A fresh start obliterated
Before I had the chance to shine.
In a gutter,
Below the surface.
On the boat,
Beneath the shallows.

I can swim.
I can flee.
I can't swim.
Never free.

The Texts

MONDAY MORNING
THE BOYS

Locke: Any updates?

Cap: None. No one in South Chapel is talking. Greedy still hasn't called back or even acknowledged my voicemail.

Kendrick: We gotta let these kids off the boats, Cap

Cap: No. Keep questioning them. Someone has to know something.

Locke: It's getting tense. Kyl has checked every phone on every yacht. Kendrick's right. We can't keep them forever

Cap: What do you think, Kyl?

LOCKE TO CAP

Locke: He's spiraling

KENDRICK TO CAP

Kendrick: Kylian's not okay. Locke's really not okay. He needs rest. We all do, man. Come home and we'll regroup

TUESDAY
LOCKE TO CAP

Locke: He won't take his meds

Cap: Tell him to call me. I'll talk to him.

Locke: He says he doesn't want to talk. He has to stay focused

KENDRICK TO CAP

Kendrick: You coming back here tonight?

Kendrick: Kyl isn't listening. Locke can't get through to him

CAP TO KYLIAN

Cap: Take your meds, Kylian.

LATER

Cap: You good?

LATER

Cap: I can't focus on what I'm doing out here if I think you're not okay.

LATER

Cap: Kylian, I'm serious. I'm going to come check on you myself if you can't take your meds. Is that what you want? You want me to stop looking for her so I can come home and take care of you instead?

Kylian: Done.

WEDNESDAY
THE BOYS

Locke: Joey's uncle is asking questions

Cap: How do you know?

Locke: He called the police. Kendrick's pops just called to ask him about it. Guess he knows her name since the girls have met her

LOCKE TO CAP

Locke: He still hasn't slept

Cap: He said he took his meds?

Locke: Yeah. He told us the same

THE BOYS

Cap: Hunter's with her. Lake Chapel General. Heading there now.

Kylian: I'll meet you there.

CAP TO KENDRICK AND LOCKE:

Cap: She's been admitted. Hunter wouldn't tell me anything else. Keep him home.

Kendrick: You serious?

Locke: Easier said than done...

Cap: I don't know what I'm walking into.

Kendrick: Pretty sure he's already on his way

Chapter 1

Decker

"Who else can I speak to?" I insist, planting my hands on the counter of the nurses' station and leaning in until my knuckles are white.

It's been sixty-one hours. Two and a half days. Might as well have been a lifetime.

I haven't eaten. Haven't slept.

Hardly remembered how to breathe or hold myself upright until Hunter called.

"We've got her. Lake Chapel General. Third floor."

She didn't elaborate. She didn't bother with any assurances. It would have been a pointless exercise. No one needs to tell me how epically not okay this all is.

"How about a supervisor?" I press. "An administrator? Someone in fundraising." I stare her down. Hard.

She knows who I am. Everyone in this goddamn town knows who I am. Rarely does my reputation get me nowhere. But here...

The nurse examines me warily. I don't blame her for the distrust she's struggling to mask. If she's worried I'm on the verge of causing a scene, she has good reason. I'm not backing down. She can either make this easy, or I can make her job infinitely harder than it needs to be.

"Please," I add, my voice hoarse with exhaustion and desperation.

Something about that single word makes her expression soften just a fraction.

"Let me make a few calls," she placates, spinning in her chair to pick up a phone at the next workstation.

I drum my fingers on the beige-speckled countertop, the surplus of caffeine and a renewed adrenaline fueling me in all the wrong ways. Every noise makes me jump. Every sound scratches against the surface of my brain. I'm barely holding it together.

My phone buzzes in my back pocket—again. It's been vibrating non-stop for the last hour. Ever since we got word that Josephine was in the hospital.

I can guess at the questions waiting for me on the screen.

I just don't know who's sending them this time.

With a long exhale, I force back some of the panic threatening to take over and slide the phone out of my pocket.

Kylian: How is she? What's the room number?

God dammit. How the hell can I mollify him if he shows up here before I even get back to see her?

I haven't slept in a solid three days. I'm exhausted—mentally whipped—but my current state is nothing compared to Kylian's. He's run himself ragged over the last two and a half days. He hasn't slept; hasn't stopped. He's a flurry of activity, and he's been trapped in an agitated, hyper-fixated state of awareness since the second I screamed his name across the lake on Sunday night. He's off his meds. He's on the precipice of spiraling out of reach.

I reply quickly, because even though I don't have answers, leaving him in the dark will just make it worse.

Decker: Waiting to see her now. I'll text as soon as I know more.

"Decker!"

My head snaps up, and the air whooshes out of my lungs like I've taken a hit to the sternum when Hunter calls my name. She's half jogging down the hall, blond curls bouncing on her shoulders despite the exhausted pull around her eyes.

"Hey," she breathes, extending her hand and running it along the length of my arm. "You made it."

I made it.

As if I've arrived at a barbeque and they've been waiting on me to bring more ice.

"Where is she?" I demand, my tone harsher than intended.

Hunter recoils.

Shit. I run a hand through my hair and try again. "Can you take me to her? Please?" I add for good measure.

Hunter darts a look at the nurses' station. It's just a quick flick of her eyes, but it's a hesitation, nonetheless.

"Follow me," she murmurs, looping her arm through mine and pulling me toward an alcove full of vending machines.

Her pace is slow, languid, even, as if she's in no rush at all. I'm teeming with restless energy, my exhaustion fueling—absurdly—the desperation coursing through my veins.

Someone needs to pay for this. Someone *will* pay.

Before Hunter is fully facing me, I pin her against a soda machine and bracket her head with my arms. She's so petite she barely reaches my shoulder, but she doesn't startle at the move. She only matches my livid gaze.

"If I find out you had *anything* to do with this—"

I haven't even articulated the threat before she's rolling her eyes.

"Save your breath, Crusade. You know damn well I have exactly one friend in this town nowadays, and right now, she's lying in a hospital bed because of your antiquated big dick rivalry."

Heart pounding wildly against my ribcage, I search her face, seeking the lie. She doesn't shrink under my gaze.

If anything, she looks defeated in the worst way. Eyes hollow, cheeks sunken and pale. As if she hasn't slept for three days, either. As if the emotions raging inside me—the anger, the fear, the anxiety, the frustration—are raging inside her, too.

After another breath, I look away. Fuck. She didn't have anything to do with this. Not if the wariness in her eyes and the weight pressing on her shoulders are anything to go by.

Lowering my arms, I blow out a long breath and prop myself up against the opposite wall.

"Take me to her."

Hunter stands tall, crossing her arms around herself and pursing her lips.

"I will. But there are a few things you need to understand before we go back there."

"Hunter," I warn.

"We only have permission to be with her because Dr. Ferguson spoke directly to the nurses on this floor," she starts, giving me a pointed look. "Otherwise, we'd be waiting out there." She points toward the waiting area near the nurses' station.

We?

Before I can ask, she continues.

"She's been sleeping a lot. They had to sedate her when she arrived. Even now that they've weaned her off those meds, she's groggy and exhausted. Every time she wakes up—"

"Is she hurt?" I demand.

I'm still in the dark. What happened? What did they do? Is she okay? *Fuck.*

Wrenching my hands through the ends of my hair, I pace the three steps it takes for me to get from one side of the alcove to the next and focus on calming my breathing.

I can't remember a time I felt this unhinged. This out of control. This... helpless.

"Bruises. Scratches. Based on what she remembers and what the guys told Greedy—"

At those last couple of words, I see red—deep crimson, the blood of every person involved in taking her, using her, hurting her.

I'm up in Hunter's face before I can temper the impulse.

"If your brother and his South Chapel goons—"

She shoves her palms into my chest to silence me.

"He's *not* my brother."

When a rumble rolls through my chest at her response, she pushes against me again. She's not strong enough to move me, but I take a couple of steps back and give her space.

We stare each other down, chests heaving. Hunter's not the enemy, and the only way I'm getting to Josephine is through her, it seems. So I have to play nice.

Shuttering my eyes, I take a deep breath and start again. "Look, I'm sorry. I've been going out of my goddamn mind—"

"It's fine," she replies weakly, sweeping her hair over one shoulder and twirling the ends. "I get it. But we're on the same side here. Just... just try to keep it together. You flying off the handle in that room is *not* going to win us any favor with the nurses."

I nod, accepting the chastisement for what it is. If I'm here by the grace of her and Dr. Ferguson, her stepfather, there's no way I'll throw away this shot.

Hunter continues. "She's not seriously injured. Everything..." She licks her lips and swallows thickly. "She did it all to herself, Decker."

My heart stutters, then beats so hard I worry it'll crack my ribs. But I can't get a single word out. Can't articulate a single question.

Tilting her head and examining me, Hunter murmurs, "Breathe. Not like that. Not on purpose. She hurt herself trying to get away from them. She told me..."

Hunter trails off as she inhales a shuddering breath.

"Please. Hunter. Tell me what happened. Tell me how I can help."

Wrapping her arms around her body again, she closes her eyes. "She told me that what happened on Sunday triggered her. She lived through some kind of trauma when she was in high school—I don't know any details," she insists as she meets my gaze, "but whatever the South Chapel guys did set her off in the worst way."

Josephine alluded to the experience the night we shared a hotel room.

That far-off look of panic in her expression. The grip of fear that was palpable as she stood before me, wilting in front of my eyes.

In that hotel room alone with her all those days ago, I really saw her for the first time. Her strength. Her resilience. The ruthless, unapologetic decision to fight, to survive, to live.

I recognized it, because it was the same choice I was forced to make after my mom died. She's been hurt. Irrevocably changed. But she's worked hard to rise above. Whatever she survived, she refused to let it define her.

If what they did on Sunday night had the power to set her back or send her to a dark, hopeless place...

"I need to see her." My voice cracks. "Hunter... please."

Nodding, she ducks around me into the brightly lit hospital hall. A glance over her shoulder and a quick wave are all it takes to get me moving.

I whip out my phone and send off a text to the group as I hurry to catch up.

Cap: Headed to her room now. Will update ASAP.

"There's one more thing you need to know."

In my periphery, she grimaces.

"She doesn't want to be alone. At all. We've been taking turns, staying with her around the clock."

There it is again.

We.

Hunter's not the only one who's been taking care of my girl.

She stops in the middle of the hallway, placing her hand on my arm and squeezing. "Do *not* overreact or make this a thing, Decker," she warns. "It'll only upset her more."

Her words have barely registered when the door on the left opens and a man backs out of the room. He holds on to the handle and pulls it shut in slow motion, taking care to release it at a glacial pace so it doesn't make a sound.

When he turns, I see red.

The deepest crimson. The blood of my enemy. The blood in his veins.

Turning from the door with a satisfied smirk plastered on his face is none other than Greedy Ferguson.

Chapter 2

Decker

"*You.*"

The word is a curse as I charge for him without hesitation. Greedy's eyes go wide, then he's spinning out of the pocket and across the hall before I can reach him. Hunter hisses behind me, trying to call me off, but it's useless. A second later, she grasps my raised arm, the touch barely registering against the blind, vengeful rage coursing through my veins.

I'm fully prepared to shake off her hold and smash my fist into Greedy Ferguson's face.

"Crusade!"

Hunter's admonishment isn't enough to stop me in my tracks. But what she says next is.

"Decker—Stop. You can't hurt him without hurting her. Joey thinks Greedy saved her."

I whip my head around so fast my neck cracks.

"*Saved* her? What the fuck are you talking about?" My demand is directed at Hunter first, then at the man of the hour. My jaw ticks incessantly, and the blood whooshing in my ears is so loud I'm sure they can both hear it.

Tension thrums between them as they turn to one another and have a silent conversation I can't interpret. Eventually, Hunter raises her perfectly arched eyebrows, and Greedy sighs.

"I'm the one who found her. Who pulled her out of the back of the truck. I was with her when she came to on Monday," he explains, back pressed against the wall behind him and his arms crossed over his broad chest. "I brought her in immediately."

Head spinning, I force myself to lean against the opposite wall. There's a pain that's blossomed in my chest that has no focal point. It's heartache and confusion and grief, all braided together into a battle rope heavy enough to weigh me down and crush me.

"She's been here since Monday?" I croak out, turning to Hunter. "The fuck?"

"I didn't know anything until a few hours ago," she says softly.

Bullshit.

"And why's that?" I turn my ire back on Greedy. "Because you didn't think to tell your sister you were chilling at the hospital with her best friend? For two days?"

"*Step*sister," Hunter mutters. She's standing smack in the middle of the hall, directly under the bright fluorescent panel of lights I swear I can hear buzzing.

The asshole across from me stands up straighter, jutting his chin toward me.

"I had no idea who Joze was until last night. Bible." He holds up both hands, as if his word is worth shit to me. "I knew she had to be important to you or one of your boys since they targeted her, but that's it. I figured she was a cheerleader or somebody's girlfriend. It wasn't until she connected the dots for me this morning that I even realized Joze knew Hunter," he offers, nodding to his stepsister.

"Bullshit," I snarl, fire igniting in my gut and licking up my insides.

"I thought so, too," Hunter pipes up. "But he has no reason to lie about this."

I snap my attention to her, and she meets it head-on.

"They only met once," she offers with a shrug.

"And it was barely a meeting. Hunter couldn't wait to get away from me that day," Greedy begrudges, his jaw clenched so tight he could give me a run for my money.

It all sounds too coincidental, too contrived, but my gut says Hunter is trustworthy. Even if she's not, my girl's in that room, and these two are standing like sentries, keeping me from getting to her.

I have to tread lightly if I'm going to uncover the truth and identify exactly who needs to pay. For now, I need to see her. Take her home. Make sure the guys are okay. Restore some sense of order to our world.

"Hold on," I mumble, remembering for the first time that the boys are waiting for me to send an update.

Cap: I still haven't seen her, but the report is that she's physically unharmed. Still trying to figure out wtf is going on. I'll let you know when I know more.

Kylian: What room? No one will tell me anything out here. I can't even find her in the system.

Fuck. He *would* try to hack into the hospital database.

"Is she here under a fake name?" I ask.

Greedy nods. "She's listed as Jane Doe on the patient manifest. Like I said—I didn't know who she was when I brought her in."

Sighing, I accept that his version of the story is the only version I'm going to get for now.

Cap: Cool it, Kyl. I'll come find you as soon as I can. What floor are you on?

I take a breath, then another, feeling completely underqualified to be dealing with all of this, even if I am desperate for answers and vindication.

Not for the first time in the last three days, I wish I had my boys by my side. I hate going this alone. I'm out of my depth, and I have no one to blame for that but myself.

Originally, they stayed behind to deal with the charter cruises. We all assumed we'd sort all this shit out and have Josephine home before sunrise on Monday morning.

When it became clear that things weren't going to play out that way, though, I panicked.

I demanded they stay back. Told them they had to stay on the boats—keep all the attendees together until we had answers.

Don't let them get you to the second location.

Isn't that the warning the experts tout? Someone on the boats had to know something, and we could force them to talk by keeping them from leaving.

Or so I thought. Fucking stupid, now that I think about it.

Maybe I was trying to play the hero, or maybe I just needed to control some aspect of the situation.

I've made more than one wrong call in the last sixty-plus hours. I just never thought it'd take this long. Or that it'd come to this.

"Who was it, and what did they do to her?" I finally grit out. I keep my focus locked on my phone while my imagination runs wild. If I don't, I'm liable to do something I might regret later.

The rivalry between the Lake Chapel and South Chapel teams has always run deep, but the pranks over the last several years have been more mild and good-natured. I never thought something like this could happen on my watch.

Greedy clears his throat and stands taller. "What they did was not sanctioned by me, my boys, or anyone else on the team. It was three underclassmen, one of which is the son of a guy who played ball for South Chapel in the '80s. They said they were taking it upon themselves to revive the rivalry to its full glory. They're nobodies. Second-string fuckers who have no idea how badly they're going to pay."

I grunt my approval. At least we agree on that.

"They also claim they didn't actually *do* anything. According to them, Joze lost consciousness within minutes of boarding their boat. She was out of it almost the entire time they had her."

Hunter squeaks out a startled whimper. Shit. Sounds like she hasn't been filled in on all the details yet, either.

Greedy glances at his stepsister, his eyes swimming with concern as he scratches at his neck. "They made sure she was breathing, but they couldn't get her to come to. I don't know what their plans were..." Greedy trails off.

One hand gripping my phone so tightly I wouldn't be surprised if I cracked the screen, the other fisted at my side, I study Greedy's expression.

He knows, just like I do.

We may not know to what extent. How far. How many. How long.

But we both fucking know.

I can't ask. Not in front of Hunter. Not when the answer has the power to send me to my knees.

Meeting my gaze, he glowers, but the look lacks the typical ire we reserve for one another. I wait with bated breath for what feels like a lifetime before he finally shakes his head twice in response to the question I refuse to speak into existence.

Relief floods my system. Fuck. For now, I'll cling to the hope that his version of the truth aligns with Josephine's experience. If they did anything to harm her—

"I believe them. They're too dumb to have come up with any sort of contingency plan once things went off script. They panicked and immediately texted a few guys on the team. I stepped up the second I knew what they had done. I swear to you both. As soon as I got there—"

"Where?"

"South Marina."

Dumbasses. They didn't even get out of the fucking parking lot?

"I brought her here immediately. She was dehydrated and not fully lucid, so they kept her sedated through Monday and Tuesday. She's been better today."

My phone vibrates in my pocket. Again.

Kylian: Update?

He's relentless. Always has been. In a lot of scenarios, his dedication works to our advantage, but this is next level, even for him.

Cap: Still haven't seen her. Stay put. I'll keep you posted.

I can only imagine the fury consuming him at the lack of updates. But I can't just shoot him a text telling him I'm having a casual chat with the quarterback of our biggest rivals, a man who's somehow embroiled in this situation right along with us.

Kylian's off his meds, short tempered, sleep-deprived, and not thinking clearly. I have to protect him. I also have to protect her.

That last thought nags at me. It's the truth of what hasn't quite evolved between me and the girl just beyond the hospital room door. We haven't had a chance—haven't had enough time. Dammit. Why didn't I do more sooner? Why didn't I act on my impulses? Tell her exactly what I was feeling. She should already be mine.

Now, though... *fuck*.

Now it's all fucked.

She's already picked him—or them, maybe—and I don't stand a fucking chance when all I've done is drag her into not one, but two pseudo-kidnappings.

"I still don't understand why it took so fucking long for me to get a phone call," I grit out, holding the device in the air to emphasize my point.

"She wasn't really lucid until this morning, but once she was, she recognized me and connected the dots. I called Hunter immediately, then she texted you, and here we all are. One happy little family," Greedy declares sarcastically.

The glare I level him with is akin to the kind I get from an entire defensive line just before the snap. What I wouldn't give to try my hand on defense right now. If only for the chance to get a few good hits and take him down.

"Sunday night," I say. "I called you the second I received the text from the unknown number. Some kid answered your phone—Pierre?"

With a slight tilt of his head, Greedy blunders. "This past Sunday?"

"Yes, this past Sunday. Three days ago. When I called your number and very clearly said 'where the fuck is my girl?'"

"Huh." Pulling out his phone, he taps the screen and scrolls. When his eyes lift to meet mine, he offers a sympathetic shrug.

"I see your name here now," he flashes the screen in my direction, "but Pierre didn't mention it. It's Shore Week, bro. He probably assumed you were trying to pull a prank of your own."

"Bullshit," I bite out.

"Bible," Greedy counters, holding up both hands as if he's sharing the gospel truth.

Asshole wouldn't admit to knowingly keeping her from me anyway.

Changing course, I try a different line of questioning.

"So if you had nothing to do with this, and you say the people involved are going to pay, then where are they now?"

He meets my gaze, lifting both brows. Likely ready to play dumb or argue. That's been his MO so far today. Deny. Deflect. Keep the upper hand. Don't give anything away.

A satisfied smirk creeps across his face. "Waiting for their captain to come dish out a punishment suitable for the crime. They've been ordered to stay in the field house, and they've been there since Monday."

His response shocks the shit out of me.

A wider smirk blooms across his face, and I have to resist the urge to match it with my own.

"What they did was wrong, no matter who she is." He waves a hand at the door to Josephine's room. "We aren't dealing with the brightest bulbs in the South Chapel locker room here. If I had to wager, I'd guess they weren't of sound mind, though that's no excuse. They *will* pay. I'll make sure of it, and I'll even extend the invitation your way when the time comes."

Satisfied, I nod, but before I can ask my next question, he continues.

"What they did was wrong, but Joze's reaction was... intense. Too intense."

Frowning, Greedy scrutinizes me, obviously questioning why this ordeal was so much heavier and overwhelming than it should have been.

In my periphery, Hunter's doing the same. I can practically feel her eyes boring into the side of my head.

I don't have the answers they seek. I don't know the what, but I do know there's something in Josephine's past that keeps her alert and constantly on edge. She practically unraveled in front of me in the hotel room at the last away game. If her fight-or-flight response kicked in when they took her, and her brain thought she was in actual danger...

"Where is she?"

My head snaps up and my back stiffens as Kylian flies down the hall. He's the leanest of us by far, but right now he's larger than life.

His hair is sticking up on end. His glasses are sliding off his nose. He's a man on the edge.

"What the fuck is he doing here?" he demands as he barrels into my space, his eyes flitting from Greedy to me, then back to Greedy again.

The rage radiating off him is so palpable I can taste it.

"You three are just out here in the hall doing what? Having a fucking tea party?" Beside me, he tenses even further and lunges forward.

I whirl around fast enough to catch his fist, but barely. Bracing one arm across his shoulders, I hold on tight as he bucks and thrashes. It takes a surprising amount of strength to restrain him.

"Chill the fuck out, Kyl."

"No," he counters, rocking back and forth against my hold. "Fuck no! Let me go!"

Locke and Kendrick said it was bad, but Jesus. This is on another level.

A sharp elbow up and under my ribs knocks me off balance and loosens my grip. The move gives him the second of freedom he needs to spin out of my hold, duck behind my back, and reach for the door I haven't even had a chance to confirm belongs to her.

He's through it one second later.

Frozen, I look from the open door to Hunter and Greedy—who are also stunned and unmoving—then back again.

There's no point holding court in the hallway now. Not with the door wide open. And although I've kept my panic reined in tight, the uneasiness rolling off Kylian matches the sense of dread settled in my gut.

I won't be okay until I see her, either.

Phone still in hand, I shoot off a quick text, this time to Locke alone. He's best equipped to navigate this kind of scenario.He'HE

Cap: Kylian just showed up. I need backup. Now. Third floor, room 3112.

Locke: In the parking garage

Wordlessly, I lumber to the door and hold it open for Hunter. Greedy also ducks under my arm—*fucker*—with a hand resting on the small of his stepsister's back.

I follow, my ears prickling at the unmistakable softness in Kylian's voice.

Fuck. Is he trying to wake her up?

Ready to demand he let her rest, I grasp his arm, but before I can yank him away, the thin hospital bed blanket rustles. She sits up, squinting against the dim glow of the computer monitors.

Blinking, Josephine focuses on me, not a hint of recognition in her expression. Almost as if she's in a dream state. She blinks again, then yawns, coming to a bit more.

On her next breath, her eyes grow wide and her jaw goes rigid.

She looks at me again, then to Kylian, her eyes darting between us as if she isn't sure who we are or why we're here. Finally, I swear I see a flame of recognition ignite in her gray-blue eyes. It's fragile and tentative, but it's there.

A croak of a whisper breaks the silence.

"Greedy... where's Greedy?"

Her voice breaks when she says his name a second time, and I swear to god my chest cracks open.

"I'm here, Joze," he murmurs, stepping toward the bed as if he belongs by her side.

I keep my disdain locked down and buried.

Kylian lets his rage.

"Get away from her," he snarls, throwing an elbow out in front of Greedy to wedge himself between the asshole's hovering form and Josephine's bed. "Don't you fucking *touch* her."

The slightest whimper escapes our girl, dragging my attention back to her. She looks drained, both physically and emotionally. Her eyes swim with exhaustion, and that recognition that ignited a moment ago is now a barely there flicker on the verge of being snuffed out.

"Calm your boy," Greedy shoots at me, perching on the end of Josephine's bed. He covers her hand with his while simultaneously holding out his other arm as if he can block Kylian's verbal assault with physical force.

"Jo! Jo, look at me." Kylian's desperate, his voice raspy and full of agony.

She's not fully with it right now. She's awake, but she's not rested or clear-headed. If she's still in survival mode... or just trying to cope...

"Jo."

It's a broken whisper, one filled with frustration and defeat.

Her eyes fill with unshed tears as she slow blinks, then refocuses on Greedy.

The room is buzzing with tension and resistance as we each stand our ground.

Finally, Hunter speaks up and ends the stand-off.

"Let's give her a minute. Could you imagine being woken from a drug-induced sleep to a room full of arguing football players?" She lets out an uncomfortable laugh in a too-obvious attempt to lighten the mood. Then, to me, she adds, "Go. He's not helping, and she's not going anywhere. You've seen her and you know she's okay. I'll stay with them."

Dammit. I don't want to leave her. I just fucking got here. But Hunter's right. Kylian can't cope. And I need to do what's best for him right now.

A quick glance back at Josephine bolsters that decision. Right now, I'm not what she needs. Her eyes are locked on Greedy's. He's murmuring words I can't hear, and she's nodding along.

She's not smiling, which selfishly soothes my ego. But she's not looking at him with disdain or panic, either.

Shaking my head, I lay down my defenses and give up the fight. For now.

Cuffing Kylian on the back of the neck, I lead him toward the door. "Come on. The guys are waiting for an update." Before he can protest, I add, "We'll come back in one hour. One hour to cool down and regroup. Then we'll figure out what's next."

I flick my gaze to Hunter. She nods, clearly aware that my warning is for her as much as for him. I don't bother looking back at Josephine. I'm not interested in witnessing any more of the scene. Of the way Greedy is comforting her. Of the reminder that I'm not what she wants or needs.

I march forward and keep my eyes locked in on Kylian's head. If I look back now, I won't find the resolve to walk out the door.

Chapter 3

Decker

"Hunter says he helped her. *Saved* her even. Brought her here."

Like a broken record, I'm repeating every detail I know. It's almost not worth the frustration that rises up each time I try to make sense of it aloud.

I'm not the only one rankled by Greedy's presence and Josephine's lackluster acknowledgment.

Kylian's pacing.

Kendrick's brooding.

Locke's bouncing his knee, alternating between cracking his knuckles and turning his neck from side to side until it pops.

"Fifty-six," Kylian informs us on his next pass, attention glued to his phone.

We said we'd give her an hour. If anyone expected any kind of buffer to that countdown, they're going to be disappointed. Kylian's been watching the clock on his phone so intently I'm not sure he's even blinked.

"So what's the plan?" Locke asks.

He looks at me, as they all so often do, but I'm at a loss. After the way Josephine basically recoiled when she saw us in her room... *fuck*. Knowing I caused her to react like that sends another kind of ache through me.

Josephine was taken, injured, admitted to the hospital, all because of her association with us. With me. To be the root cause of this situation, then to make it worse for her just by being near...

God dammit. This is all me. It's on me. It happened because of me. The South Chapel asshats who took her did so to get to me—because they've seen us together, or they know she lives at the house.

The injustice of the scenario is cruel. She was only in that position because I forced her into it in the first place.

Any way it breaks down, this is my mess. My problem. My responsibility.

"We owe it to Josephine to get her out of here and help her work through any... fallout from this whole ordeal."

I have no idea what that'll entail, but I'll see to it that Josephine wants for nothing and has every resource she needs to move past the trauma. Care. Counseling. Extra time for her school assignments. Financial support. There's nothing I won't do or give her, and yet it won't be enough. It could never be enough.

"She's here—in a damn hospital, recovering from who the fuck knows what—because those South Chapel douches thought they could get to us through her." Fisting my hands on my thighs, I suck in a deep breath to rein in the fury threatening to overtake me. "I don't care what Greedy says or what sort of savior role he thinks he's going to play. We need to get her out of here and get her home. Do whatever it takes to make this up to her. Then kick their asses and hand them their teeth on the field on Saturday."

Kylian grunts his approval, and Locke nods in agreement.

"You know his pops is big-time around here," Kendrick offers, his elbows on his knees and one brow cocked at me.

That he is. I looked up Dr. Ferguson's information on the hospital website when I arrived. He's the chief physician at Lake Chapel General. Sounds more like an administrative gig, but still.

I eye Kendrick warily. This could go one of several ways with him. I knew he would be the hard sell. He'd like nothing better than to be done with Josephine and the fiasco that his text message started in the first place. We all know it.

He doesn't know the extent of what she did for me a few weekends ago, though. Or what's transpired between us since then.

The realization slams into me with the force of a roughing the player penalty hit.

She's changed me.

She's changed us.

In the weeks we've known her, she's changed at least three of us in unexpected ways.

Even more surprising: I don't want to go back to how things were before.

I want her fire. Her playfulness. Her sass. Her spark.

She calms Kylian like no one ever has.

She lifts up Locke when he's down, peeling back the layers of pain and resentment he wears like armor.

She pushes me, tests the limits of my patience, and obliterates my sense of control. Who I am, how I carry myself, takes on a different shape when she's near. I'm a rubber band that's been stretched a little too far. Paint that's been watered down until it's a different color completely.

When I'm with her, I'm practically unrecognizable to myself. I should hate it. I should want nothing more than to get her out of our lives for good and forget she even exists.

Only I want the complete opposite. That's the truth I'm beginning to accept. She's worked her way into parts of me I didn't think existed anymore. Warm parts. Soft parts. Emotions I've never experienced before bubble to the surface when I'm with her. That alone has significant implications.

Dr. Ferguson's position has surely influenced the level of care Josephine is receiving. And probably the blind eye that's been turned at the number of non-blood related visitors in and out of her room.

"You're sure this isn't part of some bigger scheme to get in our heads before the game on Saturday?"

I hold Kendrick's gaze, searching for the heart of his question. Is he concerned about Greedy and Hunter pulling one over on us, or is he looking for any excuse to get rid of the girl?

"I'm not sure," I admit. "But we've been a fucking mess since she went missing. All of us. I can't even imagine what she's been through or how this is going to play out. If we have a chance to get her back and make this right, we need to take it."

"Fifty-nine," Kylian declares, pocketing his phone. "It took thirty-eight seconds to walk from her room to here. I'm going back now, and none of you are going to stop me."

His delivery is eerily calm and authoritative, albeit unnecessary. We all know better than to push. He's clearly a man on the edge—none of us want to watch him tumble.

"I'm going, too," Locke announces, rising to his feet. He stretches his arms overhead and winces. He tries to cover the reaction, tries to hide the pain. It's useless. I know him too well not to gauge his pain level from that move alone. But I'll let him conceal it for now. He knows damn well we'd all try to convince him to rest if he was up front about it. Three days until game day, and we're a mess.

I stand as well, looking from Kyl to Locke, then warily at Kendrick.

Hands still on his knees, he bows his head in a seemingly silent prayer. When he sits up and meets my gaze, his intentions are etched in every line of his face.

Without a word, I hold out a hand and pull him to his feet, slapping him on the shoulder once he's upright.

"K, you don't have to come with us if you—"

Kendrick cuts off Locke with a menacing glare.

"Is she your girl?"

Locke's eyes widen, and he shoots a look at Kylian, then me. "Well, she..."

"She's my girl," Kylian declares as his phone alarm blares. He holds it up for emphasis before silencing it. The hour's up. "She's his girl, too," he adds, jutting his chin toward Locke.

He doesn't bother looking my way. I can't make any sort of claim on her. At least not yet.

"Well, you're my boys," Kendrick reasons, nodding at me. "All of you. We're a family. And family protects their own. Let's go get our girl."

Chapter 4

Josephine

Intense onyx black. Cool cerulean blue. Warm, comforting hazel. Heated espresso brown.

Their gazes bore into me with simmering intensity. Barely blinking, they form a semi-circle around my hospital bed, all crossed arms and surly expressions.

It would be funny if the room wasn't stifling with tension.

Hunter and Greedy are here, too. Just like they have been all afternoon.

I've never experienced such a profound sense of relief as I did when Hunter walked through the door a few hours ago.

It was only slightly more comforting than when Greedy pulled me out of the truck bed the asshole South Chapel players had kept me in.

Thankfully, I remember very few details of what occurred after I stepped off the yacht on Sunday night or the events of Monday morning. Though Greedy has filled in many of the blanks and has helped me piece together the timeline.

He showed me an immense amount of care and kindness, even before he knew who I was. That's the hallmark of a good human in my eyes. Treating a person with compassion, regardless of who they are or where they're from.

That instinct is in stark contrast to how I first came to know the guys from Lake Chapel.

My guys.

The four scowling men surrounding my hospital bed.

I'm happy to see them. Relieved. Calmed, even. At least on the surface. But there's a rampant uneasiness still humming through my veins. It's leftover adrenaline. It's the aftershocks of being taken and held captive. First by them, and then by their enemies.

What's transpired between me and Locke, and Kylian, and even Decker—physical connections, intimate moments, and maybe even something deeper—doesn't change how I came to live at the Crusade Mansion. Or why I'm lying in a hospital bed now.

I focus on Decker first, drawn in by the frazzled energy radiating from him. It's so uncharacteristic for him.

My eyes find Kylian's next.

"You look awful," he declares, his bottom lip wobbling.

I'm not offended by his bluntness—I never am—but I'm struck by the blistering concern in his expression. So much so that I'm suddenly compelled to comfort *him*. I've been wrapped up in keeping my own head above water since they started weaning me off the sedative early this morning. Until now, I haven't even considered how each of the guys may have been affected by my disappearance on Sunday night, Kylian most of all.

"Can I—"

He doesn't have to finish the sentence. I'm already nodding and shifting to the side of the bed to make room.

His movements are frenzied, a desperation humming between us as he climbs into the bed and awkwardly wraps me in a hug.

He engulfs my shoulders as I bury my face in his chest. A silent sob rips through me. Though no noise comes out, the sorrow connected to it spans from my throat all the way to the pit of my stomach.

Kylian says nothing as he holds me, but he doesn't have to. The scent of him—citrus and eucalyptus—and the familiarity of his touch are all the calm I need. They're enough to immediately slow my breathing and to soothe the frayed nerves that have been shooting off rapid-fire intrusive thoughts for hours. For the first time in days, those notions have settled like silt on the bottom of the lake. I didn't know how much I needed him until this moment.

A throat clears somewhere in the room, and it's then that I remember we have an audience. An audience waiting for answers.

"I'm sorry," I murmur, first into Kylian's chest, then again to Decker, who's gripping the frame at the foot of the bed. "I'm sorry for how I reacted when you first came in."

Decker shakes his head, dismissing my apology. Ever the protector trying to shield me from any additional pain.

Even if he doesn't need an explanation, Kylian does. "Every time I wake up, I'm back there..." I trail off and leave it at that. Warily scanning the room, I find all eyes on me.

Kylian nuzzles into my neck, his lips warm when they find the soft skin below my ear. "You're okay," he murmurs. He kisses me, brushing his mouth against my skin with a timidness I'm not used to with him. "You're okay," he repeats, his assurances as much for himself as they are for me, I realize.

"I'm not," I object, pulling back until I can catch his gaze. "Not yet. Every time I wake up, I'm in a daze. Then the panic sets in. When you came in here earlier, that's what happened. I saw you, but I wasn't really seeing you. I was... I was back there. I was seeing *them*."

He nods and drops one hand from my shoulder, fisting it and averting his focus from my face.

"God dammit. This can't stand."

My heart lurches, and I'm pretty sure my jaw drops at the outburst that comes from the last person I'd expect to have my back.

"They fucked with the wrong girl," Kendrick announces, crossing his massive arms over his chest as he homes in on me. He's studying me in a way he never has before. The look is intense and totally disarming.

My shoulders sag, and my posture loosens as I shrink under his assessment. Like my body doesn't know how to handle the scrutiny. It's a completely foreign experience.

"We need to regroup, then we strike back. This can't stand," Kendrick repeats, turning to Decker, then glaring at Greedy.

"I don't disagree," the captain of the South Chapel Sharks asserts from the corner of the room. Greedy's propped up against the wall closest to Hunter. "But they're detained for now. Let's tackle this one issue at a time," he suggests, nodding at Kendrick before turning back to Decker.

They share a silent, heated exchange. The tension in the room is on the precipice of detonating when Decker finally sighs.

"Josephine," he hedges. "When you get out of here..." He pauses and takes in the entire room.

If I didn't know better, I would guess he's nervous.

Clearing his throat, he starts again. "When you get out of here, we'd like to take you home."

Home.

A sense of place. A physical shelter.

The mansion *has* felt more like a *home* over the last week than just about anywhere I've lived as an adult. And yet it was my very presence in that *home* that landed me here.

My mouth goes dry at the prospect of putting myself back in such a vulnerable position.

I'm not purposely being obstinate, though I'm sure Decker will assume otherwise, given our typical dynamic. But he's completely unaware of how hard this hit for me. I'm not the person I was three days ago. The woman who stepped onto the emerald yacht on Sunday. And I can't imagine going back to the way things were.

Even from across the room, Locke exudes so much empathy it hits me in waves. Kylian's feelings are abundantly clear by the way he hasn't let me go. It's the other two I'm concerned with.

Maybe to them this was all part of their stupid rivalry. Par for the course. Collateral damage. But the implications are far weightier for me.

Curling into Kylian's side, I tilt my head to meet Decker's gaze.

"They told me you sent for me," I whisper, cheeks heating with the confession. "That's how they got me to go with them. They asked if my name was Joey, and they said you wanted me to come to you. It was stupid," I mumble. "So fucking stupid..."

"Hey. No," Decker insists, his face turned down in a heavy frown. The shadows in the dim room only amplify the distress painted there. "You can't blame yourself for any of this, Josephine."

Hunter hums in agreement from her perch in the corner.

I shake my head and swallow back the tears, determined to go on.

"As soon as I realized what was happening, that I was a pawn to them, I panicked. The last thing I remember is being grabbed..."

I gulp past the fear but can't bring myself to go on.

"Baby, you're shaking," Kylian murmurs, his voice soft and just for me. "It's okay. You don't have to tell us—"

"Yes," I grit out, wiggling out of his suffocatingly tight hold and sitting up taller. "I do have to tell you. You all need to hear it. You need to understand."

Kylian tenses. Locke is stationed against the wall opposite the bed, his face screwed up in anguish. Kendrick hovers by the door, one arm propped on the jamb, his focus locked on me.

Taking my time, I look at each of them, determined to convey the severity of the situation.

"Tell us who hurt you, Josephine."

Through unshed tears, I lock eyes with Decker.

"You did. You hurt me. All of you. This happened because of you. Taking me from my uncle's. Forcing me to go where you went. To be seen with you in public. They took it too far, but you set me up and made it all possible. Your rivalry and your stubbornness. What could have..." I trail off again, the words trapped in my throat.

To illustrate what I can't say, I hold up my bare wrists. The skin is raw where they bound me. Bruises pepper a lot of my body: down my arms and all along my hips and torso.

"They did that?" Kylian snarls. The fury in his voice is in juxtaposition with the way he gingerly lifts my arm to inspect the underside of my bicep.

Before he can even focus, Decker snatches it out of his grasp and examines my battered arm.

"They gave you these bruises? They put their hands on you?"

His words are thick and cutting. Barely restrained. Despite how hard he's trying to keep it together, the anguish in his eyes proves how miserably he's failing.

"This goes beyond the rivalry," Decker growls, dragging his glare over to where Kendrick's still braced against the doorjamb. "We need to call your pops."

"No!" I rip my arm out of his grasp, wincing at the sting of the motion. "They didn't... I mean, there's nothing to report..."

Fumbling through the shame of the truth inspires new tears to well in my eyes.

"Greedy?" I murmur, resigned to let him explain it. Otherwise, I don't think I can keep the tears at bay.

He's the one who filled in the blanks for me. I didn't believe it at first. Didn't want to. But the details are consistent with instances in the past where my conversion disorder was triggered. When I press my own fingertips to the discolored spots on my skin, the perfect way they line up is hard to deny.

"Most of the marks are self-inflicted. She gave herself the bruises and most of the scrapes. The few bruises caused by one of the guys are only there because he had to fight her pretty hard so she wouldn't jump."

The room is silent for a beat, and every head in the room is turning from one person to another. They're all scrabbling for understanding, while shame threatens to bubble up inside me.

"Off the boat," Greedy finally clarifies.

"Are you fucking kidding me?" Kendrick curses from the doorway.

Locke makes a pained sound from where he's perched, and Kylian's hold tightens around my shoulders.

Decker doesn't move a muscle or make a sound.

"It was a subconscious reaction," I whisper. "The urge to flee, even if it was into the water. That's part of it—one of the many facets of the disorder. When I shut down, I lose control. I don't even remember—"

"Enough."

Decker looks around the room, jaw ticking, his eyes an impossibly dark obsidian.

"We can't change what happened. God dammit. I fucking hate that they used you to get to me, to fuck with us... *fuck*. I never meant for it to be like this."

Decker rakes his hand through his hair again, tugging on the brown strands until they're all mussed and messy. In the time that I've known him, he's never looked so frazzled.

With a deep sigh, he takes a step forward.

"Please, Josephine. Come back to the mansion. Let us take care of you. We'll protect you—and one way or another, the fuckers who did this will pay."

I swallow past the sense of dread that springs up when I think about the boat ride required to get there.

But as I look between them—from Decker to Kylian, then to Locke and even Kendrick—I see the resolve. The anger. The need for redemption and revenge.

They want to make this right. And I'm pretty damn close to letting them.

The tension in the room snaps like an overstretched rubber band, but it quickly morphs into an awkward silence when a nurse knocks twice and steps inside.

"Oh," she murmurs. "*Oh*," she says again, this time a little more drawn out, as she takes in the crowd.

Every guy in the room is tall, broad, and ridiculously good looking. They take up a substantial amount of space, their energies all dueling for dominance. It only takes her a second to lift her chin and pull her shoulders back and make a beeline for me.

"I've got your discharge orders here, dear," she informs me, holding up a clipboard as she squeezes between Locke and Decker to get to her computer. "Would you like me to come back later?" she asks, peering around the room.

"No," I insist. "I want to get out of here as soon as possible. Please," I add, a little softer.

Being here is actually making my anxiety worse. Like my subconscious is firing off over and over again because of the parallels to my last hospital stay.

After my mind finally cleared, I decided to insist I check out today, whether against medical advice or not—a point I had made clear to Greedy and Hunter. They didn't argue, even if they didn't look pleased with my declaration.

"Given your..."

The nurse takes a moment to assess every one of my guests, then focuses on me, one brow raised, clearly unwilling to discuss my medical conditions in front of a crowd without my consent.

With a quick nod, I signal for her to proceed.

"Given your *situation*, Dr. Ferguson recommends that you be discharged with at-home support."

"Meaning?" Kylian asks.

"Someone, or *someones*," another curious glance around the room, "needs to be responsible for her care over the next few days. You've been through quite the ordeal. You need time to heal."

She's talking about so much more than the bruises and scrapes covering my limbs. The bone-deep exhaustion of trauma and depression keeps trying to pull me back under, and if I don't rest, I'll lose the battle with them both.

What do boxers call it? Getting back to their fighting weight? Although a football analogy would be more appropriate, given the circumstances. There's no way I'm game-day ready.

"Bedrest for a few days. From there, you can resume daily activity, but listen to your body and ease back into things."

The nurse turns back to the computer, clicking away, then deftly leans over to place a pulse ox on my finger and the blood pressure cuff around my arm.

"You've got two prescriptions for cross-tapering, as well as the PNR you and Dr. Ferguson discussed. I just need a few signatures from you, as well as the name and contact information of the person who'll be responsible for your care. Who's taking you home, dear?"

At her question, the room crashes into a static silence that lasts all of two seconds. Silence has never weighed so heavily or sounded so loud. Then a cacophony of voices erupts around me all at once.

"I am."

"We are."

"Jose, if you want—"

"No. Don't even fucking think about—"

A piercing wolf whistle cuts through the chaos.

My heart leaps in my chest at the sharp sound, but then I bite back a snicker as my sweet nurse plants both hands on her hips and scowls at one guy after another.

"Dr. Ferguson may have approved your visitation, but you will *not* interfere with patient care or coerce this girl into doing anything she doesn't want to do. Is that clear?"

The prolonged silence is awkwardly comical. Maybe I need to bring this nurse back to the mansion with me to keep these boys in line.

Turning back to me, she sighs. "Very good. Now, *Josephine*," she emphasizes, "who is taking you home?"

Kylian's arms tighten around me.

Greedy has the gumption to mutter under his breath again, as if he can't stand the idea of being counted out.

Every eye in the room is boring into me. Decker's with more intensity than the rest.

But my friend in the corner is the person I seek. Our eyes meet, and I don't even have to ask to know she's in. Wordlessly, Hunter steps up to the end of the bed.

"Will you stay with me?" I ask quietly.

She gives me a tight, sympathetic smile. I don't know how she does it, but the expression, one that's been directed at me a dozen times from a dozen people, doesn't make me feel less than or weak. If anything, it makes me feel seen. She doesn't know all the details of what I've been through. But she knows I've been through it, and that's enough for now.

"Of course," she says, squeezing my ankle affectionately.

"Temi."

Greedy's nickname for Hunter is a low and cautionary rumble. Their dynamic is so strange—she's standoffish with her stepbrother, and yet that doesn't deter him. He treats her with the utmost respect. Reverence, even.

Hunter rolls her eyes and shuffles past Decker to fill out the release form, ignoring Greedy completely. "I have to list an address. Where are we going, Joey?"

Oh.

Shit.

That's probably what Greedy's wondering, too.

It would be easier, quieter, better, in almost every way, if I could go to my uncle's for a while. I'd have the time to rest and the space I need to get my head on straight and sort out all that's taken place over the last few weeks.

But there's nowhere for Hunter to sleep if we go back to the small space attached to the office of the junkyard. And I'm not prepared to answer Sam's questions. The wounds—physical and emotional—are still too raw. The bigger aspects of the last few days are clear to me, but I haven't had nearly enough time to process them or to figure out how to cope with the aftermath.

Hunter would let me stay at her place in a heartbeat, but the last time—the only time—I was there, the house was teeming with South Chapel Sharks. Just the thought of bumping into anyone from that team right now sends a frisson of panic down my spine.

That leaves one option.

Sighing, I lift my chin and regard Decker. His onyx eyes are scrutinizing me, just as they have been since he walked into the room.

"Can Hunter come back to the house with us?"

"Of course." The response is immediate. "You don't even have to ask."

"No fucking way," Greedy growls, stalking toward Hunter. "It's Shore Week. You shouldn't even be on the LCU campus until after it's over. I can guarantee there are people over there just itching to take a shot at us."

"I'm not a Shark, Greedy," Hunter counters.

"Yeah. So I've heard. But you are—"

Hunter crosses her arms and raises her brows in such an aggressive flex that she may as well have thrown a punch. "I'm what?" she hisses.

Snapping his mouth shut, Greedy holds both hands up and takes a step back.

"That's what I thought," she jibes before turning back to me. "I need to go home and get a few things, but I can be back here in less than two hours, okay?"

"That works," Kylian answers for me. "It'll probably take that long to process the paperwork anyway. Once you return, we'll leave together. I'll text Mrs. Lansbury and ask her to have dinner ready and to pick up the prescriptions that have been called in."

He's already pulling out his phone, obviously eager to be productive now that we have a plan.

"Better tell her to set two extra places," Greedy announces, nodding toward Kylian, then regarding Decker. "I'm not letting Hunter out of my sight if she's staying at your mansion."

Kendrick and Locke scoff in unison, the noise echoing in the room like surround sound.

"You're welcome to join us for dinner," Decker replies coolly. "But I can assure you, no harm will come to Hunter. Not on my watch."

Now it's Greedy's turn to sneer. "We've all seen what can happen on your watch, *Cap.*"

Beside me, Kylian's head snaps up, and Hunter's eyes widen to saucers where she still stands at the workstation.

"And I won't just be joining you for dinner," Greedy says as he saunters to the door. "If she's staying at the Crusade mansion, then so am I."

With that, he's out the door, with Hunter hot on his heels, already arguing with him as they head down the hall.

Chapter 5

Josephine

I'm sandwiched between Kylian and Locke in the back row of Kendrick's Suburban as he coasts along the long stretch of highway that crosses over the lake.

It's late afternoon, but not quite dusk. The sky's taken on a dreamy, hazy pink and orange tinge as the sun begins its descent.

Locke keeps looking over, his eyes swimming with hesitancy. Each time I meet his gaze, he offers me a tight smile rather than the enigmatic grin I've come to expect from him. It's like he's worried I'm about to break. As much as I hate that he's worried, I don't have the strength to assure him I'm okay—and honestly, his assumptions aren't totally off base.

At least Kylian isn't bothering to keep his distance.

He hasn't stopped touching me since he helped me into the back row and fastened the seat belt around my lap. His hands are everywhere, and although I've never been a touchy-feely PDA girlie, the constant reminder of his presence is hypnotically soothing.

Each graze of skin is grounding, a reminder of where I am and who I'm with. Nothing is suggestive, but it's intimate all the same, like he's getting reacquainted with the outline of me and reassuring himself that I'm really here.

It's a reassurance I didn't know I needed until now.

Decker and Kendrick are in the front of the vehicle, talking quietly. Greedy and Hunter are seated in the captain's seats in the middle of the vehicle. Greedy's attention is firmly locked on Hunter, while she looks out the window, body angled toward the door.

She obviously lost their argument, as evidenced by the overnight bag each held when they returned to the hospital. What could Greedy have said or done to convince her to let him tag along when she's been nothing but standoffish in his presence since I met her?

Decker's willingness to allow Greedy to come with us is just as surprising. And alarming.

It's Shore Week. The game is three days away. What's it going to be like for the quarterbacks of the rival teams to cohabitate under the same roof?

I lean forward, taking in the tightness around Greedy's eyes as he watches my friend.

"Hey," I whisper, cupping him on the shoulder. "Thanks for this." Until today, I don't think he's left the hospital since he brought me in on Monday. I can't imagine what he's missed out on and given up to be with me over the last few days. Classes. Practice. And now the comfort of his own bed.

My guys hate him because of who he is and where he goes to school. Hunter has her own beef with him, obviously, but she's never shared details about the why. She's my girl, and I'll always be Team Hunter, but right now, there's nothing anyone could say or do to convince me that Greedy Ferguson is anything but a good guy.

Covering my hand with his, he squeezes once and meets my eye over his shoulder. "Anything, Jose. I promised to make this right. I'll do whatever it takes."

Locke scoffs quietly, and Decker's got his attention trained on the rearview mirror. It's not me he keeps looking at, though. I watch him for a moment before I realize what he's actually focused on.

I slide my hand off Greedy's shoulder and sink back into the seat.

Kylian traces the hem of the soft cotton shorts Hunter brought for me to wear home from the hospital. She agreed when I told her to toss the clothes I was wearing when Greedy brought me in. I couldn't stand the idea of wearing them again, and not just because of the lake stink I'd never get out of them. The memories... The way the gauzy linen shirt did nothing to protect me from the cold as I lay in the bed of a truck all night...

Shivering involuntarily, I distract myself by looking out at the highway over Locke's shoulder. I've only lived in Lake Chapel for a handful of weeks, yet I already recognize so many landmarks. The occasional missing post separating the highway from the express lanes. Idiosyncrasies in the curvature of the overpass because of the natural shape of the lake. The exit for Sam's Auto Parts and Salvage.

At that last thought, I catch Kylian's hand.

"Could I borrow your phone? I think I need to call my uncle."

I'm almost certain my phone is at the bottom of the lake.

Beside me, Locke sits up a little straighter, and before Kylian can respond, he's interjecting.

"Here—use mine. Kyl's not real keen on sharing." With one hand, he fishes his phone out of his pocket and hands it to me.

"Just when it comes to my devices," Kylian amends, cocking a self-deprecating smirk that showcases that one dimple.

Hunter turns around then, craning her neck to watch me enter the number I memorized before moving from Ohio to North Carolina.

"What are you going to tell him?" she asks.

Shrugging, I consider my options. "The truth, I guess. Or at least as much of it as I can stand to share. He won't grill me, but I owe him some sort of explanation."

Decker's eyes find mine in the mirror again as I lift the phone to my ear.

It rings, then rings again, and again. I let out a relieved sigh at the prospect of leaving a voicemail, then immediately feel guilty for wanting to avoid speaking to him.

Maybe it's better this way, though.

"Hey, Sam. It's Jojo. Just checking in to let you know I'm okay. I lost my phone over the weekend, so sorry if you've been trying to call. And sorry I haven't been around the last few weeks. Adjusting to school and work has been a lot. I've been spending time with my friend Hunter, and you can call her cell if you need to reach me until I get a new phone."

Hunter quietly rattles off her phone number, and I repeat it for my uncle.

"Anyway, I'll visit soon. Just let me know which days you'll be around the shop. Tell Jeannie that I haven't forgotten about the cleaning and filing. Oh! And check on Scout, please. I just want to make sure she's okay. Okay. That's it. Um... bye."

I end the call, feeling all sorts of awkward about leaving a message in front of an audience. At least he won't worry now. I owe him that much.

I hand the phone back to Locke, and in return, he offers me another one of those halfhearted, tight-lipped smiles. Before I have a chance to call him out for acting so strange, Kylian pulls me into his side.

"I'll get you a new phone tomorrow," he murmurs, his fingers already back to tracing the stitching of my shorts. "And I'll take you to see the armadillo if you want. Next week? Maybe Monday?"

Yawning, I nod. As if the act is contagious, just about every person in the car yawns, too. I'm not the only one who's exhausted and sleep-deprived, and it's really starting to show.

I'm desperate for a good night's sleep, but before I crash, I need to figure out how to handle the panic that will inevitably wash over me when I wake up. It happened every time at the hospital—hence the sedation. Though that didn't help the inevitable terror that hit when I woke, it quieted my mind enough to allow me to sleep.

It would be silly to think it won't happen at home. Hunter and I will have to come up with some sort of plan for her to ease me awake if and when I startle in the morning.

Yawning again, I rest my head on Kylian's shoulder and let his soft ministrations comfort me while I blink to avoid the pull of slumber.

Any concerns I had about falling asleep or getting too comfortable fly out the window of the damn Suburban as Kendrick makes one last smooth turn and pulls into the marina.

Lake Chapel stretches out before us.

On Lake Chapel is the literal last place in the world I want to be.

I agreed to go back to the mansion.

Only I've conveniently blocked out one very important part of the trip there.

My heart rate skyrockets, and blood whooshes in my ears.

Panicked, I announce "I can't do this; I can't get on a boat again" to no one in particular.

Kylian's energy ratchets up ten levels and his body goes rigid as he shifts in his seat. He's assessing me quietly, intensely, like he's working something out in his head.

Before I can question him, Locke brushes the back of his knuckles along my thigh.

"What if we use one of the ferries? You could sit in the middle, away from the sides. That may be easier since the ferry is so big."

I hold in a shudder at the thought of any and all floating vessel transportation options.

In my current state, I doubt I could even board a cruise ship without panicking. The few memories I have from Sunday night are still too real and raw, festering right below the surface.

It's a lesson I learned years ago: at our core, we're all just animals. Not even smart animals. We're reptiles, compelled by our baser needs and survival instincts. My lizard brain has worked overtime over the years to shield me from memories of atrocities too harsh to bear. It has perfected the art of repression, and as absurd as it sounds, I'm grateful.

Pulling in a long, shaky breath, I meet Locke's gaze.

"I can't do it," I admit. Turning to Kylian, I make my plea. "Please don't make me do it."

Kylian's eyes are full of a surprisingly smug resolve when he gently catches my chin in his hand and tilts my face upward.

"You don't have to get on a boat, Jo. There's another way." Pride oozes from him as he regards me.

His declaration makes little sense. Their home is across the lake, but if anyone could come up with a way to walk on water or airlift us to the isle, it's Kylian. Right now, I don't care what his plan involves. I'm just grateful. So damn grateful.

"Dude," Locke says, stunned.

"Kylian," Decker scolds from the front seat with a sigh.

"What?" he snaps, first at Decker, then at Locke. "There is. And if there was ever a time to make the most of our resources, it's now. Don't you think we owe her that much, Cap?"

His huffy edict sounds more like a scolding than a question. It's *so* not Kylian, and I don't have the first clue what he's talking about.

Finally, Kendrick parks the Suburban, unbuckles, and swivels in his seat.

Lifting his chin toward Kylian, he asks, "You got the Sherp ready?"

Kylian smirks, an unexpected cockiness rolling off him. "Yep. Fueled and ready to roll. What do you think I've been doing for the last two days?"

The smallest hint of a smile—one I've only witnessed when he's speaking to his sisters—graces Kendrick's face as he chuckles quietly. "All right, Boy Genius. Let's fucking go."

He rights himself in the driver's seat, buckles up again, and pulls out of the marina parking spot without another word. Decker's scowl is visible in the rearview mirror, but my attention is quickly diverted when Kylian wraps an arm around my shoulder and combs his fingers through my hair.

I can't help but gravitate closer, tilting my head toward his.

He kisses my forehead and massages my scalp. "It's going to be okay, baby," he murmurs quietly. "We've got this."

Chapter 6

Kylian

The magic crackled that night, fading in and out like a poor Wi-Fi signal struggling to connect.

Weak connection? Ours was anything but.

The second Decker shouted my name from the crimson yacht, I knew.

It doesn't make sense on an intellectual level. It wasn't clear. It wasn't even opaque. His scream dripped with emotion, a million colors and shades and tones I shouldn't have been able to discern. But I knew.

Is this what people call intuition? Instinct?

A gut reaction?

More like a gut punch.

First, it was a prickle of awareness. Then goose bumps erupted all over my body.

When I heard the panic in his voice—the way he barked out my name—I knew. I fucking knew.

They'd have to hook me up and drain the adrenaline from my veins to make me physically relax at this point. I never want to let her out of my arms again.

"Belt check," I order, pulling on the yellow safety strap across my lap, then peering back to make sure one of the guys is checking Jo's for her.

Surprisingly, Kendrick is doing it, deftly testing the tension and announcing that "she's good."

Jo is seated between Kendrick and Locke on one side of the armored all-terrain. Garrett Reed Ferguson the Third and Hunter are seated across from them, having left the middle seat open as a spacer.

Decker's by my side, ready to play copilot if I need it. I won't.

Fiddling with the myriad of switches, I tap my foot against the floorboard over and over, ready to fucking go. There's an energy to this thing, hydraulics and power. Advanced tech and unmatched horsepower coalescing into an unstoppable hybrid.

Decker and Locke go crazy for cars. Kendrick loves all the watercraft in our fleet.

They can keep them all. This baby is mine.

It's more machine than vehicle. A beast of engineering, designed specifically to navigate swamp lands and off-road terrain. It even floats on water, seamlessly transitioning to land when the landscape changes. The flat front and oversized tires give it a tank-like appearance. It's not street-legal, and we've never needed to use it for its intended purpose, as an emergency escape option to get off the isle, but I'm sure fucking glad we have it now.

The Sherp lugs forward, churning against soft mud as it finds purchase in the marshy earth. I timed our departure from the hospital with this in mind. It's low tide, which minimizes the water we have to navigate. The Sherp can handle it, but I don't know if my girl can.

More determined than ever to get her home and keep her safe, I grip the lever that controls the throttle, poised to slam the brakes or accelerate as needed. I'm locked in and focused on the marsh, mentally carving out the best path to the mansion. My focus on our surroundings doesn't stop me from glancing in the mounted mirror every six seconds so I can check on Jo, though.

"Keep your bodies relaxed," I instruct, eyeing a particularly wet patch of terrain up ahead. "Lean into the bumps, and don't panic if it feels like we're airborne or rocking back and forth in the same spot. We won't get stuck. We can't."

Decker grasps my knee, pulling me out of my head, but he doesn't break my focus. The squeeze against my kneecap is almost ticklish, so I bat him away.

"Kyl. She's here. She's okay. Cool it."

I say nothing. He just watches me for a long moment, lips pressed together in my periphery, before he removes his hand and settles back against his seat.

But then he speaks again.

"When we get home, you need to take your meds and get some rest. We're good now, and you've seen her with your own eyes. She's okay. We've all been through it. You have to sleep."

I chuckle, low and sardonic, at his attempt to tell me what to do.

I've deferred to Decker for years. Allowed him to bark orders and take charge as he saw fit.

But that was before her.

When I don't bother arguing, he pushes.

"Something funny?" he asks under his breath.

"Define funny," I hedge.

His eyes are boring into me again, but I stay focused on the screens and gears ahead, navigating the Sherp with ease.

Finally, he answers. "You just laughed. Usually people laugh when they think something's funny."

"People also laugh when they're uncomfortable. Or when they can't believe the audacity of a situation or circumstance."

"So which is it?" Decker grunts as I guide the Sherp over a jagged segment of rock. The vehicle wobbles, sinking from side to side as it works overtime to chug onward.

"Audacity," I offer simply. "I'm laughing at the absurd, audacious, *outlandish* assumption that I'm interested in following any of your instructions right now."

I grit my teeth over another sticky spot, and once we've smoothed out again, I meet my best friend's eye.

His expression is a mix of shock and outrage.

The urge to laugh again bubbles up inside me, but I hold back. He needs to understand the weight of this moment, and I won't undermine the severity with what he might perceive as humor.

More often than not, I like when Decker takes the lead. Life with him is cushy and accommodating in ways I could never create for myself. He takes the guesswork out of many facets of day-to-day life, and he's excellent at anticipating the needs of others.

But over the last few weeks, things have changed. I've changed. And it's time he knows it.

"I've followed your commands for the last seventy-two hours, Cap. From Sunday night until now, I did everything you asked of me, complied with every order you gave." Flicking my attention to the mirror, I give Jo a quick scan, then assess the screens in front of me again. "None of them kept her from being harmed or got me to her any faster. *None.*"

Beside me, Decker's silent. He knows I'm not finished.

"Now you have a choice. You can let me be—let me cope with the fallout of this ordeal and do what I need to do to convince myself she's okay, too—or you can try to control the situation. 'Try' is the operative word in that sentence, because I'm done doing things your way when it comes to my girl."

Chapter 7

Josephine

Traveling to the mansion by all-terrain vehicle is an entirely different experience than traveling by boat. We circle the house and park outside the garage that until now I thought only stored WaveRunners and fishing gear. Not sure how I missed the massive armored vehicle they've been keeping in there, too. Though I suppose I've been more than a little preoccupied since taking up residence in the Crusade Mansion.

As I step through the side door, my body eases. The vibrant colors of the setting sun flood through the floor-to-ceiling windows that line the great room, immediately filling me with a small shred of peace I haven't felt in days.

We all shuffle into the house, discarding shoes and stifling yawns. The smell of butter and garlic wafts from the kitchen, and Mrs. Lansbury's humming from the same direction takes another pound of weight off my chest.

Hunter blows past me, with Greedy hot on her heels. They're no doubt locked in another battle of wills. From what I've gleaned over the last six hours, that's their default setting. It doesn't bode well for the atmosphere in the house over the next few days. It's going to be all managing egos and navigating an intense rivalry, sprinkled with the tension that constantly swirls around the stepsiblings, while we figure out how to coexist.

Kendrick heads off to his room. The move is unsurprising, though I can't say the same for Locke's exit. To my surprise, he makes a show of skirting along the edge of the corridor, almost as if he's trying not to touch me.

"Emo Boy," I call to him softly.

He stops dead in his tracks, peeking over his shoulder and wearing a sheepish grimace.

I tilt my head and take him in while I formulate my question. "What's wrong?" feels too trite when so much of what went down over the last few days isn't okay.

"Can we talk?" I ask.

A spark of guilt ignites behind his hazel eyes, turning their usual warmth into a heat that's just a little uncomfortable, but he offers me a sympathetic smile in response. "K and I have to be at the field house in less than an hour. Later?" he offers.

I nod, resigned to waiting to clear the air with him. At least we have a tentative plan to talk. I can't stand the aloofness and the hesitancy in every one of his looks and actions. He's treating me as if I'll break. Or as if I'm already broken.

He takes off toward the stairs without another look back. As he hauls himself up the steps like his feet weigh fifty pounds each, Decker's voice echoes from the upper deck—likely because he's on the phone.

Despite knowing the whereabouts of every person in the house, I startle when Kylian crowds my back and wraps his arms low around my waist.

Tracing my fingers down his arms, I melt into him, letting him support my weight. God, it feels so good to let him hold me. The panic and the sedation left me in a haze for hours, but I had this bone-deep sense—this physical ache—that kept reminding me there was a balm. My heart knew the remedy; my instincts knew there was something—someone—out there who could make the darkness less bleak.

It was him all along.

Kylian's been my safe place for weeks. I need him like I need my next breath.

When I rest my head on his chest and tilt my chin, I suck in a harsh breath, and my heart, which has finally fallen into a comfortable rhythm after days of disorder, lurches. I might need him, but the look in his eyes makes it clear that he needs something else.

He looks wrecked in the worst possible way. Sleep-deprived. Agitated. Worse than any of the other guys now that I really take the time to assess him.

"I overheard Decker say you haven't slept," I confess, tracing the muscles in his forearm as he rests his chin on my shoulder.

He exhales near my ear, his breath a warm caress along my collarbone as his arms tighten around my middle.

But then the silence drags on, and he doesn't answer.

"Kylian," I urge. I try to turn in his arms, but his grip is too strong. There's an intense determination in the way he's holding me, like he never wants to let me go.

"You need sleep," I admonish as softly as possible, straining against his hold until he finally lets me free.

He blinks at me instead of replying, cool cerulean blue eyes bloodshot and watery behind his glasses. His Adam's apple dips with a rough swallow, then he clears his throat and grits out, "Not yet."

Like a shot, he takes off down the hall. He doesn't say a word, but instinct tells me he wants me to follow.

My body aches with each step. I'm wobbly and off-kilter, but I'm determined to stick with him.

Mrs. Lansbury calls out to us as Kylian tears through the kitchen. All I can do is offer a placating smile and a quick wave as I trail after him as fast as I can.

He pushes into the dining room, of all places, but he doesn't bother to flick on the lights. So in the quickly darkening room, he stalks to the far wall, then paces the length of the table—hurried, rhythmic steps followed by a sharp pivot with a precision so severe it looks mechanical.

I watch, and I wait, my anxiety ratcheting up with each pass.

Shoulders sagging, I finally lean against the back of a chair opposite him, trying my best to be patient as he works out the thoughts consuming him. He's still pacing when my fingers start to tingle and my feet go numb. I shift from hip to hip. I'm bone-tired and eager to sit or lie down, but I won't rest until he does.

"Kylian," I plead softly.

He whips his head in my direction, hitting me with a cold, hollow glare from behind his glasses. He softens the expression slightly when we lock eyes—almost as if he's only now remembering where he is and who he's with—but then he shakes his head resolutely. "Not yet."

I'm so out of my depth. I don't know what to do—how to help. Should I text one of the guys? Call in backup? Locke and Kendrick have probably already left for practice, but Decker is here somewhere.

No. My gut instinct says that'll only make it worse.

But I'm not helping Kylian by just standing here, dead on my feet.

The pressure of unshed tears pulsates behind my eyes, and it's all I can do to keep my body upright. I feebly track his path along the other side of the table.

His pacing is rhythmic, creating a *thwomp-thwomp* on the hardwood floor with each stride. The sound of his shoes hitting the floor, along with the metronomic whoosh of his harsh inhales and exhales, lulls me into a state of exhausted detachment.

After what feels like hours, he stops.

The abrupt silence jars me out of my trance. Snapping my head up, I survey him, looking for signs of his emotional state, wary of what comes next.

Kylian shoves a chair away from the table with so much force it clatters to the floor.

He steps up to the table, taking the place of the chair, and braces his arms wide on the glossy surface. Panting with the erratic vitality of a caged animal, he finally lifts his head and locks me in his sights like a predator assessing its prey.

The veins in his forearms become more pronounced with the strain of containing himself. He's breathing like he's just finished an intense workout, but the energy emanating from him is nothing like the relief and sense of accomplishment one might expect after a session at the gym.

He maintains eye contact for another breath before dropping his head so it hangs between his outstretched arms.

Spoken into the table, his words are almost indiscernible.

"There's something I need to know."

"Okay," I hedge, swallowing back the lump in my throat.

Though I'm reluctant, it has nothing to do with my willingness to cooperate. I know how Kylian's mind works: Black and white. Numbers and stats. I would never bullshit him or be purposely evasive. But with him in such an agitated state, my honesty might do more harm than good.

He lifts his head, seeking my gaze. He homes in on me, like he actually wants to look me in the eye. It takes concerted effort for him to do so and to maintain that contact; that I know for sure. That alone is evidence of how desperate he is for me to understand the gravity of his next words.

"I need you to tell me right now if this isn't a thing for you."

The statement comes out harsh and accusatory. Not an ounce of sugar coating.

Before I can digest the implication and formulate a response, he continues.

"This. Us. If it's a no for you... If you're going to leave again—"

Anger flares inside me, igniting a flame in my stomach and fueling my rebuttal.

"I didn't *leave*, Kylian."

How dare he. The fucking *audacity*. I was taken—my guard was down for one night just as I was settling in and beginning to trust in these guys, in this house, in our relationships. I never expected—

"Willingly," he amends, his chest puffing as he works to control his breathing. "I know you didn't go with them willingly, but the summation of your departure was cataclysmic, nonetheless. I can't do that again, Jo. I won't survive it. If there's a chance you'll leave, tell me now."

Silence thrums between us, the tension so painfully acute it aches deep in my chest.

"Please," he adds, his eyes full of anguish. "Cut me out right now while I'm still low. While the distance I have to fall isn't so great."

With his plea, all the anger, resentment, and tension building in me melt away.

Utter agony drips from every word of his request. The depth of my pain grows tenfold as his admission registers and I realize just how deeply he's hurting.

Not because of me, but *for* me. *For us.*

Desperate to get to him, I pull back the chair I'm leaning on. The legs scrape hard against the floor, screeching with the force of the motion.

Despite all my aches, bruises, and bone-tired weariness, I climb onto the table.

Kylian watches, wide-eyed, as I shift forward, testing my weight and balance.

My battered kneecaps and my scraped palms press into the smooth surface, but I barely feel it.

All I feel is the gravity of him.

Of us.

The power of our connection, the inexplicable pull driving me forward.

I crawl across the tabletop, shaky but sure. When I'm close enough, Kylian's fingers graze my neck and find purchase in my hair.

Trusting that he'll hold me steady, I lift onto my knees and sit back on my heels. I splay my hands against his chest, then smooth them up and around his shoulders until I lace my hands behind his neck and pull him close enough that his lips brush against mine.

"I didn't leave, Kylian," I repeat, whisper-soft and placating.

Digging my nails into the short hair along his nape, I rest my forehead on his.

"I don't want to leave you ever again," I vow, my heart aching in my chest.

His eyes shutter behind his glasses. Though he hasn't moved, hasn't spoken, he trembles as he inhales. A single tear escapes, the moisture fogging just the corner of one lens.

And then he crashes his mouth against mine, lightning fast and with so much intensity I'd have tipped over if he wasn't holding me so securely.

His tongue plunges into my mouth, claiming mine with a force I couldn't match even on a good day.

So I don't try. Without conscious thought, I submit, letting him feed me his tongue and moan into my mouth and nip at my bottom lip until we're breathless.

"You're mine, Jo," he pants, strong hands gripping the hair at the back of my head as he moves me where he wants me. "You don't get to leave. Anyone who tries to fucking take you—"

"I'm here," I promise, meeting the demands of his mouth and clinging to his shoulders. "I'm here, Kyl. I'm here now."

"Come up to the Nest," he demands, cupping my ass and hauling me off the table.

I'm ready to agree, until I home in on his strained, bloodshot eyes.

Nuzzling into his shoulder, I shake my head. "I need you," I whisper into his neck. Then I pull back so he can see my sincerity. "But I need you rested."

A growl rips through his chest as he plops me unceremoniously back onto the table. From the determined set of his jaw, it's obvious he's ready to argue, so I bring one finger to his lips.

"You're not okay," I determine, unwilling to let him dispute the obvious. "And I'm not, either."

His mouth snaps shut.

"I'll be okay, but in order to get there, I need sleep. In my own room." I add the last part quickly to discourage him from trying to sway me.

"Neither one of us will sleep if I come up to the Nest right now." I give him a pointed look. "You need rest, and I need to convince my adrenals that I'm finally safe."

"I'll always keep you safe," he grinds out, his persistence somehow even more intense. "Now that I know what's at stake, no one is getting to you. I meant what I said, Jo. You're mine. I'm never letting you go."

If anyone else tried to claim ownership of me like that, I'd scoff and roll my eyes. But I know better than to push back against Kylian's resolve. He means what he says, always.

And more importantly, I want to be his.

Changing tack, I loop my arms around his torso and gently tug on his body until he steps forward and settles between my legs.

"I want to be yours," I promise. "But you could do an even better job of keeping me safe if you were rested."

Looming over me, he wears a skeptical frown. I'm working an angle, and he knows it. If I'm right, though, his sense of self-preservation is strong enough that he'll let me get away with it. Squeezing tighter, I breathe him in, filling my nostrils with the vibrant, lively blend of citrus and eucalyptus that has always calmed my anxiety.

"Haven't you ever heard the phrase 'put your own oxygen mask on first'?"

Brow furrowed, he assesses me.

"Those instructions are for people traveling on aircraft with children, Jo."

"Fair point. If I call you Daddy, will you go upstairs and sleep?" I tease.

"If you call me Daddy, neither one of us is going to sleep anytime soon, and you know it."

A grin blossoms on my face as I lean into our embrace. His hands travel up and down my back, and he takes another step closer, cocooning me in the safety of his hold as he returns my affection.

He kisses the top of my head, and I crane back to catch his lips.

"Sleep, Kylian. For me?"

He searches my face for so long I think he'll argue, but then he kisses the top of my head again.

"For you," he concedes. "But tomorrow, you're in my bed."

Chapter 8

Josephine

With Kylian settled up in the Nest, and Locke and Kendrick at practice, dinner was a smaller affair. Hunter, Greedy, and I ate at the barstools along the kitchen island.

Decker didn't make an appearance, but I swear I could feel his brooding presence lording over the house. For the first time, maybe ever, I didn't have the energy or fire to match him. I still don't. Avoidance is probably the best strategy for now. Especially given who sat beside me while we ate.

His biggest rival. In his house. All because of me.

Greedy's been uncharacteristically quiet since we arrived, which makes sense—I'd be on edge too if I had invited myself into the den of my enemy just days before I had to face them on the field.

Mrs. Lansbury kept a watchful eye over us as we ate, insisting on scooping out second helpings for all three of us, despite our protests. Not that we put up that much of a fight. Her creamy lemon chicken pasta was the comfort food equivalent of a hot bath and a stiff drink.

Whether for my benefit or Hunter's, Greedy mostly kept to himself. He'd ask a question now and again, and he spoke to Mrs. Lansbury when she came by to check on us. But otherwise, it was like he wasn't even there.

Hunter and I talked nonstop, as if by filling the lulls in conversation, we could avoid talking about topics too heavy to tackle right now.

We worked out study plans for midterms, and she explained the Logic homework I've fallen woefully behind on. We also made plans to go to lunch after class on Monday, although I warned her that Kylian would most likely tag along. I can't imagine he'll let me out of his sight once he fulfills his end of the bargain and actually sleeps. Plus, he said he'd take me to Sam's on Monday, and I'm anxious to check in with my uncle.

Needing something to do with my hands, I insisted Mrs. Lansbury allow me to clean up the kitchen, but I shooed my friends out of the room so I could have my first moment of alone time today. Greedy excused himself to the in-home gym, but only after helping rinse the dishes, and Hunter eventually ambled out onto the deck to listen to her audiobook after she asked me half a dozen times if I was sure I didn't want help.

I'm wiping down the island for the second time to keep myself occupied when Locke and Kendrick get home from practice.

"Have you eaten? There's still plenty," I offer, indicating the container of leftovers I have yet to stash in the fridge.

"We ate," Locke confirms, his attention jumping all around the kitchen, yet never landing on me.

Kendrick saunters past his friend and drops his bag at the foot of the stairs before he circles back.

Prowling toward me, he takes me in from head to toe in an assessment that makes me squirm.

He stops less than two feet in front of me—so close, I'm surrounded by the intoxicating aroma of his aftershave, musk, and warm vanilla. They swirl together in a scent I secretly want to roll around in.

His signature scowl pulls his brows together. "All good, Ohio?"

Gulping past the trepidation rising up inside me in response to his uncharacteristic behavior, I nod. "Yep," I confirm with a false sense of cheer. "All good here. Hunter's on the deck, and Greedy asked if he could lift in the weight room, so Mrs. Lansbury showed him the way." I bite down on my lip, hoping that's enough of a report.

"And Kylian?" he presses.

In my periphery, Locke's focus turns to me. *Finally.*

"He's okay," I hedge. "It took some convincing, but eventually, he went up to the Nest to sleep."

A smirk pulls at the corners of Kendrick's mouth. "I'll bet," he murmurs with a pointed look. Then, softer, he adds, "You should try to get some rest, too."

Before I have time to reply, he turns and strides to the stairs, scoops up his bag, and disappears.

I blink in slow motion, unsure of what to make of the longest and most civil exchange I've ever shared with my most tempestuous roommate.

Worrying my bottom lip, I glance at Locke.

"Did that really just happen?" I joke.

He shrugs, offering the same too-tight smile he's been doling out since this afternoon.

He comes closer, dropping his bag at his feet, and with a sigh, he lowers his forearms to the back of a barstool and angles a little closer. "Kendrick's a tough guy on the outside, but he was worried about you. We all were."

Nodding, I accept the admission for what it is and let the knowledge warm me just a little.

"Why didn't Decker go with you to practice?"

I didn't connect the dots at first, but Decker was still on the phone when we sat down to eat. After that, he headed to his room without uttering a word to any of us.

Locke grips the back of the barstool and cracks his neck from side to side.

"Concussion protocol. He can't participate in team workouts. The training staff will assess him in the morning, and if he meets all the requirements, he can come to practice tomorrow afternoon."

Shit. Between the flurry of activity leading up to Shore Week and then my stint in the hospital, I had all but forgotten about Decker's concussion.

"He's okay though, right?" I ask.

"Yeah. He's going to be okay." Locke gives me a single nod, but he doesn't elaborate.

I don't dare push. We're at a standstill, out of topics to discuss that don't relate to the one the thing we desperately need to talk about. An awkward charge buzzes between us, leaving us separated by the island and all that's gone to shit over the last few days.

The half smiles and standoffishness confuse the hell out of me. I didn't expect him to go full out like Kylian, but my reunion with Locke has been prickly at best and downright cold at moments. It's so incongruent with the passion we shared just last weekend. I think that's what hurts the most: all that's changed is something that happened to me—that I had no control over, nor did I have a hand in orchestrating. Prior to the Charter Cruise, Locke and I were in an amazing place. And now we're just... not.

My life has taken a nose-dive because of situation and circumstance more than once. Time and again, I've persevered, yet I thought I had already survived the worst of it. I thought life here—in this place, with this fresh start, with this man—would be different.

That I could be different.

That maybe I really could rewrite my story.

Hope and optimism drift away with each exhale. So much of the life I dreamed of creating evaporates into the ether as we stand in awkward silence.

"Are you sure you're not hungry?" I try, desperate to busy myself with a task.

"I ate," he assures me. "I'm good."

"How about that chat, then?"

Grimacing, Locke blows out a long breath. He rakes an inked hand through his still-damp hair, then inclines his head in my direction.

"Yeah. Okay," he relents.

The hesitation in every one of his movements does nothing for the deep sense of dread pooling in my gut.

"Media room?" I suggest.

It'll give us some semblance of privacy since we can close and lock the door. With Greedy in the house, that separation feels necessary.

He follows me down the hall while memories of last weekend poke at my resolve. Our conversation, the way we razzed each other about movie choices, the hope that had bloomed inside me at our reconnection. It was days ago, yet I'm already feeling nostalgic about that time.

Locke plops down on the couch and spreads himself wide: arms splayed on the back cushions, his feet planted shoulder-width apart.

I accept his standoffishness for what it is and elect to perch on the armrest.

It all feels painfully distant. Awful, and so wrong. But we need to come clean and communicate about where things stand between us if we want to move forward.

I want him. I haven't stopped wanting him since the moment he put his number in my phone on the first day of class. I won't force him to accept the version of our relationship that I have in my head if he's not okay with all that's transpired, though.

"Kylian and I talked earlier," I start, cracking my knuckles in my lap. It's a bad habit, but one I've never been able to break.

He sucks in a long breath, then lets his head loll along the back of the couch so he can see me.

"I figured." The disenchanted smile that accompanies the statement makes my stomach twist. "You two are together," he guesses, turning away from me again and focusing on the blank projector screen across the room.

"We are."

"Yeah. Okay. Well, that's good, I guess. The last few days have been horrible for all of us, but especially Kyl. He really needs you." He's quiet for two breaths, then he lets out a humorless laugh. "Damn. I honestly didn't see it coming, though. It's usually Decker, ya know? Once or twice it's been Kendrick. It's never been Kylian before."

I open my mouth, ready to ask what he means, but before I can, he continues.

"I'm happy for him—for you, too. When I saw how he reacted..." He sighs, then stares down at his hands resting in his lap. "Look, we don't have to do this. After everything you've been through this week, neither of us needs any more pain." He casts another sympathetic half smile in my direction. "We're all exhausted, and I've read enough Nietzsche to accept that this is what it is." Hands still in his lap, he squeezes them into fists, then flexes his knuckles tenderly.

"Take care of yourself, Hot Girl," he laments, pushing to his feet in a slow but sure motion. "Assuming you're sticking around, I'll do my best to stay out of your way."

Confusion fogs my mind and a razor-sharp pain lances my chest as I scramble to sort out the meaning of his words. Because of the bleakness of the moment, or maybe the highs and extreme lows of the last few days, tears well in my eyes without my permission.

He moves to skirt past me for what feels like the umpteenth time today, but I can't let him. Not again. I reach out to stop him on instinct, desperate to unravel the confusion burrowed in my gut.

"Locke," I plead, though I don't even know what I'm asking of him.

He freezes when my fingers circle his wrist.

I'm careful not to squeeze or to put too much pressure on his joints. I can only imagine the way his arthritis is flaring if he hasn't slept much over the last few days. Maybe this conversation would be better left until the light of day, after we've both had a chance to rest.

But Sunday night and all that went down with the Sharks has created this urgency inside me: to take what I want, to be with who I want, and to fulfill my promise to Alice.

I want to live.

I want to thrive.

I want to fall in love and to feel every moment on the way down.

I want to stop Locke from walking out of this room—to stop this, the moment where he seemingly gives up on us and walks away.

I know I'm a lot. My baggage is so heavy. And he already carries enough of his own. But if he's just willing to try... to let us recover from this and see what tomorrow brings...

My touch isn't in vain, because he at least slows and meets my gaze over his shoulder as he tries to circumvent the couch and move past me.

"Joey," he breathes, the sound sorrowful, when his pained eyes meet my tear-filled ones. "Why are you crying?"

With a scoff, I swipe the moisture from my cheeks with my free hand. "Why am I crying?" I sneer. "Gee, I don't know. Maybe because you just broke up with me?"

His brows shoot into his hair-line and his Adam's apple bobs under the red and black ink of his throat piece. Before he can respond, I snap.

"Guess it's not much of a breakup, though, since we barely even got started. I'm sorry it didn't work out how you wanted, but I didn't expect it to be like this, either. Everything we did... all the things we shared? I thought it was worth it."

I'm rambling, but between the tears leaking out of my eyes and the snot threatening to drip out of my nose, something has to give, and the words escaping one after another are impossible to stop.

"What did you just say? *It is what it is?*" I mock, sniffling again. "Where was your nihilism when you pulled me away from the party on Saturday night and swore you wanted me? Where was this callous exterior when you made me admit I wanted you, too, over and over again, before we had sex in your bed?"

I close my eyes, embarrassed, and release my grip on his wrist so he can leave.

Before I can retreat in on myself, he catches my fingertips, startling me enough that I peer up into his face.

The anger flaring in his eyes is enough to break me all over again.

Low and agitated, he asks, "You think *I'm* breaking up with *you*?"

I watch him blankly, blinking away tears.

"You literally just told me to take care of myself and that you'd try to stay out of my way. Pretty sure that's the universal sentiment people use during a breakup. Surprised you didn't throw in an 'it's not you, it's me' for good measure."

He cracks a smile—a real, genuine, squinty smile—and my heart lights up with hope.

Half a second later, though, it crumbles into a million little fragments. Because he was set to walk away. Just like that. Without putting up a fight. I tuck my head and hold back fresh tears, desperate for him to leave so I can properly fall apart.

"Just go," I mutter, refusing to let him see any more of my heartbreak.

"Joey," he whispers, catching my chin and tilting my face up. "I want you so bad it hurts. But you picked him. If you want to be with Kylian..."

He trails off, glancing at the door.

Kylian is his best friend. Not just his best friend—his first friend after years of feeling unwanted and impossible to love. This is as much about him and Kylian as it is about him and me.

Finally, his standoffishness makes sense.

And although I can't stand the prospect of being rejected a second time in the span of ten minutes, I shoot my shot.

"I want to be with Kylian," I confirm, then quickly add, "And I want to be with you, too. Kyl and I talked about it... Before..." I trail off, afraid that referencing the incident with the South Chapel team will send me right back to that headspace.

"He thought you'd be on board. That you wouldn't be bothered by... by..."

"By what, Joey?" He takes a step closer. "Sharing you?"

My cheeks flame at the callout.

Locke doesn't leave me in suspense for long. He tilts his head back and forth, as if he's considering his words carefully.

"Kyl's not wrong. But I'm *not* okay with an open arrangement. I don't want to be with anyone else, Hot Girl," he challenges. "I want you and only you."

I cover my face with my hands. "I don't want you to be with anyone else either," I admit, wrinkling my nose at the clear double standard.

"Yet you want to be with us both."

The statement is just that—a statement. It came from Locke, but it's so Kylian. I bite down on my lip to keep from smiling, but I do allow myself to peek up at him through my fingers while he processes the possibility. Because despite how optimistic I want to be about his response so far, I can't help but steel my heart for rejection.

After what feels like a lifetime, his warm hazel eyes zero in on me. "Kylian already agreed, didn't he?" Locke smirks, the amused look on his face proving just how well he knows his childhood buddy.

He stares down at me for another breath, then that smirk transforms into the bold, genuine smile I've grown to love.

"Okay. Yeah. Fuck. I'm in. I want you any way I can have you, Hot Girl—in *every* way. If that means I share you with one of my best friends, I'm game."

Butterflies riot in my stomach, a tickle of delight combined with the effervescent lightness that so often consumes me when I'm around this man. He holds the key to parts of me I haven't had access to in years. The way his smile lights up my insides thrills me every time.

He circles back around the couch without dropping my hand. As soon as he's close enough, he interlaces our fingers, sits down, and pulls me off the armrest and into his lap.

Once I'm settled, his body deflates and the tension oozes from him. "Fuck," he says, relaxing into the cushions. "Come here and let me hold you."

Hooking one arm under my legs, he uses his free hand to cradle the back of my head.

I sink into his embrace, savoring the bliss that comes with being wrapped up in all things Nicholas Lockewood. I breathe him in and exhale all the darkness of the last few days, along with the despair that gripped me when I thought I'd lost him.

"This is why you've been acting distant all day," I muse, nuzzling into his chest and tracing the intricate lines inked along his throat.

His Adam's apple bobs under my fingertips, then he's ducking and running his nose along my jaw. The kiss he presses to my neck before responding makes my heart practically float in my chest.

"I didn't think this—you and me, and you and him—was a possibility. I assumed you'd choose. And I'm used to not being picked first."

My heart aches at his admission. It's only been a couple of weeks since he opened up to me about his childhood, about how he bounced around various foster care arrangements as a kid until he finally found a real home with Gary and Brenda.

"Can I tell you something?" he asks, placing a kiss on my shoulder as his fingertips dance up and down my arm. "In the beginning, I wanted you to pick me."

I still, self-reproach creeping in again as guilt washes over me.

"But that thought is fleeting compared to the need I have to see you happy. Happy. Safe. Loved. If that means others are involved—"

"Just one other," I correct.

He smirks. "Yeah. Okay, Joey."

He's not even trying to placate me, his tone a playful, deliberate tease.

"I'm serious," I insist, squirming to sit up straighter so I can look him in the eye.

"I bet you are," he muses, digging his fingers into the back of my scalp and tilting my head right where he wants it. He leans in to kiss me, and as much as I crave the connection, I arch back until I'm out of reach.

Shaking my head, I give him my best deadpan expression. "I know what you're trying to do, Emo Boy. Do you really think you can flirt your way into making me forget how you just tried to break up with me when we weren't even officially dating?"

My words are in jest, and he's not buying my shit.

He smacks a peck on my lips, then kisses me again, longer and deeper. Warmth settles in my belly, percolating through all my limbs until I'm putty in his capable, tatted hands.

He nips at my earlobe, sending a shudder down my spine and an ache pulsing in my clit. "I'm just making sure you know where I stand, baby. It's me and you. Plus him. And maybe them."

I try to glare, but his smile is so wide and the sparkle in his eyes so charming it's hard to look at him and feel anything but happy.

Still.

I do my best to set him straight.

"Kendrick can barely tolerate me on a good day. And Decker..."

Decker. He's become an enigma in my life. He's the root of so much pain, yet a sanctuary when I least expect it. He may never give in to the chemistry that tries to boil over when we're alone together, but if he did, I can guarantee he is *not* the sharing type—so if we're really doing this, I have to count Decker out on principle.

"Okay, Hot Girl. Whatever you say."

"Locke," I huff in warning, but his name comes out sounding more like a moan.

He captures my lips again, teasing the tip of his tongue against the seam until I open for him.

Desperate for a better angle—a deeper connection—I grasp his shoulders and shift in his lap so I'm straddling him.

Rising to my knees, I grip the hair at his nape and force his head back, loving the way he lets me move him wherever I want him.

With his throat extended and exposed, the rapid pulse of the veins in his neck are visible beneath the fine red and black lines of his tattoo. It's all the confirmation I need to squirm against his body until I feel the hard, demanding length between his legs.

Bullseye.

Or I guess he'd be the arrow? Bazooka launcher might be a more apt description for all that Locke's packing.

I purr my pleasure as I grind against his cock.

Eager, he lifts his hips slightly to give me an even better angle and delves deeper into my mouth. The pressure is exquisite, sending sparks ricocheting through me. Arousal so strong an ache gathers in my core.

After being so wound up, so anxious and scared, then hollow and terrified, it feels good to feel good. To feel wanted. *To feel alive.*

He teases along the hem of my shorts, fingertips leaving goose bumps in their wake. His other hand travels under my shirt and up the bare skin of my back, lighting me up with each and every caress.

Fuck. Yes. This is what I need. His hardness beneath me. The distraction. To be consumed by him. It's everything, and yet it's nowhere near enough.

"Locke," I murmur, grinding my hips forward, so damn eager for more.

He catches my chin with one hand, thumbing over the tender flesh of my bottom lip. "That's not what I want to hear from this mouth when you're in my arms."

The words and the low intonation make my core clench, and without my permission, my tongue darts out to lick the tip of his thumb.

In response, he tracks the movement, his hazel irises igniting in twin amber flames.

"Nicky," I whisper.

His eyelashes flutter, and the heated look instantly melts. At the sound of his name, a smile so soft it's almost bashful splits his face. "I'm so glad you're back," he murmurs, smoothing both hands over my hair. "We missed you, Hot Girl."

Dragging his hands from my head to my shoulders, he pulls me into his chest. Though I expect a fire to ignite at the contact—stoked by the make-out session that I thought was just getting started—all I find is a warm embrace.

I revel in his touch and give in to the sweetness he loves to dish out for a moment, but when I try to lift my hips, I realize I can't move. He's holding me so tightly I can't grind against him anymore.

"Nicky." His name is a whimper this time as I struggle to press my center against his dick.

"You need sleep, Joey," he murmurs against my ear without loosening his embrace.

"I need *you*." I roll my hips a fraction, desperate for the feel of him again.

"Baby, we can't."

Oh yes we fucking can.

"Nicholas Lockewood," I snap. "I swear to god, after everything I've been through the last few days, then tonight with Kylian, and then you trying to break up with me, talking like—"

"What happened with Kylian? Is he okay?" he interrupts, his brows pulled together.

Tension drains out of me like water through a sieve. For as much as I care about my guys, they've been looking after and caring for each other for years. Since long before I showed up.

Giving up my fight against his hold, I go soft in his arms. "He wasn't okay. I've never seen him like that before."

Locke grits his teeth, nodding. "Yeah. He's been a mess without you."

Gulping past the misplaced guilt that threatens to bubble up—it's not like I kidnapped myself, after all—I try to ease Locke's concern.

"It took some convincing, but I got him to go up to the Nest, and he promised to sleep. I don't know if that was the right thing to do, or if I should have tried—"

He laces one hand through my hair and guides my head until our foreheads touch.

"You did good, baby. He does need sleep. Speaking of..."

I let out an indignant *hmph*, then try—in vain, I might add—to rock my lower body again before cursing him out.

"Dammit, Locke! I spent the last few days either sedated or hyper-aware and anxious. I don't need sleep. I need *release*."

"Hot Girl," he chides, rubbing his forehead against mine and caressing my skin under the hemline of my shorts. "We can't, baby. You need rest."

"I need *you*."

His thumbs still, and I swear I feel his resolve waver.

"Joey, they'll kill me if I keep you up any longer than necessary. Not just Kylian, either. All of them."

"That's what you're worried about?" I snap. "Pissing off Nut Cap and Grumpy McGee? I can't believe I'm being cock-blocked by Decker Crusade. *Again.*"

He fights back a smile and tries to look serious.

But I'm serious, too. And I'm not backing down. "You think they'll kill you for keeping me up? I'll kill you if you don't make me come."

His pierced brow shoots up, then he shakes his head.

"I like it when you get violent on me, baby."

I snort out a laugh. "You would, Emo Boy."

Softer, angling my lips so they brush over his as I speak, I beg, "Please let me ride you, Nicky. I want to sink down on your cock and be so full there's no room to feel anything else."

"Joey..." he groans.

I run my nails down his torso then tease at the waistband of his shorts.

"I don't have a condom."

Dammit.

But I'm not giving up.

"What if I used you and your pubic piercing to make myself come, then?"

His lips part and his pupils blow out, all but eclipsing his irises.

Licking the pout of his bottom lip, I double down.

"Would you like that, Nicky? Do you want me to use you? Can I grind my pussy on your enormous cock and rub my clit against your piercing until I make a mess in your lap?"

"Jesus Christ, Joey," he groans, one hand gripping my hip and the other tugging on his hair. "Fucking filthy girl."

"You love it."

"I do."

Yet he's still wavering, his eyes a storm of indecision.

I want him. No, I need him. And I think he needs me right now, too.

"Please, Nicky," I whisper against the warm skin of his neck. "I promise I'm okay. I'll be even better if I can feel connected to you."

He peers up through his long, thick lashes and brushes his knuckles over my cheekbone, but he doesn't respond.

"What's happening in there?" I ask, tapping his forehead with mine.

"I'm negative. I got tested at the beginning of the season," he offers hesitantly.

Oh.

Oh...

"I am too," I breathe, "and I have the implant." One of the last things I did before moving to North Carolina was visit my OGBYN for my annual appointment to get tested and get the long-term birth control option inserted.

"It's your call, Hot Girl."

That's all I need to hear.

Having the power of choice and autonomy over my own body is what seals the deal for me.

"I want to feel you inside me with nothing between us," I murmur, shimmying out of my shorts and ripping off my tank top.

"You're sure?" he hedges, hands pulled back like he's afraid to touch me. "You've been through so much this week. It feels wrong to do anything but tuck you in tonight."

"So sure," I promise, clawing at his T-shirt until he leans forward enough that I can pull it over his head. "You don't always have to be the nice guy, you know."

He eyes me up and down, then comes to a stop at my bare tits that are conveniently now at eye-level.

"I want to be good for you."

I grin and rise up on my knees.

"Then be a good boy and peel off my panties. I want a distraction. I need to lose myself in pleasure and ecstasy and happiness so I don't get lost in the dark. Please, Nicky."

Done hesitating, *fucking finally*, he hooks his fingers under the fabric at my hips, but peel them off he does not.

With the slyest smirk, he tugs, forcing the fabric to go tight around my body for a moment before a distinctive, undeniable *rip* cuts through the quiet around us.

"Fuck," I groan, fumbling with his waistband so I can free his cock from his pants.

He just ripped my panties right off my body. Hell. Yes.

"Kiss me, Nicky," I demand, pressing my lips to his in a fevered, hungry kiss.

His lips find mine, and they're just as frenzied. I moan into his mouth, licking and sucking as he finally—*fucking mercifully*—leans in to what we both want and crave.

Gripping his length in one hand, I move. Just slow pulls up and down his length at first. It takes all my restraint not to rush this.

Lust courses through my veins as I peek open my eyes and take him in. From the piercing in his eyebrow to the tats that blend together so beautifully, he's a work of art.

Paying special attention to his neck, I trace my tongue up and down the intricate lines of the ink I love so much. He smells clean and crisp, fresh from practice. The distinct scent of mint and sugar cane I've come to associate with him only stimulates me further.

He tastes divine. I want to sample every part of him. But I'll have to save that for another time. Right here, right now, I need to feel him inside me.

Nothing between us.

Forever in front of us.

I free his cock from his pants, pressing into his chest until he leans back and offers me the angle I want.

"Eager, Hot Girl?" he teases, gripping his dick and giving it a few pumps.

Breathless from kissing, I meet his gaze. "Right now, there's nothing I want more than you, Nicky."

"Fuck, baby. Say it again."

"I want you," I plead, grasping his wrist gently so we can guide his hand together. "Put it in, Nicky. I need it."

Every nerve ending lights up when the crown of his cock surges forward, causing my whole body to shudder and my mouth to fall open in a silent moan.

He takes his time, thrusting just an inch or two at a time so I can adjust to his massive size. But by the time he's halfway in, I'm done waiting.

"Nicky," I moan, bucking my hips forward in warning. "I need you *now*."

I spread my legs wide and slide down his dick until I'm taking him to the hilt. Once I'm fully seated, his pubic piercing presses against my clit, the metal noticeably warm and deliciously unyielding when I grind down harder.

"Fuck, Joey. Nothing's ever felt as good as this," he pants, gripping my shoulders and holding me to him.

"Wait until you feel me coming on your cock without a condom," I tease, clenching around his length for emphasis.

Worrying his bottom lip, he considers me.

"I know you like to be on top, Hot Girl... but can I fuck you from below?" he asks.

As if it's even a question.

"Yes, please," I reply in an instant, rising up to give him room.

His dazzling smile is the only warning I get before he's thrusting up into me, enough power to the movement that I jolt with the force of his cock fucking all the way inside.

The full-body shiver that follows sends tingles through my extremities. "Holy shit."

"My thoughts exactly."

He does it again, and again...each thrust perfectly timed and powerful enough to fuck all rational thoughts from my mind.

"Fuck, you're good at this," I praise, holding on to his shoulders so I can grind my clit against his piercing each time our bodies connect.

I'm hot all over. Heat creeps from my belly to each one of my limbs, following behind the tingles. I can barely keep up with his thrusts, but I'm desperate to give as good as I'm getting.

"I'm close," I warn after just a few minutes, a surge of numbness followed by telltale tingles coursing through my toes.

"Thank fuck," he grunts, his head thrown back. "I'm ready to fucking blow. Nothing has ever felt as good as you, Joey. Nothing."

He thrusts up once more and holds it, bridging his pelvis and squeezing my hips to create the perfect amount of pressure and hit just the right angle.

"Yes, yes, yes…" My words die off as my mouth drops open, and a silent scream escapes me as my pussy convulses in ecstasy.

"Hell yeah," he grunts, finding his own release as I spasm around him.

We come undone as we come together, reclaiming who we are to each other in a blissful, simultaneous release.

Panting, he finally lowers his hips and settles onto the couch, all while holding me firmly in his lap.

I kiss the piercing in his eyebrow. Then I trace the ink along his throat and chest, studying every line of him and committing this moment to memory.

"We're definitely doing that again," he eventually says, his eyes sparkling with adoration.

"Tonight?" I'm half hopeful, but I'm also half concerned. Now that I've finally found release, I'm desperate for a chance to sleep in my own bed.

"Not tonight, Hot Girl." He kisses me reverently, then presses his lips into my forehead.

Smiling, I loop my arms around his neck and cuddle closer so our chests are pressed together and the warmth of him seeps into me. With one last kiss to his shoulder, I savor how it feels to finally be back where I belong.

Chapter 9

Josephine

Worried about waking my guests, I pull the bedroom door closed as quietly as possible, but it turns out it's not necessary.

Hunter is awake, sitting cross-legged on my bed, gnawing on the end of a pen with her nose buried in a textbook.

"Is Greedy in here?" I whisper.

Rolling her eyes, she shakes her head, then, at regular volume, she says, "He's using the bathroom in the hallway. He insists he's sleeping in here. There, specifically"—she points her pen at a pile of blankets and one sad-looking pillow shoved into the corner of the room—"but I drew the line at letting him use our bathroom."

"Good call," I quip. "Boys are gross."

"You're not wrong." She shoots me a cheeky grin, but her smile quickly drops. "I'm sorry he's here. I legit had no idea—"

"Hunter," I interrupt, crossing the room and perching on the edge of the mattress.

I was up here earlier to shower and change, and just like then, the space feels familiar. Comforting. Safe. How is it possible that this place feels like home already? This isn't just a room—it's mine.

"I don't mind. If Greedy thinks this is what he needs to do, I'm not going to object. I owe him big-time."

She lets out a *tsk* and sits up straight like she's ready to argue, but I continue.

"You being here means the world to me. Greedy is a bonus."

"If you say so." She snaps her textbook closed, then sets it on the corner of the nightstand closest to her side and hops up to pull back the covers.

"I'm serious." I run a hand over the duvet. "I'd rather have you here with your old ball and chain than be by myself tonight."

She chuckles, then before I can react, a pillow smacks me in the head.

"I'm going to let you get away with that because you've been through hell these last few days," she teases.

I grab the pillow and throw it back. "Good to know that being kidnapped and slipping into an anxiety spiral has its perks. I wonder what else I could get away with."

Yawning, she pulls back the sheet on my side. "I assume you're not going to class tomorrow, but I am. We both need sleep. Are you ready for bed?"

Her yawn triggers my own, but I shake my head. "I need to shower first."

Hunter snorts. "I bet you do. Who was it?"

I don't even pretend to be offended by the question. If we're doing this—Kylian, Locke, and me—I refuse to be ashamed of what we are and how we operate.

"Locke," I breathe out, not bothering to temper the reverence in my voice. With a fresh pair of pjs from my dresser, I head for the en suite.

"And *how* was it?" she calls after me.

Glancing over my shoulder from the doorway, I shrug, but my coy act lasts a total of three seconds. The biggest smile takes over my face as I look back at my friend. "Fan-fucking-tastic," I whisper giddily.

Hunter squeals, kicking her legs under the covers and making a scene. She freezes and schools her expression in an instant when the bedroom door opens and Greedy enters the room.

Once the door is shut behind him, they lock eyes, but a breath later, she lies back and rolls over without a word, effectively dismissing him.

I take that as my cue to close the bathroom door so I can quickly scrub myself clean.

I did the whole long, luxurious, deep-conditioning, shave-every-hair and scrub-every-inch shower after Kylian went up to the Nest earlier. I just need a quick rinse so I can climb into bed without smelling like sex.

When I'm done, I slip on my clean pajamas, brush my teeth, and quietly sneak back into the bedroom.

It's dark. But not dark enough to hide the lump on the ground.

Greedy isn't sleeping in the corner where his pile of blankets was when I stepped into the bathroom. And he isn't on the love seat near the door to the balcony, which would probably be his most comfortable option.

No, he's on the floor, close to Hunter's side, positioned between her and the door.

Shaking my head, I climb into bed and get comfy. There's so much I don't understand about these two. But I trust them both, despite the unknowns and the bad blood between the Crusaders and the Sharks.

Greedy saved me. More than that, he stayed to make sure I was okay. He was by my side at the hospital, and he advocated for me when I couldn't make sense of what was happening.

Then there's Hunter. She isn't just my bestie—she's the best friend I've ever had. There's a soul-deep connection between us. An effortless, platonic kind of love.

The dynamic between them baffles me. There's history there, and there's also chemistry and connection and undeniable fire.

From the longing looks he gives her and the reverent way he speaks to her, it's obvious Greedy is after more than Hunter is willing or able to give. But based on what I've seen today, I don't think he's one to back down or give up without a fight.

I fidget a bit, eventually rolling to my side to find Hunter awake and watching me in the dark.

She readjusts her pillow, and a section of blond hair fans out in front of her face until she sweeps it away and tucks it behind her ear.

"Thank you for being my person," I whisper.

"Don't let your boyfriends hear you call me that," she teases.

I give her shoulder a shove.

"Seriously. I don't think I could do this without you."

That's the truth. And the reality is that it's not over yet. There's a very good chance I'll wake up in the middle of the night disoriented or in a state of panic like I did in the hospital.

We have a safety plan in place, and Hunter knows what to say and do if I spiral. I'd never tell her, but I'm grateful that Greedy's in the room with us, too, because he saw firsthand what it was like each time the panic crept in at the hospital.

"Yes, you could have. You're amazing and strong as hell. But even if you wanted to, I wouldn't have let you do it alone. That's what best friends are for."

Taking my hand under the covers, she squeezes twice before flopping to her back.

I lie there, still as stone, so overcome with gratitude that emotion clogs my throat. I don't know what I did to deserve her; I don't know what I did to deserve my guys either, but for perhaps the first time in my life, I feel cherished, loved, and seen.

Chapter 10

Josephine

I wake with a start, heart racing and too hot, but not completely unaware of where I am.

At the mansion. In my room. Still in my own bed.

I am here. This is now.

I'm safe.

Exhaling a long, slow breath, I will my heart rate to slow so I can drift back to sleep. I feel surprisingly rested, probably thanks to the lack of beeping monitors and nurses coming in and out. My gut tells me it's nowhere near morning, but I've slept longer and more soundly than I have in days.

Coming back here had the intended effect. This room... this place... it all feels so right, even though it started so wrong.

The stupid-comfortable bed doesn't hurt.

Nor does the heavy arm wrapped around my waist and holding me close like my personal weighted blanket.

An arm, I'm now realizing, that does *not* belong to Hunter.

Ironically, I don't panic. I do, however, blink a few times, until my eyes adjust to the dark and her side of the bed comes into focus. Sure enough, she isn't there. A quick peek at the floor confirms that Greedy is gone, too. Maybe it's closer to daylight than I thought. The blackout curtains in this room are exceptional.

I snuggle into the body behind me, assuming the little spoon position so whichever of my guys has joined me knows I'm awake. Maybe Locke decided he wanted that round two after all.

As I cuddle closer, I'm enveloped in a masculine scent tinged with a hint of savory sweet. In my sleepy haze, it takes a few extra seconds to identify the combination, but once the musk and warm vanilla register in my olfactory senses, I go stiff.

The scent is delicious, but over the weeks, it's one I've come to associate with anger and resentment. Which means the last person I ever expected to find in my bed is *in my bed*.

"Kendrick!" I hiss. A million questions race through my mind, but the only gobbledygook my groggy, confused mind can string together is "what the fuck?"

I try to roll over, but his grip is too tight. His massive arm is pinning me down, the deadweight anchoring me to the mattress.

"Kendrick," I growl, louder this time, bucking against him. The big guy is out cold.

I wiggle my hips and arch back to try to free myself from his grip. My heart leaps into my throat on contact, and I fly forward the instant I feel the not-exactly-soft length between his legs.

My cheeks heat, which pisses me off more. I'm not the one sneaking into someone else's bed in the middle of the night, so why should I be embarrassed?

"Wake up," I hiss through clenched teeth.

"Sleep," he mutters, deep and growly, but also a little whiny.

Sleep, I will *not*.

Not until the man who hates my guts explains why he's in my bed.

I have a boyfriend. Two, in fact!

Locke's teasing remark about Kendrick comes crashing back into my consciousness like a freight train.

But no. That's not what this is. It *can't* be.

Kendrick hates me. *Hated* me, I suppose.

For the sake of the rest of the guys, we've settled into a mutual tolerance. A tolerance that involves a wide berth and the occasional civil exchange. A tolerance that does *not* involve spooning.

"*Kendrick*. What are you doing?"

He inches closer and hitches one leg over mine, inadvertently—I think?—pressing his hardness against my ass.

Dumbstruck, I freeze in place. My mind can't form words or signal my body to take self-preserving measures when he's this close. Or when he smells so good.

"Snuggling you," he yawns. Casually. As if it's a regular thing for us.

"Why?" I demand, still trapped in his warm, comforting hold.

Another yawn. Then I swear I feel a featherlight touch brush along my side and bare hip where my shirt has risen up.

"You were whimpering."

"I was not," I huff. As if I'd know what I was doing in my sleep.

This time, he chuckles. "You were. It wasn't one little whine, either. You were going on for a while. As soon as I got into bed, you stopped. I'm here. I've got you. Go back to sleep."

I fight back a yawn, determined to do the opposite of what he says. "Where's Hunter?"

He grunts, then silence ensues.

"Where's Greedy?" I press.

"Don't fucking care," he murmurs, running his fingertips more deliberately over my hip and pressing into the soft skin of my belly, anchoring me in place.

"Kendrick…" I warn.

"Jojo…" he mocks.

"Jojo? Really?"

So few people call me Jojo anymore. It's a nickname that makes me feel both nostalgic and like I'm wearing a turtleneck that's two sizes too small.

"It's what my sisters call you," he reminds me softly. "What your uncle calls you, too. I like it."

A lump of emotion clogs my throat. There's no way this man is willingly lying in my bed, soothing me, and declaring that he likes the new nickname he's using.

Uncomfortable with it all, I crane my neck, putting a little space between us and peeking over my shoulder. His eyes are closed. He looks relaxed. Peaceful, even. It's the softest expression I've ever seen on him.

"Where I'm from, a jojo is a fried potato wedge."

The corner of his mouth quirks up, which might as well be a full-blown smile for Kendrick Taylor. Damn, his lips are even more appealing than I realized. He's never let me get this close to him before. I've never noticed the length and volume of his dark eyelashes. Or the way the stubble along his jaw makes it appear even more chiseled and makes his neck seem even broader.

He cracks one eye open, and I quickly look away, praying he didn't catch me ogling him.

"Would you rather I call you potato?" he asks with a playful squeeze of my hip.

The squeeze tickles. Or maybe it tingles. I can't make sense of his hands on me, the feelings he's inspiring, or the depraved place my mind wants to go as my body relaxes into his hold without my permission.

His hands... ugh. His hands.

Except I can't do this. I'm not thinking clearly. This moment of sweetness doesn't cancel out all the anger and accusations he's lobbed at me over the last several weeks.

I try to squirm away, only to have him grip me tighter.

"Nope. Sleep."

As if he's calling a play or commanding a dog.

"I need some space, Kendrick," I grit out.

"You need some sleep, Jojo."

Frustrated, I try to squirm away. *Try* being the operative word.

"*Kendrick*," I growl. "I can't sleep with you crushing me. Do you even know how big you are?"

Shit. The moment the words leave my mouth, heat creeps up my neck and settles in my cheeks.

He doesn't take the bait—small mercy, I guess. But he doesn't let me go, either.

"Just try to go back to sleep," he implores.

"I'm not going to be able to sleep with you in here," I argue.

"You were sleeping just fine right here beside me for the last two hours, Mama."

I was?

Heart thumping in my chest, all I can do is blink. No counterargument comes to mind, no matter how badly I want to tell him he's wrong.

"Jade used to get night terrors. She still does occasionally. Snuggling always helped. After my Ma passed... it helps. Let me help you."

His fingertips drum against my skin, the warmth and rhythm of the contact lulling me into a trance.

"Okay?" he asks.

Though I'm not used to being taken care of, least of all by someone I could have sworn viewed me as the bane of his existence, I nod in acquiescence.

"Your mom died?" I can't help but ask.

The silence that ensues probably means I've pushed too far. Leave it to me to stir up his grief when he's sharing in an effort to comfort me. But if he insists on tearing down my walls, I'm at least going to try to scale a few of his.

"She passed away when I was thirteen. Right about the time Decker lost his mom."

My heart clenches in agony for their individual and shared losses.

"How did she die?" I whisper.

Kendrick is silent for so long I assume he's not going to answer. So I settle in, resigned to his proximity.

Working in hospice for a few years dulled my discernment around grief. I forget that people tend to shy away from the nuances of death and dying until I've already made them uncomfortable.

But then he spreads the massive hand out so wide along my hip that it covers half my stomach. He lets it rest there, holding me like he needs the support almost as much as I need the balm.

"Kidney failure," he grits out. Clearing his throat, he uses that splayed palm to pull me just a little closer. "She had lupus. Passed it on to me. Emilia, too. Jade hasn't shown enough symptoms to qualify for a diagnosis yet, but..."

Instinctively, I reach for his hand. I trace his fingers with mine, from knuckle to knuckle, wrist to tip.

On the third pass, he catches me, interlacing our fingers and resting our joined hands against my skin.

Tension rises between us. Not a frenetic crackle, but a gradual simmer. Measured and steady. Deep and pure.

It's a slow build. A tightness that crescendos, then keeps climbing higher.

He's not touching me anywhere other than where our hands rest on my hip.

And yet...

A warmth is blossoming inside me.

It's delicious. And powerful. I subtly shift back, seeking the shelter of his arms, the comfort and warmth I crave.

Five minutes ago, I wanted him out.

Now I'm trying to steady my breathing and quell the clench of my thighs as every part of my essence screams at me to let him in.

"Kendrick," I practically plead. "What are we doing?"

His breath hitches on the inhale, and he shifts closer to my back and brings his face to the crook of my neck.

Placing a featherlight kiss there, he exhales, sending a bolt of desire coursing down my spine.

"I thought you were smart, Ohio," he says, his lips at my ear now. "Didn't you win the Crusade Scholarship?"

Is he... flirting with me?

"*Kendrick.* I'm serious. What are we doing?"

My voice is breathy. My chest feels tight and full of helium at the same time. The tension continues to coil at a steady pace, like it might never stop. What happens to a spring that's twisted in perpetuity?

He shifts closer, the sheets rustling around us, and pulls me back into his body. I fight back a moan as a dozen touch points spark to life between us: His chest to my back. My ass on his stomach. His arm wrapped around me, while the warmth of his lips inspires goose bumps to erupt along my neck.

"I told you," he scolds, his voice nothing but a rasp. "We're snuggling."

"You hate me." The second I say the words, I have to gulp down a wave of trepidation. Because that statement doesn't feel true anymore.

"I wanted to hate you," he corrects.

My heart lurches in my chest. "Wanted?"

"Shh," he soothes. "Less talking. More snuggling. Or sleeping." He yawns to punctuate his command.

"I'm not going to sleep until you answer me."

What is this? I was just starting to accept the cool neutrality between us—like we were finally finding our footing on opposite sides of the group dynamic.

There's been an energy between us since the moment we met. If he doesn't hate me anymore, then what's the source of that energy? And what's fueling it? If he's holding me this tightly and whispering his truth through the darkness, that has to mean something, right?

I can't risk being toyed with—not now, when I'm so unbelievably raw. Not when it isn't just my heart in the mix anymore.

He squeezes my hand, then places a tender kiss on my shoulder.

"It was easier to hate you than to admit I wanted you, too. You've been in my head since the moment we met, Jojo. I'm done fighting it. I know the deal. I don't know the details yet, but I want in, too."

I'm shocked silent by his declaration.

And he's not done.

Brushing his lips back and forth over my collarbone, he hums and nuzzles closer.

"I know I was cold. Crass. Downright cruel. I had my reasons. I thought I was protecting the others. But it was bullshit, and I'm sorry."

Shrouded in darkness, I gape, floundering for an appropriate response. He hasn't stopped touching me. Hasn't stopped whittling away at everything I thought I knew about him and our dynamic.

"The boys and I... we don't compete. Not with each other. Never have. Never will. It was easier for me to bow out in the beginning than to entertain the idea of interfering. Plus, I really did think you were trouble when you showed up in town."

Teeth graze my skin, sending me writhing. This man, who's been nothing but serious and abrasive since I met him, is nipping at me playfully? What sort of alternate reality did I wake up in?

I'm emotionally raw and physically buzzing. Hope and desire both surge through me, leaving me an absolute strung-out mess.

"Kendrick..." I don't even know where to begin. He's right—he was harsh. Cruel. Casually indifferent at his best. Downright awful at his worst.

All because his buddies liked me? And he didn't know how to deal?

I shift on the mattress, ready to make him own up to his shit.

But he beats me to it.

"I'm sorry, Jojo. It was immature and stupid. I'm sorry for how I treated you, and for the part I played in forcing you to move in here. I know an apology isn't enough, but I'll do whatever I can to make it up to you now."

Shit on a crumbly cracker. Of course it'd be the grumpiest among them to also be the most emotionally intelligent.

I could push back. I could punish him for all the ways he hurt me over the last several weeks.

But in truth, I'd be hurting myself just as deeply.

Because right now? In this bed, wrapped up in his arms?

I feel really, really good.

And I don't want to let this feeling go.

"Okay," I whisper, nodding and craning my neck so I can look him in the eye.

"Okay?" he confirms, deep brown eyes meeting mine in a smoldering assessment.

Tipping my chin up, I give him a small smile. "Yes. Okay. I forgive you."

His fingers catch under my chin, and he dips his head until his lips brush mine. He doesn't kiss me, but he comes close. Sliding his hand around to the back of my head, he searches my face.

"Don't forgive me yet, Mama. I'm going to fucking earn it. You deserve to be fought for, not fought over. You deserve to be vindicated—which is exactly what I'm gonna do. The motherfucking South Chapel Sharks need to know what happens when they try to take what's ours."

"Ours?" I ask, hypnotized by his closeness, his presence, the intensity of his gaze.

"*Ours*. We were a mess without you, Jojo. When I saw how the boys all responded, saw how they need you... I couldn't keep denying that I need you, too."

His admission steals my breath and makes my stomach dip. Is this what swooning feels like? A ridiculously delighted hum escapes me before I can stop it, and I blush when I notice the hint of a smirk on Kendrick's lips.

A small voice in the back of my mind whispers that I'm not worthy. That this is all too good to be true. But I tell that bitch to hush and revel in the feeling of being wanted. Being chosen. Being claimed.

Desperate to hide my grin, I shift again so I'm facing away from him, then sink back into his hold, savoring the warmth and adoration radiating off him.

Kendrick wasn't supposed to be part of the equation. Yet he's a perfect fit—a belt buckle finding its usual notch, or a perfectly worn-in pair of sneakers laced up just right.

"Be good to us. Don't make us compete."

"Never," I whisper, my heart aching at just the thought. "I would never do that to any of you."

He kisses the back of my neck once more, then goes still behind me. After a long moment, when I'm almost positive he's drifted off again, he speaks. "I believe that now. I didn't at first. But I was wrong. I believe you, Jojo."

Chapter 11

Josephine

Stretching my arms overhead, I roll out my neck and squint as I tip my head back and bask in the late afternoon sun. I've been out on the deck for a few hours, alternating between working on my laptop at the table and dozing in the hammock.

It's been a quiet afternoon, for which I'm grateful. Kylian FaceTimed me between his last class and a meeting with the coaching staff. Locke checked in via text every hour or so.

I received an email this morning confirming that I've been excused from classes for the rest of the week. My assignments have been magically excused as well. Thank god for Kylian or Decker or whoever made that happen. I couldn't focus on logic or technical writing right now if my life depended on it. I'll take the reprieve and get back into a routine come Monday.

I squint at the screen of my MacBook and adjust the brightness just as Mrs. Lansbury comes out to refresh my sweet tea. Again.

She's nurturing by nature, but I'm beginning to suspect that she's got some sort of timer set and is required to check on me at regular intervals. This setup also has Kylian and Decker written all over it. Whether the directive came from one or both, I'm not sure. I wouldn't put it past either of them. Or hell, maybe all of them.

Regardless, her quiet company is comforting. I smile appreciatively at her, and when she heads back into the house, I hit play on the tutorial I'm working through.

I don't have the attention span to focus on reading for school today, so I brought my laptop out on the deck to watch a few photo editing videos.

Before the day Decker handed that DSLR camera to me, I had no interest in photography, but working to capture the grit and brutality on the field through the lens of my camera is undoubtedly thrilling.

After finishing the video I have cued up and watching a small portion of it again to get it all just right, I practice quick actions in Photoshop. So much of the post-production comes down to presets and shortcuts, but I want to learn all the ins and outs of manipulating raw files, too.

I'm working to reduce the motion blur on an action shot of Kendrick when the telltale sounds of a boat float in on the breeze, warning me that I won't be alone for much longer.

The whirl of the pontoon engine grates on my nerves almost like nails on a chalkboard, but it doesn't send me over the edge like it did yesterday. I blow out a steady breath, relying on the mantra I've used for years to edge out the panic.

I am here. This is now.

I am here. This is now.

It's a lot like photography, the way I cope and calm myself. Capturing a mental snapshot of what's actually happening around me helps ward off the terror that threatens to run rampant.

On the deck, with the sun kissing my face, I'm safe and out of harm's way.

I feel the stickiness of the humid afternoon air on my skin.

I smell the roasted vegetables Mrs. Lansbury is preparing for dinner.

I hear my friends bounding up the stairs from the beach to the upper deck.

Pulling in a centering breath, I rise from the table, then I make my way to the overlook that offers a view of the entire isle below. Each step I take is slow and deliberate while I force my movements to remain smooth and relaxed. The lower decks, the docks, the rocky beach, and the lake—it's all part of the private kingdom of Decker Crusade.

Below me, my friends approach the house, unaware that I'm watching them. The guys all have wet hair, and Hunter and Greedy are with them, too. I wasn't sure if either of them would be back tonight, but I'm glad they are.

Kylian leads the pack, laser focused on the sliding glass door ahead of him, no doubt on a mission to get to me first.

Locke and Hunter are behind him, laughing together like old friends. Which is accurate, I guess. They've known each other for years. My best friend and my boyfriend. Or, well, one of my boyfriends.

Kendrick and Greedy trail behind them, heads bowed, deep in conversation. They don't look like enemies to me. They don't even look like opponents right now.

Decker brings up the rear.

As soon as I set my sights on him, his head snaps up, as if he can sense my energy.

His scowl deepens, and his gorgeous onyx black eyes drill into me with startling intensity.

Rather than follow his friends, he alters his course and beelines for the lower patio, then climbs the stairs to the upper deck where I stand.

His hair is still wet, and his cheeks are flushed. All signs that point to him clearing concussion protocol.

"You got to practice today?" I ask, shuffling to the top of the stairs.

His hard expression softens just a smidge, and the hint of a smile teases the corner of his mouth.

"I did," he confirms, coming to a stop in front of me. Our height difference is nonexistent as he hovers one step below.

"And you feel okay?" Concussions are no joke. He was in rough shape last week, and, knowing Decker, he let the drama of the last few days and my well-being supersede his own health.

"I'm okay. Tired," he admits. "But that's to be expected after the week we had. It was good to be out on the field... to get my head back in the game and to show up for my team." He scans me from head to toe as if he's trying to reassure himself that I'm okay.

"How do you feel?" he asks, turning the question on me.

I consider him, standing eye to eye for maybe the first time ever.

"I'm alive," I snark, though it's immediately clear my joke has fallen flat.

His irises darken until they almost match the pupil, and his scowl deepens.

Pivoting, I offer a more detailed assessment. "I'm still really sore," I admit. "I'm keyed up *and* exhausted at the same time. I can't focus on much of anything, but I don't want to just sit around all day, either." Dropping my chin, I study my bare feet for a moment, getting my thoughts in order. He wants the truth. He needs all the details. "I'm glad I don't have to be back in class until Monday. It's going to take a few more days for me to fully shake this."

"Makes sense." He shoves his hands in his pockets. "Your adrenals haven't recovered. You need more rest. What about the panic?" he asks, one brow cocked and his focus boring into me.

"It's there. On the periphery. But it's under control."

"Even when you wake up? How do you feel then?"

His questions are intense and disarming. Dr. Ferguson has me cross-tapering meds with the hope that a different SSRI can target the acute sense of dread that rises up when I'm on the precipice of spiraling. His theory is that if I can stay out of that almost-panicked state, then my brain won't default to that setting when I'm unaware of my surroundings. Switching meds means the world is a bit blurry around the edges, a sensation I'm hoping wanes with time.

Decker doesn't need to know the finer details about my medication regimen. But I want to open and honest with him...with all of them, so I lay it all out for him.

"I was totally fine when I woke up this morning. And when I woke during the night." I leave out the part where one of his best friends had to crawl into my bed to snuggle me into submission. "I think it's under control for now."

He dips his chin, brushes his knuckles along my cheek, and nods once. "Hold on to that, okay?"

His words are whisper-soft and wary, so different from the way he usually operates.

Before I can ask what he means or reflect on the exchange, he's bending low, letting his bag slide off his arm, and scooping me up behind the knees.

I'm so disarmed my first instinct is to giggle.

I fucking *giggle*.

Like I'm a damsel being swept off her feet by the gorgeous knight in shining armor. Or in this case, the gorgeous Crusader in red.

Except, for me, that's not the way the story ever goes. And Decker isn't just a hotshot football player trying to impress a girl.

He's been the antihero in my story since day one.

Apparently, this moment is no different.

I bounce in his arms as he turns and takes off down the deck stairs. A squeak of surprise, followed by a grunt of objection, escapes me, but my lungs are tight, and my mouth can't articulate actual words.

When his feet hit the sand, his arms tense around me, and a shout rings out from the direction of the house.

"Hey!"

It could be Kendrick or Locke, or maybe even Greedy, but I can't see a damn thing or lift my head because of the way he's bracing me.

Decker tightens his grip but doesn't slow his pace as he strides along the uneven lakeshore.

"The actual fuck? Crusade!"

That one was definitely Greedy.

And then, *"Put her down, Cap!"*

Kylian's howl pierces the heavy, humid afternoon air, and I swear Decker falters for just a moment.

I twist in his arms, desperate to get back to the house, but instead of yielding to me, he glares down as I struggle, homing in on my mouth, then my eyes, the chiseled muscle of his jaw working overtime.

"Decker," I pant, breathless, my mind spinning as I fight to get away and stay in the moment all at the same time. I can't slip back into the dark. Not now that I know what it feels like to live in the light. "What the hell are you doing? Put me down."

He whips his head away and raises his chin, ignoring my plea.

I crane back, straining against his hold, desperately searching for one of my guys.

Kylian comes into view just as he reaches the lower patio. He's running at a full sprint, powering toward us.

It's in that moment I realize just how far out we already are.

We're not on the rocky beach anymore.

We're nearing the end of the landing, on the side where they dock the pontoon.

Decker heaves me up higher and hurtles over the side of the vessel, his grip never loosening and his stride never slowing.

He holds me so tightly it's a struggle to fill my lungs.

It's not until the boat moves that the sound of the engine registers and I realize he's released me. He's got one hand on the throttle and the other on the steering wheel, while I'm the one clinging to him, my arms looped around his neck in a death grip.

Screams and chaos are just audible over the roar of the engine, the whooshing of the water slapping against the sides, and the rushing of blood in my ears.

I want to scream.

I want to protest.

I want to smack Decker Crusade upside the head until he gets it through his thick, over-inflated skull that he can't manhandle me and make me go where he wants me to go.

But all I can muster the energy to do is slither away from him and sink to my knees.

To let go. To crash. To will my mind to stay in the moment. To beg my consciousness to hold on against the torrential storm of anxiety threatening to pull me under.

All I can do is bury my head in my hands and dig the heels of my palms into my eyes as I sob. And scream. And try not to puke.

Because I'm on a boat.

I'm on a boat, against my will, being taken to places unknown, again.

Because of Decker fucking Crusade.

Chapter 12

Josephine

My hearing comes and goes, as if each sound is circling on a racetrack.

The whoosh of the water. The squawk of seagulls and the chirp of chickadees. The rustle of the leaves on the trees along the shore. The distant shouts of the people I love... the people I *need*.

Any of them.

All of them.

Just not him.

My shins ache as my weight presses into the rough carpet of the pontoon.

Shoulders hunched, head hanging, unable to rise.

Trapped. Forced into this situation. At the mercy of this man. At the mercy of my mind.

I'm conscious, but the all too familiar black orbs dance in my vision, taunting me, beckoning me to get lost in the recesses of my mind. I can't get a grip on the volume of the world around me. I'm so close to being gone... I'm always so damn close.

"You're okay. You're doing it, Josephine. You're okay."

The words oscillate from one side to the other, then back again, as tingles race along my back. The repetition helps—focusing on the syllables, on the pressure creeping up and down my spine.

Time is abstract in this state, but eventually, my mind calms enough to register my surroundings and the details of my situation.

I'm still on the floor of the boat—squarely in the middle of the vessel, desperate to stay as far away from the sides as possible. Decker is beside me—petting my hair, rubbing my back, awkwardly holding me without getting too close.

"You're okay," he repeats for what might be the hundredth time.

I've lost track of time, place, space. I've lost track of it all.

Damp hair clings to my forehead. I bat it out of my eyes, then wipe the sweat from my brow.

Beside me, Decker is laser focused on my face, his expression marred with intense, authentic concern.

As if he isn't the cause of this breakdown. *Motherfucker.*

"Why?" I demand on a shaky breath.

With a long exhale, he visibly relaxes, shifting off his knees until he's seated beside me instead of hovering.

He crosses his arms over his bent knees, regarding me with cool concern, but he doesn't speak.

"Why, Decker?"

He owes me some fucking answers.

He owes me so much, but I can't even consider collecting until he stops racking up debt with all the offenses he continues to launch against my autonomy and sense of self.

"Get your phone out and text Kyl. Let him know you're okay."

Bossy motherfucker.

"I'm pretty tired of you thinking you can force me to do whatever you want, whenever you want, *Cap.*"

His eyebrows shoot into his hairline. "Suit yourself. My suggestion was more for his benefit than mine. He's freaking the fuck out on the shore. I figured you'd want him to know you're okay."

We glare at each other, neither of us blinking, but my concern for Kylian wins out in the end. Agitated, I pull out my phone and shoot off a text.

Tucking my phone back into my pocket, I squint against the setting sun. "What now, *Cap?*"

"Now..." He hops to his feet and offers me a hand. "We see if you can keep it together."

Panic shoots through me as I consider his extended arm and the idea of pulling myself off the floor. Down here, I can't see the water, can't gauge how far we are from shore.

Yet here he is, still expecting me to push past it and fall in line—do what he says, go where he wants me to go, react how he wants me to react.

I swat at his stupid big hand with enough force that an audible *slap* rings out.

Crossing my arms over my chest, I sit back on my heels, glaring and getting comfy.

"Don't be mad," Decker says, like he's scolding a bratty child. As if those three words are a simple request rather than a dismissive order that belittles just about every one of my traumas—both recent and long ago.

"Mad? You think I'm *mad*? I'm so far beyond mad, Decker." I have to fight back the impulse to literally stomp my feet. "You're insufferable. Unforgivable. I *hate* you."

He glances back to shore, his jaw ticking and his breaths deep. Right now, he's doing his best to hold back the fire he wants to spew right back at me.

Blowing out one more breath, he pulls his hand back and plows it through his still-damp hair, then he runs it along the back of his head and scratches at his neck.

"I can take it." He gives me a dark look, his head bowed. "I'll do what it takes to help you, Siren. Even if it means being the bad guy in your story."

The *gall* of this motherfucker.

It's the ego. The arrogance. The silver-spoon lifestyle he's used to. The lifetime of being surrounded by yes-men and people willing to do his bidding, no matter when or where.

His cockiness is *infuriating*. And it ends fucking now.

Scrambling to my feet, I steel myself. It takes two strides to reach him before I'm shoving my fists into his chest. It does next to nothing to dislodge his footing, but it still feels good.

"You think you're helping me?" I challenge.

His lip quirks. "It's working, isn't it? You're doing it."

"Doing *what*?" I demand.

"You're on a boat. On the water. *Not* spiraling. Not succumbing to the panic."

I jolt back as if he's struck me, all the air knocked from my lungs.

He's not wrong.

Dammit, he's not wrong.

Doesn't mean what he's doing or the way he's going about it is right.

"You're on a boat, Josephine, and you're keeping it together. You're doing it, and you're doing it so beautifully. You've got this. And I've got you."

His attempt at placating just fans the flames of my rage.

"Really? You've *got me*?" I mock.

Nothing about this situation is right. My blood is absolutely boiling. I won't know peace until I temper the audacity of this man and knock him down several pegs.

"You know what you've got? A one-track mind and an ego the size of Atlanta. You don't fucking *got me*, Cap. You grabbed me and forced me onto a boat... again! I swear you're as bad as them!"

I don't have to elaborate for the insult to land. This time he recoils, turning away from me and grumbling as he stalks toward the helm.

As soon as he gives me his back, the anxiety creeps in, slowly darkening the edges of my vision and tingling up my extremities. The longer he doesn't look at me, the harder I have to fight to keep the panic at bay.

Shit on a crumbly cracker.

My chest tightens with each step he takes. And with every second that ticks by, it gets harder to pull air into my lungs.

Though I loathe the revelation, it's obvious I need him to look at me to keep me in this moment.

But I sure as hell don't want to admit that to him.

Stalking after him, I grab his arm and pull until he's facing me again.

"What's this really about? Is it about Kylian? Locke? *Greedy*?" I challenge.

His scowl deepens, and the anger swirling around him intensifies. "Why are you trying to fight me right now? I'm trying to *help* you, Josephine."

"Yet you just keep *hurting me*!"

I pace a few feet away, toward the stern, careful to stay as far from either side as I can, but enough that I can put a bit of distance between us.

Though this pontoon is enormous, I can't go far, and when I turn, prepared to continue my argument, he's watching me, wearing a satisfied smirk.

"What's that look for?" I demand, chest heaving. Dammit. It's not lost on me that it's easier to breathe now that he's facing me again.

"You want to fight," he surmises. "You need to fight." Chin held high, he stalks toward me until he's towering over my frame. "Want it. Need it. Crave it, even. There's so much fire in you, Siren. You need an outlet. And you know you don't have to tamp it down with me."

God dammit.

I hate that he's right. And I'll never admit how close he is to my truth.

It does feel good to unleash this tension. Especially after the last twenty-four hours. Though I'm the one who experienced the trauma, I've spent most of my time since being released from the hospital placating everyone else and assuring them all that I'm okay.

I'm not okay. I haven't been fucking okay for years.

But I haven't stopped trying, either.

My efforts go unnoticed more often than not, but not with Decker. He sees through every coping mechanism, every layer of the carefully constructed mask I wear.

He sees them, and he's not afraid to rip them away and face the ugly, raw parts of me forged over the years as I struggled to survive.

Reaching out, he twirls a loose strand of my hair around his finger. "You want to fight." He tugs, pulling just hard enough to piss me off. "So let's fight. Give me your worst."

I glare up at him, resisting the urge to swat his hand away as he baits me.

But then he tugs on my hair again. "What were you going to do?" he challenges. "Never leave the isle? Make Kylian bust out his military-grade ATV to take you to campus every day? Move away?"

The last question sends me.

"That's what this is about, isn't it?" Planting my hands on my hips, I glare up at the man who's held me captive in his mansion for weeks. "Keeping me."

"No." His response comes far too quickly.

"It is," I taunt, calling him on his shit. If he wants to dish it, I can serve it right back to him.

"It's not," he grits out through clenched teeth.

"I don't believe you."

If Decker wants to fight, I'll show him just how calm and docile I can be.

Decidedly, I plop down onto one of the plush leather benches, then cross my legs and lean back, as if I don't have a care in the world.

It's Decker's turn to rage.

Satisfaction surges through me when his gaze narrows and he clenches his jaw so hard it looks like he might crack a tooth.

Good. He deserves the pain of extensive dental work at my expense.

Sneering, he shakes his head. "You're serious right now? After everything that's transpired, you still think that little of me?"

Expression successfully schooled, I blink at him through my lashes. "So am I free to go?"

Silence ensues.

On his end, that is, because I can't help but press the issue.

"Am I free to leave, Cap? Can I start packing when we get back to shore?"

He looks across the water, back toward the mansion. We're far enough out that we can't hear or see the details of what's happening, but all five of our friends are still there, watching. Waiting for us.

I'm shocked that neither Kylian nor Locke has attempted to get to me. But I'm grateful for the opportunity to fight my own battle and put Decker in his place once and for all.

Sounds of evening on the lake rise up around us as I wait for his response. The buzz of water vessels in the distance. The whoosh of cars coasting down Route 77 a few miles north. The hum of insects and frogs just waking up to greet the dusk.

The soft ripples in the lake soothe me as I scoot closer to the side of the boat and watch tiny fish dart under the surface. When I chance a glance at Decker, he looks just as irate as before. So I poke him again.

"Answer me, Decker Crusade. Am I free to leave your house?"

He closes his eyes, his long lashes brushing against his stupid-high cheekbones.

When he opens them, fire blazes.

"No."

This controlling hypocrite. Angry, indignant tears erupt behind my eyes. The dull headache that bloomed as I crouched on the floor of the boat in a panic throbs as I try to hold them back—but it's useless. There are too many of them. They're coming too fast.

"No, Josephine," he repeats. "You can't leave."

I shove to my feet and stalk toward him, filled with so much hatred and vitriol I feel like I might blast off into space. I don't even bother wiping away the tears.

Palms out in front of me, I shove his chest, but he captures my wrists and pulls me into his body before I can find purchase. It's a fitting dynamic for the power imbalance between us.

"You can't leave," he whispers, bowing so low his minty breath is hot against my face.

The scent of amber and sea salt assaults my senses, distracting me for a nanosecond from the hatred thrumming through my veins.

"You can't leave, but not because you're a captive. Or because I want to hold you against your will, lock you in my room, throw you onto my bed, and keep you all to myself."

I gulp down a surge of hot desire as he digs his fingers into the delicate skin of my arms.

"You can't leave, because the sixty-one hours we suffered without you were torture. Pure, unrelenting torture. That's how long it was, Siren. Sixty-one hours. I counted each and every one of them. It was all I could do—all I could control. I didn't eat. I didn't sleep. I searched and I counted. That's it. For sixty-one hours, I didn't stop looking for you."

He pauses, just long enough to glare down at me. He's staring at me so intensely I'm afraid I'll catch on fire.

"I would have searched for a thousand more. I wouldn't have stopped until I found you. For them. For me.

"We can't go through that again. You can't leave, because we need you. You belong with us. I won't let anyone come between us now that we have you back, Josephine—not even you."

Shit on a crumbly cracker.

Fresh tears well behind my eyes, but they're no longer fueled by outrage. Why does he always seem to surprise me? He's fierce and fiery in the way he cares, sometimes to his own detriment. He's a protector. A leader. A relentless defender in every sense of the word.

On the field. With his friends. And, apparently, with me.

"Decker..."

I don't know what to say to any of that.

He swears he doesn't hate me...

I think I might finally believe him.

Concealing the effect his confession has on me, I lean forward, resting my cheek against his LCU T-shirt.

Slowly, as if I'm a bomb set to detonate and his touch is the trigger, he smooths his hands up my back. The warmth of his palms travels through the thin fabric of my shirt, the security of his hold a comfort, when moments ago his hands on me would have felt like a prison.

I wrap my arms around his waist and squeeze, willing him not to let me go.

He's right. He's so fucking right. I crave the fight. The push and pull. I crave it, but it's never been mine for the taking. Not like this. I need a safe place to unleash when it's all too much. Could he be that place for me?

He nuzzles the top of my head, then he dips lower, speaking directly into my ear.

"I won't hold you captive, Josephine. But I'll do everything in my power to make you stay."

Shuddering, I squeeze him tighter, silently pleading with him to be true to his word.

I'm not easy to love. There's too much trauma, too much anxiety and residual pain in my blood for any of this to be easy. I struggle enough to love myself some days.

My impulse is to lash out—don my armor and rally hard when the world's working against me. The truth is, I'm too soft to spend the rest of my days fighting. Decker sees that, and though it's a relief to know he'll hold me together when I need it, I hate showing him that vulnerable part of myself.

It's dangerous to be this raw with someone. He has the power to heal me. He also has the power to destroy me.

"You're strong, Siren. Stronger than you realize. We need you, and we need you whole. I thought bringing you out on the water and helping you get over this quickly was the right call. This may have been a bit too much too soon, though."

I snort at his half-assed admission. Tipping my head back, I rest my chin on his sternum so he can see my truth, despite my inability to say the words aloud.

This *did* help. I'm grateful.

I'm also hurt, and I'm still healing. I'm a mosaic of trauma and hope, but I don't need to explain that to him. No one sees me, truly sees me, more clearly than Decker Crusade.

Shaking his head, he releases his hold and takes a step back. "You're okay?" he asks.

It's a question this time. Although he already knows the answer, I appreciate that he's trying to course correct.

"I'm okay," I confirm, wrapping my arms around myself on instinct, already missing his touch.

He tilts his head, assessing me. "I really am sorry. I don't know how to do this."

"Do what?" I whisper.

He grips the back of his neck, staring me down. "Take care of someone who desperately doesn't want to be taken care of."

My heart weighs heavy in my chest at that admission. Every time I think he has me figured out...

Planting my feet wider, I focus on the gentle sway of the boat as we move with the current. Once I'm sure I'm steady, I let my arms fall to my sides.

"It has nothing to do with *want*, Decker. It comes down to who I am. What I've survived. What I've had to do to keep it together. I've been on my own for years. I don't know how to need someone, because that's never been an option before now."

With his attention set on the horizon, he nods, but I'm not convinced he understands.

"Bringing me out here like this... You could have explained it to me beforehand. How it might have helped," I reason, shifting my weight and trying to catch his gaze. "This would have gone down differently if you had just discussed it with me and gotten my consent."

"And you would have done it?" he challenges with a knowing look.

I slow blink, regarding him and holding in a scoff. This man in front of me may be a force to be reckoned with on the field and among his peers, but he has the emotional intelligence of a toddler.

"Maybe. Maybe not. Getting your way isn't the point, Cap."

Scowling, he retreats to the captain's seat at the helm. Without another word, he stands in front of the cushy chair, wrapping his hands around the wheel and keeping his focus fixed on the water ahead.

I trace an invisible line with my big toe and debate my next move. Should I give him space, or does he need reassurance?

There's more distance between us now than there has been since before he brought me out here. And that distance aches. Not because of fear or anxiety, but because of my need to get through to him, to move past this disconnect where he tries to control me. I struggle against his dominance, and every interaction between us feels like a near-miss.

Slowly, I approach him, and he tracks me out of the corner of his eye, that control waxing—that incessant beast that lives inside him desperate to make me do what he wants, when he wants, how he wants, without compromise.

He cracks his neck, and I see my in.

Crowding his personal space, I press myself into his side and hover until he lifts one arm and gingerly places it around my shoulders.

"I would have done it," I admit, wrapping my arms around his waist in a side hug. It's a peace offering and an indisputable truth. I rest my head on his chest, feeling the steady beat of his heart just below my temple. "Maybe not right away. But when I felt ready, on my terms, I would have asked for your help. I want to trust you, Decker. I want to let you in. But if you want to ever move past this sense of conflict, you have to accept me as I am and let me live."

Chapter 13

Decker

I've always trusted my gut.

Leaned into that deeper sense of knowing that lives just below the surface.

Used instinct and sensation and belief when calling plays on the field.

I relish control, and my position as quarterback gives me that. It took time to adjust when Kylian was recruited to assist the offensive staff with play-calling. Sure, we'd been best friends and he'd been helping me analyze film for years. We talked offensive strategy nonstop, and the way he explained the statistical probability of certain plays in specific scenarios was fascinating.

But having a voice in my headset telling me what to play based on the stats instead of instinct wasn't an easy adjustment. Thankfully, we've adapted over the years, finessed our process. Anymore, I know what he's going to say before he even calls it. We've found a rhythm, and we both lean into the security of that connection.

Josephine and me? We're ten times more combative than Kylian and I ever were. And I'm starting to lose hope that we'll ever find a rhythm of our own.

When I brought her out here, I knew she'd get all fiery and pissed off at me, but I can take her fire. Hell, I'll gladly burn in her flames if it means her tenacity and spirit come back in full force.

Seeing her in the hospital... watching the trepidation that cast over her face as she looked past me and searched the room for Greedy...

I can't fucking stand to see her like that. That's not who she is. That's not my girl.

I want to empower her. Lift her up.

But according to her, all I keep doing is hurting her.

It's like I don't know how to stop.

It's like I don't know *anything* when it comes to Josephine Meyer.

Nothing exists by halves in her world. If it isn't laughably simple, then it's mindbogglingly complex. She's like Kylian in that way: Cut and dry. Black and white. Her worldview is nuanced and emotive, and yet her reactions are straightforward and distinct.

More often than not, I get it wrong with her.

But in those rare, precious moments when I get it right...

At the bow of the boat, she's looking out across the lake, eyes set on the horizon, where the sun melts into a hazy twilight. She's sprawled out on one of the bench seats, her hands tucked under her chin. There isn't an ounce of tension in her shoulders right now. Her breathing is steady.

She looks peaceful. She looks *beautiful*.

I want to bring her peace. I want to be her safe place.

But she's right. I keep pushing, forcing, trying to control her, as if I can bend her without concern for how I might break her in the process.

Internally, I condemn myself for fucking this up—forcing her onto the boat like this, even if it's what I know. It's what my dad did to me all those years ago.

"Josephine."

She turns her head and inclines it slightly, smiling as she considers me. Her hair cascades in a waterfall over her cheek for an instant before she tucks it behind her ear and peeks up at me with those crystal blue eyes that reflect the light glimmering off the lake.

God, she's pretty. The plush, peachy hue of her lips. The smattering of freckles across her nose. I could stare at her for days and never tire of memorizing every detail; of studying all the pieces that make up this gorgeous force of a woman.

Clearing my throat, I snap myself out of it. I open my mouth on instinct, ready to tell her to come over here. "Come" is on the tip of my tongue, but I catch myself. Before it can escape, I snap my jaw shut and change tack.

With a small shake of the head, I reset and try again. "Would you like to steer?"

A glint of mischief sparkles in her eyes—she knows I had to course correct just now.

I might get it wrong most of the time, but I'm coachable. I'll learn. I'll put in the work, learn all her tells. Run drills and perfect every play until I get it right.

She leaves me in suspense for a few torturous seconds, but finally, she rises, stretching her arms overhead in a way that pushes her tits out against the thin fabric of her T-shirt.

Mouth set in a straight line, I watch with even coolness, pretending to be unaffected by the way her tight little body stretches and preens. Though I can't help but track the shape of her mouth as her lips form a silent O when she yawns.

Her spirit and no-holds-barred attitude are enough to do me in. Add in her perfect, full tits, curvy hips, and long legs, and it's enough to send me somersaulting over the edge of desire.

Or inspire a semi in my shorts.

Ignoring the pulse of my now very interested cock, I focus on the task at hand: giving her some semblance of control.

To do that, I have to explain to her why I thought this whole "exposure therapy" situation was a good idea, and the more I study her, the more I find that I actually *want* to tell her. I *want* her to know this side of me, to understand where my instincts were formed.

When she finally approaches, she doesn't bother waiting for instructions. Instead, she ducks under my arm, squares her shoulders and steps right up to the helm, placing her hands on mine.

"Like this?"

Sliding my hands out from under her hold, I shift back, intent on putting space between us, just in case she brushes up against my shorts and discovers something she shouldn't.

Her delicate fingers wrap around the wheel, and she peers over her shoulder at me.

"Just like that," I nod. "Good girl."

Her eyes spark with a wanton heat I wasn't expecting.

I clear my throat, determined to get through this without getting distracted.

Another breath.

An extra layer of Teflon wrapped around my heart.

And then...

"My mom died when I was twelve."

This time when she regards me over her shoulder, her expression is full of an entirely different kind of intensity. One full of pain and compassion.

"She died out here, on the lake."

My words are cool and collected thanks to extensive media coaching. Over the years, I've learned that the more I can detach my delivery from the constant ache that's lived inside me since that night, the easier it is to convince people I'm fine.

Josephine watches me, wide-eyed, but she doesn't speak. She just gives me the time and space to continue when I'm ready. There's a willful openness to her gaze. She doesn't shy away from the dark or the heavy. She isn't easily scared off. I've learned that over the last several weeks. I don't know why I thought this would be any different.

If she keeps staring at me like that, I won't make it through any of this. Dropping my chin, I run my palms over her hands and refocus.

I pull back on the throttle, putting the boat in neutral. We drift with the current, swaying as the wind picks up slightly.

"My dad brought me out on the water the very next day," I confess, setting my hands on hers again. "Exposure therapy, he said. He didn't want me to fear the lake after what happened."

Her breath hitches as she scans my face, and her hands tremble beneath mine.

"Hold the wheel steady," I instruct. "Easy. You'll feel if she starts to drift too far one way or the other, then you can correct it however you see fit."

Once I'm sure she's got it, I pull away.

But she doesn't let me get far.

"Decker..."

She leans back, seeking my touch, and in response, I catch her hips and hold her in place.

"I'm right here," I assure. "You've got this, Siren."

Each one of my fingertips ignites with a sparkling, pulsing energy where it rests against her. It's the same warm, sure sensation that courses through me when I hold a football. The confident, perfect-fit kind of hold that reminds me that I'm alive. That I was made to do this. That I belong right here, in this moment, with her in my arms.

Clearing my throat, I rush to recite the words I've tormented myself with for years. Words that don't even begin to measure up to the emotion and grief they represent.

"We were coming home at the end of a regular day. My dad was out of town, so Mom had picked me up after practice. We dropped Kendrick off at his house first, then headed to the marina. When we arrived, there were a few paps waiting, like usual.

"The media was always following her and my dad. They were obsessed with them as a couple, but they were absolutely feral about snapping pictures of them individually. There were... rumors... that they had been unfaithful to each other. Tabloids and local media were offering ridiculous sums of money for photographic proof.

"It didn't matter that she was with her kid. Or that we were just trying to get home, to make dinner, to turn in early and call it a night. None of it mattered to them. She wasn't human. She was a meal ticket. Or maybe a lottery ticket. They were willing to gamble everything to strike it rich at her expense."

I take a quick breath through my nose, then forge on.

"We made it out onto the lake okay. But as we approached the dock at the mansion, my mom realized she had forgotten a few bags in the car. In all the hustle to get me away from the photographers, she had left groceries in the front seat."

"We were so close, and I was desperate to get home and get my homework done so I could log on and play Madden with Kylian. I asked her to drop me off before she went back. I made her...I made her drop me off at home and go back to the marina alone."

"Decker." My name is nothing more than a choked sob.

At the sound, I snap out of the trance I drop into when reciting this story. I'm so used to feeling nothing when I tell it, but Josephine's voice breaks through the numbness like a shot to the heart.

"You don't have to..."

My heart drops into my stomach, and I dig my fingers into her arms at the look of horror on her face. A look that divulges an almost impossible truth. She's never heard any of this before. How that's possible is unfathomable. *Everyone* knows.

The story of Danielle Crusade's tragic death made national headlines. My picture was plastered on every website and news outlet for months. Every season, it makes a resurgence. Decker Crusade, the phoenix risen out of tragedy, the son of the GOAT.

"Let me finish," I whisper, fighting the agony swirling in my gut. For so long, I've successfully kept it buried, but the sorrow in her expression threatens to set it free.

She nods, gripping the steering wheel unnecessarily tight as her knuckles pale.

"When she turned the boat around to head back to the marina, two paps were waiting. I don't know why they were still hanging around. Maybe they thought she was sneaking out to participate in the illicit affair they'd created to keep the public engrossed in our family. They were on jet skis, and they worked together to wedge her into the shallows so she'd be stuck and at their mercy."

They wanted to make her a sitting duck. What happened was so much worse.

"The rocky lakebed damaged the bottom of the boat, and my mom must have panicked. No one knows for sure." Dropping my head, I close my eyes for just a moment. "No one else was there. The boat was stuck, and the paps left her like that. Just abandoned her, even though they *had* to know she was in distress. The water where they pulled her out wasn't even that deep... Then there was a picture." I swallow past the lump in my throat, determined to get the rest of the story out. "One of her on the boat, with the bow clearly crushed in on one side..."

The nausea that always sets in when I think about that night roils around my stomach.

"I wasn't paying attention to the time. Didn't notice that she hadn't made it back. I was too wrapped up in my game with Kylian. It wasn't until Mrs. Lansbury found me and asked where my mom was that I realized how long she'd been gone."

Nearly two hours had passed.

One hundred and twenty minutes.

Seventy-two hundred seconds.

She'd been dead for almost all of them.

Josephine leans back into me again, catching me so off guard I startle as she sinks into my hold. My reaction doesn't stop her, though. She only angles in closer, trusting me to take her weight. Instinctively, I wrap my arms around her waist, then rest my chin on the top of her head.

I blow out a breath, desperate to make room for a deep inhale that'll hopefully settle my nerves.

The sense of dread that shrouded me that night never truly dissipates—but it burns hotter when I think about the things I didn't do and all I could have done to contribute to a different outcome.

Craning back, Josephine searches my face with those clear blue eyes. She holds my gaze, brushing her fingertips along my knuckles until I spread my hands wide on her stomach and let her interlace our hands.

"You couldn't have saved her, Decker," she whispers into the almost-dark night. "Even if you were there... You were a child. You couldn't have saved her."

It's a nice thought. A reassuring sentiment.

But she has no way of knowing for sure.

Neither do I.

And that's what haunts me.

The uncertainty—the lack of control. I won't forgive myself for it anytime soon, if ever.

"How do you know I wanted to save her?" I counter.

A knowing smile paints itself across her face as she twists in my arms. Tilting her head back, she pushes up on tiptoes.

I bow low, pulled into her orbit by her gravitational force and the juxtaposing simplicity and complexity of this woman.

"Because you can't stop trying to save me."

She's close enough to kiss. And damn, do I want to kiss her.

"I meant what I said," I murmur, inching closer, breathing her in. "We need you, Josephine. I—"

A rumble of thunder reverberates in the distance, miles away.

Josephine jolts back as if she's been struck by an actual bolt of lightning. Instantly, her body goes rigid and her shoulders creep up to her ears. With her focus still locked on me, she shudders, and tears well in her eyes.

In the span of two heartbeats, she transforms from steady and empathetic to trembling and panicked. Pain flashes across her expression as she silently pleads for a request she hasn't yet made.

"Take me back."

I have every intention of agreeing and am about to tell her to sit down and let me take over at the helm, but she doesn't wait for my response.

"Decker. I need you to listen to me. This isn't about anything but...but the storm. If you care about me at all, turn the boat around and get me back to the mansion as quickly and safely as possible."

Though it might have surprised her, I wasn't going to argue. I wouldn't have even hesitated. But dammit, she still thinks that with me, all the additional justification is necessary.

"I've got you," I assure her through gritted teeth. "Sit down. We'll be back to the isle in a couple of minutes."

Chapter 14

Kylian

I could forgo most of the emotions required of the human experience, but layered feelings are the ones I loathe most.

Experiencing more than one emotion simultaneously is not only frustrating but exhausting. It takes my brain too long to break down and catalogue each feeling individually. It takes even longer to make sense of what the combined sensibilities are supposed to convey.

It's like ordering two flavors of soft serve—two or more emotions, twisted into a symmetrical helix. Sure, the individual flavors are there, but when you lick it, they're indistinct. An indiscernible mashup, creating a new and unfamiliar taste. Each bastardizing the other. What's the fucking point?

In this moment, inside my mind, worry and panic are battling against fury and resentment.

The first for my girl.

The latter for the man I used to consider one of my best friends.

I've been allowing Decker to call the shots when it comes to Josephine because that's how the two of us work. I analyze the data, give him information, offer my suggestion, and he makes the play.

But this isn't a game.

And this time, he's gone too far.

"They're headed back."

Narrowing my eyes, I search the horizon for evidence of Greedy's declaration.

He was as livid as I was when Decker carried my girl onto that boat and into open water without her consent.

Decker didn't mention a single thing about his ludicrous idea to any of us.

He knew better.

He knew we'd stop him.

And despite insisting that we're a democracy, he decided he knew best and forwent any vote or consensus gathering before enacting his strategy.

There's a false sense of leadership bestowed on the members of a group like ours.

We all take on the role of lead from time to time, flexing our prowess when a particular skill set or life experience makes one more knowledgeable than the others.

But at our core, *because* he's our core, we inevitably defer to Decker.

He has the charisma. The charm and the magnetism. He has the ability to make each person feel seen and heard, valued and respected, even if, in the end, he's still going to do whatever the fuck he wants.

Like now.

Like *always* where Jo is concerned.

It ends today.

It ends the second he pulls up to the dock.

It took both Kendrick and Locke to hold me back, to physically restrain me as I considered taking one of the jet skis—or even one of the fucking ferries we use to get people from the marina to the house on party nights.

As they held me back, they talked me down. Forced me to listen to their reasoning.

Once they had my attention, their explanation made sense.

Despite every instinct raging inside me and all the sticky, confusing sensations ping-ponging around my brain, there's an undeniable reason why hopping on a second vessel and chasing after them would have been a very bad idea.

Not much rattles Decker Crusade.

The guilt and the shame and the anger he harbors over his mother's death have coalesced into an insidious cancer that lives inside him. It's dormant most of the time—a disease in remission, a trauma response he keeps locked down and tucked away.

But pursuing him in the same way his mom was chased across the lake and left for dead has the potential to trigger the beast.

Once I made that connection, I knew my only option was to sit back and wait.

Even now—seventy-one minutes later—I'm certain it was the right call. In this situation, inaction was the best reaction. Even if it hurts like hell to endure.

Hunter's been sobbing since she realized what happened.

Locke has been crouched on the rocky shoreline, head hung low, silently seething.

Kendrick's been standing guard at the end of the dock, curling his hand into a fist, then flexing it open over and over again.

Garrett Reed Ferguson the Third has been pacing, drifting from Kendrick to me, from Locke to Hunter, trying to comfort and soothe and make sense of the situation.

He thinks we're too weak to chase after our girl—to defy the great Decker Crusade.

He's ignorant to the excessive amount of power we must harness to keep from tipping the scale of this shitshow barreling toward a fate we can't fathom.

We're holding back, because the fallout of chasing after him would inevitably make matters so much worse.

It could always be worse.

But the worst is nearly behind us.

The pontoon boat is approaching. Not just approaching. It's practically flying across the water, coming in fast.

Kendrick barks an order to Locke, who hops to his feet and races to meet him at the end of the dock.

Thunder rumbles in the distance. Low and long. Distant but noxious, nonetheless.

I seek out Locke as he spins on his heel to meet my eye, horrified.

A storm's rolling in.

Josephine is out there, on open water. She's on a boat, against her will, on the water, as a storm brews in the distance.

Our girl doesn't do storms.

Pulling up the weather app, I zoom in on the live radar. There's plenty of green. But it's the jagged, angry line where green transforms to yellow and orange that concerns me.

The boat is less than fifty yards from shore.

Decker doesn't slow. In fact, it looks as though he increases his speed once he sees that K and Locke are ready and waiting to help him dock.

At the last second, he throws the engine into reverse, giving just enough resistance to allow the pontoon to scrape along the edge of the landing.

A single raindrop splashes on my glasses' lens, blurring the scene in front of me.

Thunder crashes miles away.

The side of the pontoon and the dock are close, but not close enough.

Jo is standing now, steadying herself on the port side, watching the gap close on approach; doing the math; gauging her chances.

"Locke!" I holler.

He's closer. Stronger, too. My shout is unnecessary. He knows exactly what he needs to do.

As if the move has been choreographed and practiced a thousand times, he positions himself at the edge of the dock, then stretches his arms out. Jo scrambles over the side and launches herself off the boat and into his embrace.

Garrett stops beside me and scoffs, surveying the scene. "So much for Crusade's brilliant plan. Looks like he did more damage than good."

He's wrong, but I don't bother arguing.

Jo's desperation right now has nothing to do with the boat.

It has everything to do with the storm in the sky; the storm in her heart.

Without a word, Locke barrels past me, Jo wrapped around him like a koala clinging to a tree.

"Get her up to the Nest," I instruct. I'm itching to follow. Desperate to peel her off him, assess her head from toe, and pull her out of her head and shelter her from the storm raging in her mind.

But before I do that, I square my shoulders, cross my arms, and wait.

When Decker finally looks up from the boat's gauges, it's not with smug victory or even defiance.

He looks just as broken as I feel.

He's clearly out of his depth. Remorseful and confused. Desperate to make things right. Desperate to do something right for Jo.

His expression is filled with more despair than I've ever witnessed from him.

I don't need to question why.

I know the answer in my gut. A resounding answer that settles down deep in my soul, if I even have one of those.

She's in his head. She's in his heart.

He's fucked up and so fucking gone for my girl.

"I'll deal with you later," I shoot his way once he's close enough to hear me.

Then, without another word to any of them, I turn on my heel and take off after the people deserving of my time.

Chapter 15

Locke

"You're okay, Joey. I've got you. We're almost there."

She whimpers in response, and my heart splits in two. I hoist her up higher in my arms as I scale the last few steps up to the Nest. My traps will be screaming at me tomorrow, but right now, physical pain is nonexistent.

Because she's here, in my arms. Her skin warm against my neck where she's got her face buried. Her heart pounding out a rhythm against mine. *Fuck*. She's clinging to my body, but I crave the connection just as badly, so I'm holding her just as tight.

Decker had her out there for over an hour.

A whole fucking hour.

Felt more like a lifetime.

A harrowing, infinite expanse that I never want to live through again.

I push in through the door, exhaling on instinct as I move us into the dark, quiet, cavernous space.

The Nest is Kylian's domain, but I spend enough time up here to be familiar with the unique features of the space.

Between the floating floor, the soundproofed walls, and the near-total blackout features, it's a sensory deprivation paradise.

But is that what Joey needs right now?

"Baby," I murmur, perching on the end of Kyl's bed. "Look at me," I demand in the softest tone I can muster as I shift her on my lap. "What do you need? What can I do for you?"

She's shaking in my arms, and her skin is clammy to the touch. Shit. If she's been panicking like this for more than an hour…

"I'm going to fucking kill him," I grit out.

Kylian flies into the room and hits the panel on the wall, casting the space in blue LED light. Every piece of furniture, from his bed to his desk to his bookshelves, glows cerulean—it gives the three of us an eerie, extraterrestrial vibe.

"Up."

I don't know whether he means me or her. We both scramble to our feet on command.

I keep one arm around Joey's torso, in case she needs the support. She runs her nails down my forearm affectionately as she leans into me and we stand side by side.

Kylian stalks forward, eyes darting from Joey to me, then back to her again. He scans her body, his blue eyes bright and unblinking behind his glasses as the LEDs reflect off the square frames.

"Turn."

Without hesitation, she does as he says, spinning away from me slowly.

It takes everything in me not to reach out and hug her back into my chest, but I clench my fists at my sides and resist the urge. I don't understand what's passing between them, but I get the sense that I shouldn't interrupt.

I trace my thumb along my bottom lip and watch as Kylian inspects our girl from head to toe. And inspect he does. He gingerly lifts one arm, then the other. Then he uses one finger to tilt her chin from side to side. She's shockingly responsive. Her submissive reactions to him stand in stark contrast to the forward, domineering attitude she typically asserts with me.

"You're not physically harmed." He nods once, the movement terse. "But he still hurt you."

A clap of thunder booms outside, though it's dulled to little more than an echo thanks to the soundproofing of the Nest.

Joey still jumps a foot in response.

Before I've taken a step her way, ready to soothe her, Kylian's got his arms around her.

"You're okay, baby," he whispers into her hair, smoothing one hand up and down her back. "You're safe. We're right here. You're safe. You're safe. You're safe."

With a deep exhale, she arches back so they're eye to eye. "This is all because of the storm. Decker and I... We talked. He explained what he was trying to do. I was okay out there with him."

"Not initially you weren't," Kylian counters.

"True. But I read him the riot act, and he course corrected."

I snicker quietly. They could easily be talking about an unruly toddler rather than a multi-millionaire team captain of one of the highest-ranked college football teams in the nation.

"Did he actually apologize?" Kylian presses.

"He told me about his mom."

That confession practically knocks the air from my lungs, and I have to snap my mouth shut to keep from sputtering. Decker doesn't talk about his mom, and he definitely doesn't talk about that day. Not beyond the soundbites he's been trained to provide when the media presses the issue. Had we not all lived through the experience alongside him, none of us would understand the full extent—and lifelong effect—of the tragedy surrounding Danielle Crusade's death.

But Decker was willing to tell Joey about what happened... while being out there, on the water... Significant doesn't even begin to explain the implication.

I shift from one hip to the other. Now that my panic has ebbed, my hamstrings are on fire. After going a bit too hard on leg day, then carrying Joey up four flights of stairs between the beach, the deck, and the house, my muscles are smoked.

It's a little awkward, watching my childhood best friend comfort my girl. But right now, Kylian is giving her exactly what she needs.

I consider excusing myself. She's up here, after all. Safe. They'll be okay.

But just as I shift a few inches toward the door, Joey peels out of Kyl's embrace.

She doesn't pull away from him, but she twists her torso and extends one arm, inviting me in.

I hesitate, unsure of what, exactly, she wants me to do.

"Nicky."

It's the softest whisper. A simple plea. If the room wasn't so damn quiet, I may not have even heard it.

It's the summoning of an angel, a siren song with the power to send me to my knees.

Without hesitation, I circle up and rest my chin on her head. "We've got you, Hot Girl. Whatever you need... whatever will help. We've got you."

I lock eyes with Kylian so I can gauge his frame of mind, hoping like hell he's okay with this.

I shouldn't have wasted my energy worrying.

As soon as I catch his gaze, he tips his chin, nodding once.

"So we're doing this?" he asks point-blank.

Joey peeks up from our group hug, looking so small in our arms. But there's no denying the magnitude of her presence. Our girl is a fucking force.

"I want to be with both of you," she declares, her voice shaky but sure.

"I'm in," I offer without a moment of indecision.

"Me too," Kylian confirms. "So that's settled. Now we have to figure out how to deal with—"

"Shh." Joey brings one finger to Kylian's lips.

Nipping at her fingertip, he cocks a quizzical brow.

"I don't want to talk about Decker tonight. Or Kendrick. He's a factor in this, too. But that can wait until tomorrow. Right now, I don't want to talk at all."

"What do you need?" Kylian demands as Joey tucks herself tighter into my side. A soft rumble of thunder reverberates in the distance. Her responding shiver is almost indiscernible this time.

"Jo," Kylian scolds when she doesn't respond right away. "Answer me. What do you need? What can we do for you?"

She peers up at me, her eyes sparkling in the blue glow of the room, and sinks her teeth into her bottom lip. Then she turns that look on Kyl.

"Distract me."

He grabs her chin, using his thumb to release her bottom lip.

"Black and white, baby. How do you want us to distract you?" he rasps, tracing her lips with that same thumb.

The repetitive motion on her pink pout is giving me all sorts of ideas about where we could take this.

"Let me make good on my promise from last night. Make me feel good. Make me forget."

Kylian squints in consideration. "With Nicky here?"

"With Nicky inside me," she sasses, catching Kylian's wrist. Without another word, she pushes his thumb deeper into her mouth.

"Get on my fucking bed," Kylian growls. "You too, Nicky." He jerks his chin. "You heard our girl."

Chapter 16

Josephine

"Spread your legs and let me see your perfect cunt."

A whimper escapes me as a heady mix of arousal and submission swirls through my veins.

At the foot of the bed, Kylian looms over me where I'm spread out on his mattress. Naked.

Locke stands beside him—also naked, per Kylian's instructions—fisting his erection and looking every bit my alt-rock, pop-punk fantasy.

"Look how pretty she is, Nicky. I bet she's already wet."

"How do you want me, Hot Girl?"

"Under me," I pant. There's nothing I love more than riding ten inches of Lockewood dick and rubbing against his pubic piercing every time I take him to the hilt.

Kylian hums and points to Nicky, then me, directing the scene.

"Sit on the edge of the bed, Nicky. Baby, you get in his lap but face me."

I scramble up, eager to comply with his instructions.

Locke hasn't even settled on the mattress before Kylian speaks again.

"Holy shit. Bro. That's..."

"Impressive?" Locke smirks, then pulls me into his lap and peppers kisses along my bare shoulders.

I lean back into his touch, letting him hold my weight as he lines himself up with my pussy.

He's right there, coating himself with my slickness, slipping his crown through my folds, when Kylian goes on.

"I was going to say intimidatingly girthy."

Locke's shoulders shake below me in silent laughter. "Bro. You've seen my dick before."

"But not in this context," Kylian counters.

"What context is that?"

"About to thrust up into and potentially tear apart my girl." Kylian's voice is so serious I have to hold in a laugh.

Locke grunts. "You mean *our* girl."

"Our girl. Right. Semantics. That doesn't ease my concern. I'm being realistic here. Have you measured it recently? What's the circumference? I don't want her getting hurt, or—"

"You guys!"

It's like I'm not spread out between them, naked, waiting for someone to fuck me.

"Sorry, Hot Girl," Locke mumbles, placing a soft kiss on my shoulder. "Your boyfriend's worried my dick's too big for you to handle."

Tipping my head back to look up at Kylian, I lick my lips. "Trust me, Daddy. It'll fit."

"*Daddy?*" Locke gibes.

"You're a philosophy major, Nicky. Don't tell me you're not familiar with the teachings of Pascal. *Daddy is a state of mind.*"

Locke chortles, but this time, he doesn't neglect me. Two fingers swirl around my opening, teasing my pussy, then tickling over my clit.

"Fuck, baby. You're so wet for us," he breathes against my neck. "But I gotta know. He makes you call him Daddy *and* he's got jokes? Who is this cyborg, and what have you done with my best friend?"

"Relax." Kylian waves one hand while he fists himself through his pants with the other. "You don't have to call me that," he says, watching Locke play with my cunt. "Unless you want to."

This time I can't help but join in. "He might be into that. Nicky loves being a good boy. Don't you, baby?"

"Only for you," he quips, pinching my nipple for emphasis.

I whimper as the pain blossoms into pleasure that shoots down to my pussy. "Enough fucking around," I demand, arching my back in search of more. "I need you," I plead.

"Hmm," Kylian murmurs low, still working himself through his pants. "She's getting impatient, Nicky."

"No shit. You should feel how wet she is for us."

Kylian stalks forward, crowding us on the mattress and caressing my jaw with one hand while he fists his cock in the other.

"She's always ready, aren't you, baby? Needy and wet. Such a good fucking girl."

Kylian tips my chin back, forcing me to sink back into Locke's embrace. "You want him inside you?"

His filthy words and Locke's scorching touch ignite a flame in my belly. It burns low and slow as I nod and clench my thighs, desperate for what Kylian's tempting me with. But I'm trapped. Locke has me spread open, with each of my legs hooked over his thighs.

"And where do you want me? Sucking on your tits? Holding a vibrator to your clit?"

"You have toys up here?" I ask, breathless, as Locke kisses up and down my neck and teases my inner thighs. The hard, pulsing length of him rests along my ass. It's taking every ounce of willpower I possess not to squirm until his dick slips inside me.

"Just your favorite." Kylian pulls his shirt off and readjusts his glasses.

The heat in my belly swirls at the memory of my favorite and the way Kylian set me off with it the last time. "You bought a sex toy for me?"

With a step back, he slides his pants down his legs, and I immediately home in on the erection straining behind his blue boxer briefs.

Fuck. I want them both. I want them *now*.

"Technically speaking," he says, stepping between where my knees are hooked around Locke's and quirking a brow. "I purchased a backup of the device you already own. For the Nest. Just in case."

Despite the way my body burns and writhes, all while Locke alternates between kneading my breasts and tweaking my nipples, I can't help but grin.

"But yes. There's a Thumper in my nightstand, fully charged and ready for you. Is that what you want, baby? Do you want me to get you off while you're full of Nicky's cock?"

Rolling my hips, I imagine the scenario, desperately chasing after Locke's dick as he teases me with the tip.

"Goddamn, this pussy. You're so wet and warm," Locke's breath is ragged and hot against my neck.

Bracing myself with one hand on his thigh, I reach for Kylian with the other. "I just want you," I plead, shuddering as Locke pushes the head of his cock just an inch into my cunt.

"Get on his dick, baby," Kylian urges, his irises twin flames lit with need. "Nicky, you lean back. And keep her legs spread open for me."

From the quick way Locke complies, it looks like he's as eager as I am to follow Kylian's instructions.

"That's it," Kylian encourages as Locke slides into me. "Nice and easy."

Inch by glorious inch, he stretches me to accommodate his absolutely massive penis. He feels even bigger than normal at this angle. Longer and wider, like I'm stuffed so full I can barely move.

Whimpering, I thrust forward as far as I can in this position and shudder when the movement makes his piercing press into my taint.

At my reaction, he moans deep and low in my ear, his abs tightening beneath me and his hands kneading my tits a little more aggressively.

"I can't ride you at this angle," I whine.

Ignoring my complaint, Kylian drops to his knees before us and kisses me fiercely, though a heartbeat later, he pulls back, leaving me arching forward in search of his mouth.

"Don't worry about riding him, baby. We'll make you feel good." Then, tilting his head to the side, he regards Locke. "You're good with this? I'm not interested in licking dick, but you're inevitably going to feel it while I'm working."

"We're cool," Locke grits out behind me. "Make her milk me until she screams." Gripping my hips so tight each fingertip digs into my flesh, he holds me in place and fucks up into me from behind. Once he's found a rhythm, he sets the pace. Even though he's barely moving, the angle is exquisite. I've never felt so full in my life.

Kylian lowers himself onto his haunches, watching, rapt, as his best friend eases his dick in and out of me for several beats. Then he heaves himself up and kisses me once more before working his mouth down my body. He sucks on one side of my neck while Locke kisses the other. With a final nip, he eases down a fraction and takes one nipple into his mouth and lavishes it with attention, then the other, sucking and licking, biting playfully and pulling on it with his teeth. Finally, he trails a path of kisses down my torso, then drops back onto his heels.

"Fuck," he hisses, caressing my cunt with two fingers as Locke maintains his slow, sensual rhythm. "Did you blow your load already, Nicky?" Kylian asks.

"What? Hell no," Locke grunts, his rhythm faltering.

Kylian wears the most devilish smile when he lifts his chin. "So you're telling me all this sweet cream is from our girl?"

Their girl. Their fucking girl. I want to be their girl, always.

And I'm not the least bit ashamed of how obvious it is that I want them.

"Did you make this mess, Jo?" He's so close I can feel his breath on my clit. He's right fucking there...

"Kyl," I whimper, desperation causing me to thrash.

"Answer me," he demands.

Behind me, Locke grunts out an unintelligible order, but I don't need to comprehend the words to understand that he wants my answer just as fervently.

"Yes." The word escapes on a whimper as the pleasure in my core sends currents of arousal coursing through me.

"Yes, what?"

"Yes, Daddy," I plead. Because that's what it is. My submission. An honest plea. I want nothing more than for him to put his mouth on me and put me out of my misery.

Massaging my swollen clit, he collects my cum, then he holds up two fingers to show us.

"Look at this mess. It's gushing out of your hole, baby. You're soaking his cock and dripping all over my sheets. Are you gonna help me clean it up?"

"Yes, Daddy," I repeat, flames licking up my insides as telltale tingles spark in my toes.

Finally—fucking finally—Kylian puts his mouth on me.

Instead of licking my clit like I expect, like I so desperately desire, he runs the tip of his tongue along the rim of my pussy where it's stretched taut around Locke's dick. Just once. Then he rises to his knees, grips my jaw with one hand, and looks me right in the eye.

"Open your mouth," he mutters, and when I immediately obey, he angles his lips near mine and spits, holding my jaw open to prevent me from swallowing.

"Fucking hell," Locke mutters, his fingertips digging into the flesh at my hips.

I couldn't agree more. The rasp from behind me sends shivers racing up my spine, and the intense look on the face of the man in front of me makes me clench around Locke so tightly I worry I'll cut off his circulation.

"Good girl," Kylian praises, licking my bottom lip and kissing me softly as I hold my cum and his spit in my mouth. "Now share that with your boyfriend while I suck on your clit."

My breath is so ragged and my heart is pounding so rapidly against my chest that I can't think straight.

Thankfully, Locke takes charge. His hand replaces Kylian's on my chin, gripping my face and turning my head. He dips his tongue into my mouth, working it in and out in rhythm with his thrusts.

"Oh, shit," he murmurs against my lips as Kylian licks us again.

Locke's dick jerks inside me, and I dig my nails into his thighs as my pussy chokes him harder.

"Doesn't she taste good?" Kylian asks, his breath hot on my inner thigh. Then he's diving back in and working his tongue into my hole alongside Nicky's cock. My pussy pulses as more slickness seeps out of me.

"She tastes so fucking good," Locke murmurs, kissing me again.

"She tastes like ours," Kylian groans into my cunt.

"I couldn't agree more." Locke toys with my nipples as Kylian absolutely ravages my clit. He moans each time I bounce on him, dipping his tongue into my mouth over and over again like he can't get enough of my essence.

"Hold her," Kylian commands, dropping his palms to my thighs and pressing into them.

Locke complies immediately. He wraps both arms around my torso and nuzzles into my neck.

An instant later, Kylian seals his lips around my bundle of nerves and sucks. Hard. I scream and writhe, flying into the atmosphere like a helium-filled balloon released into the heavens, Locke's hold on me the only thing keeping me on this earth.

Kylian licks at my oversensitive clit as I spiral, pulling off eventually but keeping his focus locked on my still-pulsating cunt.

"Fucking perfect," he murmurs, his voice full of adoration. "Such a good girl. Keep gripping him, baby. Milk his cock until he fills you up."

Beneath me, Locke's thrusts become frantic. "Fuck, fuck, fuck... I'm close," he grunts, as his thighs tense below me.

"Hold it, Nicky. She's got another one in her. I know it."

Like hell I do. I'm locked up so tight around him I fear we'll be trapped like this.

"Open your legs farther, Jo."

Despite my own doubts, I do as he says, spreading wide and exposing myself to him.

Kylian rubs my clit furiously, fusing fire and ice, creating an impossible sensation that's building into another orgasm.

"*Fuck*," Locke grits out. "I can feel every stroke of your hand, bro."

"Both of you come. Right now," Kylian demands.

Locke's thighs tense below me as the first pulses of his release shoot into me.

"Jo."

I squeeze my eyes shut and hold my breath. I'm so close, so fucking close—

Kylian lifts his hand and slaps my clit, and I fragment.

I shatter and crumble and cease to exist in this dimension as pain and pleasure, heat and desire, control and reckless abandon all rip through me with such force there's no room in my head for anything but this moment.

This moment.

With these men.

Being cared for, and being taken care of, in ways I never thought I'd experience.

When I'm sure I'm not going to black out, I flop back into Locke's arms, reveling in the tingling aftershocks of post-orgasm bliss.

He holds me tight, face buried in my hair as he murmurs words I can't fully comprehend. As we come down from the high, my release, mixed with Locke's, drips out of me, making a literal mess on the floor.

Kylian swipes his hand through it and paints it across my chest, teasing my nipples on each pass. I revel in his touch—in Locke's hold—in this moment I don't ever want to end.

He grunts, and I open my eyes in time to watch him finish in his hand. Panting, he stands, then hovers over us and mixes his release with the mess already smeared across my stomach.

"Ours," he whispers as he traces one finger from my clit over my belly button and up my chest, before finally resting his open palm over my heart.

More Texts

THE BOYS

Kylian: Tonight was eye-opening. It's apparent that I cannot count on you to understand consent, implied boundaries, or the lengths I'll go to protect her.

Cap: You need sleep, Kyl. Go to bed.

Kylian: No. I will not sit back idly while she suffers at the hands of a man I considered my friend.

Locke: Bro. Chill. We can talk about it tmrw

Cap: Aren't you up there with him?

Locke: Yeah, but he's over at his desk, not in bed with us

Kendrick: TMI

Kylian: I will not chill. There is no chill to be had until you all agree to the following terms.

Kylian: 1. No one makes Jo go anywhere she doesn't want to go. This includes forcing her to relocate through co-ercion, incentive, manipula-tion, blackmail, or physical re-moval.

Kylian: 2. If it storms and we're at the house, get her to the Nest. If we're not home, get her to me or Locke, whoever's closer or more readily available.

Kendrick: I'd like to be considered for a position on that list.

Kylian: No.

Kylian: 3. She's the boss. You will seek her approval and deliberate consent in all matters. If it's not a clear yes, then it's a hell no. I read that on the Internet, but it's applicable here. I will not let anyone inside or outside this house treat my girl with anything but the utmost respect and deference.

Locke: You mean our girl

Kylian: Fine. Our girl.

Kylian: I will inform Garrett Reed Ferguson the Third
of these developments. Any
questions?

Kendrick: I know boats are
a touchy subject right now...
but maybe if she knew how
to operate one, she'd feel more
comfortable...

Kylian: Good point. With her
consent, Kendrick may teach
her and help her acquire a
boating license.

Cap: I'll teach her.

Kylian: No. Kendrick is the
better boatsman. And the
more patient teacher.

Cap: I can be patient.

Kylian: Noted. Still no.

KENDRICK TO LOCKE

Kendrick: We're on our way.
Take care of her. We'll be back
before sunrise

Chapter 17

Kendrick

"You make a habit of keeping tubs of alcohol wipes in your car?" Greedy asks.

With a frown, I watch him run a wipe over each finger. "Between your fingers and all along the nail beds, too," I instruct, ignoring his jab. "And this isn't my car."

He balks, but the glare I shoot at him in the mirror shuts him up.

I don't know why he's acting surprised. I wasn't about to drive my own car across town to commit multiple counts of aggravated assault.

His father's a surgeon, so I have no doubt he's privy to plenty of auxiliary medical information. I just happen to possess a wealth of knowledge about expunging evidence. Learned a lot from my pops over the years, whether he realizes it or not.

With my attention on the road again, I cruise at speed and stay extra alert as my wipers slice across the windshield. Honestly, I'd feel better driving my Suburban in these conditions, but the Toyota Decker keeps at the marina was our safest bet, seeing as how it's a nondescript gray and registered under a pseudonym.

"You're sure they won't squawk?" Decker asks beside me. The dude's jaw ticks incessantly as he opens and closes his fist, inspecting his throwing hand.

We all have a lot on the line, but Decker has the most to lose.

He shouldn't have come with us. But it didn't matter what I said or how Greedy and I tried to reason with him.

He refused to be left behind.

Greedy regards his rival, none of his usual bravado on display. "They won't. They're done and they know it. My guy in the ER is set to text me the moment they come in. We'll know what they tell the staff as soon as they open their mouths."

"*If* they can open their mouths," I add.

Three on three should have been a fair fight, but the second-string punk-ass Sharks were so sleep-deprived and dehydrated they could barely lift their fists to defend themselves.

Greedy did us a solid by ensuring they were ill-prepared and scared shitless before we even showed up. We wore masks as a precaution, but it wouldn't take a genius to figure out who we are and why we were there.

Not that any of that puts us at any real risk.

Between his connections at the hospital and my familiarity with the department, we've got multiple fail-safes in place.

"You think it was enough?" I ask Decker quietly, my focus fixed on the road.

We fucked them up, and the precedent has been set. But even after inflicting that amount of damage, Decker's desire for revenge still burns so hot it's stifling. And I can't shake the feeling that he wouldn't have stopped had I not pulled him off the last guy.

In my periphery, he turns my way. "Nothing will ever be enough. But it was a start."

"Amen." I hold out my knuckles, and he pounds them. Then I swing my arm back and offer them to Greedy, too.

We may hate the guy on the field, and we may be preparing to beat his ass in the game on Saturday, but we couldn't have pulled this off without him. For that, I'll always be grateful.

Chapter 18

Kendrick

Soft footsteps alert me to her presence.

Decker and I have been here since before dawn, trying to get our heads back in the game and physically recover from the days of stress and disjointed sleep. There was no point in trying to come home and sleep.

Our in-home gym is pretty damn impressive. It's outfitted with state-of-the-art equipment, and Thomas replaces or swaps out machines each season based on our individual needs and the latest technology.

Technically, this is his house, even though we've all lived here since our senior year of high school.

When Nicky was set to age out of the system, the four of us came together and made this place our home. Brenda and Gary would have loved to adopt him, but the boy was too smart to let that happen. He has access to significantly more financial assistance and medical support from the state as an aged-out adult.

Living together was the logical thing to do. We usually ended up here on the weekends anyway, and both Decker and Kylian function better with the privacy and security the isle provides.

I'm finishing a set of heavy-ass squats on the Tsunami Bar when she turns the corner and comes into view.

When she stops in the doorway, I watch her reflection in the mirror and tip my chin to let her know I see her.

And fuck, do I see her.

Messy auburn hair. Sharp blue eyes. A smattering of freckles across the bridge of her nose. Either I've only recently noticed them, or they've developed since she's been here. Regardless, I find myself seeking them out anytime she's near. Like craning back to find the first star in the night sky after stepping outside.

She leans against the doorframe, arms crossed as she yawns and searches the room.

I know who she's looking for.

Just like I know when she spots him where he's sprinting full-out on the treadmill at the opposite end of the room.

"He's gonna make you subscribe to his OnlyFans if you keep ogling him like that, Mama." I toss her a smirk when she turns back to me.

She snorts, not even a little embarrassed by the disgusting sound she makes.

"Cap doesn't have an OnlyFans," she quips.

I bite down on my bottom lip and fight back a grin. "You tried to look him up already, huh?"

She pushes off the doorframe and waves one hand at me as she strides into the room.

"Didn't need to look. Misty wouldn't allow it."

Yeah, Misty and Thomas would flip the fuck out if he so much as posted a personal photo on social media without the proper hashtags. No part of his life can be shared without their input.

With a sigh, she straddles the weight bench, spreading her fingers and pushing them into the cushion between her thighs before leaning forward.

"What are you doing up so early?" I ask. I force a nonchalant tone despite the worry creeping up my spine.

Deadpan, she watches me in the mirror.

"Thought maybe you needed a spotter. That looks heavy."

It's my turn to snicker. Damn right it's heavy. Four hundred pounds, but nowhere near my limit.

"Be real with me, Jojo. You're okay?" I check.

Kyl and Nicky took care of her last night. Though the implications of exactly how they coaxed her out of her panic and kept her calm during the storm make my blood pressure spike.

Not because her relationship with either of the guys or what they were up to bothers me, but because I wasn't in the room with them. The Nest is a soundproof fortress that I wouldn't dare enter without Kylian's direct invitation.

I never had much interest in spending time there. Until now. *Fuck.* I only want to be wherever she is these days.

I want to hold some of her fears for her, wipe them from existence. Support her while she works through all the bullshit. She made it through last night, but getting through something and being okay are two different experiences entirely. She survived Decker's ambush, yeah. She didn't lose herself during the storm, either, but that doesn't mean she's okay right now.

Wearing an even expression, she tips her head back, exposing the smooth skin of her neck as she considers me. Damn. She's showing me she's okay—She hasn't said a word, but the message is loud and clear in the way she opens up for me.

But I've still gotta hear her say it out loud.

"So?" I press.

"I'm okay-*ish*," she offers, giving me a halfhearted smile that feels genuine.

With a huff, I shake my head. "I don't like that 'ish,' Mama. What do you need?"

Her halfhearted smile blossoms into a smirk.

"Bodily autonomy would be a good start." She sits up straighter and pulls her shoulders back. "Maybe a way to keep big brutes from snatching me and taking me wherever they want, whenever they want?"

She side-eyes Decker on the treadmill, but he still hasn't noticed that she's here. He's too focused on hauling ass, hitting a full sprint like he always does at the end of his workout. He won't stop until our session is over.

Which, apparently, is now.

The alarm on my phone blares through the Bluetooth sound system, but he's still in the zone, attention fixed on the treadmill's control panel.

"Time's up, Cap," I call out, hopping up to rack my weights for the day.

His head snaps up at the sound of my voice. Then his eyes bug out when he spots Jojo sprawled out on the bench.

His stride falters, and he loses his legs, but before he can take a tumble, he smashes the safety and hops off. I spin to the weight rack to hide my smirk. I'll let him think I didn't see him almost fall off a damn treadmill.

It'd be funny if it wasn't so pathetic.

I see him. I see him working overtime to shapeshift and mold himself into what he thinks she needs him to be.

He hasn't figured it out yet. But he's getting closer.

And once he does...

She peers up at me again, dark lashes tickling her cheeks when she blinks.

I shuffle closer and bump her chin playfully with my knuckles. "You're tough, but you don't have to keep that up all the time." With a step back, I pick up my towel and run it down my face. "I've got to go into town for an infusion this morning, but I'll be back by lunchtime. I'll be around all day after that. Come get me if you need me."

She tilts her head and opens her mouth, probably to dish out a sassy remark.

"*Jojo*," I scold, hovering beside the bench she's still straddling. "Promise me."

She snaps her mouth shut and bites on her lower lip, distracting me from what I should be focusing on. Always so fucking distracting.

She's in my head. She's under my skin. I should hate it. Rally against it. But I'm tired of fighting it. All I want to do nowadays is let her in. Pull her in farther. See just how deep we can get—how far she's willing to take this.

"I will," she whispers. "Thanks."

On instinct, I duck low and drop a kiss to her forehead, trailing one hand along her spine. "Be good today," I tease.

I want her to be okay. Fuck, I want her to be more than just okay. I want her well. I want her back so I can have another shot at not fucking this up.

Reluctantly pulling away, I turn to the door and come face-to-face with a brooding Decker. He's propped up against the doorframe, glare firmly in place and set on me.

With a final wave, I leave her in the gym so we can get on with our morning.

I'm prepared to part ways with Decker, hit the shower, and make sure Locke's slow ass is awake and ready to go. He's got an appointment at the medical spa today, too.

Decker has other plans, though. Instead of turning left and heading to his wing like usual, he stalks after me.

"So that's a thing now?" he grits out when we step into the kitchen.

There's a bite to his words. They're dripping with jealousy.

His question raises my hackles and puts me on the defense, which I assume is exactly what he intended.

Running a hand over my tightly cropped fade, I look him in the eye.

"Would it be a problem for you if it was?"

He glowers at me like he can intimidate me—the big goon—but when I stare right back, square up, and cock one eyebrow, he drops his chin and turns his head.

If he's not willing to answer, I'll take the opportunity to make myself abundantly clear.

"It's not a thing yet, but it's about to be. You can't expect me to believe you wouldn't do the same in my shoes. You're big mad that you're not in my cleats right now, but I can't help you there, Cap."

Arms crossed over his chest, he focuses on something over my shoulder and gives me a derisive grin. "Have you talked to Kylian? Or Locke?"

I bite back a chuckle. Because, damn, there's the rub. That's why he and Jojo aren't clicking. Why he may never be included in the dynamic brewing in the group.

He has control issues, and those issues are about to cockblock his ass so hard he won't know what sacked him.

"I have not," I offer, sauntering to the fridge to grab an electrolyte water. I hold out a second bottle to Decker, but he ignores it.

"Do you think you need to?" he challenges.

I slow blink, which is the opposite of the reaction he was hoping to pull out of me. "I think that's for her to decide."

I swear the faintest hint of steam billows out of his ears at my lack of reaction. "You're honestly okay with her just stringing you all along?"

Cap. Poor Cap. No Cap. He's still not getting it. Maybe he never will.

Sighing, I close the fridge door and head for the stairs. But not before looking over my shoulder and throwing one last truth his way. "I don't think that's what's happening here, Crusade."

I leave it at that. He's got to figure it out on his own. Whatever that looks like and however much time he needs. He'll either get there, or he won't.

The odds are fourth and long, and he's trying in vain to whip out a quarterback sneak when he could really use some play action.

His hostility won't work. Hell, it'll probably make things worse. But it's not my place to coach him through this. Only he can make the final call where our girl is concerned.

Chapter 19

Josephine

Greedy and Hunter are graciously clearing the table after Friday night family dinner. Kendrick cooked, and we all did our best to act like it wasn't intensely awkward to dine with rival quarterbacks the night before they face off at the biggest game of the season.

Hunter offered to stay one more night, and I gladly accepted. It's not that I don't feel safe in the house with the guys. If anything, I feel like we're in a better place now than we've ever been.

I'm okay. I'm more than okay when I'm with them.

But her presence brings with it an extra softness. I don't have to navigate uncharted territory or try to figure out where things stand with Hunter. I can just be. There's serenity in the type of friendship that requires no pretense or preamble. We exist on the same wavelength. Our connection, though new, is already soul deep. It goes so far beyond words or action. I feel most like myself—like my best self—when I have her by my side.

It also helps that she and I are rooming together. If she weren't here, Kylian would surely lure me to the Nest and lock the door forever.

Decker's in a particularly grumpy mood tonight, which doesn't bode well for what I'm planning to share.

But we're all here.

I don't want to have to tell this story more than once.

If I'm going to tell them—if I'm going to commit to being my most authentic self with them—they need to know what they're getting into. Even if it wrecks me to stir up old memories, I need to share my truth.

I want Hunter to know.

I trust Greedy enough.

I need to give Kylian the facts.

I crave Locke's comfort.

I hope Kendrick doesn't overreact.

I pray Decker understands.

Clearing my throat, I rise from my seat, wincing when the chair legs scrape against the deck. "I was hoping... I was hoping I could talk to you guys. All of you. About what happened."

I scan the group, finding all eyes on me.

"Joey..." Hunter shuffles close and takes my hand. "We don't need to rehash it. Greedy will take care of it." She looks to her stepbrother, who's nodding in agreement over by the sliding glass door.

My heart leaps into my throat. I want to take the out, but I can't. I have to see this through. "No, I don't mean about last weekend. I want to tell you about... before. About why I hate storms. Why being taken was so... triggering. About why I panic."

Wringing my hands, I search for Kylian in the small crowd, desperate to connect with him now in case he shuts down before it's all over. I've promised myself that I'll give him time, space, distance... whatever he needs to process all this. Even if it hurts me. Even if it affects our relationship. Even if it all ends because of this. He deserves that much.

And I hope, more than anything, that he understands that it was real. What we shared. How he made me feel.

If everything changes tonight, I want him to know that he was worth it. And that I would do it all again if given the chance. He's been my safe place. He's been so much more than I ever imagined I could have with another person.

Next, I shift my focus to Locke, silently pleading with him to not be upset with me. I should have opened up to him weeks ago. I undoubtedly should have told him before we established our relationship.

I needed to be the new me for just a bit longer before I brought the past I can't escape into my present. I wanted to bask in his affection and soak up every moment where I was just the Hot Girl he met on the first morning of Logic class.

When I find Kendrick, I don't shrink under the intensity of his stare. He's going to be hurt. He'll probably feel duped. His reaction will be fiery and instant, but I have to believe he'll forgive me for not telling them sooner.

Finally, I turn to Decker and will myself to stand tall and keep my head held high.

"You thought I was hiding something." My voice is hoarse with emotion. "And you were right. I was."

Heavy silence settles around us. Hunter sits back down in her seat, and Kendrick leans forward, steepling his fingers against his forehead.

"My name wasn't always Josephine Meyer," I admit. "It used to be Jolene Neuer."

I survey the faces around the table, eager to gauge each reaction, though I don't allow myself to actually meet anyone's gaze.

There's a moment where the world around me is paused—suspended as the bits and pieces start to click. *Processing, please wait.* I crack my knuckles and fight back the nausea swirling in my stomach. For now, I force myself to just exist in this space where the first of many secrets is out, but no one has responded or reacted just yet.

It's Decker who speaks first. But he's not looking at me.

"You knew."

He's standing, brooding like he does, dominating with his arms spread wide at the head of the table. His scowl is one of pain and disdain. And most surprisingly, betrayal.

I follow his gaze across the table to Kylian.

"You knew?" I ask, my heart lurching in panic. Is my secret not even a secret after all?

Black and white. Cut and dry. His response should be nothing more than a simple, single-word answer.

I know I'm in trouble when Kylian peers up at me through his glasses, his cerulean eyes a mess of emotion.

He holds eye contact in a way that makes me want to physically recoil. It's not just that he's making a concerted effort to get the delivery right. It's the realization that he won't need time to process or come to terms with what I thought I was revealing tonight. None of what I'm about to say is news to him.

Shaking his head, he swallows thickly and whispers, "Those files should have been redacted, Jo. You were a minor. They shouldn't have been so easy for me to find... why weren't they redacted?"

It's a question I asked so many times. But in Ohio, there's no law that requires a victim's identity to be protected. Minor or not. "Redaction is a courtesy" is what I was told every time I asked, and the members of the Blakely Ohio Police Department were never particularly courteous where I was concerned.

Rage surges through me as the truth comes barreling to the forefront of my mind. Kylian knew. I didn't disclose the information... but he knew.

"And if my name had been redacted from the case files?" I spit out with a vitriol I've never used with Kylian. "You wouldn't have been able to figure it out? You wouldn't have kept digging? Doing his bidding"—I throw an arm out toward Decker—"until you found something worth having on me?"

If it was quiet before, it's eerily silent now.

I had no intention of getting distracted from what I intended to tell them, but it's too much.

"I wouldn't have gotten as far as I did before I realized it wasn't my business and stopped digging."

Angry, indignant tears well in my eyes. I pull in a deep breath, willing them not to fall.

How far did he get?

How much did he see?

This is the exact opposite of how I wanted this confession to go down. They're awful truths. Wretched secrets. But they're *my* secrets. My story to tell. I went to excruciating efforts to leave the past in the past. I would have left it there forever if I could guarantee it would keep.

But with the way my conversion disorder has been flaring, I needed them to know. I *wanted* them to know.

Now all I want is to dig a hole in the sand, crawl inside, and stay there forever.

"You've known all along." The accusation catches in my throat.

The night they brought me here. The morning after, when he came out to talk to me at the end of the dock.

He knew even then.

Kylian doesn't deny it. He holds my gaze, his throat bobbing with a heavy swallow.

The reality of just how thin my veil of discretion really is slams into me with the force of four football players.

I don't realize I'm crying until I open my mouth, ready to tear into him, and taste the tears that drip onto my tongue. A salty reminder of all that I was and all that I'll never be.

"Baby," Kylian murmurs, tracking the movement of my tongue. He pushes to stand and storms around the table. As he approaches, he grasps my upper arms and spins me to face him, then wraps me in an embrace.

Though the last time he held me wasn't more than a couple of hours ago, his touch suddenly feels foreign. Stiff and distant, despite the dozen touch points between our bodies.

"Baby," he whispers again in what I'm sure he thinks is reassurance. "You're okay. We're okay. This changes nothing."

"This changes *everything*," I counter, clinging to him as I sort through my feelings about his knowledge of such deeply personal information—information I wasn't ready for anyone to know until now.

"Jo. Look at me."

Reluctantly, I obey. The tension melts away a little more with each second as I search Kylian's face.

He knew. He fucking knew.

And yet...

He's never treated me like I'm damaged or broken.

He's never pushed me to reveal more than I was willing to share.

He knew, but he kept my secret safe, as is becoming more apparent by Decker's outraged reaction.

Dropping my forehead to his chest, I press into his hold and take a steadying breath. When I finally look up at him, I see the truth he's already declared: I'm okay. We're okay.

With a slight nod, I take a step back.

Just like I knew he would, he gives me space to retreat as I temper my anguish, wipe my tears, and assess the rest of the group.

Naturally, Decker inserts himself then and presses the issue.

"You knew something about her, something obviously important, and you said nothing?"

The accusation is sharp, dripping with venom. I don't know what Decker's more upset about: not being in control of the situation, or Kylian breaking his trust on my behalf.

Kylian side-eyes Decker, takes a deep breath, and shrugs. "Wasn't my story to tell, Cap."

As I look from one person to another around the table, I realize Decker isn't the only one in the dark. It's clear that Kylian did not share details about who I was or what I've endured with any of them.

That's further confirmed when Locke interjects. "Uh, someone want to fill us in? What's there to tell?"

Chapter 20

Josephine

"Do you remember seeing headlines about Steubenville, Ohio, back in the early 2010s?"

"The high school rape case?" Kendrick asks, head whipping up from where his attention was fixed on his lap.

At the same time, Hunter screeches, "That was you?"

I drop into my chair and dig deep into my resolve before turning to my friend. "No," I deadpan. "My rapists did their homework and weren't dumb enough to record penetration on camera like in Steubenville."

"Jesus, Jojo," Kendrick huffs, pounding his fist into the table, then bowing his head again.

"You were..." Locke starts, his usually warm hazel eyes filled with sorrow.

I clear my throat, garnering my strength to make it through as many details as possible before I lose it.

This is my past. It *was* my story. I've put in the work to heal as best as I can from the trauma of that night, but in the end, it shaped me. Changed me. It happened. It was real.

I'll never be over it. But I can live with it. Most days, at least.

The lasting effects of that night—and the fallout after—made the rest of the world go fuzzy around me for several months. But with years of counseling, the proper combination of meds, and a shit ton of time and self-care, I've moved on.

Correction: I was moving on. This week, it's as though I ran into a brick wall, and I'm still slamming my body into it over and over again, desperate to get out of this feedback loop. I'm trapped in my head, transported back.

Inhaling and calling on all the courage I don't feel strong enough to muster, I begin to explain.

"When I was sixteen, I went to a party. I was drugged. I was raped. Probably gang banged. I don't know exactly what happened, because I was unconscious, dumped on the side of the road, and left for dead. It was storming that night."

I look first to Locke, then to Kylian. They're all too familiar with my deep-seated aversion to storms.

"The rain was relentless. It soaked through my clothes, washed away evidence. All the semen, and the blood."

Greedy curses under his breath. Beside him, Hunter places her hand on top of his.

"Lightning split a tree along the side of the road where they left me. I saw it strike. It's one of the very last things I remember—the night sky splitting in two, then the tree cleaving down the middle. I still see it. When I close my eyes. At night, when I dream.

"I wanted to vanish into those cracks of bark and burning wood. I lay there, semi-conscious, wishing for the sky to swallow me up and take away every ache, every pain, all the memories. I just didn't want to feel anything anymore."

Hunter sniffles, and my gut reaction is to reach out and comfort her, but I can't be the friend I want to be in this moment. Not until I get through this.

"The tree fell across the road where they left me. That's the only reason I wasn't hit by a car. The road was blocked, so not a single vehicle passed all night long."

"The clean-up crews were out early the next day. It was a massive storm. They eventually found me, but it wasn't until the late afternoon."

"They called 911, and I was transported to the ER. I was in such a fog. I had definitely been drugged, but I couldn't access the words or wherewithal to explain that. The last thing I remember from the night before, besides the lightning, was chugging a cup of lukewarm beer to shut up the second-string quarterback."

I close my eyes and sit up straighter, willing myself to press on.

"It wasn't until the next week when I went back to school and saw the first recordings that I started to piece it all together."

Chapter 21

Kylian

Six videos were recorded that night.

Grainy, poorly lit videos.

Videos meant to serve as trophies of their conquest.

Videos that now function as the guide map I'm using destroy them.

One hundred eighty-nine seconds of footage.

Six videos.

Five years for them to circulate, migrate, swell, and reproduce.

In those five years, technology has evolved. Access to pornographic content has improved. Circulation of said videos has dwindled significantly.

It's an easier job than I expected it to be.

But it's the most important job I'll ever complete.

For her. For us.

For who she was, and who she deserves to be.

I'll destroy them.

Not just the videos, but the perpetrators who thought they could put a fucking hand on my girl before I even knew she was mine.

I'll plant a cancer in their systems; be the insidious disease that rots all the parts of life they cherish.

All the parts they tried to take from her.

Six videos.

One hundred eighty-nine seconds of footage.

When I'm not working for the team, jumping through the inane hoops required for classes, or spending time with Jo, I'm pursuing my personal vendetta passion project. I've been working around the clock for weeks to issue DCMA and child endangerment complaints on dozens of sites. Where the videos still exist, I take the time to go in and scramble servers.

I won't stop until the scum who did this are personally and professionally reduced to ashes. My new purpose in life is to track them down and expose them to every social circle. To make sure their wives and neighbors, bosses and pastors, know who they are. What they did. How they tried to ruin her.

It's tedious work. Slow, deliberate. But I've got a lifetime ahead of me to accomplish it.

A lifetime to avenge her.

Several seconds have passed in which no one has spoken. Even I can pick up on the thick, awkward energy humming around us as our friends process the unfathomable and Jo tries to push through the residual trauma intent on trapping her.

"Then what happened?" I prompt.

She's lost in her head. She's lost in the world.

She wanted space.

As a person who often needs space, I get it.

I get it, but I hate it.

I just want to hold her.

If she doesn't want my embrace, that's okay. For now. She has my loyalty. My devotion. My lifelong commitment to avenge her and make them pay.

She has me.

Chapter 22

Josephine

"There... there were six videos, all from different phones and angles." I keep my face downcast and my focus locked on the tabletop. The shame is insidious—always festering below the surface, despite the work I've done to heal and come to terms.

"I don't know for sure, but because there were six videos, I think there were six of them."

Hunter cries softly beside me. I'd give anything to take away her tears. To assure her that I'm okay. But I'm not. And right now, I don't have the energy or the courage to pretend otherwise.

"Their voices are audible on the video. You can see a few of them with their dicks out, standing around me, jerking off. One of them tells the others that I'm so tight."

Shame transforms into anger that burns hot in my stomach at the memory of the videos. At the way they were distributed not only to my classmates, but on the internet.

I let the anger lick up my chest like flames climbing the walls of a burning building, soaking in the blistering pain. It's better than the ache of shame that threatens to weigh me down. It's the more productive emotion.

Because it wasn't just my assailants and what they did that night that threatened to destroy me. It was the events afterward that were the hardest to come back from.

"But like I said, there's no physical or video evidence of penetration." Greedy huffs with what I assume is indignation. He's been still as stone throughout most of my trauma dump. Reserved, respectful. They all have. But I would welcome their ire and outrage, too. It might make me feel less alone.

"But you went to the hospital," Greedy presses. That would be his first line of thinking, considering who his father is. "Surely they checked you out when the ambulance brought you in? Did a rape kit?"

I laugh a cold, emotionless laugh.

"No. At the time, I didn't remember anything from the night before—I still don't remember much, aside from what's on the videos—and the hospital had no reason to suspect I had more than a sprained ankle and a concussion, plus a hangover from mixing alcohol and recreational drugs." I glance at Decker and offer a sad smile. "Now you know why I'm so well-versed in concussion protocol."

Dropping my forearms to the table, I sit up straighter, determined to get through this part. It's not even the worst of it, and I need to power through so I can focus on the more critical fallout and how it's affecting me now.

"By the time I saw any of the videos, too much time had passed. It had been *days*. I had laid outside in the swale on the side of the road all night, soaked to the bone from the rain. Even if they had attempted a rape kit, it's unlikely any evidence would have survived."

Mutters of outrage and pained protests echo around the table, but I push on, determined to get through this.

"I was conscious when I arrived at the hospital, so they didn't do a catheter. I was dehydrated and needed fluids. It wasn't until I got up and went to the bathroom for the first time that I suspected..."

Hunter slides her hand across the table and grips mine, garnering my attention. With one tight squeeze, she meets my gaze, a sense of solidarity rolling off her in acknowledgment of what it's like to be a woman in this world.

I blink, inhaling deeply and holding the breath in my lungs, willing myself not to lose it. At least not yet.

"They were charged?"

Decker's question is self-assured. Of course it is. In his world, things work in his favor. Why wouldn't they? He holds tight to the control he has over the people around him and the rule of law on his side.

"There was a trial," I confirm with a single dip of my chin.

Picking up on my lack of detailed response, he presses. "What were their sentences, Josephine?"

I look him dead in the eyes, laser focused, desperate to convey the ire that's burned in my soul for five years now.

When I answer, it's hard not to laugh. Not because it's funny. Nothing about this is fucking funny. But because the absurdity is almost comical.

Pursing my lips, I fight back any inflection.

"Twenty hours of community service each for the three guys they were able to identify."

Chapter 23

Decker

I'm on my feet before I know what I'm doing.

The urge to avenge—to protect—surges through me with an intensity so explosive I can't harness it.

My fist is driving into the wooden railing that lines the deck before I can stop myself.

The smooth stained wood splinters on impact. But one hit isn't enough. I'm wound too tight, my fury too strong.

I wasn't there. I couldn't have known. It was impossible for me to protect her back then.

But fuck if I didn't contribute to her more recent suffering.

Her words reverberate in my skull, bouncing around my brain as I pound against the railing, relishing the pain as punishment for my role in all that's gone down since she moved to Lake Chapel seeking the fresh start she deserves.

Every hit.

Every shockwave radiating through my knuckles and wrist.

It's not enough.

Nothing could ever be enough. Not in comparison to what she survived.

I'm in an echo chamber of despair. Unseeing. Unhearing. Unable to make sense of anything aside from the soul-deep need to make things up to her—to make them pay.

I don't stop. I can't stop. Not until my arm is caught mid-swing, breaking the rhythm of my jabs.

Panting, I flex my hand into a fist. Pain radiates through my knuckles and up my forearm. But it's not enough. It's fucking nothing compared to what she's been through—what she's survived.

"Cool it, Cap."

I practically jump out of my skin at the sound of Greedy's voice in my ear. Frantically, I turn, looking for my guys.

They're on their feet. All three of them.

They're surrounding *her*, offering support.

Kendrick's arms are draped over the back of her chair, his head bowed in anguish.

Locke is hovering close to one side, brushing a tatted hand up and down her arm.

Kylian's on his goddamn knees, his chin propped on his hand, murmuring soothing words I can't make out over the whooshing of blood in my ears.

I would ridicule just how far gone he is for this girl if I wasn't itching to take his place at her feet.

Greedy squeezes my bicep, calling my attention back to him. "I get it, brother. I do. But punishing yourself will only hurt her more."

His words are low, just for me. His tone is placating, but not condescending. There's a sense of truth and understanding in his delivery—as if he knows from experience what it's like to blemish something so pure and beautiful and then keep fucking it up over and over again.

Louder, he lifts us both out of the despair that's threatening to take hold.

"I want to beat your ass tomorrow because I earned it, Crusade. Not because you fucked up your throwing hand."

Then, softer, with his fingers still wrapped around my upper arm, he asks, "You good? She needs you to get it together."

Sucking in a jagged breath, I nod.

I'm loath to admit it, but Greedy's right.

I can't punish myself for not protecting her back then. I can't blame myself for triggering her trauma when I had no context for what she's endured.

What I can do is course correct, get my shit together, and lead our family the way they deserve to be led.

My hatred will keep.

The opportunity to pivot will not.

If I'm going to make this up to her—to stop hurting her once and for all, and to be part of the new story she's writing—I need to rise above my baser instincts and be the man she needs.

Chapter 24

Josephine

"There was a trial," I confirm again once Decker and Greedy take their seats. The other guys—my guys—hover close, although only Kylian is touching me now.

"Three of them were identified, so only three of them had to take the stand."

Kylian *hmph*s softly from where he's crouched at my feet. I don't dare look his way, though. If I do, if I see the look on his face, I may not get through the rest of the story.

"I sat in the courtroom for days and watched as each one talked about their plans for the future, about how sorry they were." Pressing my lips together, I shake my head. "In the end, their lawyer worked his magic. His closing arguments featured a slideshow that included a handful of photos of me looking shitfaced at other parties. The photos of the boys showed them playing sports, receiving awards, and volunteering in the community."

"Wait. Character evidence can't be entered into a sexual assault trial," Hunter counters.

Nodding sadly, I explain. "Good thing it wasn't an actual rape case, huh?" My flippant response takes concerted effort. It wasn't until I was older and had distance from the town of Blakely, Ohio that I realized just how biased and unjust the case was.

The police. The judge. Every adult involved. They had all decided my fate before I even stepped foot into the courthouse.

My mom wanted nothing to do with it, which is on-brand for how she's regarded me my whole life. I didn't have anyone else on my side, least of all someone to advocate or offer advice.

"It wasn't a trial," Hunter deduces through tears. "It was a smear campaign."

Nodding, I swallow past the trepidation burning in my esophagus. The next part is what makes my heart ache the most—because it was so unnecessary and cruel.

"It was. And it didn't stop there."

When I'm met with nothing but the sound of crickets chirping all around, I continue.

"One boy's mom, Karen McGilvery, rallied a whole bunch of parents. And not just the parents of the other guys charged. *All* the parents of high school-aged students in Blakely, Ohio. There was a Facebook group. There was a Change.org petition. They wanted to have me expelled."

"The fuck?" Kendrick mutters.

Hunter watches me, brow furrowed, calculation in her eyes. She knows exactly where this is going. "Did they succeed?"

With a tilt of my head, I shrug. "I guess it depends on how you define success. I dropped out of high school. Eventually, I got my GED so I could get my cosmetology license.

"I didn't have a choice. Every day was something new. Posting old pictures of me. Pulling screenshots off my social media."

"That's awful," Hunter murmurs.

An emotionless laugh bubbles out of me. "There's still more."

"How could there possibly be more?" Kendrick growls out, pushing off against the back of my chair and pacing the length of the table.

Locke catches his arm and halts him. "Let her talk, bro."

Silent again, they all turn back to me.

"McGilvery's mom was relentless. It didn't matter that I dropped out of school. That I was practically a shut-in, isolated from the people I once considered friends because I never knew who might take my picture and post it in one of her online groups."

"She organized a fundraiser for the three guys who'd been sentenced to community service. Since they were too busy dealing with the trial to apply for scholarships that year."

Hunter snorts.

"She also held a vigil in the town center."

"For what?" Locke asks at my side. Though he still isn't touching me, he's hovering so close I can feel his heat.

Shuttering my eyes, I push down the nausea that threatens to make me lose my dinner. "For the loss of innocence that occurred because of my accusations."

"What the actual fuck? Where did you say you're from? Blakely, Ohio?" The outburst comes from Greedy this time. Although their voices are starting to blend together in my mind.

I'm slipping, just slightly. There's a disconnect between my words and the emotions that should be associated with this conversation.

"Why didn't your parents do something? Stop them?" Locke's questions are valid. Ironically enough, he'll understand the answer more than anyone.

"My mom's an emotionally absent alcoholic, and I haven't seen my dad since I was four." Need I say more?

Before anyone can press further or offer me condolences for winning the shitty parent lottery, I continue.

"I would have been okay if it was just the rape."

Gruff protests rumble across the deck like thunder, but I don't stop.

"Or maybe if it was the rape and the trial even. But once Karen McGilvery sank her French-tipped acrylics into me, it was too much. The constant chatter. The incessant worry. It's one thing to deal with whispers at school and to have most of the student body calling me a slut. It's another to have an entire community holding pitchforks and doing all they can to run me out of town."

"Eventually, I moved away. I rented a shitty apartment in a shitty part of Cleveland and started working at a long-term care and hospice facility. It wasn't my dream, but it had great health care benefits, and I was able to get help."

"I spent years in counseling. I started on anti-anxiety and depression meds. When I wasn't working, I volunteered in the art and music therapy rooms at the hospice center. You learn a lot about yourself when you spend time with people at the end of their lives."

Except for the lapping waves in the distance and the humming of insects, silence surrounds us, giving me a moment to breathe. I sit back in my seat and close my eyes, listening to the frogs and crickets sing as dusk sets in over the lake.

With one more deep inhale, I open my eyes and sit up straight, ready to finish this conversation and leave the past where it belongs.

"What happened to me is just that—something that happened. It isn't who I am. It isn't even the most significant part of me. I've put in the work to ensure that. The work may never be done, but I'm okay with that, because I'm not giving up."

"That's my girl," Kylian croons, lifting his head and hitting me with a deep, sultry stare. As I consider him, the wheels begin to turn. He's assessing me. Really taking in what he's seeing.

"We need to wrap this up. Jo's exhausted and still recovering. Tomorrow is game day." He rises to his feet, looks around at our friends, then focuses on me, though his next words are directed toward the group.

"Can we get some privacy?"

Chapter 25

Josephine

"Who's we?" Locke asks, shifting his gaze between Kylian and me.

"Jo. You. Me." Kylian lifts his chin and regards Kendrick. "K?"

"Yes," the big guy replies instantly, coming around my side and crossing his arms over his chest.

"Let's go on a walk, Tem." Greedy stretches an arm out, offering his hand to Hunter.

She nods and stands, but she turns back to me before she goes. Bending at the waist, she wraps her arms around me without hesitation. The gesture alone speaks volumes about our friendship. She doesn't see me differently or view me as weak because of what happened.

"You're so fucking strong, Joey. I hate that you have to be, but I'm so proud of you." She kisses my cheek and gives me one more squeeze, then pulls back and trails after Greedy down the stairs toward the beach.

Once they hit the grass, Greedy rests his hand low on Hunter's back. It remains there for all of three seconds before she swats it away and takes a longer stride away from him.

When I turn back to my guys, Decker and Kylian are glaring at each other from opposite ends of the table, engaging in a feverish but silent debate.

"You don't need to be here for this," Kylian declares, eyeing Decker up and down.

Anger flares behind Decker's eyes. "Interesting. You seem to be making a lot of solo decisions along those lines lately. What the actual fuck, Kyl?"

Kylian shrugs, keeping his head high. "I learned from the best."

Next to me, Locke hisses at the jab. Kylian doesn't do sarcasm. Amendment—Kylian rarely does sarcasm.

"Please don't fight." I'm exhausted enough without having to navigate the rest of the night around their big dick energy. "I think I know what you want to talk about, Kyl. And I want Decker here for it," I declare.

"But he's not—"

"Is it my choice?" I ask.

"Always yours," he vows, the double meaning clear.

"Then Decker stays."

I don't dare look over at him, because I couldn't justify any of this if pressed. I know what I want. They all need to be here so we can get everything out in the open and I can finally move forward.

Dropping my head against the back of the chair, I close my eyes and steel myself for the myriad of reactions bound to hit me once we start this conversation. It's got to be a blow to discover a person so close was victim to a heinous, senseless crime. Then there's the lying. Technically, I've lied to them all from the very beginning...

I lift my head and open my eyes, finding four sets of eyes watching me with so much intensity it hits me like a violent gust of wind.

Looking around the table, I offer the only thing I have to give them in this moment: the truth. "I didn't change my name to pull one over on anyone, and I didn't come to Lake Chapel with the intention of deceit." Turning to Locke and Kendrick, I add, "Seeing you at the medical spa that day really was a coincidence."

"Josephine."

My gaze snaps over to Decker's.

"Not one of us is judging you or upset with you about anything you shared just now."

Murmurs of agreement rise up around the table.

My heart warms a little, though I can't help the sad quality of the smile I give him.

My narrative was out of my control for so long, and thus, I still struggle to grasp that my truth is just that: my truth.

Locke clears his throat and stands tall. "Fuck, Joey..." He regards me, regret tainting the warmth in his hazel irises. "If I would've known, I never would have—"

"I'm gonna stop you right there. Don't for one fucking second think that anything you and I have done wasn't okay. I wanted it. I was into it. It was toe-curling and mind-blowing and incredible."

"That goes for all of you," I declare, even though Decker and I haven't even kissed. They need to know. I need all of them to understand.

"Everything we've done has been hot, consensual bliss. Sex isn't an issue for me. I sat in therapy for months wondering and worrying if it would be, but it just... isn't. What they did... that wasn't sex. So far, not a single sexual act has triggered my panic."

Kylian nods, taking my words at face value like I knew he would, though Kendrick and Locke watch me with furrowed brows and concerned frowns.

"Don't get me wrong. I have weird as fuck triggers. You've witnessed most of them already. I'm anxious at parties. I hate to have my picture taken or to be recorded without consent. I'm terrified of storms, which you've seen more than once now. But sex isn't traumatic for me. Honestly, it gives me the freedom *not* to overthink. I love sex. The adults involved in my case tried to use it as a weapon against me, but in the end, they didn't win. I did."

Kendrick cracks a smile and tips his chin in approval.

"So now you know. I'm the girl from Ohio who got roofied and gang banged, but not the one who made the national news. My name wasn't always Josephine Meyer, but it's who I am now. I'm not broken, and I'm no delicate flower. I'm a survivor, and I came to Lake Chapel so I could finally start living."

Chapter 26

Kendrick

Never in my life have I been more regretful.

Yes, my instincts were spot-on about Josephine Meyer, but there's no vindication in that discovery. Not after she poured herself out to us tonight, her tone even and practiced. Like her story isn't the most fucked-up load of bullshit I've ever heard.

What's more: she went through it all alone.

During the hardest times of my life—losing my mom, getting my diagnosis, Emilia's diagnosis, too—I needed people. I had them. My boys. My dad. My uncle and auntie. The girls, even though they're a decade younger than me. I needed my family. I needed them, and they were there for me. I'm not sure I could have done any of that alone.

And yet, she did. Because she had to.

She suffered the unimaginable, yet she pulled herself out of the trenches, put in the work, bided her time, and created a fresh start.

She moved here for a new beginning, but only after jumping through hundreds of hoops to even get to a place where a fresh start was possible.

And to think, the moment I saw her, I jumped to all the wrong conclusions. Then I used my connections to flip her world upside-fuck-ing-down.

"Oh."

At the sound of her voice, I zero in on the woman I look for first now. On campus. In a crowd. At the games. Around the house.

I've been seeking her out more and more, the need to be near her catching like wildfire the more time I spend in her presence.

"You okay, Mama?"

My question sends a flush creeping up her cheeks and a secret smile playing across her face. Yeah, she's okay.

She's a terrible liar. Her truth is always right there on full display. She can't even pull the smallest prank over on Decker or get to the punchline of her own joke without giving herself away.

It's wild to think that, in the beginning, I looked at her and saw her candor, yet I couldn't see all the beautiful parts of her truth.

Arms out, I beckon her. "Come here."

That hint of a smile blossoms across her face as she saunters across the room, her hair wet and braided in two plaits.

I'm perched on the end of her bed, legs spread wide.

Without hesitation, she walks between them.

Looping my arms around her hips, I tip my head back and consider her.

"I asked Hunter and Greedy if they'd switch rooms with me for the night."

She frowns a little, catching her pouty bottom lip between her teeth, but she doesn't pull away.

"If you'd prefer to have them here, just say the word. Or I can take the floor or pull in a lounge chair from the balcony—"

She guffaws. "You have a game tomorrow, Kendrick."

"Yeah, and I have my girl to take care of tonight."

Her eyes go wide as she gently rakes her nails along my fade. "Your girl, huh?"

"I want to be with you, Jojo. But I need to make things right between us first. What I did... what I assumed, and how I handled things that night I saw you at the spa—"

Her hands freeze in place for a moment, then she grips my head and tilts it back so sharply I grunt.

"Don't."

"Don't what?" I challenge.

Her blue irises turn stormy as she glares down at me with an intensity she usually reserves for Cap when he really pisses her off.

"Don't apologize. Don't treat me differently now that you know."

Hoping to quell my temper, I pull in a deep breath. This girl has the power to wind me up and leave me spinning. I don't even think it's intentional most of the time. The chemistry between us is potent enough to incite a cataclysmic event every time we come together. It's a chemistry I can't wait to explore, but not until I can ensure our tempers won't burn us both to ash.

"I was wrong about you. And I'm so damn sorry."

"Kendrick," she warns, her body going rigid in my hold.

"No, Jojo. You don't get to shut me down. Not on this. Every fucking issue you've been forced to face since you showed up at LCU was because of *me*. You can't honestly insist I shouldn't apologize for fucking up and sabotaging your chance at the fresh start you deserve."

She breathes in, bowing her head low enough that her lips tickle the skin below my ear.

"I don't want to fight with you. Not anymore."

"I need to make this up to you, though," I reason.

Her warm breath hits my neck at the same time her low sigh registers. "You don't think you being here is enough?"

"It's not. It never will be. It's—"

My words end abruptly, then, and all reasonable thought flees when she presses her lips to mine.

The move is so much more than a kiss.

It's the kind of connection that demands full attention from both participants. The kind that inspires all sorts of visceral, physical reactions throughout the body.

One of the very few benefits of the chronic pain that flares inside me is that I have an extra sensitive pleasure gauge, too.

Every touch. Every caress. When it feels good, it feels so fucking good.

She licks the seam of my lips, and I gladly open for her, tilting my head back and angling it so she can tease the tip of her tongue along mine. Sweet mint registers on my taste buds as each caress turns up the heat of the fire growing in my core.

She lets out a wanton, primal purr when I cup her ass and pull her against my body.

For another moment, I'm lost in the taste of her, in the desire prickling down my spine, but then a flash of reality strikes.

"Wait." Though I'm hesitant to do it, I pull back. I'm even more distraught when I see her puffy, swollen lips turn down into a pout.

"Can I stay in here tonight? I promised Hunter I'd let her know."

She shoots me a coy smile, pushing back the game clock and making me sweat for a handful of excruciating seconds.

"You can stay," she sing-songs, angling over me again and resting her forehead on mine. "But you have to deal with the fallout when Kylian finds out."

There's playful mirth to the statement, a testament to just how okay she really is.

Maybe it's because she's learned to survive on her own for this long, or maybe it has a little to do with me. Regardless, that sassy tone sends me every fucking time.

"Why do you think I waited until we were alone before I made my move? Text your friend so she knows you're okay, Mama. Then go lock that door."

With a cheeky grin, she turns and scurries away to take care of business, but not before I give her ass a playful swat. Then I duck into the bathroom to get ready for bed.

By the time I emerge, the room is cast in the dim glow of the bedside lamp.

I climb under the sheets, reveling in the certainty that she wants me here—that she wants *me*—and make my way to the middle, draping an arm around her and pressing my forehead to hers.

"What can I do for you right now?" I'm at her mercy. I'll do anything she wants. Any favor, every whim. I want to honor her and cherish her. Because she deserves that. She deserves that and so much more.

She presses her torso into my chest, her tight little body straining against mine in the most tantalizing way.

In response, I place a chaste kiss on her forehead. I refuse to push my luck tonight. But apparently, that's the wrong move.

"Don't treat me like I'm breakable, K. Don't pity me. Please don't let what I shared tonight change how you view me." She hitches one leg over mine, tangling our lower halves beneath the sheets.

"Never," I vow, stroking a hand down her back.

"Prove it," she challenges, her sass turned all the fucking way up.

Frozen—because I'm so fucking turned on by her snark yet still so fucking distraught over my transgressions—I croak, "What did you say?"

She ghosts her lips over my neck and up to my ear, eliciting goose bumps in her wake. "Prove it, Kendrick. You want me to believe that tonight's revelations don't change how you view me? Prove. It."

She runs a hand down my torso and brushes against my cock, making her request abundantly clear.

I could argue. Push back. Hesitate. Question her.

But none of that would serve either of us right now.

So I roll over and cover her body with mine, shucking my boxers along the way, then fumbling to pull her sleep shorts down to her ankles.

I kiss her fiercely, intentionally, claiming her mouth as I roll my hips and press my cock against the apex of her thighs. Every move sends bolts of desire through me, lighting up every one of my nerve endings.

Rising to my knees, I capture her tits in my hands, smashing them together and biting at her nipples through the thin fabric of her tank top.

"Fuck... yes," she hisses through her teeth, bucking her hips up to meet mine, chasing the connection we both know is inevitable.

"Let me hear you, Jojo," I grunt, biting and sucking at the fabric over each breast until her nipples are peaked.

"Kendrick," she moans, scraping her nails down my chest and abs before she heads straight for my cock.

"Thatta girl. Let the whole house hear you," I command, burying my face between her tits and pinching her nipples.

She finds my length, fisting me from root to tip, and smears the pearl of precum around the head.

The utter euphoria it elicits sends me shooting up. Hands pressed to the mattress on either side of her head, elbows locked, back rigid. *Fuck.*

Beneath me, she eyes me coyly and slips her other hand down her belly and between her own legs. The temptress doesn't look away as she gathers up her arousal, then coats the head of my cock with it.

"Goddamn, that was hot." The words scrape out of me, my breaths escaping in ragged pants.

She pulls me forward, clawing at my ass with one hand while the other guides my dick between her thighs.

"Where you putting me, Mama?" I tease.

"Are we okay to not use a condom?" she asks instead of answering my question.

"You want me to pull out?" I grimace, because damn, I don't know that I can fulfill that promise with how out of my mind she's got me. I won't take that risk with something so precious.

"I have the implant. I just wanted to make sure it was okay with you."

"More than okay. I'm clear. I want to feel you—all of you, all the way. Put me inside you, Jojo. Let me give you what you need."

She lines me up and shifts her hips, urging me to meet her. Obediently, I slide in to her tight, wet pussy, calling out as our bodies come together in the most intimate, amazing way.

"Proof, Mama." Lifting up, I pull all the way out, then thrust until I'm buried to the hilt. "You feel that?" I roll my hips, meeting her for every single thrust. Forearms pressed to the bed, caging her in, I run my nose along her neck, then bring my lips to hers. "You feel all that proof?" I grunt, punching up and burying my cock in her sweet, warm cunt as far as it will go.

She bites down on her lip and moans again, fixing those gorgeous blue eyes on me as I fuck her into the mattress.

"Squeeze me."

She does as I command, clenching her inner walls as she keeps pace with the slow, sensual, rolling thrusts of my hips.

The tightness around my cock is incredible. Pleasure sparks with each clench, desire spikes with every passing second. I pound into her with ferocity and reverence. I don't take one second—one thrust—for granted.

"Fuck, Jojo. My heart beats for you. My body burns for you. I'm gonna fill you up with so much proof you won't ever doubt me again."

"*Kendrick.*"

Hell yeah. She's close already. I brace myself on one arm and reach between our bodies, never breaking pace. I press my thumb into her wet, swollen clit, giving just enough pressure to send her over the edge as I fuck into her at the perfect pace.

"You feel so fucking good. Give it to me, Mama. Come on my cock while I fill you up."

The first spasms of her pussy milk the orgasm right out of me. My hips falter as pleasure and release, happiness and joy, radiate through my limbs and light up every cell in my body.

She told me to prove to her that nothing has changed between us.

I didn't realize until this moment exactly what I was proving to myself, but now it couldn't be more clear. I'll never be the same because of this woman.

I hold myself above her, creating a sated, blissful cocoon for the two of us as we come down together. I kiss her everywhere—from her needy, eager mouth to her heavy, supple tits—waiting until I'm totally soft before slipping out, rolling over, and pulling her into my arms.

"Fuck... I needed that." She presses her ass into my crotch to emphasize the admission.

"It was a privilege to give you what you need," I murmur, stroking my hands up and down her bare hips and legs. I can't get enough of this girl. "I want to be here for you, always."

She sighs, curling back into my arms, conveying that holding her and just being here is enough.

Stifling a yawn, I run my hand along her smooth skin. I refuse to fall asleep until she dozes off. She's my priority, and I want to make sure she sleeps soundly. Her care is my greatest concern. I wait patiently, tracing a pattern from her shoulder to her hip, then down her thigh and back up again.

For now, her breathing is even, and she lets out a contented hum at the contact.

When I brush my hand over one ass cheek, she instantly pushes back, seeking more.

Tentatively, I tease one finger between her cheeks, toying with the rim of her ass.

"You let your boys play back here, Mama?"

With a moan, she whips her head around to look at me over her shoulder, her eyes full of smoldering desire.

"Not yet, I haven't."

"Good," I grunt, applying a bit more pressure against her puckered hole. "I want this."

"I bet you do," she teases, grinding her hips with just enough force to have the tip of my finger nearly pressing in.

"I want everything where you're concerned, Mama. But I can be patient. You're more than worth the wait."

Dragging my hand back up to safer territory, I loop an arm around her and pull her into me. Kissing the back of her head, I settle in to wait for her to sleep, so damn grateful to have a second chance with this woman.

Chapter 27

Locke

"You're an asshole," Decker snarks at Kylian.

"I learned from the best," Kyl fires back, lifting his chin.

I knew this wouldn't be easy. The tension has been simmering between them all week. Tonight's revelations finally sent it bubbling over.

The three of us are still on the deck, despite how late it is and how early we have to be up for tomorrow's game. This can't wait, and we all know it.

Decker is standing on one side of the table, Kylian on the other. They're facing off in a way I've never witnessed before. After all the years we've had together and everything we've been through, I hope like hell this isn't what breaks us. There's no way I can choose between them if it comes down to it.

Decker huffs, glaring from Kyl to me, then back to our friend again. "I can't believe you kept all that from us. We don't do secrets. I can't fucking stand secrets."

Clearly exasperated by arguing in circles, Kylian sighs. "It wasn't my story to tell," he says for the umpteenth time.

Decker paces the length of the table, muttering to himself. He's hurting. We all are. But he's having a hard time coming to terms with what Joey shared. He's failing at keeping his shit together, and, apparently, he's decided Kylian should be the punching bag for his self-loathing.

Raking his hands through his hair, he spins and strides back so he's directly across from Kylian again and thrusts a finger in his direction. "We could've avoided all of this. All the shit we put her through—"

"I didn't do anything wrong," Kylian grits out, hands planted on the tabletop. "And I'd do it again, if given the chance. You knowing about her past wasn't going to change your decision about keeping her here." Leaning forward, he squints behind his glasses. "You just can't handle knowing you weren't as in control of this situation as you let yourself believe."

Yikes. Shots fired.

But also... Kylian's got a point.

Propping myself against the railing, I cross my arms over my chest and examine them both. They've never really had to duke it out before—not like this. They need to work through this so we can all move forward.

"I should have known," Decker groans, his hands clenched into fists. "I should have fucking known."

Now we're getting somewhere.

He's not upset that Kylian didn't tell him.

To his credit, I think Kylian knows that.

Decker's pissed because he can't fix this. Because so many of his decisions and actions probably made things worse for her over the last several weeks.

With a final huff, he slumps into a chair, lifting his head to regard me before focusing on Kylian again.

"What can we do?" he laments.

Kyl stands up straighter, a glint of mischief in his smirk. "What we do best. Analyze. Strategize. Make a plan and hit them where it hurts. Cut them off at every pass. We play the long game, and take down our enemy in ways they never expected."

"How?" Decker demands, glowering. He won't be satisfied until he figures out a way forward.

Kylian can't control the smugness that drips from every word. "We could start by tracking them down, quietly dropping hints that someone knows their secret. Harass them for months to make it that much more unbearable. Then, eventually, we expose them to their families and communities with irrefutable evidence."

Decker's eyes practically bug out of his head. "The fuck, Kyl?"

"That's what I've been doing. Ever since I found out. I've been working to destroy the videos and weave together a revenge plan worthy of our girl."

Decker nods, then blows out a long breath. "That's a start. But be careful, Kyl. She can't..."

"She won't. Not until it's done. It'll take time. Years, even. But I won't rest until I see this through."

"What can I do?" Decker presses. "How can I help?"

"We can't outsource this," Kylian contends. "I wouldn't trust anyone else with this job anyway. I need time. Money. New equipment dedicated to this project so it isn't tangled up with anything related to football."

"Consider it done," Decker declares, sitting a little straighter. That position, and the satisfaction it conveys, only remains for a heartbeat, though. A second later, he's hunching forward in his chair, and his expression fades to one of remorse. "Do you think... Do you think she's really okay?"

She is. Or she will be. I know that. Kylian knows that, too.

There's a vivacity to Joey that life hasn't dimmed, despite all the trials and hardships she's endured. She's okay. And now that we're all on the same page, maybe she can move past okay and finally thrive.

"Unequivocally," Kylian assures him. "It's important that you believe her, Decker. That might be the most important piece to all of this."

"Should someone go check on her?" Decker asks, tapping his foot against the boards of the deck—he's clearly anxious to volunteer.

"Kendrick's with her," Kylian informs us, double-checking his phone. "And it's late. We all need to go to bed."

How Kylian knows Kendrick's whereabouts, I have no idea. But I'm glad he has it covered. She's got the support of all of us, and she's going to need it.

Never one to mince words, Kylian shuffles toward the sliding glass door. "I assume we're done here?" He regards me, then nods to Decker.

"We're done," Decker confirms.

He grips the door handle but pauses before sliding it open. "And we're good? As in, you no longer feel compelled to slam your throwing hand into inanimate objects or my face?"

Decker gapes in response to Kyl's question, but I can't hold back my snicker. Kylian has never cracked jokes like this. She's changing him. She's changing all of us.

"We're good," Decker eventually confirms, his eyes wide as he watches Kylian retreat into the house.

Turning to me, he blinks a couple of times and nods toward the closed door. "He's got jokes now?"

With a grin, I push off the railing. "Apparently." I come to stand before him and extend a hand. When he's on his feet, I pull him into a hug and give him a smack on the back. "She makes us better. All of us individually; all of us together. I know your first instinct is to protect, but there's no danger here. She doesn't need protection. She just needs you."

I don't give him time to respond before I turn on my heel and head to bed.

Chapter 28

Josephine

The vibe is alarmingly tense this morning, as proven by the way both the Lake Chapel Crusaders' and South Chapel Sharks' quarterbacks are aggressively shaking their blender bottles on opposite ends of the kitchen island while giving each other haughty looks.

Worrying my bottom lip, I look from Decker to Greedy and back again, willing my heart to settle.

"They're fine," Locke quietly assures me, claiming the barstool beside me and sliding a plate of scrambled eggs my way. "Their heads are just in the game already."

Makes sense. But the conflicting energy rolling off them is so thick it's hard to breathe in here.

Kendrick slipped out of my bed around six this morning. He must have texted Greedy to coordinate movements, because just as I was coming back from the bathroom, Hunter crept into the room.

My coquettish grin was enough to tell her exactly what happened the night before.

Waggling her brows, she whispered, "Good for you, girl. But you're out of your pretty little head if you think I'm about to crawl into your love nest and bask in those sex sheets."

I snorted, only to be caught by surprise by a yawn.

"You need more sleep," Hunter lectured, circling the bed and rummaging through the bedside table she'd laid claim to.

"Will you be okay if I sit on the balcony and read?" she asked, holding up her Kindle.

With a false confidence she could no doubt see right through, I gave her a nod and a small smile. Unburdening myself of my darkest secrets admittedly lightened the weight on my chest, but flashes of Sunday night still haunt me, and in turn, they spark visions from that night five years ago.

The semiconscious moments are the worst. When I'm almost asleep or just starting to wake, visions cloud my mind, and the intrusive thoughts play out on repeat. I know I need sleep, but I hate the idea of having to awake again.

"I'll keep the door cracked, so just holler if you need me."

I crashed for a few hours, only to wake up in a stupor. The fog of confusion was far more preferable to one swimming with panic, but I struggled to rouse myself. Then I had to hustle downstairs to catch the guys before Decker, Locke, and Kendrick had to leave for the game.

"You didn't have to make me breakfast," I chide through a yawn. Although the eggs and toast in front of me look delicious. "You have to get your head in the game, too, Emo Boy."

His dazzling smile hits first, followed by the cock of his pierced eyebrow. "Maybe this is my favorite game, baby. Just because I'm a team player doesn't mean I can't make big plays." He stabs a huge bite of egg on his own plate, then shovels it into his mouth.

Decker has barely acknowledged my existence this morning, which is par for the course for QB1 on game day. He's laser focused and in the zone, already locked in and mentally preparing to dominate, despite having to share the kitchen with his biggest rival.

Speaking of...

Greedy and Hunter packed their bags last night. When they leave for the game today, they won't be coming back to the Crusade Mansion to stay. My friend has done more for me over the last few days than she could comprehend, and my state of mind is far less fragile than it was even forty-eight hours ago, but anxiety still simmers just below my skin, threatening to spike when I think about falling asleep without her beside me.

"Hey." Locke brushes his tatted hand up my thigh, teasing precariously close to the hem of my sleep shorts. "You're not hungry?" He nods at my untouched plate.

It's not that I'm not hungry. I'm just convincing my body—specifically, my brain and my stomach—that I'm safe, and that there's no need to fear any sort of spiral today, despite the potential of coming face-to-face with members of the South Chapel football team.

I'll be with Kylian, and if I know him the way I think I do, he won't leave my side. But I'm still sapped from all I divulged last night—metaphorically raw and bleeding out of the wound I've cauterized ten times over throughout the years.

"I'm just not looking forward to the game," I confess.

Locke frowns in concern, the glint of his eyebrow piercing catching my attention momentarily as he assesses me.

Shuddering, I wrap my arms around myself. "I want to watch you guys play, of course. But knowing I'll be in such close proximity to the game, right there for all the Sharks to taunt or jeer..."

I trail off, only to feel every eye in the room on me.

Great.

Another captivated audience for my emotional trauma.

An awkward silence buzzes between us. Thankfully, Greedy clears his throat and takes one step closer before I melt off the barstool into a puddle of humiliation.

He looks from Decker to Kendrick, then tips his chin at me. "They won't come anywhere near you, Joze. The three stooges from that night will be on the bench the entire game." He pulls his lower lip between his teeth and squints. "Actually, one of them might not even be there today. Injury, last I heard."

The guys involved are all second-string players, so that makes sense. Still.

His assurance doesn't calm the roiling in my stomach or the dread pressing against my ribcage.

There's no guarantee they won't get called up, or that they won't make a point to hassle me or get under my skin from the bench. I'm not sure I'd even recognize them. The panic from that night and then the sedation at the hospital have made all the images I can conjure hazy.

"You're okay," Kendrick whispers in my ear from behind, startling me so severely I almost slip off the barstool for real this time. Bringing my hand to my heart, I focus on steadying my breathing, only to have him wrap his arms around me and engulf me in his soothing, masculine scent.

I lean back, going soft in his arms, and bask in his comfort as best I can, willing myself not to worry about what I can't control.

"We took care of it, Mama. Decker, Greedy, and me. While Nicky and Kyl were taking care of you in the Nest a few nights ago, we were out there taking care of you, too."

The words are whispered in my ear, the sweetest murmur. They're a reverent oath and a quiet confession.

"What—"

"We took care of it." Kendrick's tone is stern, effectively cutting off my questioning.

Gulping past the dread over any of them risking their safety or reputations for me, I crane back and meet his gaze. "Thank you," I mouth, too vulnerable to trust my voice not to shake if I spoke the words aloud.

K cups my chin, kisses my forehead, and retreats to the other side of the island.

This time when I look around the kitchen, no one is watching me. The guys are conspicuously busying themselves with finishing their food and packing up for the game, and Hunter has her head buried in the fridge.

Sighing, I turn to Locke and find his hazel eyes on me.

"You'll be okay, Hot Girl." This time, I'm tempted to believe his assurance. "Plus, you'll be with Kylian. Just like always."

I scrunch my nose and try to quell my anxiety. "I know. He has a job to do, though."

I leave it at that. Every person in this room knows how hyper-focused and fixated Kyl can be during a game.

"Move," Kylian demands, brushing past Greedy and Hunter and shooing Locke from my orbit so he can have my full attention.

Swiveling the barstool so I'm facing him, he cups my face in his hands and levels me with an intense look I've come to crave. For several long seconds, he's silent, inspecting me from behind his glasses.

"You think I can't do my job and keep you safe," he finally says. It's not a question. It never is with him. It's an observation, and maybe a bit of an accusation. "You don't think I notice every move you make when the guys are on the field?"

He smirks, then bows lower, brushing his nose with mine in an adorable way that's so unlike him.

"Baby, you underestimate just how well I can compartmentalize. Don't think for one second that I'm not tuned in to you every second you're on the bench by my side."

He releases my face, his fingertips tickling down my neck until his thumbs brush my jaw, and tilts my head back, holding me at the exact angle he wants me.

"I see you. Every movement. Every reaction. The way you squeeze your thighs together when offense runs off the field and the boys hustle over to the sidelines."

My cheeks flame at the callout. There's no way I do that.

"The way you yelp and jump in your seat when Locke takes a hit, even though it's his damn job to be ready for impact. The way you can't stop cracking your knuckles on third and long, despite witnessing K find his route more often than not."

Kendrick scoffs across the kitchen and lifts his chin. "You mean almost always."

Kylian side-eyes him without turning his head. "I manage the stats, K. More often than not is nonspecifically generous by design. It's certainly nowhere close to the realm of *almost always*."

Greedy snickers where he's propped up against the counter near the stove, eliciting grumbles from the rest of the guys. But then Kylian focuses on me again, and all distractions around us fade away.

The thumb that was just brushing my jaw traces my lower lip.

"The way you bite your lip when you hear me call play action, because you know more than one of your guys is going to be involved."

I suck in a breath. I had no idea I did that.

"The way you glance over at me an average of twenty-six times per quarter, your gorgeous eyes searching my face and reading my body language to check on me. Always concerned, always right there. Even though I can't give you the attention you deserve."

My heart stutters in my chest, and my bottom lip quivers. I do check on him. Remind him to breathe. Bring him water when I think he needs it. I wouldn't put it past him to not notice, but what I didn't realize was that not only does he notice, but he's so in tune with me that he's *calculated the average.*

"I see you, baby. Always. You're safe by my side. Nothing and no one is getting to you ever again."

Kylian pulls back so fast I nearly fall forward. On instinct, I catch myself on his chest, then right myself on the stool. When I've found my balance and lift my head, I discover that we have a rapt audience.

My cheeks flush with embarrassment—*again.* I was so transfixed by Kyl I didn't register that he was talking loud enough for anyone else to hear.

Whatever. They're all aware of the tangled relationship dynamics we're braiding together anyway.

The alarm on Decker's phone sounds, and the guys throw back the last bites of food and dredges of protein shakes.

As the crowd shuffles out, Greedy swings by and snags my attention.

"Kendrick told you we handled the three guys from last weekend," he murmurs low, keeping the conversation private.

I nod, my heart panging with appreciation.

"In case you need an extra layer of defense, I left something for you upstairs."

Confused, I purse my lips and peer over at Hunter. Maybe she can clue me in. She shrugs and shakes her head in response, though. Looks like whatever Greedy's up to was his idea alone.

"Think of it as my parting gift, Joze." He squeezes my shoulder.

I'm more than grateful for all he's done. A parting gift is unnecessary, but he continues before I can insist that I don't need anything else from him.

"You've been through hell. I've never seen someone fight that hard to pull themselves back from the brink, but you fucking did. More than once. You're scrappy, and I admire that. Plus, you're an amazing friend to Hunter."

A little uncomfortable with the praise he's lavishing me with, I open my mouth to discount his claims, but he raises his eyebrows and cuts me off at the pass.

"You don't need any more help, but if you want an extra layer of armor, it's there for you. As soon as you put it on, the message will be clear: you're a Crusaders girl, but you also have my respect and protection."

Chapter 29

Josephine

Rubbing the hem of the jersey between my fingers, I adjust it again, tugging it down my torso as if stretching it out might make me more comfortable somehow. I fiddle with my camera settings, but my heart's not in it tonight. Crossing one leg over the other, I stash it back in the bag and give up on taking pictures for now.

"Jo."

Beside me, Kylian's watching the field, so I inspect his profile: The scowl of concentration hidden behind his thick, square-framed glasses. The sharp angle of his freshly shaven jaw. His game-day headset and dual devices in place and ready to go.

He looks locked in on the field and nothing else.

Except as I scrutinize him, his words from earlier in the kitchen replay in my mind. Despite his intense focus on preparing for the game, he's undeniably aware of my every move.

"I know you're uncomfortable, but you're going to have to scoot down the damn bench if you squirm like that through the whole game."

"I'm not uncomfortable," I snap back too quickly.

He doesn't turn to face me, but he calls bullshit with a simple quirk of a brow.

"Do you think it's a bad idea?" I hedge.

This time, he does glance my way. Just long enough for me to see the trepidation in his eyes. Then he's homed in on the field again.

"You're literally wearing the jersey for the quarterback of the South Chapel Sharks whilst sitting on the Lake Chapel Crusaders' bench." He drops his chin slightly and taps the screen of one of his tablets. "Decker has been shooting daggers our way since the second he came out of the tunnel. You already know the answer to that question."

I huff, feeling more insecure with each passing second as the captains and refs come together for the coin toss.

"Why didn't you say something earlier?"

Kylian and I rode to the game together like usual. Well, not exactly "as usual" since he insisted on taking the Sherp and navigating the marshes to get us to the mainland. But it was low tide, and he swore he'd have to make the trip this weekend anyway so he could perform routine maintenance before returning it to the garage.

Kylian squints at the field, sitting stone-still, then exhales a long sigh when the Sharks win the coin toss and defer. Tapping away on the device on his right leg, he bounces his left knee. He spends another ten seconds or so inputting data and analyzing the recalculations before he gives me his attention again. "You're a strong, independent woman. You most certainly don't need me telling you what to do."

Reaching over, he hooks a finger through one of the belt loops of my ripped boyfriend jeans and tugs until I get the hint and scoot over so we're sitting hip to hip.

"Besides," he murmurs, tucking a strand of hair behind my ear and lowering the microphone of his headset. "Who am I to stop you if you want to be a bad girl tonight?"

My cheeks heat at the callout. They warm even more when Greedy rushes to the sideline, the smuggest smirk plastered on his face when he sees me sitting on the bench wearing number two. He spits out his mouth guard, grins lewdly, and hollers in our direction.

"Hot damn, Joze. I was *not* prepared for just how good you'd look sitting in a sea of Crusaders red wearing *my* number."

Without waiting for a response, he sprints toward one of the players' benches, an energizer bunny brimming with excitement. He does some sort of side shuffle, jumping up and pumping his fist to get the Crusaders' attention.

"You boys seeing this?" he taunts. "Taylor. Lockewood. Are you seeing what I'm seeing?" He throws his head back and cackles, then runs back toward me, pointing wildly. "Who am I kidding? How could you not?"

Greedy's right. How could anyone not notice me?

In a sea of crimson, I'm a homing beacon of bright aquamarine.

I duck my head and shrink back in my seat, wishing it was more than just Kylian and me on this entire bench so I'd have someone else to hide behind.

Greedy sprints past us, hollering over his shoulder as he passes.

"I'll be back for you, Joze. I'll sign that jersey just as soon as I beat these boys on their home field."

Cocky son of a bitch.

Have we grown closer over the last week? Yes. Do I trust him implicitly? Also yes. Did he help me immensely, in the most significant and selfless ways over the last week? Yes, yes, yes.

Did I allow the care and generosity of his time to overshadow the bigger picture? The one where he's the quarterback of my team's biggest rival, and by default, the arch nemesis of the four men I desperately want to win this game?

Also yes.

I fight back a grimace and silently scold myself for not anticipating how this would play out.

Greedy's jersey was meant to be armor—an extra layer of protection between me and any asshat Sharks who may have heard about last weekend's prank. I assumed that, at best, I'd go unnoticed. At worst? Anyone from South Chapel who tried to run their mouth would be confused and beguiled by my choice of attire.

I hadn't considered its effect on anyone but the second and third string South Chapel players.

Hopefully my guys are secure enough in our dynamic to not let something so minuscule rile them.

Surely the indisputable ire radiating off Decker Crusade has everything to do with football and tonight's game, and nothing to do with me.

This can't be happening.

Maybe it's a coincidence.

Or maybe it's because of the bye week.

Decker's concussion protocol and lack of practice could be contributing factors.

Or maybe the Sharks are just the better team.

For the first time all season, the Crusaders are *losing*.

Not only are they losing, but they're not playing well.

At all.

I'm still a novice when it comes to football, but I've been on the bench during every game this season, and not once have things gone so poorly.

The guys keep fumbling, both literally and figuratively. There's a flag on almost every drive, and the refs are calling penalties left and right. There's no rhythm or finesse on the field. They haven't picked up any of their usual momentum.

Three sacks for Decker and two plays resulting in negative yardage. This is not the Crusaders way.

As the offense comes off the field and special teams takes their place on the line of scrimmage, I blow out a long exhale and scan the sideline to keep an eye out for my guys.

Kylian curses, calling my attention back to the field. "Why the hell is he kicking end-over-end?" he mutters, tapping against his device at an impossible speed.

The punter's kick comes down just shy of the thirty-five yard line. The Sharks make it all the way to midfield before the Crusaders can take down the kick returner.

"At least that wasn't my fault," I mutter under my breath.

Kylian glowers at me. "If you think any of this isn't related to what you're wearing and how it's affecting our guys, and in turn, the entire team, you're sorely mistaken."

"Seriously?" I snap, reeling back.

"Jo."

"Kylian," I mock.

The one person I consider my safe place is calling me out, and that's got my hackles rising and a heavy weight sinking in my stomach. Gulping past the trepidation clogging my throat, I bury my face in my hands. Regret and shame wash over me because, though I'm loath to admit it, this was a bad idea. A very, very bad idea.

Conceptually, it was solid. Greedy's reasoning made sense.

And even though deep down I *knew* it would piss off Decker, I didn't put enough thought into it to really consider the consequences of showing up in his rival's jersey.

Pissing off Decker is what I do. I push. He pushes back. Then I push harder. It's never affected him like this before, and eventually, he cracks. We recalibrate. And the whole song and dance begins again.

Except this? What's happening right now, during this game, on the field, because of me?

This is something entirely new and wholly unexpected.

Maybe it's because of how our dynamic has changed and changed again over the last two weeks. From his concussion and the out-of-state trip to the hospital, to the quiet moments we've stolen, the ones brimming with emotion and potential.

Maybe it was his dedication to finding me—the confession that he hadn't eaten, hadn't slept, could barely function until I knew I was safe.

Could it have been what went down on the boat? His horrific attempt at helping me, the one fueled by his deep desire to heal me and banish my anxiety and pain? It was awfully executed, but his intentions were pure. Then there was the way he opened up about his mom...

Or maybe it's that he finally knows. He finally knows who I am, who I was, what I've survived, and instead of pushing him away like I originally feared, it only makes him want to protect me more.

"Do you really think they're losing because of me?" I whisper.

"Undoubtedly." Kylian doesn't even hesitate. There's not an ounce of sugar coating his explanation. "You couldn't have picked a more perfect way to get under Decker's skin and throw him off his game. You donning Garrett Reed Ferguson the Third's South Chapel Sharks jersey is the equivalent of a total knockout for Cap. I know it. He knows it. Greedy knows it. You pretending *not* to know it only makes it worse."

Shit on a crumbling cracker.

"Why didn't you say something earlier?" I hiss. Suddenly, the bright teal polyester covering my shoulders and torso is too hot, too sticky, too itchy to endure. I scrape my nails against my upper arms, but it does nothing to alleviate the discomfort.

The neckline is too tight. The fabric is stifling. I don't have anything on under the jersey besides a cropped bralette, so I can't just take the damn thing off.

"Baby," Kylian murmurs. "I would never tell you what to wear or hold you back from what you want to do. Unless we're in my bed"—a flash of heat sparks in his eyes, but it's gone as quickly as it came as he focuses on the game again—"you're the boss."

While using his left hand to keep up with his tablets and keeping his attention on the field, he works one hand under the itchy fabric of the jersey and grazes my right hip before he rests his hand on the small of my back. The skin-to-skin contact soothes me in a way that only Kylian's touch can. What I wouldn't give to rip off this stupid jersey and ask him to hold me right now, football game and stands full of angry fans be damned.

"Besides," he says, turning from the data on his screens. "I no longer prioritize Decker's opinion above all others. He's not my number one, Jo. You are."

He squeezes my hip once more before turning back to his devices just as the star running back for the Lake Chapel Crusaders jogs over to our bench.

"Get up," Kendrick demands, his chest heaving as he hovers over me and spits out his mouth guard.

"Why?" I snap. I'm already drowning in vulnerability and regret. I know I fucked up. I don't need Kendrick Taylor pulling out his grumpy big dick energy to—

"Because I need you to hear me when I say this, Jojo. And I need to physically block you from Cap's view so we don't piss him off even more."

Oh.

A glance at Kylian confirms he has eyes on us. That small comfort galvanizes me to rise from the bench and square up against number 24.

Kendrick is massive in his street clothes. Add in his pads and helmet, and his presence is colossal.

Sweat streams down his face as he scowls at me from behind his face mask. He's so close the warm musk and vanilla of his cologne mixed with the scent of fresh sweat, grass, and upturned earth overwhelms my senses. It's a supremely masculine smell, entrancing enough I could get lost in his aura if I don't keep my head on straight.

With my feet firmly planted, I rest my hands on my hips and lift my gaze. The position is so reminiscent of when he laid into me during the last home game—pissed off and raging that Kyl called a time-out because I knew something was wrong with Decker.

That first time, I was right.

I already know I'm wrong this time around.

Fueled by the memories of the hatred he shoveled my way for weeks, I tip my chin defiantly.

"Say what you need to say, K."

Fire erupts behind his eyes.

"*Goddamn*, this mouth." He catches my chin with two fingers, tipping it up with the gentlest touch. "I'm gonna fuck the sass right out of it and teach you some southern manners one day soon." He bows his head, his words heavy and guttural. "You're gonna suck down every drop I give you and say 'thank you, Kendrick, can I have some more please?' when I'm done."

I squeak in surprise while simultaneously being hit with a wave of hot desire. Forcing my spine ramrod straight, I choke back the response and try to quell my reaction.

The threat—*more like a promise*—was not what I was expecting. I sink my teeth into my bottom lip as he grips my chin tighter.

"You're fucking with him big time, Mama."

He doesn't actually need to say the words. I see that clearly now, but I remain silent, letting him get it out.

"He can't keep his head in the game. Out of all our years playing together, I've *never* seen him like this."

I ignore the little thrill that rises in my chest.

"I don't think it was your intention to make us lose, but intention doesn't mean shit on game day. It's about action. Choices. You did this. You made a bad fucking choice. The damage is done, but the damage isn't irreparable. Not yet. Fix it, Jojo. Fucking fix it right now."

He's right. But I can't help myself from pushing back and resisting his request.

He shakes his head like he's snapping himself out of it, then drops my chin, turns, and jogs three steps before I can call after him.

"What's in it for me, K?"

He spins around and freezes, then smirks.

God, he's so fucking hot. Larger than life. Enigmatic, passionate, and sensual. Now that he's not constantly scowling and hiding his true nature from me, it's so blatant it's like a smack in the face every time he turns his attention to me.

His eyes are full of a mix of playfulness and blazing intensity. He knows I'll make this right. Just like I know he's about to say something that'll make me have to squeeze my knees together.

"Fix it, and I'll give you all the southern hospitality lessons you want." He gives me a long once-over, virility and masculinity rolling off him in waves. "So many lessons, Mama. I'll make it so good for you. I may even throw in some extra credit."

Done.

Chapter 30

Josephine

"I'm going to find Hunter," I declare the moment the clock runs out on the second quarter.

Kylian throws an arm out and catches my wrist before I make it two steps.

"You have your phone on you?"

"Got it," I confirm.

He's still homed in on his iPad, rapidly scrolling through data on the screen, but he doesn't release me.

"Text me when you get to Hunter. Don't leave the stadium. And be back before the start of the second half."

My instinct is to clap back and sass him, but I snap my mouth shut and nod instead.

Kylian is not the controlling one of the group. He's black and white, straight to the point. His directions are rooted in a deep concern for my safety and well-being. He can't leave, but he's not going to force me to stay. I don't take his concern for granted. We've come too far—we're in this too deep—for me to be anything but wildly appreciative of the way he cares.

He doesn't wait for my acquiescence before releasing me, and once I'm free of his hold, I turn on my heel and make my way through the crowd, blowing out a long breath when I join the stream of fans heading to the bathrooms and concession stands. It's so much easier to blend in with the sea of people.

Hunter is already waiting in our designated meet-up spot—the aisle of section 130, closer to the alumni and premium seating section than the student section in the end zone.

"Joey!" she squeals, her eyes as wide as saucers and her pretty blond hair pulled back in a high ponytail that bobs as she shakes her head. "This is bad," she declares. "This is *so* bad."

"I know," I relent. "But I have an idea." I quickly shoot off a text to Kylian, as promised, then stash my phone away.

"Will you help me?"

"Of course, girl," Hunter starts. "But I don't know how you think we're going to—"

Grabbing her hand, I tear off with one destination in mind.

"Wait. Where are we going?" she demands.

"Bathrooms," I answer over my shoulder, weaving in and out of the crowd.

"*Which* bathrooms?" Hunter huffs as I drag her farther into the stadium.

Her irritation is justified. I just dragged her past the nicest, least crowded bathrooms in the entire place. I bypassed it because I'm less likely to find what I need in there. Instead of explaining my reasoning, I quicken my pace and pull my friend behind me into the bowels of the student section.

Colors shift around us, the juxtaposed aquamarine and reds transitioning to almost all crimson the closer we get to the curve in the concourse.

Students stand shoulder to shoulder, waiting in massive lines to use the bathrooms or grab a drink. I ignore more than a few jeers when I rush past in my Sharks jersey.

Out of breath but more determined than ever, I reach the women's restroom between the football players' and cheer team's locker rooms.

It's the largest one in the whole stadium, and it's overrun with Lake Chapel students all dolled up in their spirit wear.

"Try and keep up," I call back to Hunter, wedging myself through the door to the restroom. A few people waiting in line protest, worried we're cutting, but I don't slow as I toss out muttered apologies and insist we just need the mirrors.

Inside, the sea of red and white and black is hazy from the glitter and hairspray being applied with reckless abandon.

I scan the girls lined up at the sink, hoping beyond hope to find what I'm looking for.

It can't be a T-shirt. Or a hoodie. Or a crop top.

A homemade fit won't work.

My attention snags on the number 24—*Kendrick*—once, twice, and a third time. Then I spot a number 9—Locke—halfway down the line of sinks. I nearly give myself whiplash doing a double take when I catch sight of a Sigma jersey. It's identical to one I designed and had specially made to wear in support of Kylian.

I'll deal with that later.

Right now, there's only one number I need to find.

There it is. At the very end of the row of sinks. The girl's back is to me, and she's reaching for a paper towel to dry her hands.

"Hey!" I call out, beelining for the redhead wearing the oversized Crusade jersey.

I catch her attention in the mirror, repeating myself once she's focused on my reflection.

"Hey. Hi. Um, this is super awkward, but I really need your help."

With a slow turn, she looks me over from head to toe the way girls sometimes do.

Shit. Maybe this'll be harder than I thought...

"Um, so. I was wondering if you would be willing to switch jerseys with me. I—I messed up," I admit to this girl I don't even know. "I messed up bad, and I really need to go out there for the second half of the game wearing number five's jersey."

Her face is screwed up in bewilderment, but I keep pleading my case. "I have these cute Crusaders friendship bracelets I can also give you." I pull off the elastic bead bracelets from my wrist. Hunter and I made them yesterday, and I intended to give some to Kendrick's sisters, so I have more than enough. "You don't have to return them. Which ones do you like?" I shuffle through them with shaky hands so she can see the designs and phrases. "No, wait, don't pick—you can have them all."

When the girl makes no move to take the bracelets from my outstretched hand, I pull my shoulders up and drop my hands to my sides.

"I'm happy to pay you for the jersey, or trade something else... I only have my phone on me right now, but I could Venmo you. I also have a really nice MacBook at home, or—"

Hunter steps up and cuts me off before I can offer up my car. *Sorry, Honey.*

"Here's the deal, Red. You give us the Crusade jersey, and we'll return it to you by Tuesday, freshly laundered and signed by *Decker himself.*"

The girl's eyes bug out, then she gawks at the crowd that's formed all around us.

"Do it, girl!" someone calls out.

"Hold out! Maybe they can set you up with Crusade!"

"Or with one of his roommates," someone else offers.

I crack my knuckles, forcing myself to remain calm while pleading with the biggest puppy eyes I can manage.

"Please?"

"Um." She lets out an uncomfortable laugh, glancing from me to Hunter and toying with the hem of the prized garment.

"I mean, I would love to help you, really, I would..."

I hold my breath and wait for it.

"But—"

And there it is.

"I can't go back to the student section wearing that." She points a painted red nail at my aquamarine Sharks jersey.

Shit. Of course not. Why didn't I think about what would happen if another student showed up in the Crusaders student section wearing this dreadful, regrettable choice?

I smile sadly and nod. I get it. I hold up one hand, ready to thank her anyway. It was a good idea, if not for—

"*God dammit*, Josephine no-middle-name Meyer," Hunter curses, bumping me out of her way and shuffling up to the girl in the Crusade jersey.

I search her face, confusion swirling in my mind. *Why the hell is she cursing me out?*

"You owe me. You owe me big-time. I want at least one guaranteed lunch date per week sans *any* of your boyfriends for the rest of the school year, plus a monthly sleepover—no boys allowed." She pulls one arm through the sleeve of her shirt. "I may have additional demands, so I'll need an open-ended favor rider for the foreseeable future." Her other arm is free now, too. "I'm never going to live this down."

She whips off her shirt so fast her hair hits me in the face.

"Hunter! What's happening?"

Shoving her cute red Crusaders T-shirt at the redhead, she purses her lips and gives me a pointed look.

"Isn't it obvious? So painfully, predictably obvious." She closes her eyes, her long lashes fanning out over her cheeks, and presses her fingers into her temples. "I'll give her my shirt. She'll give you Decker's jersey. And I'll wear..."

"*Hunter!*"

"It's fine," she insists, tipping her head back as if calling on a higher power to get her through this.

I don't blame her. She's going to need universal, holy support if Greedy catches sight of her with his name on the back.

"Thank you," I whisper, my throat clogged with emotion as I squeeze her hand.

"And thank you," I add, regarding the redhead. "What's your name, by the way?"

"Ashley," she offers, peeling off the number 5 jersey and handing it over as she accepts the T-shirt from Hunter. "And you?"

"I'm Joey. And that's Hunter," I explain with a sheepish grin. "Here, have this," I insist, offering one of the cute red bracelets and keeping a few for myself.

Snapping back to attention, Hunter holds out her hand, scowling.

"You best understand we're now in this for the long haul, Josephine Meyer. If this isn't some romance novel-worthy grand gesture, I don't know what is. I want to be maid of honor in your wedding. Weddings? And you'll name your first child after—"

"Okay! Okay!" I snap, desperate to shut her up. We've gained quite the audience, and halftime has got to be close to wrapping up. We've got to make the swap and get back out there.

"Thank you, Ashley. Seriously. Let's exchange numbers so I can get this back to you."

"Signed?" she asks, her eyes sparkling and her face split in a wide grin.

"Signed," I promise.

"This better work," Hunter mutters as she dons the South Chapel Jersey with her stepbrother's name on the back and tightens her ponytail.

"It'll work," I declare, pulling Decker's jersey over my head.

I give Ashley a quick one-armed hug and rattle off my phone number. When she's typed it in and has sent me a confirmation text, I snag Hunter's hand once more and power walk out the door so I can make it back to the bench for the second half.

"It has to."

Chapter 31

Decker

Never in my life have I let an opponent mentally best me. I train my brain just as hard as I condition my body. I've had as many mindset coaches as I've had trainers throughout the years. My mind is an impenetrable fortress of focus and determination. Or so I thought.

I didn't even have the wherewithal to process the words coach spit at us in the locker room. He might have chewed us out, or he might have delivered a motivational speech. Either way, my head is not in the game.

At least not the one being played on the field.

Jaw locked tight, I ignore the bench, desperate to purge the vision of Josephine wearing Greedy Ferguson's jersey that's branded in my mind. I sure as hell don't need another dose of her to send me spiraling.

The two-minute notification comes through my headset, followed by our offensive coach asking Kylian which fullback to send in.

The rest of the team rallied at the half, and K scored on our second possession in the third quarter, running the ball for nearly forty yards on what should have been an impossible route. Kylian's gonna flip out when he analyzes the play. I don't know what got into him, but he's been on fucking fire in the second half of this game.

Locke is more solid now, too, although he's hurting. A few early hits rocked his world. South Chapel came to fucking play.

But this is our field. This is our home. *That's my fucking girl.*

We're down by six. It's third and inches, and there's exactly two minutes on the clock.

Kyl's gonna call a sneak.

I know it. The Sharks know it. I'm already visualizing plowing through their defensive line to lock in the first down.

Which is why I do a metaphorical spit take when Kylian calls a timeout instead.

It's our last timeout, and we're down by six with two minutes left to play, which makes it a wasteful, egregious call.

"The fuck?" Kendrick chides, jogging over to me. "Was that Kyl?"

I grunt my confirmation, then chomp down hard on my mouth guard to hold in the string of curses fighting their way out of me.

"Cap."

"Yeah, Kyl?"

"You gonna come to the sideline?"

Rolling out my shoulders, I bite into my mouth guard again.

"Just call the play and let me finish this," I counter without so much of a glance his way. I don't need to see the stats on his screens. We both know what needs to happen here.

Besides, I couldn't go to the sideline even if I needed to consult with him. I can't stand the thought of catching a glimpse of her right now.

I need to power through. Complete the sneak. Keep possession of the ball. Tuck in the motherfucking South Chapel Sharks and kiss them goodnight.

"You should at least look over here," Kylian bites out.

He's still mad at me. Livid, in fact.

I get it. I really do. I'm mad at me, too. But if he thinks for one goddamn second now's the time—"Dude," Locke murmurs, coming up on my right side to balance out where K's flanking me to the left.

Kendrick chuckles under his breath, then whistles appreciatively.

Despite the ironclad grip I've been maintaining over my self-control, I break.

With a growl, I follow Kylian's command and find him on the sideline. He's watching me, both his devices at his sides, in a stance far too casual for the last two minutes of a game.

Heart in my throat and already silently berating myself, I scan the bench in what feels like slow motion.

My heart drops back into its rightful place and beats double time while my dick springs to life the second I register what I'm looking at.

Josephine. Standing proud. Wearing the number that's been mine since I was ten years old.

"Kylian," I croak into the headset. "What number's on that jersey next to you?"

He *tsks*, but he plays along.

"You've got twenty-twenty vision, Cap. You know she's wearing number five."

Pulling his mic from his face, he tilts her way and brings his mouth to her ear like he's speaking to her. She immediately springs into action, climbs onto the bench, and cups her hands around her mouth to make sure her words reach me.

"Let's fucking go, number five!"

Let's. Fucking. Go.

I can't fight the grin that erupts on my face. I don't even care that both Kendrick and Locke instantly hound me, punching into my pads and running their mouths.

Her grin matches mine, and in that moment, as my team rallies around me and the Sharks continue to circle, as the band erupts into the fight song in the stands and the crowd chants "Crusade," all I see, all I want—my entire purpose in this life—is her.

Josephine.

In Crusaders' red.

Wearing number 5.

With *Crusade* across her back.

My Siren.

That's my fucking girl.

"Let's go, let's go, let's go!" I scream, shoving my teammates and rallying the fucking troops. We have a game to finish. We have a game to *win*.

"Spoon check, brother," I murmur to Kendrick.

This'll only work if he's got a full drawer.

"I'm good," he assures me. "Whatever you need, I got you."

"Kylian," I bark into the headset. "Call Nacho."

Silence ensues for exactly one second.

Then coaches start talking over each other, all in opposition to my request as the offensive line makes their way back to the line of scrimmage.

I line up with Kendrick by my side, more confident than I've felt the entire game. Maybe more confident than I've felt during any game, ever.

"Stats support the sneak," Kylian advises, just like I knew he would. It's how his mind works. There's a clear, statistically supported call for this situation.

"I hear you, Kyl. I do." I can't criticize him for pointing it out. "But you and I both know something the stats don't know."

Despite how black and white he can be, Josephine's opened him up to a world of color over the last several weeks. He feels it. He knows what seeing her in my jersey fucking does to me, and he knows what I can fucking do in turn for this team.

Kendrick's on board.

Locke is keyed in.

I won't settle for anything less than a nontraditional quarterback sneak that results in me scoring on this field.

I want the touchdown.

I want to fucking end this.

I want her in my arms.

I just want her.

"Roger that. Nacho, fake cheese spread," Kylian calls into the headset.

Clenching my fist in anticipatory victory, I call over my shoulder to number twenty-four. "Get us there, K. I want to get our girl home."

"Aye, aye, Cap. Let's fucking go!"

My guys fan out in a spread, confusing the shit out of the Sharks as they scramble to reconfigure their big set formation.

I call us up.

The ball snaps.

The pebbled leather sits perfectly in my hands as I take a step back, and then another.

I know the route I want. Players part, and I fucking swear the sun beams down on it, guiding me forward. Kendrick side-steps to divert one of the Sharks' biggest linebackers.

I pump-fake, then spin out of the pocket.

"Let's go, let's go, let's go!" I cry as I chase Kendrick, his big-ass body working overtime as my lead blocking back.

So often football is a mental game. A game of awareness. A game of control—knowing who's positioned where, ferreting out the opponent's weaknesses, searching for their blind side. There's a hell of a lot of strategy that goes into the sport.

But on rare occasion, it's not a game at all. It's a feeling. An emotion. A collection of sensations and commotion, all swirling together into surreal kismet alignment.

I feel like I'm taking flight and flying down the field.

Nothing can match the roar of the crowd punctuating the whoosh of my pulse in my ears.

I love this game. I love winning.

As I follow K into the end zone, running the ball in and scoring the touchdown we need, the realization hits me like a three-hundred-pound defensive end.

I've never felt anything that touches my soul and lights up my insides the way football does—until her.

Chapter 32

Josephine

They won. They won! The Crusaders fucking won.

Decker ran in the touchdown, then Lake Chapel got the extra point.

For all of twelve seconds, the South Chapel Sharks had possession of the ball. Then Greedy fumbled, and the game was ours.

Decker took a knee a few times, the cacophony of cheers escalating with each kneel.

Leave it to football to be the one game where the crowd goes wild when the players snap the ball and literally do nothing.

I'm still standing on the bench, screaming my head off. By my side, Kylian is muttering to himself about outliers and standard deviation while he keeps one arm wrapped around my legs, supporting me.

The crowd is chaos behind us, and my phone is blowing up with texts in my back pocket, probably from Hunter. I don't bother pulling it out to check or even turning around to take in the scene.

Right now, in this moment, I only have eyes for him.

QB1. Number five. The captain of this team. The heartbeat of our group. The only man with the power to bend me to his will and bring me to my knees.

Jogging off the field, he pulls off his helmet and gives me the most devastatingly handsome grin.

He stops in front of me, tosses his helmet to the grass, and wraps his arms around my thighs. With one quick jerk, he lifts me off the bench and spins around in circles.

"Decker!" I squeal, clasping my hands behind his head and digging my nails into the sweat-drenched hair at his nape.

That contact ignites a spark. Jubilation transforms into heat. Then heat transforms into need.

This man would never let me fall, but I wrap my legs around his torso and hold on with all my strength anyway.

"*Decker*," I repeat, his name a prayer on my lips.

We're eye to eye, contemplating each other in a way we've never allowed ourselves to fully embrace.

Chest still heaving, he licks his lips and lifts his chin, just slightly.

"Do it," I demand.

"Say it," he counters.

Grinning, I clasp his face with both hands and allow myself to get lost in his onyx irises.

To get lost, and to, in turn, be found.

"Kiss me, Decker Crusade."

I've given him the order, but I don't wait for him to comply before I dive in.

Our mutual desire arcing like an electric current between us, I pull myself closer and kiss him, inciting a cataclysmic sizzle of push and pull. Everything we are and everything we haven't allowed ourselves to be comes together as he kisses me back, and all the stars finally align.

He tastes like sweat and mint and *victory*.

He won his game.

And he's won my heart.

It's not just about power and control between us. In the end, it comes down to compromise and transparency.

Seeing him so rattled—shaken, unhinged, unable to keep his head in the game—because I was wearing someone else's jersey?

He showed every one of his cards tonight.

His vulnerability won't be in vain.

Tentatively, I tease my tongue along the seam of his lips, seeking entrance. He opens for me and matches my strokes, digging his hands into my ass as our kiss grows more frantic.

Every second that passes, every moment when his mouth is on mine and his tongue worships me, solidifies just how much I want him.

In my life. By my side.

I want him with me. I want him with us. I want to be together, in whatever way that makes sense. I hope to god he wants that, too.

Breaking away on a pant, he whispers against my lips. "What are you doing to me, Siren?"

I grin, resting my forehead against his sweat-slicked skin, and loop my arms around his neck so I can kiss him again.

But a flash of the brightest light startles me so badly I jolt in Decker's arms and scream.

It's followed by another. And another.

It takes a moment for my brain to catch up and make sense of the source. It's not lightning. That knowledge soothes my panic. There was no rain in the forecast. There's not even a cloud in the sky.

Another breath. Another succession of flashes. My heart pumps faster again and dread creeps up from my stomach.

Shouts echo around us. His name is repeated over and over, from difference sources and different angles, pummeling me like physical blows.

Photographers have swarmed the field, some of them crowding so close they're within arm's reach. They shout their questions as they snap picture after picture.

"Put me down," I plead, my tone urgent. The ache in my chest grows stronger by the second, threatening to steal all the breath from my lungs.

"You're okay," he assures me, keeping me close. He sets me on my feet and wraps one arm around my shoulders, keeping my body pressed to his. "We're okay," he grunts again, shouldering past the overbearing media and shielding me from view as best he can.

"I won't be taking questions until the presser," he informs the crowd. "And I won't be calling on anyone out here harassing me or trying to capture a private moment," he adds.

The reporters and photographers simmer down. The racket around us hushes to a murmur, and the flashing ceases immediately. Whether it's because he's Decker Crusade, QB1 and son of Thomas Crusade, or because of the connection between the press and his mother's death, they give him the space he commands without argument.

"Let's get you back to Kyl," Decker whispers, guiding me to the sidelines with an unyielding rigidity that's in stark juxtaposition to the fervent way he was just kissing me on the field.

Chapter 33

Josephine

Kylian's in no rush tonight. Unlike after the last handful of games, he lingers on the sideline to talk to some of the assistant coaches and interns before weaving his fingers with mine and guiding me toward the locker rooms at a leisurely pace.

"We're going to take the boat back to the house as a unit, if that's okay with you."

Now the delay makes sense.

My heart clenches in appreciation. All of us, together... *as a unit*. We have a lot to figure out as that unit. But we're off to a pretty damn good start. Nodding, I lift our joined hands to my lips and kiss his knuckles.

"Thank you," I murmur, cuddling into his side when we come to stop outside the locker room to wait for the other guys.

He wraps his arms around me, holding me close enough that I can smell the citrusy eucalypts scent of his body wash. Inhaling, I allow myself to sink into the moment. To bask in the security of being in his arms. To honor the care, and maybe even love, I share with this man.

He kisses the top of my head, then keeps his face buried in my hair. When he pulls in a breath, then lets out a long, satisfied sigh, it dawns on me. Maybe I'm becoming a safe place for Kylian, too.

He puts on a front a lot of the time—mentally steeling himself to be in a crowd or garnering all the fortitude he can muster to be "on" and focused even when surrounded by the sensory overload that happens on and around that field. It takes him hours, sometimes even a full day, to recover from a game. If there's any way I can bring him peace, I want to do that for him.

We stand like that for what feels like ages, just holding each other while we block out the rest of the world.

People move around us. Minutes tick by. His steady heart beats against his ribs, syncing with my breath. No matter the place, the setting, or our surroundings, this man settles me. He is the very definition of safe—a physical and mental dwelling where I can just be. It should scare me how much his arms feel like home. But from the beginning, there's been a natural reciprocity to the way we lean on and care for each other. If my home is inside him, I'll do whatever I can to be that safe place for him in return.

We're two of only a handful of people still waiting when Kendrick's voice echoes down the long hallway that leads to the locker room.

"Will you come up to the Nest with me tonight?" Kylian whispers, his voice nothing but a rasp.

He's always bone-tired after a game. Mentally spent. Physically exhausted. Masking does that to him—mimicking social cues and presenting himself a certain way with the coaches and players, while also tuning out the sensory overload that is all things college football in the South. He's burned out, exhausted, and often agitated after a game. As much as I crave his proximity, he doesn't sleep well when he's not alone.

"You need sleep," I remind him with a gentle squeeze around his torso.

"I need *you*, Jo."

Pulling back, I regard him for a moment, taking in his bloodshot eyes and the lines on his face, then nuzzle into his chest again and nod. Tonight's party is sure to be chaos, given that it's Shore Week and the Crusaders won by the very skin of their teeth. I wouldn't mind a few hours of quiet to hide away from the world myself.

"I'll come up until you fall asleep," I compromise.

"Then you'll come back up in the morning and let me eat your pussy for breakfast."

I crane back in his arms and laugh, only to smack my hand over my mouth when I register the seriousness in his gaze.

"Is there something funny about me wanting to start my day with my head buried between your thighs?"

"No," I squeak, warmth tingling through my core at the prospect of what he's promising.

"No, what?"

I bite down on my bottom lip and give him a coy smile.

"No, Daddy."

"Good girl," he murmurs, lowering his head to whisper directly into my ear. "Don't you dare come up to the Nest wearing his jersey. You and I both know exactly who you belong to when you crawl into my bed."

A breathy whimper escapes me. "Yes, Daddy."

"Good fucking girl." Kylian weaves his hand into the hair at my nape, tilting my head back and kissing me. "You did so good tonight, baby. You did so good for Decker and this team. Good girls deserve all the rewards."

I'm so wrapped up in his words that I startle when Locke wraps his arms around me from behind.

"Hot Girl," Locke murmurs, kissing my neck, even while my mouth is still inches from his best friend's. "Sit with me on the boat?"

I nod like a bobblehead, basking in their combined affection, at their willingness and eagerness to comply with almost any request. The sentiment is only compounded as I catch sight of Decker and Kendrick making their way over to us, ready to head home.

As a unit.

Chapter 34

Josephine

After the week I've had, it's bizarre how soothing it is to be on the pontoon boat with all four of the guys. Between our school schedules, their NIL commitments, and the drama of the last few weeks, we're rarely all in the same place at the same time.

The lake is calm tonight—inky black and smooth as glass, the surface illuminated by a crescent moon and countless stars. I snuggle closer to Locke's chest, relishing in the comfort of his hold.

Decker is at the helm, driving us across the lake.

Kylian is sitting beside us, playing with the frayed denim along the edges of the hole in my jeans. The sparks that zap through me each time his fingers tease along my thigh make me squirm. Which makes Locke even harder beneath me, his rigid cock pressing into my ass as he kisses up and down my neck.

Kendrick is spread out on the bench seat across from us, watching with a surly scowl.

Locke smiles against my skin and licks a path up my neck to my earlobe, then takes it between his teeth.

"So this is how it's gonna be?" Kendrick snarls.

I tense at the anger in his voice, but Locke just shifts me up in his lap and holds me tighter.

Scoffing, K shakes his head. "Every man for himself, out here callin' dibs on our girl?"

Our girl.

Our. Girl.

"We'd be happy to create a master schedule," Kylian chimes in. "I could send out calendar invites if you prefer."

Locke chortles into my hair, not-so-subtly grinding me against his cock as Kylian lets his fingertips linger in the hole of my jeans.

"Joey does what she wants, man. You're just big mad she doesn't want *you*," Locke offers.

Kendrick leans forward and drops his elbows to his knees, a wicked smirk on his face visible even out here in the dark.

"*Ah*, but you see, brother, that's where you're wrong. I know exactly what Jojo wants, and it just so happens that she and I discussed—"

"Enough," I scold. I squirm out of Locke's grasp and plant my ass firmly on the bench seat between him and Kylian. Whipping my head from one side to the other, I shoot them each a warning look, then set my sights on Kendrick.

"I'm fully committed to making sure you follow through on those lessons, big guy." He raises both brows, his gaze narrowing with an intensity I could easily get lost in. "But I promised Kylian I'd go up to the Nest when we get back to the house." Softer, I add, "I'm not really feeling the party scene tonight, ya know?"

Kendrick darts a look at Decker, and I follow his line of sight. He's still in position at the helm, but his attention is on us. With his lips pressed together in a frown, he glances from me to K and back again, but he doesn't speak.

Before I can ask what all the looks are about, Locke tucks my hair behind my ear and nuzzles my neck again.

"There's no party tonight, Hot Girl," he whispers. "Cap canceled it the second we knew you were safe."

There's *always* a party.

Emotion swells in my chest, catching my breath and making me light-headed.

"He did it for you, Jo. Didn't ask us our opinion or need any sort of persuasion," Kylian says on my other side, answering the question I didn't ask. "He did it for you."

"Tell her about tomorrow," Locke adds.

Kylian squeezes my bare thigh under my jeans, then carefully dislodges his hand so he can play-punch Locke in the arm.

"You have no chill. You know that, right?"

Across from us, Kendrick chuckles, obviously in on their little secret.

"Tell me," I plead, sounding a hell of a lot needier than intended, but if they've got a surprise planned, then I'm desperate for at least a few hints. I turn to Locke, knowing he'll be the easiest to crack, and drag my nails up his thigh.

"Easy, Hot Girl," he hisses, snatching my hand mid-stroke.

"Tomorrow's a beach day," Kylian declares without fanfare.

"Like, the beach-beach?"

Kendrick chuckles at my question, then holds out a hand, inviting me over.

Carefully, I rise and steady myself. The instant I do, Decker eases up on the throttle, and he doesn't resume speed until after I've shuffled to the other side of the vessel and am seated.

I've barely settled on the bench when Kendrick pulls me into his lap, steadying me with one arm around my back and caressing my jaw with his free hand. With a sigh, he presses his lips to the pulse point below my ear.

"We're going to the beach. A quiet spot. Just the five of us. We'll pack a lunch and make a day of it. You should wear your pink bikini," he suggests, his voice low and gravelly.

"I don't know if that suit can hold up against the ocean," I tease.

"Exactly." He nips my earlobe, then helps me to my feet and smacks my ass. "Go on, then," he directs, tipping his chin toward Decker. It's hard to be annoyed by his bossy, domineering post-game swagger when it has my pulse racing and my heart thudding in my chest.

I find my balance, then carefully make my way to the helm.

At my approach, Decker takes a step back, making room for me to squeeze between his body and the steering wheel.

Wrapping my arms around his neck, I tilt my head back and study him as his eyes flit between the water and me. Always alert. Always so in control.

"It's Shore Week," I state.

"It is," he replies with a small dip of his chin.

"You won the game."

This time, a genuine smile takes over his whole face. "I sure fucking did."

"You canceled the party."

He zeroes in on my mouth as I speak, then he nods.

"You canceled it for me?"

Another nod.

"And tomorrow we're going to the beach?"

A sly smile creeps across his face in response to that question.

I can't help the matching grin I wear when I say, "I've never been to the beach. I've never even seen the ocean."

Pressing up on my toes, I pull his head down to meet mine. I place a quick kiss on his lips, then release him just as quickly. I know him well enough to know he's focused on navigating the lake and getting us all home safely.

"Thank you, Decker," I whisper, adjusting my hold on him so I'm hugging his torso and resting my cheek on his chest. I don't want to distract him, but I need him to know just how much it means to me.

The parties aren't just for fun or a way to boost his ego, like I originally assumed. Decker, Kendrick, and Locke all have season-long sponsorship deals that require a certain number of social media posts each week. Hosting the weekly post-game party helps them fulfill those commitments and allows them to create content without having to add another to-do to their already very full plates.

Canceling the party is a bigger sacrifice than I ever expected.

But it's so very appreciated.

"You're really good at taking care of the people you lo—" I falter, catching myself before I can say something stupid.

But I wasn't quick enough.

"Say it," he growls, echoing his demand from earlier, his eyes still trained on the lake.

Peering up, I muster my courage and finish that sentence. "You're really good at taking care of the people you love."

Looking at me now, he nods, a satisfied smile teasing at the corner of his lips before he surveys our surroundings.

"Am I one of those people now, Cap?"

The question slips out before I've thought through the repercussions, but something inside me has to know. I feel bolder under the cover of darkness. As I wait for his response, I play with the soft, short hairs on his nape.

"You are *the* person, Josephine. The one and only."

I tip my chin up, hoping he'll kiss me again.

Instead, he grasps my shoulders, spins me, and pins me between his body and the console. "I'm gonna need you to stay right here until we get back to the house," he whispers into my ear.

"And why's that?" I can't help but sass over my shoulder. Leave it to Decker Crusade to manhandle me when I'm trying to be sweet and show my appreciation.

He drops his focus from the horizon ahead of us, his fiery smolder practically scorching me.

But Decker's not studying my face the way I'm studying his. He's looking at the back of my shirt.

"I need to memorize exactly what it looks like to see my name where it belongs before we get back to the isle and one of my brothers rips this jersey off your body."

Chapter 35

Josephine

The wooden planks are rough and warm under my bare feet as I trail behind my guys. Locke laughed at me when I whipped off my flip-flops as soon as we reached the edge of the parking lot, but I couldn't wait another second.

The sun is already high in the cloudless sky, the air warm but breezy the closer we get to the ocean.

The ocean.

The actual ocean.

I grin as I take it all in.

Over the side of the boardwalk, there's water as far as I can see. The rhythmic sound of the waves crashing against the shore is far louder than the gentle lapping along the edge of Lake Chapel. Though it's more intense, it's surprisingly soothing. When I lick my lips, I can actually taste the saltiness of the air.

It took us nearly two hours to get here. The last thirty minutes of the drive consisted solely of twists and turns on a winding two-lane road canopied by trees with Spanish moss hanging from the branches.

Now that we've reached our destination, I can see why this place is so special.

The sand is pale and the beach looks almost untouched for what feels like miles in both directions. A few mansions dot the shoreline farther down, and there are several umbrellas set up on the opposite side of the boardwalk. But just like Kendrick promised, the beach is private, like we've got it all to ourselves.

"The ocean's that way, Hot Girl," Locke teases as he circles back and comes to stand behind me. "It's the big blue thing over there."

With a laugh, I turn to finally take in the expanse of water, only to discover all the guys are waiting for me. Each one is watching me, looking nothing but relaxed and hot as hell in their board shorts and sunglasses with umbrellas, towels, and coolers tucked under their arms.

"I told you; I've never been to the beach. I want to soak it all in."

Locke rests his chin on my shoulder, then plants a soft kiss on my cheek. "I know, baby. You deserve this day. Let's go have some fun and make the most of it, yeah?"

Nodding, I grab his hand and head toward the rest of the guys, determined to do just that.

Adjusting the strings of my bikini top to ensure everything's in place, I turn, ready to head back to our spot. I couldn't wait another second to get down to the water, so I left the boys bickering about umbrella placement and wandered down to the shoreline on my own.

The ocean is colder than I expected, in stark contrast to the warm tide pools carved out of the sand. According to Kylian, we arrived at low tide, so it's a bit of a jaunt back to my guys.

We're all alone on this section of the sand, despite the gorgeous weather and the pristine beach. The signs in the parking lot where we left the Suburban boasted public beach access, but I wouldn't put it past Decker to have had a hand in coordinating all this.

The boys packed a lunch and carted a massive cooler of water and sports drinks out here. But I eyed a little ice cream shack near the boardwalk on our journey, and that sounds way better than what I can only imagine is a cooler full of health food Decker and Kendrick deemed appropriate for a picnic at the beach.

Kendrick's the first to notice me as I make my way back toward them. Two fingers beckon, and that's all it takes to get me in his lap.

"You wore the pink bikini," he observes, running his hands up my thighs and gripping my ass through the thin, slinky fabric.

"Wore it just for you," I tease, shifting so I can straddle him and wrap my arms around his neck.

A hint of a smirk graces his face, then he runs his nose along the length of mine. "You look so damn fine, Jojo. I've been dreaming about you in this bathing suit since that day you smacked into me in the hall."

His lips meet mine in a sultry, unhurried kiss.

"So. Fucking. Fine." He punctuates each word with a peck, brazenly brushing his hands down my bare stomach and letting his thumbs rest along the juncture where the fabric of my bathing suit meets my thighs.

"Should I point out the double standard here? Why are you still fully clothed?" I tilt my pelvis forward just a bit, grinding against him, and run my fingertips up the sleeves of his tech shirt. Swiping the hat from his head, I place it backward on mine and swivel my hips again.

Big hands clamp down on my thighs. "Behave, Mama," he scolds, though the fierce look fades as he angles back and supports himself on his elbows.

"The sun and I don't get along," he explains, drinking me in slowly. "Never have. UV exposure on a cloudy day is enough to cause a pretty severe rash or even make me nauseous or cause joint pain. A day at the beach could easily turn into a full-blown flare for me if I don't take precautions."

"That's why you always wear sleeves at the games," I say as the realization hits me.

Sitting up again, he wraps me in a hug, then digs his heels into the sand and lifts his knees. He presses on my shoulders until I lean back against his massive thighs and allow him to prop me up like he's my personal lounge chair.

"Yep." He nods, tracing the triangles of my bikini top with one finger. "Better safe than sorry. You'll find me here under the umbrellas all day."

Makes sense. And he'll have plenty of time to just chill out and rest. After yesterday's game, they all need it.

"I'll take a nap with you later," I promise, dropping my head to the side, then letting it loll to the other as I look for each of the guys. "But first, I'm going to make the most of this day. Know what I want to do first?" I ask, biting on my lower lip.

"I can think of a few things," Kendrick quips, cocking one brow at me and tweaking my peaked nipple through the fabric of my suit.

"Not that," I insist, rolling my eyes and smacking him playfully in the chest. "At least not right now."

A quick glance over to Decker confirms he's watching us—always watching—his onyx eyes hidden behind turquoise-framed Ray-Bans, his tan, muscular legs spread wide where he's sitting in a low-rise folding chair.

"I want ice cream. I saw a stand near the parking lot."

"Ice cream?" Locke asks from a few feet away, hopping to his feet like a puppy who's just found a ball. "I could go for some ice cream. Kylian?"

On the far end of our setup, Kylian's made camp. He has two large umbrellas staked in the sand, providing total shade to what looks like a suspension cot hovering six inches off the ground like a mini trampoline. It's big enough for one person to stretch out on. Two, maybe, if the occupants don't mind cuddling.

I look from the setup to my boyfriend, puzzled. "Did you bring a bed to the beach?"

I don't care how good my guys look in their swim trunks. There's no way I'm getting freaky on the beach and risking sand in certain places.

"He doesn't like sand," Decker offers, motioning to Kylian's setup with the dismissive sweep of one hand. "The less contact he makes with it, the less whining he subjects us to."

"I do not whine," Kylian counters in a huff. "What's there to like about sand, anyway? It gets everywhere. It clings to all the wrong places. You find it for days after leaving the beach, even after multiple showers. Sand is the glitter of the sea."

Locke snorts, and Kendrick snickers, the action jostling me where I'm propped up along his front.

"Does that mean you won't go swimming with me later?" I fake-pout, crossing my arms over my chest and frowning.

Kendrick will be camping out under the umbrellas. Kylian doesn't want to touch the sand. I'm not sure I'm prepared to deal with Decker's vibe today. At least I have Nicky to play with.

"I'll escort you down to the shore and watch you swim," Kylian offers.

"You can swim, Hot Girl?" Locke asks, still on his feet and casting a long shadow over me as he edges closer.

Decker snickers under his breath and cocks a sardonic smirk. "Believe me. She can swim."

My cheeks heat at the recollection of the last time I was submerged in the lake with Decker. He almost kissed me that day... and he really did kiss me last night.

But that's all that's happened as of now.

When we got back to the house after the game, Decker disappeared behind his bedroom door. Nicky, Kendrick, and I tried to watch a movie, but we all fell asleep in the media room before it was even halfway through.

I woke up to the warm glow of the rising sun peeking through the blinds and to the smell of Mrs. Lansbury's Sunday morning feast. Once I checked the time and confirmed it wasn't too early, I snuck up to the Nest as promised.

Decker and I haven't had a chance to talk. Not that I was ready to delve into anything with him after the game. Even now, I've barely had a chance to process what happened between us last night. Or what should happen next. This could be the perfect opportunity for the two of us to break away from the group and have a few minutes to ourselves.

"What do you say, Cap? Want to buy me an ice cream cone?"

Decker shifts forward, lifting the back of his chair off the sand a couple of inches, and yanks his wallet out of his pocket. Without a word, he slides a black card out of his wallet and holds it out.

"I don't want your AmEx, Crusade." I bat at his forearm with the back of my hand. "I wanted you to get off your ass and come with me."

Peering over the top of his sunglasses, Decker scowls and keeps his hand in the air.

"Take it. I'm good. You guys go."

Bossy, grumpy, moody man.

"Fine," I declare, snatching the card out of his hand. "Let's go, boys."

I don't have to turn around to know that Kendrick, Locke, and Kylian will all follow. But I pause and wait for them anyway.

"You're a dumbass," Kendrick mutters to Decker, pushing lightly against his shoulder.

Decker sighs. "Tell me something I don't know. I'm still waiting on that call." He holds up his phone for emphasis as he slips his wallet back into his shorts.

Kendrick's face pinches with a twinge of concern as he assesses Decker for a couple of heartbeats. A silent exchange passes between them, then finally, Kendrick nods.

The interaction is another reminder that these men have been caring for each other since long before I ever entered the picture.

At least their conversation confirmed that Decker's surly attitude and standoffishness isn't just about me or our kiss. At least not today. That should make me feel better, except now I'm concerned about things I'm not even privy to.

His plate is constantly too full, and I want nothing more than to relieve him of some of his burdens, but in my experience so far, he's not interested in sharing the load.

"Want anything, Cap?" Locke asks, winding an arm around my midsection as we step out from under the umbrellas.

Decker declines with a succinct shake of his head and unlocks his phone, effectively dismissing us.

The warmth of the sun on my skin melts away the trepidation that's begun to bubble up as I watch Decker shutter himself again. The sensation also serves to remind me of the conversation Kendrick and I just had. I pluck his LCU hat off my head and turn back to hand it to him, but he's already got a new one on. This time, he's rocking a khaki bucket hat with a wide brim all the way around—he looks like a little old man about to go fishing.

"Better safe than sorry," he repeats when he catches me eyeing his new attire. He snatches the hat from my hands and places it back on my head.

"Let's go, Boy Genius," he calls back to Kylian.

Chapter 36

Josephine

"We should order ten ice cream cones each, just to stick it to Decker," I muse, surveying the menu tacked to the siding of the ice cream hut. A blast of cold air and that ice cream shop smell—sugar and artificial sweetness—wafts out from the order window as a young kid slouches against the counter, waiting for us to step up.

"Go easy on him, Jojo." Kendrick squeezes my hip. "He wasn't trying to be a dick, whipping out his credit card and blowing us off like that. He's got a lot on his mind."

"Yeah, yeah." Just because he wasn't trying to be a dick doesn't mean he wasn't acting like a dick. Whatever.

"I'm at least getting an add-on," I declare, perusing the menu of fifty-cent options, debating about whether I want chocolate coating, fudge drizzle, or sprinkles.

"*Oh.* They've got vegan fro-yo and non-dairy whipped cream. I'm ordering a banana split with extra nuts," Locke announces.

I snort. "That sounds more like a fruit salad than a treat, Emo Boy."

He gives me one of those dazzling Nicky smiles and winks. "True. But I know just what to lick if I'm craving something sweet later."

"Hey-yo," Kendrick murmurs.

I elbow him in the stomach and shoot a glare at Locke.

"Order one for me, too," Kendrick tells him. "We're still early in the season. Gotta make good choices."

I let the nutrition bros step up to the counter and slink back so I'm shoulder to shoulder with Kylian.

"What are you getting?"

"Vanilla," he replies without any preamble.

"*Just* vanilla?" I tease.

The irony. Between his dirty mouth and his lack of inhibitions when he's sharing me with his friends, Kylian is anything *but* vanilla.

"Just vanilla."

I loop my arm through his and tug him toward the counter. "You should at least get an add-on. Ooh. Get sprinkles!"

He cocks one brow and looks down his nose at me like I'm delusional. "I'll do no such thing."

I fight back a grin, love drunk, sun kissed, and a little punchy after my encounter with Decker.

"But I love sprinkles," I murmur in his ear, rubbing up against his bicep.

"Then you should get them," he encourages, rapping the fingers of his free hand on the chipped blue countertop while we wait for the employee to come back and take our order.

"Kyl."

He side-eyes me under his glasses, then turns to face me completely once he sees my smirk.

"We could share," I suggest. "Your vanilla *covered* in my sprinkles?" I push my tits out for emphasis, just in case he needs a little more context.

"No."

Denied.

With a huff, I stick my lip out, teasing him with a pout.

"It's a texture thing," he explains. "Sprinkles are pervasive, especially when paired with soft serve. I don't stand a chance of taking a bite without getting one in my mouth."

Affection blossoms in my chest. I should have known. "So sprinkles are the sand of the ice cream world?"

"Exactly."

The kid working the counter comes back with Kendrick's and Locke's orders and slides open the partition to dole them out.

"Bro," Locke calls to Kylian as Kendrick takes the bowls and napkins. "Get the damn sprinkles. She's not being direct enough," he explains. "But with the way she's looking at you right now, I bet she'll lick them off you. All of them. Anywhere you put them."

The kid behind the counter drops the spoons he's holding out to Kendrick and sputters out a cough.

Kylian peers at me through his glasses, scanning me up and down. "Is that an accurate assessment of what you had in mind, baby?"

"Maybe." I smile coyly.

"Black and white, Jo. Tell me what you're thinking."

I lean in close, emboldened by the other guys' eyes on me. Gripping Kylian's shoulder, I pop up on my toes and bring my lips to his ear. "I'm thinking we should order an ice cream cone covered in sprinkles so I can smear it all over your cock and lick you clean. Don't worry. I'll find every last sprinkle. I swear."

Kylian goes rigid, and his spine snaps straight. "Give me the car keys," he demands of Kendrick before leaning against the counter below the window and hollering, "One soft serve vanilla cone, extra sprinkles!"

Chapter 37

Josephine

"Back seat," he demands, swatting at my ass as I climb into the Suburban.

"We'd have more room in the front if we put the seat all the way back," I suggest, though I follow his orders regardless, clambering over the captain's seats.

"No way. I have no problem sharing you with the guys, but don't think for one second I'd let you be on display for anyone else. No one gets to see what's mine."

My pussy clenches. *Mine.*

I want to be his. I want to be claimed by Kylian.

The very idea of what we're about to do makes me lust drunk. I'm only pulled from the haze when a trail of ice cream drips down my hand. The sensation is a reminder that we're pressed for time.

Kneeling on the bench, I lick the side of the cone, my attention fixed on him.

"Let me taste," Kylian grits out, sliding into the middle seat and capturing my mouth in a frenzied kiss.

Our tongues dance, his dipping in and licking the ice cream out of my mouth before I have the chance to swallow.

"So sweet," he purrs, sucking on my bottom lip and pulling until I whimper. "But I think I prefer the taste of your cream more."

"Nope," I declare, denying him before he can flip the script. I'm a woman on a mission. "I made you a promise. Every single sprinkle," I vow, nodding toward the dripping cone.

"Get out your cock for me, Kylian."

"Get on your knees for me, Jo."

With a pang of desire coursing through me, I position myself beside him on the back seat and watch, enraptured, as he unties his black and blue board shorts and shoves them down. I pull on the hems of each leg to give myself better access as he spreads his legs wider.

"Top off," he instructs, plucking at the strings of my bathing suit with one hand.

In a hurry, I undo the knot at my back and around my neck and push my tits together as I reposition myself between his legs.

His cock is fully erect, pulsating and smooth, already weeping a drop of precum from the slit.

Licking my lips, I watch him, waiting for him to call the play.

"You want it?" he asks huskily.

The timbre of his voice ignites a low flame in my belly. "So fucking much."

He holds my gaze as he guides my hand, cone and all, and coats the tip of his dick with the ice cream. At first contact, he hisses from what I assume is a startlingly cold sensation, but he doesn't stop. He leaves a generous path of sprinkles all around the crown, taking care to make sure there isn't a centimeter not covered in them.

He's methodical in the way he swirls the half-melted ice cream on his shaft. He even leaves me a little loop on the tip.

I giggle at his handiwork, but the heat in his gaze makes it clear he's not fucking around.

"Open."

Dammit. Why are his commands so hot? Without argument, I open my mouth wide, but I gasp when he grips me by the throat and tips my head back farther. The anticipation prickling along my spine is heady as he holds the melting cone above my face and white cream runs along the textured grooves of the cone and eventually drips into my mouth.

I mewl when the first drop hits, then, greedily, I stick my tongue out for more.

"Look at you, pretty girl. Ass up, tits out, and on your knees for me. Desperate for anything I'm willing to give you."

I purr at his praise and have to press my thighs together for a moment to stave off the need pulsing in my core before I arch my back and tip my chin so I can catch the next few drips on my tongue.

"Tease," I chide.

Growling, he takes the bait. Rather than forcing me to wait for trickles of sweetness, he tips the cone upside down and coats my lips, chin, neck, and breasts with melted ice cream.

There are sprinkles *everywhere*—clinging to my neck and clustered on my chest. But I don't dare complain.

"So fucking messy, baby," he tsks. "Now we're both covered in cream. Ready to clean me up like you promised?"

"So ready."

"Good girl. Every last sprinkle, you understand?"

The sight of him, coated in sugar, expression firm, and the low way he issues his command make my mouth water with the need to taste him. "Yes, Daddy."

"Fuck, you're perfect. Such a good fucking girl."

Aiming to please, I lick him from root to tip, capturing as much of the melted liquid as possible and slurping it down. Then I take him in my mouth and hollow my cheeks around the smooth, warm head of his cock. I repeat the motion until he's completely clean.

"I want more," I hum, popping off the top of his dick and mouthing up and down the length of him as he spreads more ice cream along the tip.

Craning back, I stick out my tongue as the cool liquid fills my mouth, and a warm gush trickles between my thighs.

I use one hand to fist his cock as I hungrily suck everything off the tip again, then wind my other hand between my legs to put pressure where I need it.

"Jo."

At the sharp tone, I zero in on his face, my entire body hot with arousal and wanton desire.

"Eyes on me. *Hands* on me. Be a good girl and eat your ice cream, then I'll take care of that needy little cunt you're trying to play with."

I whimper, clenching my thighs together in anticipation.

Doubling down, I take him so deep the crown of his cock hits the back of my throat.

"Swallow," he grits out, bucking his hips even higher as I gag on his length.

I do as he says, even as pressure builds behind my eyes and tears form.

"Again," he encourages, weaving one hand through my hair and thrusting harder.

I hum around his length, sucking and licking so quickly that saliva dribbles out of the corner of my mouth as tears roll down my cheeks.

"Ease up."

I back off instantly, sitting on my heels and catching my breath, playing with my nipples as I peer up at him.

Lip pressed between his teeth, he caresses the side of my face, brushing his thumb over my swollen, puffy lips. The reverent touch is in direct opposition to the way he was just making me choke on his cock. "Fuck, Jo. This mouth is incredible, baby. I've never felt anything so perfect." He peers into the partially crushed cone in his hand and turns back to me. "There are still a few sprinkles left."

"Gimme."

"They're yours. Everything you want from me is yours."

Prepared for him to drip the remaining ice cream on his dick, or maybe into my mouth, I balance on my hands and knees again and lick my lips. Instead, he fists his erection, pulls it flat against his stomach, and shifts forward on the seat until his balls are on the edge of the leather.

He hisses when the cold liquid hits, and I watch, totally enraptured, as he drizzles the melted ice cream all over his sack.

He zigzags it over both balls, and sure enough, a few sprinkles escape the cone.

Holding his cock out of the way, he grins down at me. "You know what to do."

I sure fucking do.

I follow the path he made me, running the tip of my tongue in an intricate pattern to lap at the cream.

"Fuck, baby. Yes. Lick it up and suck me clean."

Pressing the flat of my tongue over his entire sack, I hum greedily. Then I take one ball into my mouth, sucking like he asked, as he fists his cock and squeezes.

With his free hand, he grazes my cheek again and weaves his fingers through my hair gently.

"You're doing so good for me, Jo. I could come just like this, with your pretty little mouth sucking on my nuts. Get the other one, baby. Put it in your mouth. I know you can do it."

Emboldened by his encouragement, I open wider, working his entire sack into my mouth, relishing the curses that fall from his lips when I do.

"*Fuck.*" He throws his head back against the seat. "So good, Jo. You're doing so good for me."

Tentatively, I tease my tongue out between my lips, licking under his sack as he writhes and tenses.

"I love my balls in your mouth. But I want more, baby. Will you give me that?"

I swirl my tongue once more, then slowly sit back.

"Black and white, Kylian." I repeat the phrase he uses with me so often.

I'm almost certain I know what he wants. It's something I absolutely want to share with him. I couldn't care less that we're in the back seat of Kendrick's car and that my tits are covered with sprinkles. But I have to be sure we're on the same wavelength.

With his hands under my arms, he hoists me up and leans forward until we're nose-to-nose. "I want to lay you down on this seat, line myself up with your perfect cunt, and slide all the way home. Because that's what it'll be for me, Jo. Homecoming. Landing right where I belong." His breath is hot on my lips, and this close, his irises swirl like the ocean waters down the boardwalk. "I've never understood the concept of home until you. But I get it. I finally fucking get it. Right now, I want to be inside you more than I want my next breath."

His wants are my wants.

His needs, my most primal desires.

More than anything, I want to welcome him home. It feels like my soul's purpose: To connect with Kylian. To let him in, and to let him stay.

"Please fuck me," I pant, shifting over and joining him on the bench seat.

"Always so agreeable for me, aren't you, baby?" He crushes his mouth to mine, licking inside once again and groaning when he tastes the remnants of vanilla soft serve and him all over my tongue.

"Lie back, Jo. Show me what's mine."

I don't even have to ask. Though we haven't done this before, I could put money on his desire to be on top. Just like I know I want to look him in the eyes as it happens.

We've bared our souls. We've spent hours skin to skin, exploring one another's bodies. We've brought each other to the brink of pleasure, held each other through the lowest, darkest times. The most significant, emotional parts of our beings have been intimately woven together, but we haven't done this.

And now? It's all I can do to not shake in anticipation as I wait for the homecoming he's promising.

It takes a bit of maneuvering, but eventually, we position ourselves on the back seat in a way that's mostly comfortable.

"You're a sticky mess," he teases, running one finger between my sprinkle-covered breasts before gently squeezing my throat.

"You could make me messier?"

I ache to be covered in him. Marked in every way possible.

"No. This is our first time, baby. I'm going to fuck you fast and hard, then fill you up and claim you from the inside out."

At the image he creates with his dirty words, I practically combust. Every filthy thing that comes from this man's mouth, every damn time, threatens to do me in.

"Ready?"

Nodding, I tilt my hips, chasing the tip of him that's so close but nowhere near where I want it.

"And you're sure?" He blows out a slow breath and swallows hard as he scans my body and homes in on where we're nearly connected.

Consent. Concern. The utmost care.

But also directness. Demands. Dominance I've come to crave in a dynamic I've never even considered until him.

Kylian gives me so much.

In return, I want to give him all of me.

"So sure."

He cradles my neck and rounds his shoulders, angling over me so our foreheads are practically touching but avoiding all contact with my ice cream–coated torso. Then he glides his cock into me in a torturously slow, drawn-out claiming.

His mouth falls open as he works himself to the hilt.

"Perfection," he whispers, kissing me sweetly once he's fully seated inside me. "God, you're fucking perfection."

On the pull-out, he groans and holds himself above me. His glasses dangle precariously off his face as he peers down, his focus completely transfixed on the place our bodies come together.

"Fuck, baby. How do you feel so good? Nothing has ever been this perfect. Statistically speaking, there's—"

"Kylian."

His eyes dart up to meet mine, blinking in confusion.

I wrap my arms around his neck and pull him closer. "No stats. Just us. I need to really feel you before I go out of my mind."

With one final blink, the toggle flips in his brain. The puzzlement in his expression melts into a feral desire. Switching gears, he pulls back, but not all the way out, scanning me from my face to where he's buried inside me.

"I'm not going to last two minutes fucking this perfect pussy. I need you to come on my dick before I fill you up, though."

With his eyes set on mine, he spits. He spits, and it lands right on my clit, making my walls spasm around the length of his cock.

"So fucking responsive," he murmurs, his fingertips spreading the lips of my pussy. His thumb finds my spit-covered clit, and he rubs it with a fervor so focused, there's no stopping him. He needs me to come.

First. Hard. *Now.*

"Give me what I want, baby," he grits out, pushing his cock into my cunt with slow, measured breaths as he works my clit, sending tingles arcing through my core.

I clench around his dick, the reaction involuntary as he plays my body like an instrument.

Heat builds, from a small flame to an inferno licking up my stomach and chest. Arousal surges, soaking his cock as he builds me up higher and higher.

I can feel every micro-movement he makes, my body and soul so perfectly tuned to his presence. I live for him. I breathe for him. I want to be such a good girl for him.

"Come, Jo. *Now.*"

He thrusts all the way in, his cock fully seated with his hand trapped between our bodies. The pressure is exquisite—an unyielding force that demands my full attention.

My thighs clench up as pin pricks spark in my toes.

"Kylian," I pant, heat rising in my cheeks as my body is engulfed in the blaze of my impending release.

Above me, he's completely transfixed, gazing down in reverence like the universe begins and ends in this moment.

And when the first pulse of pleasure crests like the ocean crashing on the shore, a supernova erupts between us.

I cry out with each wave. They build in intensity, every crescendo higher than the last as he relentlessly pounds into my pussy and rubs my clit.

"Mine," Kylian grunts, his rhythm faltering. "Keep going, baby. Milk me, take it all, and give me everything you've got," he demands as slickness gushes between us.

He sweeps a hand through where our bodies come together and brings it to my mouth.

"Open," he murmurs, his eyes ablaze as he feeds me our combined release mixed with a hint of vanilla.

Groaning, I lick his fingers clean, letting a hazy, dreamy satisfaction settle in my bones.

"Such a good. Fucking. Girl." He punctuates the last three words with kisses, easing out of me and blowing out a long breath as he sits back on his heels.

"Come back," I whimper, reaching out. I miss the weight of him above me already.

Smirking, he eyes my sticky chest and torso, then sits back against the seat and scoops me up, being sure to keep an arm behind my back and one under my knees. The man has absolutely no problem with any and all bodily fluids, even if sprinkles are still a hard no.

But he compromised. He played my game. He was willing to adapt and be flexible.

"That was everything," he murmurs, running his nose along mine as he cradles me in his lap. "Everything, Jo. More than I could have imagined, in one perfect moment I'll never forget."

I hum, nuzzling against the lean, taut muscles of his chest. "Makes me wonder why we didn't do it sooner," I tease. Careful not to transfer any of the sticky ice cream onto his body, I kiss his sternum.

Two fingers catch my chin and tilt my head up. When I blink, I'm met with his intense, fanatical, singularly focused stare.

"I had to be sure, baby."

Anxiety rushes my body, and my limbs go rigid.

"You doubted me?" I hedge, unease creeping up my neck.

"No. Never." He kisses me quickly and smooths one hand over my back. "I had to be sure you were okay. And I had to be sure I could manage the inevitable fixation sex with you would inspire. This is it for me, Jo. *You're* it for me. I knew the second you let me in that I was done. There'll never be anyone else. There'll never be anything else I want or need."

Then, after a breath: "Is that okay?"

I cuddle closer, tears pricking behind my eyes as I bask in his resolve and adoration.

"More than okay, Kyl. I've never wanted anything more than I want to be yours. Completely. Forever."

Chapter 38

Decker

I'm laid out on one of the blankets, lounging in the sun, while K snoozes under the shade of our umbrella. No matter what I do—scroll on my phone, check the highlights from the other games in our division, or just zone out and listen to music—my gaze lands on her time and again.

I've been watching the three of them for almost an hour now. Josephine and Locke might as well be little kids for the boundless energy they possess as they chase each other into the waves. She's good for him. Locke's RA means he's never not in pain, but he can be distracted enough to not allow it to be his sole focus. As evidenced by the way he keeps chasing after Josephine and screaming in victory when he catches her.

Kylian might as well be playing the role of Kendrick Taylor today, given the near-constant scowl he's got plastered on his face. I give him ten more minutes before he retreats and leaves them to their games. The guy hates the sand. And the ocean. He's only pretending to tolerate all this for her. He's noticeably more chill now than he was earlier—she's good for him, too.

Smirking, I lift my phone and zoom in on Kyl. I snap a picture to send to the group chat, but before I can hit send, the device vibrates in my hand.

I tighten my grip around it, allowing myself two seconds of resentment before I clear the emotion and spring to my feet.

I can't avoid him forever. I've been expecting this call all day.

He doesn't always call after my games, but he always calls on his bye week.

"I've gotta take this," I mutter to Kendrick.

He acknowledges me with the lift of one hand, and I retrace my steps to the boardwalk.

"Hey, Dad," I answer, slowing my stride as I climb the wooden steps. I pivot at the top, immediately scanning the shoreline until I find her again.

"Decker! It's great to hear your voice, son."

"Yeah, you, too. It's your bye week?" I ask, simply to make conversation. I know his team's schedule as well as I know my own.

"It is. I won't have a chance to make it to North Carolina this week, but we'll see each other later this month for the photoshoot."

I still, gripping the wooden railing along the boardwalk.

I visualize my calendar and try to recall exactly which photoshoot he's talking about, but I draw a blank.

"What are the dates of that again?" I hedge.

"That's what I called to talk to you about. That, and your Cleveland-worthy performance last night," he jibes. "You thinking of joining the ranks of the cardiac kids?"

Gritting my teeth, I fight back a growl at the backhanded joke.

"I don't know," I reply when I'm sure my tone will come out even. "Stefanski's an outstanding coach. He's got a strong grasp on the stats game, too."

A disgruntled huff is all the response my wisecrack earns.

As much as I like the idea of following in my dad's footsteps and playing for the South Carolina Cougars, I'm open to other opportunities. Especially if those opportunities allow me to stick with Kylian.

Kendrick and I would love to play together when we go pro, but that dream isn't all that realistic. Not with the way the draft is expected to go. He's got the speed, yards, and power to hold his own. He'll get picked up within the first few rounds if we keep showing up big this season.

And right there's the rub.

He got it together and pulled us through the second half of the game yesterday, while I was totally off-kilter until the last two minutes.

I'm drawn to the shoreline again, where Locke is picking Joey up from behind and spinning her around in the surf. I can't hear them, but joy radiates from both of them. It's in every carefree movement and the smiles that seem to grow bigger with every passing minute. I can practically feel the lightness and happiness rolling off them, even from here.

Dammit. Maybe I am jealous. I yearn to be the one holding her, playing in the surf, burying my head between her thighs when we get home—

"—you play after a tough game speaks volumes. All eyes will be on you next week when you're in Texas. Keep that in mind—"

He drones on, but the words don't register. The entirety of my focus is on her.

"I'll arrive the following week. The first photoshoot will happen at the house, as long as the weather cooperates and the lighting is good."

That gets my attention.

"Remind me again about the shoot?"

A beat of tense silence passes. Obviously, this is something I shouldn't need to be reminded of.

"It's for the SportsZone double feature," he offers. "The collector's editions? Four special edition covers, one of each of us, then two of us together. Father and son. The reporter and photographers will want to start setting up at the house in the next week or two. Misty should have gone over the details already."

"She has," I rush to assure him, making a mental note to ask Misty to resend the schedules and requirements as soon as possible.

More often than not, I don't pay attention to the details of the NIL commitments and terms laid out each season. I just show up where I'm supposed to be when I'm supposed to be there.

But now that it's not just me and the boys...

This acute need to shield her from the media and protect her from the spotlight hits me hard in the gut. With her history, she'd hate every second of it. If she got caught up in this publicity, would it jeopardize the fresh start she's worked so hard for?

"Hey, Dad?"

I've completely lost track of the conversation, but it doesn't matter. Because my gut is churning at just the thought of allowing cameras into our home.

"Maybe now isn't the best time to have people at the house. Reporters. Cameras. It's a little much, with it being mid-season and all of us trying to stay on top of our schoolwork, too."

Silence ensues.

Rather than wait him out like I should, I fill the emptiness with more thin justifications.

"I've been having a hard time focusing since the concussion," I admit. That's not a lie. He doesn't need to know that for the most part, my inability to concentrate can be attributed to the girl in the hot pink bikini playing in the waves.

Between everything Josephine has been through, then what we all endured when the Sharks took her from us, we could all use some time to rest. Recover. We need a minute to settle into this new version of whatever it is we're doing.

"Do your coaches know?"

I blow out a long breath, leaning back on the railing, and survey the wooden planks covered in sand.

Kylian's right. It's pervasive.

Just like the media and their pursuit of private information.

Just like my dad and his insatiable desire for fame.

"They're aware. They know I'm still working my way back to 100 percent. That timeline might speed up a bit if it was quieter at the house."

His slight scoff raises the hairs on the back of my neck.

"Is that why you canceled your party last night?" he asks.

My heart drops into my stomach, and I shake my head. Of course he knows. Of fucking course.

It was the right call. For her. For them. For all of us. But I knew it wouldn't be without consequences.

I spent hours on the phone on Wednesday afternoon, moving things around and making alternate arrangements. Misty had to do all sorts of schedule shuffling to make sure we could still meet our content quotas for the week without hosting the party. She wasn't happy with me, but I didn't give her much choice in the matter. In the name of compromise, I'll be spending all day Tuesday taking pictures and filming brand footage.

Before I can formulate a suitable reply, he presses on.

His tone far too haughty for a father talking to his son, he asks, "Or does this have something to do with the girl you were kissing on the field after the game?"

God dammit.

A breath passes. Then another.

If I acknowledge her, name her, tie her to me in any way, I put her at risk.

If I pretend she's no one...

God-fucking-dammit.

"It'll all be fine, son," my dad reassures me, instantly flipping back to his chipper, media-trained tone. His questions weren't questions at all. They were warning shots. "Real and raw is what these special features are all about. They want to see you in action—at school, at home, on the field. They want to see how the son of Thomas Crusade does it all."

Running my hand through my hair, I grip the back of my neck. Anything I say will be met with opposition. All I want to protect is at risk because of this feature.

I squint toward the shoreline, suddenly hit with an urgent need to set eyes on each one of them. Kendrick's joined them now, standing beside Kylian at the water's edge, hollering and egging them on as Josephine and Locke play in the water.

Hit with a wave of determination, I shoot my shot. He already knows my whole playbook. I might as well come out with it and go for the Hail Mary.

"What would have to happen for the coverage to only feature Kendrick and me?"

More silence. Consideration, maybe?

If only. The second he speaks, it's obvious he's going to shut me down.

"That's not the agreement, son. SportsZone wants unbarred access. They're planning twenty-four seven coverage. In fact, a camera crew will be by to set up equipment for B-roll in the next week or so. When you signed that contract, you agreed to full access, and your roommates are included in that. The scope of this feature is covered by the NDA they each signed when they moved into my house."

The reminder of whose name is on the deed hits as intended.

As does the mention of the guys. One of my "roommates" hasn't signed an NDA. And there's no fucking way I'm sticking her in front of a camera or giving anyone access to her in any way.

Blowing out a long breath, I relinquish any hope that my dad will help me with this. I'll have to figure it out with the guys, or on my own.

"Cameras will be installed in a week?"

"Next weekend, I believe. Double-check with Misty. She has the full schedule." Voice low, he adds, "I worked hard to make this happen for you, son. This isn't just another media spot. It's the equivalent of your professional debut as you transition from college ball and prepare to go pro."

A few weeks ago, I would have been thrilled.

Now I'm filled with dread. Unease. Worry. After what we've been through over the last few weeks... after everything she's endured to have a chance at the life she wants to live...

"See you in a few weeks," I force out. With that, I end the call before I end up throwing my phone off the boardwalk.

Chapter 39

Josephine

"You want us to go in with you?" Kendrick asks, navigating the Suburban along the gravel driveway, his eyes fixed on the road ahead.

I know what he's looking for. Or rather, who.

While Kendrick is desperate not to have a run-in with Scout, the junkyard armadillo who roams around my uncle's home and place of business, I'm eager to put eyes on her for the first time in weeks.

Or maybe I'm hoping for a distraction from the overdue conversation about to take place. It's time to put my tail between my legs and apologize to my uncle for disappearing on him. Though initially, it was against my will—not that I'll fill him in on that tidbit of information—staying gone for so long without checking in was my choice.

"I say we all go in." Kylian reaches back from the front seat and squeezes my hand. "But we need to get our stories straight before we head inside."

"Hmm. So you don't want me to explain to my uncle how you removed me from my bed in his home and forced me to live in the mansion?" I muse, leaning forward so I can kiss Kylian on the shoulder.

Kendrick made Kylian deep clean the Suburban last night after it was abundantly clear what we'd gotten up to in the back seat.

He shrugged like it was no big deal, then admitted to me this morning that he would have cleaned it out anyway. He hates tracking sand onto the boats or into the house.

"I don't want your uncle to suspect that I'm the reason he's been on a wild goose chase throughout Georgia and the Carolinas for the last month," Kylian clarifies.

"Wait. What?"

Kendrick scoffs as he puts the Suburban in park outside the door to my uncle's office.

"How do you think we got rid of him in the first place, Jo? I set up a series of fake accounts and buy-sell-trade listings for early '90s Honda Preludes with no rust and low miles. Sam's been after one for years. Over the last month, he's been going after one listing after another, but each time he arrived at the location, the car had *just* sold or was mysteriously no longer available."

"That's—" I snap my mouth shut. I'm suspended somewhere between being impressed and being wildly irritated by the way Kylian can seemingly manipulate any situation.

"Heads up. We're being watched," Kendrick murmurs, nodding at the back entrance that leads into the residence side of the building.

Sam is standing in the doorway, arms crossed, peering through the screen door.

"I agree with Boy Genius," he adds. "We go in together, and we leave together. We'll follow your lead, Jojo."

Theoretically, it's a sound plan. But I have no experience being the leader of the group. Or any group, for that matter.

Climbing out of the car, I smile at my uncle, but I hold back, waiting for Kylian and Kendrick to join me so we can present a united front.

A couple of spots over from the Suburban is my beloved Civic, Honey—the car Sam gifted me when I arrived in Lake Chapel. The guys all agreed when I insisted I drive her to the marina today. Decker winced when I brought it up, but I let it slide. He's concerned about my safety first and foremost. It's not about controlling me anymore. At least most of the time.

Having access to her whenever I want is another step in solidifying the autonomy I've worked so damn hard to secure, and none of the guys, Decker included, want to infringe on that.

My uncle watches us approach, his gaze fixed on me for the most part, though he flicks a few skeptical glances toward the boys.

"Jojo," he greets when we're close enough to speak. "It's good to see you."

"Hey, Sam. Can we come in?"

Nodding, he holds open the door, though his expression turns surly when the boys get close.

Kylian breezes right past him without a word, but Kendrick stops to introduce himself.

"Kendrick Taylor, Sir," he offers, extending a hand. "I'm a friend of Josephine's."

My pulse races. I don't have the slightest clue about how my uncle will respond, but I don't dare look back at the exchange.

Kylian's already halfway down the hall, heading toward the office area at the front, but I'm still sorting through my thoughts, moving much more slowly. Shuffling along the worn carpet, I peek into my old bedroom as I pass, then stop in my tracks when I see that it's exactly how I left it.

"Wasn't sure when you'd be back," Sam murmurs close behind me.

I jump, startled by his proximity, and bring a hand to my chest.

"I kept it just as you left it." Squeezing my shoulder, he slides past me. "Just in case."

My heart catches in my throat.

Sam gave up his bedroom when I moved in. He's been sleeping in the living room/kitchen ever since, even though I've been gone.

I don't have time to apologize or explain my absence, though, because as soon as we step into the office area, Jeannie is out of her seat.

"Sugar! I thought you'd gone and disappeared on us! Where the hell have you been?"

The middle-aged woman rushes me. The scent of her soapy perfume, followed by the distinct whiff of stale cigarette smoke, engulfs me when she pulls me in for a hug.

She holds on for too long, and even when she lets me go, she grasps my shoulders and keeps me close.

In my periphery, Kylian slides closer, hovering, no doubt in tune with my discomfort. Jeannie isn't a threat, but she's a lot. I haven't spent more than a couple of hours with her since I met her, but that fact was obvious the moment we were introduced.

Wearing a conspiratorial grin, she squeezes my upper arms. She's practically vibrating she's so giddy. "I saw the picture in today's paper, Sugar. I knew. I just knew! I already clipped it and showed it to Sam."

"Picture?" I balk, looking from her to Kylian, then past him to Kendrick.

K shakes his head. He's in the dark, too. Kylian whips out his phone and taps away. Looks like he doesn't know what she's talking about , either.

"I haven't seen any picture," I hedge as a bead of sweat tracks down my spine.

"Leave the girl alone, Jeannie," Sam chides. He strolls into the office, plants his hands on his hips, and looks from me to the boys and back again. "Can I get y'all anything to drink?"

Both Kendrick and Kylian decline, but I request a water, so Sam heads back toward the kitchen to retrieve it.

Jeannie releases me so quickly I stumble, then she turns on her heel before rushing back to her desk.

Closing my eyes, I let out a long breath, only to pull another in quickly at the warm touch on my hip. Kylian is beside me now, steadying me. He drums his fingertips against my low back in a soothing rhythm while he inspects the screen of his device.

A quick squeeze is my first warning. "You're not named," he murmurs, inclining his head to signal Kendrick to join us.

Once Kendrick's at my side, Kylian turns his phone so we can both see the image he's pulled up.

It's a black and white picture: the front page of a newspaper, it seems.

It's clearly me. In Decker's arms. On the field after they won Saturday's game.

My stomach sinks, and a million questions swirl in my mind as I take in every detail of the photo.

Snatching the phone from Kylian, I zoom in. The grainy picture blurs even more, so I squint as I absorb every detail. Frantically, I zoom out again and read the headline: *LCU Crusaders Sink the SCU Sharks.*

I'm fixated on the screen as I'm engulfed in another hug. Unlike Jeannie's, this one is warm and welcome, comforting and all kinds of right.

Tension leaches out of me as Kendrick holds me. His lips find the pulse point below my ear, then he whispers, "Breathe, Mama. You're okay."

He's right.

I am here. This is now.

I'm not pleased, but I'm okay.

"This photo wasn't featured in any of the online coverage," Kylian explains, extracting his phone from my vise-like grip. "That's why this is the first time we're seeing it. But the caption only names Decker, and we can only see your profile. None of the keyword alerts I have set up for you pinged any results because of this."

I nod, tamping down the anxiety clawing up my chest by focusing on my breathing. My lungs expands with each inhalation. Kendrick's breathing along with me, helping to ensure panic doesn't take over.

After a handful of deep, steady breaths, my anxiety wanes.

But then Jeannie speaks, and a shot of disquiet courses through me again.

"Well, what do we have here?" She struts past us toward the couch in the waiting area of the office, waggling her fingers at K and me.

"You're full of surprises, Sugar. I was sure you were with the Crusade boy. This *is* you in the picture, isn't it?"

She holds out a newspaper clipping almost the size of the entire front page. The photo itself takes up most of the space above the fold now that I see it in print.

The unease slithering through my veins makes me squirm, but Kendrick tightens his hold.

"Dammit, Jeannie," Sam says, returning with a water bottle in hand. "I said leave the girl alone, and I meant it. We just got her back."

Blinking rapidly and with a deep crease between her furrowed brows, Jeannie looks at Sam, her mouth opening, then snapping shut when she takes in his expression. Grumbling under her breath, she rises to her feet and scurries back to her desk across the room.

Shame trickles through me, now for an entirely different reason.

I'm not back. At least not for long.

"Sam, can we talk?"

I peel K's hands off me, and this time, he relents. Turning, I nod, and Kendrick takes the hint for what it is.

"Come on, Boy Genius. Let's take a walk," he mutters, cuffing Kylian on the neck. Kylian kisses my cheek—a move I'm sure Jeannie no-tices—then lets K lead him back down the narrow hallway.

Sam holds out the water bottle, watching warily as I accept it, then take a seat on the worn vinyl couch Jeannie occupied for a whole thirty seconds.

He sits on the armrest, perched above me, eyes darting over to his receptionist.

"She's fine," I assure him. I have to stifle a scoff at the way she's got herself positioned. Her head is down, and she's mindlessly flipping through a stack of papers, but she's sitting ramrod straight on the edge of her seat with an ear tipped in our direction.

"First things first. You're okay?" Sam asks, assessing me with narrowed eyes, no doubt searching for any hint of reluctance or uncertainty in my answer.

"I'm good. Great, even." I hold my palms up for emphasis. "School is going well. Midterms are coming up. My professor just posted grades for the big project I was working on in business and technical writing." The smile that splits my face is impossible to fight. "Ninety-eight percent."

"And it seems like you're making new friends."

It's not a sarcastic remark, but it is a searching one.

A clattering sound from across the room startles me. Both Sam and I turn and find Jeannie bent behind her desk, fumbling to pick up a stapler off the linoleum floor.

"Don't mind me," she chirps too quickly. "Carry on, carry on..."

I stifle a snort. She couldn't be more obvious if she tried.

Doesn't matter. I didn't intend to reveal my relationship status and current living situation to my uncle anyway.

"I've made great friends. I've been staying with them," I admit, though the explanation stops there. "I'm sorry I didn't loop you in sooner. The weeks have been flying by, then on the weekend, there's football—"

Sam chuckles, crossing his arms and resituating himself on the arm of the couch. "Didn't know you were such a sports fan, Jojo."

I smile coyly but keep my lips glued shut. I can take the teasing, but I draw the line at divulging personal information that he doesn't need to know.

Though I open up and give him all the pertinent information.

"I'm really happy in Lake Chapel, Sam. School is great, and my new friends..." I trail off. How could I even begin to put into words what Hunter, Greedy, and the guys all mean to me, both individually and collectively? "I sincerely appreciate you helping me get settled and offering up your home, but I think it'd be okay if you went back to sleeping in the bedroom."

Sam raises both eyebrows and rolls his lips, but he remains silent.

"I hope you don't think I'm ungrateful. I didn't expect things to happen the way they did. But I'm genuinely happy where I'm at. Hell, for the first time in years, I actually know what happiness means. If you want to keep the car, I under—"

"No, Jojo." He shakes his head fiercely. "Honey is yours. And that bedroom is yours, too," he adds, pointing down the hallway. "I'm glad you're okay. I can see the truth in your eyes, so I won't try to change your mind. But I'm heading back out on the road in a couple of days, and I'll be gone for a few weeks, so the bedroom will be unoccupied indefinitely, regardless of whether you're here. Just in case."

Tears well in my eyes. I don't deserve this level of generosity or kindness. Especially after accepting so much from him already, then ghosting him the way I did.

Not that I had much choice in the beginning. Truth be told, I never expected to be at the Crusade Mansion as long as I have been—first unwillingly, and now of my own volition.

"Thank you," I choke out while fighting back tears. The two words don't even begin to scratch the surface of the depth of my gratitude, but they'll have to be enough for now.

"Let's do dinner when I'm back in town," Sam offers, rising and extending a hand to help me to my feet. "Just because you don't need a place to stay doesn't mean you're off the hook from hanging out with your family."

He's teasing again, but his words strike a chord I wasn't expecting. I'd love nothing more than to have dinner with him. Not because either of us feels obligated to do so, but because we are family.

"I'd love that. Thanks, Sam." I wrap my arms around his middle, and he *hmphs*, obviously surprised by the gesture. "You have my new number, right?"

Before he can reply, Kylian hollers through the screen door.

"Jo, we gotta go. Cap just saw the picture. We've got some Big Decker Energy to work through."

My heart lurches and my breath catches as I look from Sam to Jeannie, who's sitting stock-still on the edge of her chair, not even pretending to not listen anymore.

She squeaks out the start of a question, but I cut her off at the pass.

"Bye, Jeannie. I'll be back again soon." Then I dash toward the back door, snagging the keys to my Honda Civic on the way.

"He's mad?" I hedge once I've stepped out into the warm afternoon sun. Shielding my eyes from the light, I scan the junkyard quickly, even though it's unlikely I'll spot Scout. Armadillos are nocturnal, and she tends to be most active in the early mornings anyway.

"He's Cap," Kylian contends.

Fair enough.

"I set up a few cameras," he informs me, nodding to the yard, as if it's as casual as someone picking up a loaf of bread or stopping for gas on the way home. "They're motion-activated with high-def night vision. I'll put an app on your phone so you can look for her."

My heart melts as we approach the Suburban, where Kendrick's already behind the wheel.

Drumming his fingers on the steering wheel, he regards Kylian and shakes his head in mock disgust. "I see how it is. Using Jojo's love of junkyard possums to pull off some techie grand gesture."

"Don't hate the player, K. Besides. Armadillos are mammals most closely related to sloths and anteaters, whereas a possum is a tree-dwelling marsupial," Kylian informs us. Then, to me: "Let's go home."

Chapter 40

Josephine

"Isn't *modal* a type of fabric?" I groan, lifting my Logic textbook off my lap and dropping it onto the ottoman in front of the love seat where I'm sprawled with my back against one armrest and my legs in Locke's lap.

Hunter peers up from where she's sitting cross-legged on a lounger. Squinting, she taps her pen against her temple. "You're totally right. It's a good one, too. I have a modal blouse that's as soft as silk."

"It's also an order of logic, Hot Girl. And it's most definitely going to be on the midterm," Locke replies, running one hand up and down my shins.

We've been out on my balcony for nearly two hours, working through the study guide for next week's exam. Hunter is freaking out and on her third iced matcha of the afternoon. I need a decent grade on this exam to tick off a general ed credit, but she needs this course for her major.

Locke is doing his best to help us, but all of this comes naturally to him, and he doesn't know how to succinctly explain things when Hunter and I don't grasp a concept. Chalk it up to him being a philosophy major, I guess.

"I bet snacks would help," Locke suggests.

Hunter snorts. "If that's a euphemism for sex, I'll excuse myself and leave you to it."

"I was going to suggest popcorn, but that's not a bad idea, either." He strokes higher up my leg, letting his tatted hand rest on my thigh. "What do you say, Hot Girl? Meet me in the pantry in five?"

With a playful eye roll, I shove his hand away.

"You wish, Emo Boy."

He clamps down on my thigh once more, even higher now. "Yeah, I do, but so do you."

I detach his hand from my leg and interlace our fingers, then open my mouth to reply, but promptly snap it shut when a commotion from below reaches my ears. Perking up, I shift forward on the love seat and peer over the ledge of the balcony.

The rest of the guys are home—tying up the boat on the dock and locked in a heated debate.

Hunter rises to her feet and comes to stand beside me. She watches them for a moment, a sly smile on her face. "It's always something around here, isn't it?" Then, looking back at me, she cocks one eyebrow. "Should I take off? Looks like you're about to have boyfriend drama."

"I'm sure it's not about me," I reply, standing and stretching my arms over my head, ignoring the way my cheeks heat at her callout.

Locke snickers. "I've seen the group text thread. It's most definitely about you, Hot Girl."

"Wait." I drop my hands to my sides and peer down at him. "There's a group text I'm not included in?" If so, then I'm going to be totally miffed.

It's his turn to blush. He averts his gaze even as redness creeps up behind the red and black ink of his neck piece. "I mean, there are lots of text threads. It's not like we purposely left you out. We've just always had group texts between—"

My pointed look silences him.

"That's my cue," Hunter singsongs. "I'm going to get another matcha and settle in for an all-nighter. Call me later?"

She gathers up her study materials, so I do the same. Once we've got everything collected, we go back through my room.

"I'll walk you out," I offer, following behind her while Locke holds the bedroom door for us both.

By the time we reach the kitchen, the guys are inside, standing in a triangle formation, all piss and vinegar and big dick energy.

Decker has his arms crossed over his chest, a surly scowl on his face.

Kylian's wearing a pinched expression somewhere between mildly frustrated and annoyed.

Kendrick's glower is all anger.

I assess them for all of two seconds before heading toward Kylian.

He lifts one arm without taking his eyes off Decker, allowing me to get close enough to nuzzle into his side.

"Hi," I whisper.

He doesn't respond, but he gives my shoulder a squeeze and kisses my hair.

"What's going on?" I ask, turning my attention from one guy to the next, hoping *someone* will fill me in.

Despite her declaration that she was leaving, Hunter is lingering in the kitchen, standing on the opposite side of the bar next to Locke.

It's Decker who finally breaks free from the showdown and sets his sights on me.

Sighing, he runs a hand through his hair, his jaw ticking. "We're working out logistics for this weekend."

"What's this weekend?" I ask, my anxiety notching up multiple levels. I wasn't aware of any big plans, and I don't like being caught unaware.

Kylian pulls me closer. "We have an away game. South Texas. Transportation is confirmed, but the accommodations are proving to be problematic."

Hunter snorts, but the sound quickly transforms into a full-on belly laugh.

At a loss for the source of her outburst, I gape at her, waiting for her to explain what the hell she thinks is so funny.

"Oh brother," she laughs, dabbing at her eyes before the welling tears can melt her mascara. "You're all fighting over whose room she's going to sleep in this weekend, aren't you?"

My heart thuds in my chest, and I suck in a sharp breath. My head oscillating like a rotating fan, I look at each of the guys, taking in their expressions. Decker and Kendrick at least look adequately bashful at the callout. Kylian just smirks.

I sag against Kylian, not mentally prepared to have this conversation but not willing to be excluded from it, either.

"What's the plan as of now?"

Kylian answers, straightforward and precise, like always. "They have to travel with the team." He nods at Decker and Kendrick, then over at Locke.

"As do you," Decker adds, one haughty brow raised.

"I have the *opportunity to*, yes. But I'm not required to," Kylian differentiates before turning back to me. "They'll leave on Thursday night. I booked tickets on a separate flight for you and me. It leaves Friday afternoon."

He looks unabashedly proud of himself. And now I'm starting to understand why Decker and Kendrick are less than excited. Locke seems fine, but for the most part, he's laid-back compared to the others.

Kissing Kylian's shoulder, I say a silent prayer that I'm not about to start World War III. "And if I don't want to go?"

Kylian tenses, and his fingers dig into the flesh of my hip. Locke presses his palms into the island, watching me with a knowing simper. Kendrick steeples his hands and purses his lips, clearly annoyed.

I swear every one of us holds our breath as we turn in unison to Decker and wait for him to respond.

"Keeping you safe is our highest priority, Josephine."

Sighing, I step forward out of Kylian's hold and come to stand on the opposite side of the bar.

I don't want to fight with Decker, but he should know by now that cutting me out, excluding me from these conversations, making decisions on my behalf, is not the flex.

"And why do you think traveling halfway across the country and being exposed to all the media attention you're guaranteed to garner is the safest option?"

Hunter lets out a low whistle. *Yeah, girl. I've got him there.*

"Josephine," Decker practically growls.

"Decker," I mock in a deep, dumb man voice that makes Kendrick snicker and Locke shake his head.

The second I register their reactions, I regret teasing him. I'm not purposely being difficult, despite my history of riling him up for fun. I guess that's one of the downsides of the group dynamic we've got going on. Relationship decisions affect a handful rather than a couple.

Standing straight and crossing his arms over his chest, he glares. "I would feel better if you'd travel with us this weekend," he tries. "Will you... Will you come with us? Please?"

His jaw ticks like mad, and I swear there's steam billowing out his ears.

"I would feel better—*safer*," I hedge, communicating in a language this man *should* understand, "if I stayed home."

He grips the counter in front of him so hard I'm tempted to march over to him and pluck each one of his fingers off the quartz. The last thing our quarterback needs is a hand injury to contend with.

"How is staying here alone safer?" he asks through gritted teeth, though his chin is dipped like he's speaking to the smooth surface of the counter.

I approach him with slow, even steps. Every eye in the room is on me when I stop at his side. He doesn't acknowledge my approach or make space for me like usual. He keeps his head bowed and his attention firmly locked on the countertop in front of him, lost in his own head, surely cycling through all the terrible what-ifs that accompany my suggestion.

Nudging his arm with my hip, I whisper, "Hey. Let me in."

On instinct, he lifts one arm, and I duck under so I can stand directly in front of him, so close our chests almost brush. I peer up, already knowing what I'll find when we lock eyes.

Concern.

Confusion.

Devotion.

It's the last one that makes it all make sense.

Wrapping my arms around his middle, I push up onto tiptoes, ignoring our audience completely. He's rock solid under my arms, an impenetrable mass of muscle and stubbornness.

Thankfully, my will is just as strong.

"Decker," I whisper, my nails catching in the short hairs along his nape as I run my fingers up and down the taut muscles of his back. "I know you're trying to take care of me, but sometimes caring for a person means loving them the way they want to be loved."

His eyes flicker with curiosity, but his scowl stays firmly in place.

"I feel safe here, Cap. Do you know that? There's nowhere else I want to be. This is my home now. I would never do anything to put myself at risk or to cause you unnecessary worry while you're away."

Deep onyx eyes assess me, searching for the lie.

He doesn't completely trust me. It's there, in the flash of reluctance in his expression. It's a strike to the solar plexus. In my heart, though, I know his distrust isn't all about me. Decker and I are still figuring each other out. We're trapped in a sort of relationship purgatory.

We'll get past it, make peace with it eventually. I'm determined to get us there. We just need more time. Time. Space. Moments like this. Where we communicate and compromise and create opportunities for the shaky trust between us to grow roots.

"There's no threat here, Cap. Shore Week is over. South Chapel won't bother us again. You and Kendrick and Greedy have made sure of that. You'll be back on Sunday. There's nothing and no one here that can hurt me.

"I know you'd feel better if I was with you... but I could really use a few days of peace and quiet. Rest. Time to study."

He sighs, and I know we're getting closer.

"Hunter could stay with me?" I offer, breaking out of Decker's orbit to glance over at my friend.

"Absolutely. I can be back with an overnight bag before Kylian leaves on Friday," she offers cheerfully. "Lord knows I could use a quiet weekend before our Logic exam."

"*Only* Hunter," Decker grunts, giving me a pointed look.

"I promise that won't be a problem," Hunter rushes out. She knows exactly what he's referring to. "They're away this weekend, too. Greedy only pulled that stunt because you all were here. Besides, he and I aren't exactly on speaking terms right now anyway..."

That's news to me, but it sounds like I'll have all weekend to get the story out of her.

The others have all been uncharacteristically quiet. I may be wrong, but I'm taking their silence as support. I don't need Decker's permission to stay back, but I'd rather this feel like something we all agree on than another thing I have to fight him on.

Spinning back into his arms, I place my hands on his stomach. His abs shudder under my touch, and I fight back a tremble of my own. Our connection—everything between us—is like two jolts of supercharged electricity. We're so well matched. When it's good, it's so damn good. But it makes navigating the tough stuff all the more difficult, because neither of us is good at compromising, let alone conceding.

"It's not that I don't want to see you play," I murmur, just for him. "It's just a lot to pack up, head out of town, then be on display on the bench, worried about the cameras, the media, who might be watching—"

"You'll check in every day." It's a demand, not a request.

I bite back the sassy quip that begs to be released and instead run my hands up his chest and circle his neck. "Multiple times a day," I promise solemnly.

"With me, Siren. Not just with Kylian."

"Of course." I agree easily, as if I was planning that all along. I wasn't, but I don't mind. For as much as we're figuring things out as a group, Decker and I still have so much work ahead of us as a couple.

He turns his head slightly, enough that I track the tic of his jaw before he sets his sights back on me. "And you won't fight me about security. I'll have our regular guys on detail the whole time. They won't be in your way, but they'll be here. That's nonnegotiable."

This time I don't hide my smirk. Though I'm still a work in progress, I can bend to his more reasonable his requests. But I also get to call him out when he's being an overbearing, controlling asshole. "Okay, Cap."

"Josephine, I'm serious." He closes his eyes and bows his head as if he's calling on a higher power to help him through this.

"I am too," I vow, exasperated. "I'm not fighting you on this. I'm on your team, Decker."

He opens his eyes and settles his typical sharp look on me, brows furrowed in a way that makes his cheekbones even more prominent.

"You *are* the fucking team, Siren," he whispers, catching my chin with his forefinger and thumb so I'm forced to meet his gaze.

Devotion.

Blanket, all-consuming devotion.

A shiver quakes through me. Instinctively, I tip my chin, so sure he's about to kiss me that I can't fight the urge to wet my lips.

"All right. Good talk." Kendrick claps, breaking us out of the spell. "If you two are done making googly eyes at each other, maybe we could get dinner going? I'm starving."

Locke snickers and heaves himself off the island where he's been stationed, and without a word, Kylian wanders off, face buried in his phone. Decker takes a step back, as if suddenly remembering that we have an audience.

"I'll text you later," Hunter calls as she heads out toward the docks.

Locke, Decker, and Kendrick spring into action, working as a unit, pulling vegetables out of the chiller and grabbing the pots and pans they'll need while I retreat to my room, reveling in what feels like a win.

Chapter 41

Josephine

Kylian rinses the last plate and loads it into the dishwasher with meticulous precision as I watch on. The others cooked, so he's on dish duty tonight. They're all surprisingly domestic for college guys. They've lived together for several years, so I suppose they've had time to fine-tune their process and figure out a schedule so they operate as a well-oiled machine.

Kylian insisted he didn't want my help with the dishes, so I made myself an ice cream cone and have been making a show of eating it with slow, deliberate licks.

He closes the dishwasher, turns it on, washes his hands, then pounces.

"You. Are. Trouble," he snarls against my lips. He dives in then, kissing me roughly and licking the ice cream right out of my mouth.

"Took you long enough to notice," I tease, leaning forward to kiss him deeper.

Holding my face in both hands, he pulls back, just slightly.

"I've told you before, baby. I notice every move you make. I've just gotten very, very good at masking my reactions over the years. Don't think for one second I wasn't watching you out of the corner of my eye and trying to ignore my hard-on."

"I love that you watch me." I kiss him again, slower and sweeter this time. "I know I'm always safe with you."

He steps forward and situates himself between my legs where they dangle off the island, running both hands up and down my bare thighs and pressing our foreheads together.

"You're tired." I realize now that I'm close enough to get a good look at him.

Kylian has very few tells. Not that he willingly shares, at least. Each time I recognize one, I'm hit with a warmth in my chest. Because I'm privileged enough to see him as he truly is. He's given me that trust, and he knows I'll always look out for him, even when he's not on full alert or firing on all cylinders.

He nods once, then kisses my nose.

"Do you want to come up to the Nest tonight?"

Do I want to? The answer is yes—it's always yes—but he won't sleep if I do. I'm not tired in the least, and there's something else I still need to do before I go to bed.

I rest my chin on his shoulder, relishing the feel of being wrapped up in him.

"I'm not tired. And I need to find Decker," I admit.

Kylian traces my spine with his knuckles as I kiss the exposed skin along the neckline of his T-shirt.

"He's probably in the weight room. Still brooding," he murmurs into my hair.

I scoff. "When isn't he brooding?"

He works his hands up my back and over my shoulders until his thumbs graze my jaw. Pulling back, he looks me in the eye. "Just be careful, Jo. Earlier... that was a lot. He's been pushed enough tonight."

The warning hits. It wasn't easy for Decker to compromise and give up that kind of control, and that's exactly why I want to go find him now.

I bite down on my bottom lip anyway.

"Yes, Daddy," I taunt, knowing full well it'll get a reaction out of my typically serious boyfriend.

Fire sparks in his eyes, and he smashes his mouth to mine in a bruising kiss. "Don't start something you don't have time to finish, baby."

I smile even as he ravages my mouth, letting him feed me his tongue as I lean back in submission. Kylian kisses like he wants to consume me—like he doesn't need food or water or air as long as he has me.

"I love you. Do you know that?" he asks, pulling back just enough that I can see his eyes behind his glasses.

Heart leaping in my chest, I rear back at the admission he just offered so freely.

"I do now." I gulp past the emotion in my throat, at a complete loss for words. What the hell is the appropriate response to such an out-of-the-blue statement? No one has ever said those words to me. Ever.

"Is that okay?" he asks, brushing his nose against mine. "For me to love you?"

My chest constricts so tightly it's hard to breathe as my eyes well with tears and my bottom lip quivers. I nod as I struggle to hold it together.

It's more than okay. So much fucking more than just okay.

But until this moment, I didn't know the extent of his feelings. Not for sure.

I hoped. Wished. Wondered.

The way in which this man loves me is more than I could have ever dreamed of—more than I deserve.

"Jo," he hedges, using both thumbs to brush away the tears I can't hold back. "Talk to me."

"Happy tears," I manage to get out through a sniffle.

Relief washes over his features, and he leans in to kiss away the paths of moisture streaking my cheeks.

"So you like when I say that? I can keep telling you I love you?"

Safety. Acceptance. Adoration. Care.

Kylian loves me.

Kylian loves me.

Kylian is so damn good at loving me.

I nod again, not trusting my voice not to waver. But apparently, that's not enough.

"Words, Jo. Use your words."

"Yes. I like it. Never stop saying it," I plead, tempted to say it back to him immediately.

"Good girl," he murmurs, kissing me once more. Then he's lifting me off the island as if I weigh nothing and setting me on my feet. Once he's sure I have my footing, he steps back and swats at my ass playfully.

"Now go find Cap."

I snort. He can't be serious.

Planting my hands on my hips, I raise both eyebrows. "Really?"

He surveys me, brow furrowed. "What?" he finally asks.

"You kiss me senseless, tell me you love me for the first time, then send me on my way to go find your friend?"

His expression softens, a smile playing across his face at my sassy recap.

He hovers closer, cupping my face in his hands once again. "That's a fair assessment. It may have been the first time I said the words out loud to you, but it's been my reality for weeks, Jo. I love you. I'm *in* love with you. Things just finally feel... *settled* enough that I thought I could say it without scaring you off."

Oh.

"Besides," he adds, nipping my bottom lip playfully. "I'm still taking that flight on Friday, so we'll have the house to ourselves on Thursday night and Friday morning. I plan to fuck you six different ways and leave you so satisfied you'll feel how much I love you the entire time I'm gone."

My core clenches at the very prospect. But the hit of desire is quickly replaced by one of trepidation.

"Do you want me to say it back?" I ask quietly, pressing a palm to his chest.

"No, baby," he replies instantly. "I don't need to hear the words." He places the softest kiss on my lips, confirming his sincerity. Not that I would ever question it. Kylian always says what he means and means what he says. "I feel your love every single day."

He pulls away then, turning me by the shoulders and nudging me in the direction of the weight room.

"Go find Decker before he goes to bed."

Chapter 42

Josephine

I'm weightless, like I'm walking on clouds, as I glide into the home gym. The moment I spot Decker Crusade, though, it's as though a half ton weight has been dropped in my lap.

He's straddling a bench, legs splayed wide, grunting through the extension of a bicep curl.

He's absolutely dripping in sweat and red with exertion. The familiar signs of self-loathing and punishment are clear even from where I stand in the doorway.

"Decker," I scold softly and pad toward him.

He sits upright, panting, when he catches sight of me in the mirror.

He's still panting, scrutinizing me, as I lower myself to straddle the bench beside him. From the look of him and his silence, he's too exhausted and wrung out from our conversation earlier to do anything but stare. Compromise isn't hard for most people, but it's fucking torture for him.

Yet he did it. For me.

Maybe he's in here this late because he can't believe it. Maybe it's because he resents the necessity of it or because he just needs to get out of his head and experience a sensation other than worry. Regardless of his reason, I can't help but feel responsible.

"How long have you been in here?" I ask, my fingertips brushing along the bulging veins of his forearms.

He's still watching me, assessing me as if he's trying to read a play on the field.

Fair.

But I didn't come in here to fight or rile him up. Not tonight.

I gingerly pluck his fingers from the textured steel of the thirty-five-pound weight until he's released it and it rests on the bench. I shift my gaze from the free weight to the floor and back again, willing him to understand.

When he eventually comprehends and sets it on the floor, I catch his hands in mine.

Then I interlace our fingers. Because I need him to truly comprehend what I'm about to say.

"What are you doing, Josephine?"

I swallow past my hesitation, then scoot forward on the bench until my knees graze his inner thighs.

"What I wanted to do earlier."

I press my lips against his cheek, closer to his mouth than his temple, because I can't ever seem to give him more than he's willing to give me.

I'm willing to bend. But he has to learn how to bend, too.

To my relief, he doesn't leave me hanging.

Capturing my lips in a real kiss, he cuffs the back of my neck with one big hand while he wraps the other around my body.

Grasping my low back, he pulls me into him. I spread my thighs as wide as they can possibly go, but it's still not close enough.

Clambering to close the distance, I hitch my legs over of his, then lock my ankles around his back. He's shirtless and dripping in sweat, but I couldn't care less. I want it. I want it all. Every drop of sweat. Every ounce of frustration. I want his fire to fuel me in a way I've never experienced before.

We're perfectly matched. Combustible in the best way. If only we'd stop resisting the pull. So in tune with one another I can't imagine ever not having his fire in my life, yet so similar I can't imagine not fighting him at every turn.

Tonight, though, I don't want to fight.

I want to thank him.

I want to show him that I see him—the full depth of what he did for me today, what he's willing to give up and how far he's willing to go to bring peace to my world.

I want to show him it wasn't in vain. That I want to be his. That I would gladly spend a lifetime challenging him and pushing him, harboring him and lifting him up, if only he'd let me.

"Decker," I pant into his mouth. Every stroke he gives, I match. Every kiss is a gift and an invitation I'm so damn eager to accept.

Grunting, he leans back, but he keeps our lower halves connected. He drops his chin to his chest, focusing on where our bodies collide, on where the hem of my shorts is pushed up and the seam down the middle is stretched tight. His erection is rock hard under his athletic shorts, pressing against the fabric enticingly.

"Fuck," he mutters. "I want you so fucking bad." With a roll of his hips, he presses up into me in the most delicious way.

"So have me," I beg, chasing the friction and heat of him.

He sighs, wearing a defeated frown.

Tears prick the backs of my eyes at the impending rejection. Every time we get here, we get stuck. In limbo. Purgatory. Existing on a plane where what we both want is so clear, but who we are, what we've been through, and what we want in the future don't mesh.

A less cautious man would just take it. Why he can't just let us have this—

"Not tonight, Siren."

I pull back, searching his gaze and finding all the fire and want I feel reflected back in his onyx irises.

"Not *tonight*?" I repeat. Of all the reasons he could provide for why we can't take this further, I didn't expect timing to be the issue.

He sighs again, but this time the sound is a stifled release of pent-up energy—not the exasperated disregard I've grown used to when we go toe to toe.

"I have to be at the field house in"—he cants to one side to look at the clock on the wall—"five and a half hours. It's late. And as much as I want this"—with another tilt of his hips, he rubs his erection against the soft fabric of my shorts—"as much as I want *you*, our first time isn't going to be rushed or reckless. When I make this pussy mine," he grits out, rubbing a thumb along the seam of my crotch, "I need to take my time."

My first reaction is to push back.

Test him.

At the very least, clarify that my pussy belongs to me and me alone, and that any claim he wants to make on it will be one of joint ownership. *Team ownership? Discussed with the other shareholders? Brought in front of the board?*

An image of Kylian in a suit with his charts and data, leading a meeting for the board of directors, pops into my head unbidden, causing mirth to bubble up inside me.

Before it can escape, though, Kylian's warning slams into me, bursting that building sensation, and I bite back all the things I could say that would inevitably piss off Decker or dismiss his concerns.

"Okay," I relent, peeking up through my lashes and reveling in the close-up view I have of his delicious lips. God, I hope he'll at least kiss me again.

His eyes narrow. "*Okay?*" he asks. "Seriously?"

"What?" I *may* be fighting off a grin at his response.

"What's the catch?"

Ducking my head, I laugh. "There's no catch, Decker."

"When have you ever just gone along with what I say?"

He's got me there.

Rising from the bench, I trace one hand across his chest, taking my time to come around and kneel behind him. I stay propped up on my knees and hug his neck, resting my chin on his shoulder and meeting his gaze in the mirror in front of us.

"I want exactly what you want, Crusade. I can wait." Cocking a brow at his reflection, I hold on to him just a little tighter. "And I can be agreeable when given the proper motivation."

He watches me—always watching, always looking for the lie. The day he finally trusts me will be a day worth celebrating.

"You're telling me I could have been using my dick to get my way this whole time?" His lips tilt up in a smirk, and his eyes dance with mischief.

Glee percolates through my body. It's good to see him smile. To know we can still banter and tease. It makes everything feel lighter—hopeful, even.

"We'll find out soon enough." I stand up and kiss his neck. "Good luck at your game this weekend, Cap. I'll be waiting for you to make good on your promise when you get home."

And with that, I walk out of the weight room without a backward glance.

The house is dark as I make my way down the hall, past the living room and into the kitchen. A blue light illuminates Kylian's face where he's sitting at the bar, focus locked on the glowing device in his hand.

I approach quietly and sidle up next to him. He side-eyes me for an instant, and after a few seconds, he closes out of the chart he was analyzing, stifling a yawn.

"Ready for bed?" he asks, hopping off the barstool and reaching for my hand.

He's wiped. He admitted as much before I went to find Decker.

"Why are you still up?" I ask, fully embracing the yawn he just inspired as we head toward the stairs together.

"I was waiting for you," he offers matter-of-factly.

"Were you spying on me?" I ask, half-joking but also slightly indignant. Kylian has no problem sharing with Locke and Kendrick. I assumed that attitude extended to Decker as well, but maybe we should have discussed it first.

"Not exactly," he hedges. He looks over his shoulder at me, then flicks his gaze toward the weight room.

"You were spying on him," I guess.

"That would be an accurate assessment, yes."

When we reach my bedroom door, Kylian stops, and I step into him, kissing his sternum and squeezing our joined hands.

"Don't you trust Cap?"

He crowds my space, one arm propped on the doorjamb above my head, and leans close.

"I trust Decker with my life," he declares. "But I don't trust him with my heart. At least, not yet." He kisses me softly, then, without another word, he turns to head up the next flight of stairs to the Nest.

Dumbfounded, I watch him go, brushing my fingertips against my lower lip and marveling at how I ever made it through my days without these men.

Chapter 43

Josephine

I sip through the pink paper straw Hunter insisted we use in our Tom Collinses and set my glass on the table where we usually have family dinner. It's a warm, breezy night; the epitome of fall in the south, according to my bestie.

"Your turn, babe," I declare, picking up the bottle of top coat and waving at her, gesturing for her to hold out her left hand. "Truth or truth?"

As much as I miss the guys, I can't remember the last time I felt as light and free as I do right this second.

For once, the mantra I rely on so often to ground me feels more like a prayer of gratitude.

I am here. This is now.

This is what living feels like.

Hunter and I slept until noon, only rolling out of bed because the growls coming from her stomach were comically loud. Mrs. Lansbury has been around all weekend waiting on us, even though she's usually off when the boys have away games.

Over and over, I've insisted that we're fine and that she should take the day off. But it's clear she revels in taking care of people, and I can't deny how lovely it's been to eat so much yummy food without having to do the work ourselves. She's spoiled us with shrimp pasta and she-crab soup and whipped up the simplest yet most incredible fruit salad and broccoli salad. The broccoli salad has called my name all day. Every time I pass the fridge, I have to reach in and pluck out another piece. It's that good.

We studied plenty. Put on our suits and sunbathed on the docked pontoon. Napped. Now we're sitting out on the deck, enjoying a plate of fresh-baked cookies and sipping drinks while I do our nails.

"Truth," she finally answers through a mouthful of chocolate chip goodness.

Holding my bottom lip between my teeth, I smooth the clear top coat over her thumb. When I'm finished, I inspect my work, then move on to her right hand.

I glance at my best friend, then focus on her nails again before I ask, "Have you ever been in love?"

I fully expect her to laugh. To blow me off. To recoil or quickly change the subject.

Hunter is amazing—brilliant and kind, beautiful and caring—but despite how much I've divulged about my past, she's still not forthcoming about a lot of hers.

I don't take it personally. If anything, I get it. Trauma knows trauma when it sees it. A person can only shine so brightly for so long before the truth peeks through the cracks.

So when she heaves in a deep breath and sits up straighter, I'm shocked.

"My senior year of high school. I was so in love I didn't think I'd ever have the capacity to feel another emotion for the rest of my life. It was... everything."

Her expression is mournful when I look up and meet her gaze. There's a wistfulness in the way she sighs, as if she's really, truly known love. Only it's in the past, and she doesn't expect to ever experience it again.

I'm so disarmed by her candor that it barely registers when she quickly flips the script and turns the questioning back to me.

"Your turn. Truth or truth, Joey Meyer?"

I finish applying the top coat and twist the cap on before replying. "Truth."

"Are *you* in love?"

I don't miss the change in tense.

I scrunch up my nose, only slightly embarrassed by the gush of emotion that takes over when I think about the guys.

"I think I am," I admit.

Her resounding squeal is so loud Mrs. Lansbury pops her head out to check on us.

"Everything all right, dears?"

"Yes!" I insist, my cheeks heating.

If she's overheard *anything* we've been talking about tonight, I'll be mortified. I've never felt judged by Mrs. Lansbury, and I'm certain she's witnessed enough of the little gestures and interactions between the boys and me to suspect there's something going on with, well, all of them, but that doesn't mean she wants to hear the sordid details.

Once the sliding glass door is firming in place, Hunter doubles down.

"Okay. Spill it, sister. Which one? Or should I say which *ones*?" She waggles her brows at me.

Now that it's just the two of us, I can't hide my grin, and I don't bother suppressing the warmth radiating from my center. I'm not embarrassed by the relationships that have emerged between the guys and me. I want them all. They want me, too. We're figuring it out—and there's no denying the end result I hope and pray can become a reality.

"Kylian for sure. He actually said the words to me the other day."

Across from me, Hunter's expression melts, and she sighs dreamily.

"And I think I'm in love with Kendrick, too, even though he was the last one I ever thought I'd end up with." I roll my eyes, still baffled by how naturally things fell into place with LCU's star running back.

The sands shifted below us so quickly and irrevocably. It's like the intensity of his loathing flipped and was instantly replaced by a love just as consuming.

There's passion and physical yearning, and he radiates this deep sense of care and sacrifice. Always. I feel it deep in my bones when he looks at me and when he holds me and when he makes love to me at night.

Kendrick's love fills a vacancy inside me I thought would remain empty for life. It's the kind of love most people only ever experience within a tightknit family. It's unconditional, soul-mate level magic.

"I think he loves me, too. Or at the very least, we're heading in that direction."

Scooting a little closer to the table, I inspect my own nails, noticing a blemish near the cuticle of my ring finger. I'll have to find an orange stick and take care of that later.

"Wait, what about Locke?" Hunter presses.

I force my attention to her again and give her a sad, sincere smile. Locke and I have had so many ups and downs in such a short amount of time. I want nothing more than to be in a steady place with him, but we just haven't found it yet, and I'm beginning to worry we might never land there.

Sighing, I sit back, surveying the sun as it sinks into the lake, then turn back to my friend. "When things are good with Nicky, they're good. Like *so* good. Effortless. Authentic."

Honestly, Locke's brand of love feels the most natural to me. He doesn't overthink it. There's practically no effort at all on my part to exist by his side. He's everything I want. Well, he and his friends. That dynamic, thankfully, isn't an issue for him, either.

Yet I don't know what to make of how easy it is for him to pull back, as if what we share isn't anywhere near as important to him as it is to me.

"It doesn't always feel like he wants me. Not fully. When things get hard, he backs off, like maybe he's losing interest. I don't know if it's from the pain, or..."

I trail off, because damn, that sounds so self-centered. Like I can't get enough attention.

"The back and forth is hard. Maybe we're not as well-matched as I originally thought."

Sighing, I sip from my drink and survey the pinks and oranges flooding the sky behind Hunter.

"I want to love him... I do. But something's missing. The ease I feel with Kylian and Kendrick, how good each of those connections is, only makes the disconnect with Locke that much more apparent."

"Do you want compassion or advice?" Hunter asks, crossing her legs and settling back in her seat.

God, I love this girl. She could teach a masterclass in friendship. Since I met her, she's taught me lesson after lesson in girl time and sisterhood I never thought I'd be privy to.

I don't have to tell her I appreciate her, though. She knows. And that's what's missing with Locke, I realize. The assurance. The security. The connection we can both count on, even when things get hard.

"I'll take some advice if you've got it," I concede, reaching for my drink and draining the rest of it through the ridiculous pink straw.

Hunter snags her glass as well, assessing the now-soggy straw she insisted on with a scowl. She sets the straw on a napkin, then throws back the rest of her beverage, too, hopping to her feet as if she's ready to deliver her closing arguments.

"You know I grew up with them," she starts, standing behind her chair.

Silently, I nod. It's one of the few things I do know about Hunter's past.

"Kendrick was in my kindergarten class. Kylian sat beside me in second grade. I was assigned to be Decker's cheerleader in middle school."

"Wait," I demand, sitting a little straighter. "What does that mean, you were *his* cheerleader?"

She rolls her eyes and purses her lips. "Exactly what it sounds like. Welcome to the south, girl. It's archaic and gross, but starting in sixth grade, cheerleaders are 'assigned' a player to dote on and support. We're supposed to make them brownies and paint their numbers on our cheek at the games. It's like a twisted southern form of matchmaking. Half the girls I graduated from high school with are already engaged to their assigned football player."

My eyes go wide, but Hunter just gives me a knowing look. "I needed a sports bra by the time I was ten," she admits, sweeping a hand dismissively over her impressive tits, "and I'm a natural blond, so of course I would be assigned to the kid who was football royalty and destined to be the star quarterback."

"*Okay.*"

She's right. It all sounds archaic and odd and disturbing. It doesn't answer any of the questions consuming me, though.

"How does any of that relate to Locke?"

"Trust me. I'm getting there," she promises, plopping back down into the chair opposite me and crossing her long, tan legs.

"When Locke started coming around, he wasn't always in the fold. He missed a lot of events because of doctor's appointments and illness. Sometimes, though, he just didn't insert himself enough. Honestly, it was probably Kylian's steadfastness and hyper-focus on having a best friend that secured Locke's place in the group once and for all."

I can't help but smile at that. I'm intimately acquainted with what it feels like to be on the receiving end of Kylian Walsh's specific brand of love.

"I don't think he's one foot out because he wants to be," she hedges. "Think of how he grew up. Think of how he talks about himself, his life, his plans. He's one foot out because that's all he's ever known, and he's waiting for the other shoe to drop."

"It's self-preservation," I murmur, the realization slamming into me with so much blatant force it takes my breath away. Not because it's a shocking revelation, but because it's one I've lived myself. How didn't I recognize it sooner?

"If I had to play armchair therapist, I would guess that he needs more reassurance... and maybe more time? He's probably your hardest to love because he's comparing himself or worried he's not worthy or concerned that he may not have the ability to reciprocate all the time."

"But he's *beyond* worthy," I protest.

She smiles serenely, nodding. "There ya go. You have your answer."

I let out a long, heavy sigh. The insight she's given me is so, so valuable, yet I can't help but chide myself for not seeing it sooner. Pulling out my phone, I check the time. The guys are probably just getting back to the locker room after the game. For as much as I resisted traveling with them, I really do miss them.

I checked in with Decker at halftime.

Kylian texted me the final score after the Crusaders won.

Kendrick posted a game-day photo on social media, then slid into my DMs with a private picture just for me. Sweaty abs and football pants do it for me. I couldn't hit *Save Image* fast enough when his borderline NSFW pic came through.

On instinct, I scroll down to my text thread with Locke and shoot off a message.

Hot Girl: Hey you. Great game tonight. Kyl sent me the highlights. I miss you and can't wait to see you tomorrow.

He replies just a few seconds later.

Emo Boy: Ya know, just because we're in separate states doesn't mean I can't see you tonight...

I grin, but I then silently scold myself. It's easy to default to the physical with Locke. He's gorgeous, and our chemistry is palpable. But that wasn't the point of reaching out to him. More than anything, I want him to know how special he is and how sincerely committed I am to him.

Hot Girl: Raincheck on the phone sex. Get some rest, Nicky. I can't wait until you're home and I can be in your arms again.

Emo Boy: You're killin' me, Hot Girl. But I'll tell the guys you checked in

Hot Girl: No need. This isn't a check-in. I just wanted you to know I was thinking about you.

I send three heart emojis to drive the point home and promise myself I'll make a more concerted, consistent effort with Locke. He deserves to know how much I want him—not just physically, but in all other ways, too.

He makes me feel so good. I want to make him feel the same.

"Okay, this is too heavy," Hunter says, smacking her palm against the table. "We've got the whole Crusade Mansion to ourselves. We're supposed to be having *fun*. What are we doing for the rest of the night?"

"Want to watch a movie, get crumbs all over Decker's favorite chair, then go to bed early?"

Hunter grins. "A girl after my own heart."

"Don't forget, tomorrow—"

"Oh, believe me. I have *not* forgotten," she assures me. "I've got everything stashed in my trunk at the marina."

"The guys expect to be back in the late afternoon, so we should probably head across the lake after lunch." I worry my lip, running through the plan I've had in place since the night I met Kendrick's sisters. I think it's funny, but things have changed drastically over the last few weeks. Is it *still* funny?

"Admittedly, five hundred might have been a few too many," I concede.

"Nah," Hunter dismisses with a wave of her freshly manicured hand. "It's perfect. Uncle Ducky won't know what hit him."

Chapter 44

Decker

"That's the way it's done, boys!" Coach McDaniels hollers as we circle up.

The energy in the locker room is palpable. We're a mass of adrenaline and infinite possibility, celebrating a big win over an excellent team on their home turf.

While the guys grin and bounce and pat each other on the back, still riding the high, my mind is far too absent to feel any of it.

I locked it in for the game. After last week's dismal display of distraction, I couldn't afford not to. But now that we've clinched the win, all I can think about is getting home.

Getting home and being with her.

We're stuck in Texas for one more night, and our flight doesn't leave nearly early enough tomorrow for my liking. By the time we get back to North Carolina and account for the time change, it'll be late afternoon.

We'll have a day or two to recalibrate, then chaos will descend on my home, and there's nothing I can do to stop it.

The camera crew will arrive midweek to go through the house and determine where to install the cameras and mics. I've reviewed the contracts. Combed through the fine print. Almost nothing is off limits.

They'll have access to it all. They'll always be watching.

A year ago, it would have been little more than an inconvenience as we went through our day-to-day lives. The irony? Once I truly studied the contracts and accompanying documents, I discovered that this whole feature has been in the works for more than a year.

Now? With Josephine at the house, and because of the way things have evolved and shifted within the group?

It's a gross invasion of privacy I can't believe I'm allowing.

It's mind-boggling how a single person can change one's entire perspective on life.

That's what she's done. She's flipped the script.

Nothing makes sense anymore.

My phone buzzes in my hand, pulling me from the fog that descended the moment the clock ran out. Kylian texted, saying he's already back at the hotel. *Good*. He needs time to unwind and decompress after a game more than any of us.

I stash my phone, pull off my jersey and pads, then strip out of my base layers and head for the showers.

Kendrick's in step with me, but Locke is standing in front of his locker, still in his full kit.

He's got his helmet in one hand, his phone in the other. And he's smiling at the screen like it holds all the secrets of the universe.

I nudge his shoulder to get his attention. "What's up?"

Locke's head snaps up, almost as if he's embarrassed to be caught. Then Kendrick starts losing it, nearly doubled over with laughter.

"What's so funny?" I demand. Fuck, I just want to be done with this night, yet my guys are threatening to pull me into whatever the hell they've got going on.

"Relax, Cap." K straightens and cups my shoulder. "It's just beyond obvious who's got our boy smiling like that."

Locke at least has the decency to glare at Kendrick.

"You gonna need a little extra time in the ice bath tonight to cool down, Nicky? Or…"

"Shove off," he grumbles, finally tucking his phone away and starting to undress.

He was clearly texting Joey. I shouldn't care about in the least, but I was messaging with Kylian sixty seconds ago, and I'm certain I didn't have any unread messages from her.

I'm tempted to go back to my locker and retrieve my device, just to double-check.

I'm clearly a masochist.

"Let's go," I grunt, shouldering past Kendrick to hit the showers.

The faster we can get out of here—back to the hotel and back home, to her—the faster we can get this week over with.

My jaw aches from clenching so tightly.

We were late getting in the air because of a storm system. It was mainly over Texas and Oklahoma, thank god. I hadn't even thought about what would happen if it stormed at the lake while we were all gone.

Then coach pulled me aside before I could leave the field house. Apparently, the camera crew from the feature had sent their access list to the communications team at LCU, and a few of their requests were deemed too invasive, so we had to get on the phone with LCU PR, Misty, and the SportsZone PA to hash out a compromise.

A compromise that included an additional photoshoot on the field next week after the game.

Needless to say, we're headed to the marina two hours later than planned.

Kendrick's driving, Nicky's slumped against the window, snoozing, and Kylian has his head tipped back and his eyes closed. He ended up flying home with the team after all, since his commercial flight was also delayed because of the storms.

"Corbin says they've been at the marina all afternoon," I grit out.

"She's fine," Kylian assures me for the umpteenth time. He's exhausted. We all are. But he's also been short with me all day.

"You know that for sure?" The words escape before I can think better of them. This isn't me. I'm not antagonistic. I don't purposely try to get a rise out of people, least of all Kyl.

He leans forward and squeezes my shoulder in a way that's supposed to be reassuring and comforting. All it does is crank up my anxiety even further.

"She texted me"—he pauses, presumably to check his phone—"eight minutes ago. The security guard you pay a huge sum of money just checked in to confirm that they're waiting for us. We'll be home soon. Cool it."

If only I could. I'm anxious to get home, sure. But I'm more anxious to get to her.

I know it's not a competition, but I can't help but compare our situations.

He'll get her in his bed tonight or sometime tomorrow. He gets to hold her and hug her and kiss her whenever he wants. I've got a few days to soak her in—from now until the camera crew descends.

Every minute that slips out of my grasp ratchets up my blood pressure another ten digits.

"Fucking finally," Locke mutters from the back as we slow to turn into the marina.

Kendrick grunts his agreement, turning the wheel so he can circle the lot to park in his usual spot near the landing.

"Why is Jo sitting on the hood of your car?" This from Kylian.

The mention of her name makes my damn heart stutter, and of its own volition, my body contorts until I'm craning my neck, looking for her. Sure enough, both Josephine and Hunter are perched on the hood of my G-Wagon, legs crossed in front of them and heads bowed low.

Corbin is just a few spots down, wearing his typical surly scowl. The extra detail I hired are nearby, as well. Three boats hover just offshore, each one waving a distinctive red, black, and white flag so I can easily identify them from afar.

I don't bother to grab my bag or gear, but I do make a concerted effort to slow my pace as I climb out of the Suburban and approach my car.

Hunter looks bored, her face relaxed and impassive.

But Josephine is trying—and failing miserably—to hide the biggest shit-eating grin.

She's up to something.

And as much as moments like this used to irk me...

I struggle to hide my own smile the closer I get to the car.

The boys call out, asking about bags, but I don't bother even glancing their way. I've only got eyes for her.

"Siren." I step up between her legs, offering a quick nod toward Hunter. Then I fix 100 percent of my focus on my girl. "What did you do?"

Josephine bites down on her lower lip—saucy little temptress—still trying to hold in her grin.

Kylian swoops in beside me to greet her, grabbing her face and giving her a quick kiss. "Missed you, baby," he murmurs before moving on toward the dock.

It's the slight lean that gives her away.

Peering over the girls' shoulders, I home in on my dash.

My all-black, always-pristine dash. Except, from the look of it, it's now covered in color.

"Josephine..." I scold, storming around to the driver's seat and whipping open the door.

A waterfall of knickknacks pours out at my feet. Yellows and reds, blues and purples. Bits and bobs of every color in a relentless stream. I scan the interior of my car, which is completely unrecognizable.

They're everywhere. Covering every surface. On the dash. Along the floorboards. All over the seats. They're even affixed, upside down, to the headliner.

"What the hell?" I grumble, looking from the mess at my feet to the even bigger mess filling my car.

"They're ducks," she quips at my side.

My chest lurches at her proximity. I didn't realize she had hopped off the hood and come around to stand beside me.

Hunter is hovering near Kendrick and Locke, letting my girl fight her own battle, it seems.

"Ducks, Josephine? Really?" I pluck one of the blue rubber toys off my driver's seat. If this isn't the stupidest idea—

"I thought you'd like them," she muses, still fighting back the mirth that's determined to escape and paint itself on every one of her features. "I always see them in cars like yours. I thought the rubber ducks were a Jeep thing."

With a huff, I shoot her a glare, though it's almost impossible to hold when a snort breaks free from her and she slaps a hand to her mouth.

I hold back my own smile and will the scowl to remain as I breathe through my nose. "You know damn well this isn't a *Jeep*, Josephine."

"Hmm," she muses, turning on her heel to head to the dock. "If you say so, Uncle Ducky."

Locke bursts out laughing. Hunter finally cracks a smile. Josephine? She takes off in a sprint that has me tempted to call after her to slow down. I refrain, but only because Kylian's waiting for her at the start of the dock.

This girl.

This beautiful, infuriating, magnificent girl.

"Cool it, Cap," Kendrick murmurs, cuffing my shoulder as he comes to stand by my side. "It was just a joke. And I'll help you clean these up. The girls will love them."

I smirk at my friend, laughing to myself as I open the back door and more ducks topple out of the car.

Kendrick's concerned about my reaction.

He must not realize that this is *exactly* what I've been waiting for.

On more than one occasion over the last few weeks, I felt her fire dimming. After the Sharks took her, obviously. Then again when I forced her on the boat. The night she told us about her past. Just a few days ago, when we squared off about her not traveling with us to the game.

Her light flickered, and I've spent an inordinate amount of time worrying that she's closer to being snuffed out than she's letting on.

"Why are you smiling like that?" K hedges, bending and snatching a handful of toys off the ground. "She doesn't deserve whatever you're plotting in your head, Cap. I'm sure it was—"

"Bro. Don't you get it?" I interrupt.

Rising to his full height, he considers me, then eventually shakes his head.

"The ducks. The prank. All this mess?" I wave one hand toward the G-Wagon, then allow myself to exhale—truly exhale—for the first time in weeks. "She's back, K. Our girl is back."

Chapter 45

Josephine

"Easy. A little slower, Hot Girl."

With a grimace, I check the rear-view mirror again.

"Slower isn't really an option. There's a pickup truck riding my ass," I explain.

Locke turns around in the passenger seat, searching for the offender.

Although I'm not sure "offender" is the appropriate term, since I'm the one driving fifteen under the posted speed limit down a residential street lined with dilapidated homes. If the roles were reversed, I'd be riding my ass, too.

When he rights himself, he turns up the music, blasting "Happy" by Pharrell at full volume.

I look over at him and can't help but grin. He's so damn adorable.

When he watches me in return, his expression transforms into an unexpectedly soft smile with a hint of self-consciousness. He invited me along today and is sharing a sacred part of himself with me now. I don't take that for granted.

He goes back to scanning our surroundings, and a second later, he whips his head in my direction. Once again, the wide, easy smile I know and love takes over his entire face as he points out the windshield.

Past his finger, two little boys, similar in size, race out of the front door of a double-wide and book it down a dirt driveway until they're skidding to a halt next to my car.

Locke already has his window rolled down and is holding up his hand so the kids freeze and don't run into the road. The truck that was riding my tail passes, thankfully, then Locke waves the kids over to his side.

He greets them and offers them knuckles. "Trey, Trenton. You got first! Good work, boys. You wanna help me gather up the team?"

Up close, it's clear the boys are related, but at least a few years apart. With bright smiles and bobbing heads, they agree and start heckling each other about who can get down to the field faster as they claim opposite sides of the road and take off.

"Next street over," Locke directs, pointing to where he wants me to drive.

He turns down the music as I make my way there. This street is more of an alleyway, and there are already a few kids watching us eagerly on approach.

"Same thing?" I ask, leaning over to increase the volume again.

"Nope," he replies, tipping his chin. "I see a few of my kids already out on this street."

His kids—my heart.

"They know to wait until we're in front of their house, but they'll come running as soon as I give them the all-clear."

"How did you come up with this system?" I muse, amazed at the patience of the little girl with lopsided pigtails who can't be more than six or seven years old. She's hovering on the last step of a rotted wooden deck attached to the front of the house, surrounded by grass that's as high as her knees.

She waits, bouncing on the balls of her feet with such ferocity it looks like she has to go to the bathroom.

"Here?" I ask. Locke nods and waits for me to come to a stop before he waves her over.

"Rosie Posie! Hi, princess." He offers her knuckles just like the boys. "You're my team lead for this street, okay? Make your brothers help, but tell them I said you're in charge."

She's wearing a toothy grin when she spins on her heel and screams, "Jimmy! Josh!" like a banshee as she heads back to the double-wide she must call home.

"Princess?" I tease, putting the car in drive and coasting down the road to the next section of houses.

"*Ah*, are you jealous, Hot Girl?" Locke smirks, raising his pierced brow for emphasis.

I return the gesture and shake my head. "Not jealous. Mostly impressed. And more than a little curious. You do this every week?"

"We take turns." He points straight ahead to guide me farther along the street. "Me and the boys. A few of the other guys on the team volunteer, too. Only a select few I know I can trust, though. With the way the schedule works out, I'm out here about once a month."

"So it's different days and times each week?"

"No, never. We pick a day and time for the whole year and stick to it," he contends. "We haven't canceled in the four years since we started the program."

Halting at a four-way stop, I survey him, curious. "Why bother going through the streets like this, then?"

Locke scowls, looking all directions before nodding me forward. "Slower on this one," he directs with a nod of his head. He's typically laid-back and more than easy-going. I've never seen him as purposeful about anything as he is about the task at hand.

"We have to be consistent. These aren't the kids whose parents sign them up for sports and camps. They're the ones who don't even make it to school some days because of lack of transportation or just negligent parents. It can't be on the kids to keep track of when we practice. Most of them are too young to have phones, and there's no one at home reminding them to head to the field. It's simple," he sweeps his hand around the car and up and down the street, "but it works."

"Typically, by the time we've made it down every street, word has spread enough that they're all waiting at the park when we get there."

"And how many kids usually show up?"

"Fifteen or twenty. Sometimes more. Seven or eight usually want to play."

"Less than half?" I challenge.

Locke hums patiently, waving to an older woman sitting on a front porch in an aluminum-frame lawn chair.

"Everyone who shows up gets a bagged lunch, plus another bagged meal to take home."

That I knew. Mrs. Lansbury, Decker, and Kylian prepared all the food this morning in an assembly-line of sorts. They worked quickly and with such precision it was obvious they'd done it before.

"All the kids have to do is show up. All I want them to have to do is show up," he emphasizes. "When they do, they know they'll have something to eat and that a safe adult is waiting. That's more than what some of them can expect on their best days."

Understanding and heartache wash over me in waves. That was me once. Home alone for days at a time. Slicing open my hand on jagged aluminum when I was too young to use a can opener on my own but desperate to get to what was inside. I was never physically abused or assaulted at home, but the neglect can be just as painful as a physical blow.

I let his words marinate in my mind. Here we are, living in a literal mansion, while there are so many kids in unsafe homes, just trying to survive. My heart hurts for Locke and for the little boy he was; he had to learn these lessons himself.

"Did you grow up around here?" I ask. I don't want to open old wounds, but I'm more than a little curious about his life before he came to live with Brenda and Gary and eventually met the guys.

"Not in this neighborhood, but in one like it. We lived closer to the coast."

Worrying my lip, I push my luck. "How old were you when you went into the system?"

"Seven."

He lets the one-word answer linger between us, sighs, then continues.

"We were playing dodgeball in gym class. I took a hard ball to the gut and promptly collapsed. Then when I got to the nurse's office..."

"Duty to report," I surmise.

It's a very real fear and one I also dealt with as a child. Avoiding the people and situations that may draw extra attention to myself became second nature from a young age. Avoiding the system was my primary goal for so long. Plenty of kids have good experiences in foster care. Some don't, though, and a child's baser instincts are often set to prefer the devil they know versus the devil they don't.

Locke nods, his expression grim. "Thank god, too."

Oh. I wasn't expecting that.

"I had internal bleeding from the beating I took the night before."

Shit on a crumbly cracker. I grip the steering wheel and bite on my inner cheek to fight back tears as emotion overwhelms my senses.

"By the time I was discharged from the hospital, it was official. I was taken straight to my first foster home."

My mind conjures up the image of a young Nicky, hurting both physically and emotionally in ways I can't begin to fathom. I was in no position to help anyone but myself all those years ago, but I find myself wishing I could go back in time and help him somehow. I want nothing more than to wipe away his pain and replace it with all the love he deserves.

He drops a hand to my knee and squeezes, pulling me from my spiraling thoughts. Melancholy fills the space between us as we finish the route. I like that he doesn't try to gloss over his truth. He doesn't sugarcoat the past, but he doesn't dwell on it, either. His tenacity is admirable. The way he rarely lets things rattle him is a skill I'd love to learn.

The last road on our route ends at a parking lot in the middle of several fields, so I peek over, waiting for instruction.

"Left up here," he points with a tatted finger. "Park next to that equipment shed."

I pull into the closest spot, put the car and park, and unbuckle. Before I can pull open the door handle, Locke grasps my wrist.

"Hold up, Hot Girl. I got you something."

He holds out a plastic shopping bag from a local business.

"You don't have to wear it now if you don't want to... I just wanted you to have the option."

I snatch the bag out of his hands. "Is that what I think it is?" My giddiness peaks when he just smiles and cocks one brow in response.

Tearing into the bag, I let out a squeal. The slinky bright red fabric is an instant giveaway.

Grinning, I lean over and kiss him, then pull the jersey all the way out of the bag. This is the first time a guy has ever gifted me his jersey, aside from Greedy's duplicitous offering, and if the warmth growing in my belly is any indication, I like the whole concept very much.

"Wait..."

I hold up the shirt, confused, as I process what I'm seeing.

It's emblazoned with a big number 9. But the name above it doesn't belong to him...

Locke tucks a strand of hair behind my ear, then caresses my jaw with the backs of his knuckles. "I know better than most that the name you're born with means nothing. More than that... sometimes it's a name you'd rather forget."

I blink at him, hit with an emotion so strong it leaves an ache gripping my chest.

"I want you to wear my number," he explains. "But I put Meyer on the back because you fought like hell to become the person you are today. I want you to know that I see you, Joey. You're so beautiful and strong, and you've had to survive and overcome so much. I'd be honored if you'd wear number nine for me, but I want you to be represented, too. I see the life you're working hard to create for yourself, and I want to be part of it."

"Nicky." I press my palms to his face and pour every emotion threatening to spill out in the tears welling behind my eyes into the kiss I plant on his lips.

Pulling back, I give him one last peck, then adjust so I can look him in the eyes.

"I love you."

He tries to shake his head, but I press more firmly on both sides of his jaw, refusing to let him shrug off my confession.

"I love you," I repeat. "I love who you are. I love who I am with you and how you make me want to be the best version of me. I'm in love with you."

Gnawing on his bottom lip, he searches my face, his eyes filling with tears that mirror mine.

"Yeah?"

I nod, sniffling back the emotion threatening to overwhelm me.

"Yeah," I whisper, kissing him again. "I love you, Nicky," I vow against his lips. "And I love this jersey," I assure him. "Thank you."

"I love you, too, Josephine Meyer. I see you. And I can't wait to watch you ride me wearing nothing but this jersey," he taunts, twisting the fabric in his fist and stealing one last kiss across the center console.

"In your dreams, Emo Boy."

He scoffs. "I think you mean *in my bed tonight*, Hot Girl."

Chapter 46

Locke

She loves me.

An admission I wasn't expecting. Words I almost couldn't bear to accept.

But now that she's said them, they're all I want to hear from her sweet, sassy lips over and over for all the days of my life.

Joey loves me.

And I love her. So damn much.

I'd do anything for her. Fight any battle. Stave off every demon. I'll be anything she wants me to be, anything she needs. I just want to be with her.

She's on the other side of the field, sitting with a few of the younger kids. One of the scrawnier boys, Ashton, holds his belly, glancing over at me every few seconds, panicked.

He ate too fast. I watched him scarf down his sandwich, then snag a few pieces of crust from nearby kids who were too distracted to notice.

If I had to guess, he's worried he'll be sick and get in trouble because of it.

I was that kid once.

Hell, I was that kid for years. Even after I was finally placed with Gary and Brenda. Survival skills and coping mechanisms don't just turn off once a child is in a safe, stable environment. It takes years of nurturing, therapy, and reprogramming to flip the switch.

I scan the group of kids who are horseplaying and still tossing the ball on the field, then make my way to the sidelines, my focus once again homed in on Joey.

She tips to one side and says something to Ashton. He nods and looks around wearing a sheepish frown, his eyes full of trepidation, but then he lowers his body onto his left side and curls up around Joey's hip and thigh.

She keeps chatting with the two little girls in front of her, but she rests a hand on Ashton's back and moves it in slow, soothing circles at the same time.

Every few seconds, she peeks down at him with a smile—reassuring him without making a scene or calling extra attention to his position.

My breath hitches in my chest as I take her in: wearing my number on her jersey, fully committed to the conversation around her, caring wholeheartedly for Ashton. She's surrounded by kids who haven't bathed or brushed their teeth in who knows how long. Yet she acts like each one of them is sacred and beloved.

Because they are.

And so is she.

Someday, she'll sit with our kids, comforting our son or laughing alongside our daughters.

She loves me.

There's no doubt in my mind that I want to spend the rest of my life loving her.

Chapter 47

Josephine

It feels so damn good to settle back into a routine. Although our routine nowadays is new and improved in a lot of ways.

I attend my two in-person classes each week and tag along to campus with one of the guys most days so Hunter and I can meet up at the library or go out to lunch. Kendrick and I spend time on the water so he can teach me how to operate the different watercrafts. I got my boating license two weeks ago, but he insists I still need more practice. Decker agrees. What Decker doesn't know, though, is that K really just wants to get me alone and finger fuck me behind the helm... after he gives his lesson and is satisfied with my progress, of course. He's an excellent teacher.

Kylian is by my side more often than not, my personal haven of safety and security, passion and pleasure.

And then there are the sweet, stolen moments with Locke.

Like now.

When we're hidden away, making out in the pantry like horny teenagers hiding from our parents, despite having nothing to conceal from anyone in this house.

He's my joy—my free-spirited happiness who's always up for anything.

"I love you," I tell him, my lips brushing his. Without giving him a chance to respond, I kiss him deeper.

"I love you, too, Joey," he says when we finally catch our breath. "And I love these lips," he groans, licking along the seam of my mouth. "So kissable. So fuckable. So delicious." His tongue dips into my mouth, teasing and swirling around the tip of mine.

With a mewl, I tease him right back, walking my fingers down his torso until they're dancing along the hem of his sweatpants.

"I could put my lips somewhere else, you know," I offer coyly, cupping his cock over the fabric as he thrusts into my palm.

"Believe me, Hot Girl. I'm well aware of all the magical things your lips can do. But we should probably—"

Unexpected brightness floods the dark space, startling us both. I whip my head around, squinting.

Kendrick's bulky frame fills most of the doorway. "Oh, shit. My bad. I was gonna grab a snack."

"Yeah. Me too," Locke deadpans. "Shove off and close the door behind you."

Resting my cheek on Nicky's chest, I smile at K so he knows the interruption doesn't bother me. Locke was about to end this anyway. Probably so we could get started on dinner. It's his night to cook, and I agreed to help.

Silence settles in when Kendrick doesn't back out of the pantry. Or make any move to leave at all.

Catching the glimmer of mischief in his gaze, I give the slightest wrinkle of my nose. He's going to push back, and I'm not sure how Nicky will react to that.

"And if I don't?" he asks in a husky challenge.

Locke's grip on my hips tightens for all of two seconds, then he bows his head and searches my face, deferring to me.

He's always so eager to please. Willing to follow my lead and submit to whatever I have in mind.

When we lock eyes, we both know which way this is about to go.

The smirk he gives me is wicked. He can read me like a book. A smutty, graphic, open-door book. He knows what I'm going to say before I even ask. Yet I still mouth "Okay?" to get his consent.

After a quick nod from Nicky, I look back at Kendrick, who's still hovering on the threshold.

"Get your snack and get out or get on your knees and help your friend."

The energy surrounding us charges in that moment. Kendrick pulls himself up straighter, like he's compelled to rise to my challenge. Locke slowly turns me in his arms so my back is to his chest.

"You're for real right now?" K asks. He closes the door behind him, but he doesn't step any farther into the expansive storage area lined with shelves of snacks and dry goods.

Nicky captures both my breasts and kneads, paying special attention to my nipples through the fabric of my crop top. I press back and sink into his touch, but I keep my focus on Kendrick.

Nicky's lips find the crook of my neck.

One finger hooks under the strap of my shirt, sliding it down my arm.

To an outsider, it would look like he's undressing me. Handling me. Offering me up to his teammate and friend.

But that's the beauty of what I share with my guys: I'm the one in control. Always.

"Come get your snack, K," I encourage. "I want to feel both your mouths on me at the same time."

Locke grunts his agreement, pushing down my top until my breasts are fully exposed.

Kendrick stalks toward us, his gaze set on my tits, then darting up to search my face. Like he can't resist the draw, he homes in on Nicky's mouth—the way it's sucking and pulling on my ear.

I crook two fingers until he's close enough to kiss. Then I cuff one of his huge shoulders and push him down.

Without resistance, Kendrick sinks to his knees, tipping his chin up and shooting me the most devilish smile.

"Let's see if you can be a team player off the field, K."

He scoffs. "Teamwork's my middle name, Mama." Then, to Locke: "Hold her for me."

In the span of two breaths, he rips down my shorts, then hoists one of my thighs up onto his shoulder. His skin is warm and sweat-slicked where it's exposed in his cutoff T-shirt, like he's just come from the gym.

His thumbs find my bikini line, caressing the skin, teasing me with his proximity to my pussy.

"Fuck, that's hot," Locke murmurs over my shoulder.

I follow his line of sight to Kendrick on his knees. The image of him, with both hands spreading me open as he hovers so close to my cunt I can feel his breath on my clit, is like gasoline to the fire Locke has already set.

"Kendrick," I whimper, thrusting forward so I can get his tongue right where I want it.

"I said hold her," he scolds.

Locke obeys, clamping an arm around my middle.

Leaning forward, he runs his nose through my pussy, inhaling and groaning in pleasure. "You got her worked up real good, Nicky. Her scent is strong. She's already fucking soaked."

Finally, he puts his tongue on me, licking from my taint to my clit. I try to buck my hips and chase the pressure, but Locke's grip on me is too strong.

"Nicky," I whimper, dropping my head back to rest on his shoulder.

"I know, baby. I know. We're going to make you feel so fucking good."

He gets to work kneading my breasts again, pinching my nipples as he sucks a mark into the tender flesh of my neck.

Kendrick seals his mouth around my clit, alternating quick flicks with long, torturous pulls of my pleasure point between his teeth.

He traces up my thigh, then teases me open with one finger, crooking it forward in the most exquisite motion.

"Fuck," I cry out. I'm lost. The euphoria is so consuming I can't make sense of all the tingles coursing through my body.

Locke's tatted hand presses into my low belly. The pressure on the outside is the perfect counterpoint to the way K's massaging my G-spot. My legs quake, and the unmistakable urge to pee flashes through me. It passes just as quickly as it came, and my body keeps climbing...

"Fuck, fuck, fuck. I'm going to come hard," I warn, too wrapped up in my own pleasure to be self-conscious.

Kendrick grunts, and Locke pinches one nipple again as he sucks on my neck.

"Come on, Hot Girl. Give him all you've got. He wants it, don't you, K?"

"Fucking come for us, Mama," he commands, pressing a second finger into me and holding it against my G-spot as he nips my clit.

That's all it takes. I scream until my voice cracks, gushing out my release and squirting all over K's hand and face.

"Fuck yeah," he praises, lapping at my thighs and pussy.

Locke moves one hand down my body to catch some for himself. "*Fuck*, Hot Girl. You soaked him, baby. That was the hottest fucking thing I've ever seen."

He rests his chin on my collarbone, then pops two fingers into his mouth, groaning. Always doting, he offers them to me next, and I lick him from tip to knuckle, tasting myself and sagging against him, giving into my boneless state.

Kendrick rises to his feet. Wiping his mouth and chin with the collar of his cutout, he eyes me up and down, the smuggest smile on his face.

"Good game, brother," he commends, raising one hand and high-fiving Locke over my shoulder.

"You did not just do that!" I scold, holding back my laughter and trying to force an outraged scowl.

K smirks and presses into me until I'm sandwiched between him and Nicky. "You said you wanted teamwork. Took us less than five minutes to make you squirt, Mama. My boy deserves a little praise too, ya know?"

I can't hold back my laughter this time, catching his face in my hands and kissing him deeper as Locke caresses the skin along my stomach and hip.

"Why don't we—"

Any and all suggestions fly out the window when the clip of heels against the hardwood floor echoes outside the door.

The three of us freeze—then bust out laughing from the ridiculous response. Who the hell would even be in the house that we'd have to hide from?

Smiling, I swivel my hips between my guys, ready to suggest we head upstairs to my room together. But then distant voices grow less distant, and I share a confused look, first with Kendrick, then over my shoulder, with Locke.

Is someone actually at the house?

Kendrick gets to work pulling up my shorts while Locke helps me get my arms back through the spaghetti straps of my shirt. I'm dressed in record time, thanks to them. I give my hair a good fluff then kiss each of my guys on the mouth.

"Raincheck?" I offer, nodding toward their crotches.

Neither balks at being left in such a state. They just herd me toward the door. With a chuckle at their antics, I smirk at them both over my shoulder as I press down on the handle on the pantry door. The second I step out into the brightly lit hall, I smack into a mass of muscle.

Horrified, I right myself, then look from the stunned expressions of Misty and another woman I don't recognize up into the eyes of a fuming Decker Crusade.

Chapter 48

Decker

"I need to speak with Josephine. Alone," I demand, shooting hard looks at Kendrick and Locke, then at Misty.

Both guys wait for Josephine to nod, effectively dismissing them. Locke pecks her on one cheek as Kendrick leans in on the other side and says something that makes her cheeks flush. Then they're gone, heading back toward the kitchen.

In that moment, I've never been more jealous of any of my brothers.

When Misty doesn't move, I pin her with a seething glare. "Excuse us," I repeat.

Misty is staring wide-eyed over my shoulder, watching Kendrick and Locke saunter away. It isn't until they're out of sight that she focuses on me and finally snaps back to it.

"Right. Okay." Smoothing a hand over her fitted black dress, she gracefully links arms with Callie, the production assistant we were just showing around the house. "Let's head outside to go over the exterior angles. We'll meet you out there in five?" she asks me.

I inhale through my nose and crush my molars together, but I nod.

I have contractual obligations to uphold.

I watch Misty and Callie head deeper into the house, waiting until they've disappeared completely before turning back to my girl.

My agitation doubles as I take her in.

Her hair's a mess. Her clothing is askew, even wet in some places, if I'm not mistaken. She looks well and thoroughly fucked, which would irritate me on its own. But it's the attitude that sends me.

Arms crossed over her chest and one foot planted on the wall behind her, she leans back and assesses me with a sneer like she can't wait to dish out the sassy remark she's surely come up with.

"You requested a private audience, your highness?" she mocks.

My teeth are clenched so tight my jaw aches as I hover closer. The boys didn't fuck her well enough if she's still this brazen afterward. There isn't enough patience in my body—maybe in the world—to deal with her haughty, bratty attitude right now.

But the clock is ticking. And this isn't a laughing matter.

"Siren," I rhapsodize, hoping the juxtaposition to her teasing is enough to catch her attention. "That woman with Misty is a production assistant. She's here for a tour so she can get a feel for the mansion—and its inhabitants—before she comes back with her camera crew to start setting up on Sunday."

She wilts right there in front of me. Dammit. My words—this situation, my obligations—are responsible for it, and that kills me.

We all know the practical aspects of what's coming for us next week: the cameras and monitoring, a total lack of privacy. We're all anxious to get it over with. The SportsZone crew is not only going to disrupt our routine, but they will intrude on what should be private moments in our home.

Cameras and media coverage are a fact of life for Kendrick and me, but a dense fog of guilt wraps around me when I think of exposing Josephine in this way.

I offered to put her and the other guys up somewhere else for the week. A rental house on the lake or a condo close to campus. They unanimously and vehemently refused.

Stepping closer, I catch her under the chin with two fingers and tilt her head back.

"I need you to behave and keep your boys in line for the rest of the afternoon. After the tour, we have a meeting to confirm the final schedule, so I suspect they'll be here a bit longer."

Understanding registers in her eyes, and she gives a quick nod—thank god—but then a smirk creeps in, because apparently, she can't resist the opportunity to rile me up.

"I'll see what I can do," she muses, tilting her face and nuzzling against my hand until I'm cupping her jaw.

"Josephine." It doesn't hold the bite it did just two minutes ago. At least we've reached an understanding. "I'm serious."

She turns her head quickly and nips at my thumb—brat. "You're always serious, Cap."

I'm done fighting her, though. At least for today. It's time I return to the hell of my own making I'm trapped in, the torture I didn't see coming because I've been too distracted to pay attention to the little details of my schedule as of late.

For one more minute, I allow myself to linger, soaking in the depth and fortitude in her blue-gray eyes and homing in on that perfect, pouty mouth.

"Why are you looking at me like that?" she breathes.

Because I want to. Because I need a reason to get through the rest of this day.

"Come out on the boat with me on Saturday night, Siren."

Her expression morphs from wanton right back to sassy. "You have a game on Saturday night, Cap."

"Afterward, then," I demand. I'm running out of time. And patience.

"What about the party?"

A thrill surges through me before I even say the words. Caressing her cheek with my thumb, I remain silent for a moment, teasing her the way she likes to tease me. "I canceled the party."

Shock washes over her. She pushes off the wall and drops her arms to her sides. "Again? Why would you do that?" Her voice is a whisper. With a long inhale, she scans the hallway, peering from one end to the other to make sure we're alone and our conversation is still truly private.

Good girl.

Double-checking that we're in the clear, I step forward, then lower my head until our mouths are close enough that we're sharing breath.

This. Her. This is what I did it for.

"Because I want to win the damn game, come home, and spend the night out on the lake with my girl."

I plant a featherlight kiss on the pulse point below her ear.

"Your girl, huh?" But her smile is softer now. And I know she'll be in my arms soon. "Are you going to let me drive the boat?" she taunts.

My phone rings in my pocket. I don't even have to pull it out to know it's Misty.

"Saturday," I repeat, walking backward down the hall so I can keep my eye on the prize.

Soft moments. Private moments. More moments with her. This is what I'm doing it for.

Chapter 49

Josephine

"Decker! Did you do this?"

We hit the landing in unison, feet tapping against the warm planks as we stroll down the dock toward the pontoon. He's got one arm wrapped around my shoulders, and he smells divine—like amber and sea salt—freshly showered after winning tonight's game.

I peek over to assess his expression, but he's focused on our destination.

Slowing at the end of the dock, he holds my hand and guides me onto the boat.

He still hasn't answered me, so I look back and raise my brows in question.

"Now you know why we took one of the ferries across the lake to and from the game," he mumbles. He's got his chin tucked, and I swear he's wearing the hint of a sheepish smile as he climbs aboard and makes his way to the captain's seat.

I do a slow spin, taking it all in. The boat is decorated with dozens and dozens of candles—battery operated, I see, now that we're closer—with twinkle lights wrapped around the poles of the bimini top that covers the helm.

In addition to the candles and the little lights, there's a massive pile of blankets laid out in the middle of the boat, along with a picnic basket and several pillows.

"Cap," I singsong, making my way over to him.

He lifts one arm when I press into his side, allowing me to wedge myself in between his body and the steering wheel. Leaning back into his chest, I tilt my face up and grip his nape so he's forced to focus on me.

"Did you make us a love nest and bring me out here to have sex?" I tease.

His brows shoot into his hairline, but he schools his expression quickly. Putting the boat in reverse, he ignores me while he adjusts the throttle and pulls back from the dock.

Finally, once we're in open water, he grumbles a reply. "I did not bring you out here to have sex, Josephine." He sighs, exasperated as always. "I brought you out here to rewrite the past and make up for the last time we were on a boat together."

Oh.

Softer, he brushes my hair over my shoulder, his lips trailing my neck with kisses. "I just want to be with you tonight. Enjoy your company. Lay beside you and forget the world for a few hours. Can you give me that, Siren?"

Shit on a crumbly cracker.

I thought I was cruising the lake with Decker Crusade, control freak, QB1, asshole extraordinaire. I had no idea I was getting on this boat with a top-tier groveler and hopeless romantic.

Shivering, I spin in his arms and look up into the onyx eyes of a man who never ceases to surprise me.

"Yes," I murmur, pushing up on tiptoes.

Our mouths connect in the softest, slowest kiss. We're both tentative, testing the way we move together. He matches my pace, weaving his hands into my hair. He kisses me like I'm the most precious thing in the world—like his happiness begins and ends in this moment.

Pulling back slightly, he scans the water around us. I ease back down until I'm sure-footed, giving him space, because ensuring our safety is critical to his mental health.

Satisfied, he focuses on me again, a smirk coming out to play as he thumbs my lower lip.

"Any other questions or sassy remarks?"

I grin.

Broody Decker is fun to poke. Swoony Decker takes my breath away. But playful, joking Decker might be my favorite. It's a rarity to see him like this: at ease, comfortable enough to let his guard down and crack a joke or two. It's a sacred side of him he so rarely shares with anyone.

Heart so damn happy I swear it's floating like a buoy in my chest, I slam my mouth closed, pretend to zip my lips shut, and throw the invisible key over the side of the boat.

I want to play. I want to revel in this night with him. Soak up every moment of what he's planned for us. I want to lie beside him and forget the world for a few hours, just like he said.

True to his word, Decker lets me drive. Though I suppose *drive* is a bit of a stretch. He does allow me to control the wheel and throttle, but he sits behind me in the captain's seat the entire time and watches my every move. After a while, when he's obviously satisfied with my skills, thanks to Kendrick's teachings, he grows bold enough to tickle my sides, kiss my neck, and graze his hands over my collarbone and between my breasts.

Not out here for sex, my ass.

Eventually, we drop anchor in the middle of the lake and enjoy the picnic he packed for us.

Now we're lying beside each other in the blanket pile he swears isn't a sex nest, despite my continued teasing and my not-so-subtle touches. But it's been over an hour, and sadly, he hasn't taken the bait.

His body is ridiculous—impenetrably hard, all sharp lines and stark definition. He's a mass of muscle. More machine than man in some ways. With me, though, he's willing to crack open his tough exterior every now and then. In those moments, he lets me see what's really in his heart. They're sometimes hard-won, but that's what makes these quiet moments together all the more precious to me.

Draped over his chest, I've got one hand under his shirt, my palm flat against his abs, and a leg draped over his thighs. The rock of the boat on the water is lulling us both to sleep, casting a dreamy sort of haze as the water laps at the sides of the vessel.

Right now, in this moment, I feel closer to him than I ever have. Physically. Mentally. Emotionally. Thoughts that are shocking yet also not surprising keep springing up in my mind.

I want him.

I might be in love with him.

I desperately want more, and I need him to get on board with the relationship that's flourished between Kylian, Locke, Kendrick, and me.

The idea of broaching that topic, though, is terrifying. So I lie on top of him in silence, running my nails along his scalp as I match my inhalations to his.

Humming, he squeezes my ass and dips his nose along my jaw. "What are you thinking about?" he whispers.

Steeling myself and calling on my inner courage, I shoot my shot. "How much I want this."

His hand falters, coming to rest on my low back. "This?" he asks.

"You, Decker. Us. All of us, together."

He exhales, teasing up the hem of my shirt until his fingertips find the base of my spine. "I know" is all he says as he trails a path up and down my back.

"I don't think you do." Pushing up, I hover above him, scanning his face and willing him to read the sincerity in my eyes. "What we're all doing—Kylian, Kendrick, Locke, and me—it feels like family to me, Decker. I want you to be part of it. The mansion feels like home. You all feel like safety... and although I sometimes still question whether I deserve to be this happy—"

"You do," he growls.

Smiling softly, I press one finger to his lips. "Let me finish. You make me believe I'm worthy. You give me hope that there's a bright future ahead if I can just stay present and stave off my demons long enough to get there. I feel capable—hopeful—with the four of you by my side. I want you, Decker. I want you for myself, and I want you to be part of what I share with the guys."

He raises his brows, silently asking for permission to respond.

I could go on forever, honestly, pleading my case, but when it comes down to it, he'll have to make the decision for himself. Either he wants to be with us—all of us—or I need to cut him loose once and for all.

Kylian's words from the day I came home from the hospital float through my mind. *Cut me out right now while I'm still low, while the distance I have to fall isn't so great.*

I don't want to lose Decker. I can't bear the thought of him not being all-in. But any further, any deeper, and we'll be too far into this for any of us to survive the carnage if it falls apart.

With a sigh, he rolls over so we're chest to chest and props his head on his hand. He watches me with his signature surly scowl while I keep my expression impassive, letting him look. Praying he finds what he's searching for in my eyes.

"What does it look like in the future, though, Siren?"

I don't have to think twice about my answer. It's a fantasy I play out in my mind every night as I'm drifting off to sleep.

"Like this," I whisper, leaning forward until my lips brush his. "Me in your bed, considering you won't fuck me on this boat..."

"Josephine," he scolds. "I'm serious."

I press a finger to his lips again. "I am too," I tease. "Close your eyes, Cap. Let me paint the picture for you. I want you to imagine the future the way I see it."

He reluctantly does as I ask, and I keep my palm on his cheek so he knows I'm right here. I'm not going anywhere.

"It's me in your bed when you're home. It's Nicky and me cheering for you in the stands while Kylian is working on the sidelines for the team you sign with.

"It's us making plans for your bye week, flying out with Emilia and Jade to see Kendrick play. It's traveling with you sometimes, and it's staying back and holding down the fort others."

He peeks his eyes open, glancing in the direction of the mansion. "You'd want us to live here?"

My heart beats double time. He sounds... hopeful. Like he's actually considering the possibility of the life I'm so desperate to create with him.

"Maybe. We'd have to see where you and Kendrick end up after the draft. I don't care where we call home, as long as we're together."

His Adam's apple bobs as he swallows, but I press on.

"It's family dinners. Movie nights. Days at the beach, and yeah, a lot of sex, too."

He cracks a smile, and I can't help but match it.

"It's a promise to ourselves that we'll put each other first. Always. It's unconventional, but it's beautiful and real. It's what I want. More than anything in the world. Can you see it, Cap? You and me... plus all of us together?"

His lashes flutter, his gaze cast down. When he lifts his eyes to meet mine, his raw, vulnerable truth is dancing right on the surface.

"I can see it," he admits. "It's a pretty fantastic picture, Siren. It might be a pipe dream... but I can see it."

Holding my breath, I push harder.

"So then, I guess the real question is, do you want it?"

A beat passes. Then another. I refuse to look anywhere but directly into his eyes, noting the way the brightest stars reflect in his dark irises as he considers me, unblinking.

Finally, he whispers, "I do. I don't know how to do this or what all the rules are, but—"

I silence him with a kiss. Because none of that matters now.

He said yes. He wants me. Us. He's in, and that's all I needed to hear.

He kisses me back with an intensity that's akin to a claiming, his mouth forcing mine to yield and react to his as he dominates the moment.

What he doesn't realize is that he doesn't have to try so hard. For as much as I like to tease and taunt him, I know he craves control. In due time, I'll show Decker Crusade just how cooperative, docile, and submissive I can be.

"Fuck," he mutters, pulling back and adjusting himself in his pants.

I don't tease him or try to take things further. He's at his limit.

And as corny as it might sound, his original vision for this night is enough for me right now. Being out here in his arms? It's more than enough.

I'm okay going slow, because what we're building to is a forever kind of love. The kind that a person doesn't recover from. There's sanctuary in the way Decker shares himself with me. He doesn't just desire me. He cherishes me. Like I'm the most precious thing in his life. Like he would sacrifice anything and everything for me, even to his own demise.

I love the soft, tender care radiating off him right now.

But he still better be a bossy asshole in the bedroom.

I yawn to stifle a laugh at my own thoughts. If Decker's plan is to edge me into submission, dammit, it honestly might be working.

He yawns, too. He's had a long, exhausting day. By now, he's usually shut in his room, already asleep, even on party nights.

"Should we head back?" I ask, snuggling closer and repositioning myself like he's my favorite pillow.

Stroking my hair, he hums softly. "Not yet. I want to hold you just a little longer. This is happiness, Josephine. This is what it's all for. I want to remember this moment with you in my arms for as long as I live."

Tears threaten to spill over as I press my cheek into his chest and cuddle closer. I want to remember this moment forever, too.

Chapter 50

Josephine

"God, I'm starving," I declare, scanning the breakfast spread. It's just as elaborate as always, and that makes it so damn hard to know where to start.

It's Sunday, so I've been up since sunrise. That's the deal. Kylian sleeps alone in the Nest on Saturday nights so he can decompress, but only as long as I promise to come up first thing Sunday morning.

Watching the filtered sunlight sparkle through the stained glass of the cupola while Kylian eats me out is the ultimate way to wake up. I don't know which one of us likes it more.

"Oh yeah?" Kylian whispers. He wraps his arms around me, then teases his hands down the front of the boxers I stole from him before coming downstairs. "I thought you were fully satisfied."

One finger dips lower, the tip connecting with my clit in the lightest of touches.

"Baby, why are you still so wet?" he asks, licking a path along my neck and pinning me to the island in front of a bowl of fruit. It's all I can do to set down my plate and grip the edge of the counter.

"I thought I cleaned you up before we came down here," he teases, his hand traveling farther into the boxers. He pinches my swollen, sensitive clit between his thumb and finger. "Unless this just happened, and you're wet again?"

His breath is hot on my neck, his words kerosene to the fire smoldering in my belly. I shudder when he gathers all the fresh arousal from between my legs and slathers it around my pussy.

"This is all new?" he asks, swirling a finger through my folds. "You're fucking soaked, baby," he purrs reverently, shallowly fucking that one finger into my pussy. He kisses along my neck again, and I can't help but grind back against his cock.

I really was satisfied when we came down the stairs. Leave it to Kylian to ignite the glowing embers settling inside me.

"Such a needy girl. You like knowing that all your other boyfriends are right through that door? That at any second, one of them could walk in and see me playing with your pussy?" He adds a second finger, then draws them out so slowly my hips chase his hand on instinct. "So fucking needy," he murmurs again, using his hips to pin me against the island. Once I'm immobile, he pinches my clit hard, and he doesn't let go.

"Kylian," I pant, moisture surging from me and coating my thighs in a way that's going to be awfully apparent if he keeps this up.

"So fucking messy," he murmurs again. Except it sounds like praise. And it makes the walls of my pussy clench with desire.

He grazes his teeth against my shoulder, only heightening the sensation. "I should spread you out on this counter right now between the berries and the whipped cream and fuck you so hard you gush all over the quartz."

Holy. Shit.

The heat is all-consuming. I'm so sensitive and well-fucked I ache.

But I can't make him stop. I never want him to stop.

"Please, Daddy," I whimper as he presses his erection into my ass. "Please, let me—"

"There you two are!" Mrs. Lansbury calls, pushing through the door that connects the dining room to the kitchen.

Kylian has just enough time to remove his hand. Once Mrs. Lansbury is focused on the coffee, he wraps his arm around my chest.

"Clean it up, naughty girl," he taunts, holding his hand in front of my face.

I pull back but can't go far. I'm trapped in his hold. There's no way in hell I want sweet Mrs. Lansbury to watch me suck my own cum off my boyfriend's fingers.

He drops his chin to my shoulder when I stall.

But then Mrs. Lansbury speaks again.

"Kylian."

Her tone is low, serious in a way I've never heard before. I shake myself out of the lust-filled haze Kylian has put me in yet again, only to catch sight of her pained, panicked expression.

"You need to get in there. Both of you. Now."

Kylian stiffens and moves to my side, suddenly on high alert. His eyes meet mine for a fraction of a second. His furrowed brow and the subtle shrug of his shoulders tell me he doesn't know what's going on, either.

"Grab something quick," he instructs, reaching past me to snag a bagel and a sausage link he pops directly into his mouth.

I reach for the closest thing available—the stupid mixed berry blend I almost got fucked beside—and spoon some into a bowl.

He grabs my hand a second later, pulling me behind him as he hustles into the dining room.

A sense of déjà vu washes over me as I take in the scene before me.

Decker and Kendrick are seated on one side of the long table. Locke is positioned on the other. Misty is standing before all of them, but this time, she's got a literal projector set up behind her.

It's the images illuminated on the wall that stop me in my tracks.

It's me.

Hoisted up in Decker's arms on the field after they beat South Chapel, our lips inches apart in what sure as shit looks like an almost kiss.

The screen changes.

It's me again.

Snuggling between Kendrick and Locke out on the lower deck, K's hand spread wide across my stomach while my arms are wrapped around Nicky's neck.

"That was just last night," I whisper, mortified.

Every head in the room turns in my direction.

A satisfied smirk paints Misty's face. "Good to know. That'll help me piece the timeline together and better respond to all the inquiries we're getting about the Lake Chapel Crusaders' *number one fan.*" Shit. The bite in her tone means we're all in trouble.

"Don't say another fucking word," Kylian growls under his breath. He guides me around the table and pulls out the chair next to Locke, then motions for me to sit.

"What is this?" he demands, jutting his chin toward the projector, then flicking his gaze to Decker.

"*This*"—Misty huffs, regarding the screen, then sweeping her perfectly manicured hand between the five of us—"is the makings of a PR nightmare."

My stomach knots with dread. I knew there were photographers on the field that day with Decker—but I never thought someone would take our picture here at the house. During a clearly private moment. When the five of us were the only people here.

Kylian clamps a hand down on my thigh in a protective hold. He barely tolerates Misty as it is, and he doesn't bother to hide his disdain as he shoots her a glare, then angrily swipes at his phone's screen. I know exactly where he stands, but what about the rest of them?

One by one, I try to silently garner their attention. Neither Kendrick nor Decker will look at me. And there's nothing reassuring about either of their expressions.

Kendrick's face is ashen, a hard glare flicking between the screen and Misty.

Decker's face is blank. His carefully constructed public mask is in place, though his jaw is working overtime. I lean forward, ready to speak, when he finally looks at me.

It's the subtle, barely there nod of his head that makes my heart rate spike. Whatever this is—whatever's about to go down—Decker is deferring to me.

With her hands planted on her hips, Misty looks from Decker to me, then follows the length of Kylian's arm where it's possessively resting on my leg.

"I need a complete and honest rundown about all this so I know what I'm dealing with here."

It's Kendrick who speaks up first. "No, you do not."

Her gaze narrows on him, but she ignores his comment and regards Decker instead. "A camera crew and two production assistants are down on the beach collecting B-roll as we speak. You'll be on camera—*on the record*—and under scrutiny twenty-four seven in one week's time."

I shut my eyes as anticipatory dread swirls inside me at the reminder of everything involved with the SportsZone coverage. Decker gave us all an out—suggested we leave and camp out somewhere until it's over—but I couldn't stand to leave any of them, let alone break up the group because of my own insecurities.

"This feature has been in the works for months. It's the biggest publicity push we have in our arsenal ahead of the draft. Thomas flies in next week. The feature is woven into seven sponsorship deals. And yet despite all the planning, all the strategy, and all the work we've put into it, I'm being blindsided by what the 'Life of A Crusader' actually entails, it seems."

She clicks back a slide to the picture of Decker and me.

"The feature is supposed to follow Decker, although you'll benefit from the additional coverage ahead of the draft, too, Kendrick. Per the contractual agreement, the crew will have complete access to the house and to your lives for up to ten days. Everything is on the record. Everyone who lives here"—she shoots a wary, peeved glance my way—"is subject to be interviewed and included."

"No." Kylian's objection is loud and absolute.

Misty barks out a mocking laugh. "You've already signed off on this."

Heart dropping to my stomach, I search Decker's face. When I get no reaction, I look to Kendrick and Locke and finally Kylian.

"I didn't sign anything," I whisper, my voice cracking on the last word as I fight back tears.

"You did not," the other woman confirms. "And that's a problem in and of itself. Everyone who lives in this house is required to sign an NDA. Decker knows this." She glances at Cap. "Thomas has already been informed."

"We're done here," Decker declares, rising to his feet.

"We're not, actually," Misty counters, pointing her clicker at the screen.

The picture comes into focus in slow motion.

Though picture isn't an accurate description. It's *pictures*. Plural. It's a collage. A collage of regrettable choices and stupid decisions, made by a young girl trying to look so much older than she actually was. Though childhood hadn't really been an option for her to begin with.

It's pictures of me at fifteen and sixteen. Grainy, red-eyed photos of me partying: double-fisting beers, pulling on a bong. It's pictures I haven't seen in years. Pictures that have been rounded up and used to deliberately destroy once before.

Near the bottom, an out-of-focus shot proves to be the worst offender.

It's me, unconscious, being carried by my hands and feet by two boys who fucking knew better but took what they wanted anyway.

Never let them get you to the second location.

I gulp past the fury—the shame, the outrage—threatening to incinerate me. It doesn't matter where she got the photos or what she knows. All that matters is that she's trying to use them against me now.

I've let these pictures pull me under once before. I refuse to allow anyone to weaponize them against me ever again.

Standing slowly, I focus on taking measured, even breaths. Beside me, Kylian matches my movements and also rises to his feet.

I smooth my hands down the front of my Crusader's T-shirt, then rest them gently on the table, steadying myself. For a handful of heartbeats,

I study the images illuminated on the wall behind Misty. I stare into the eyes of a girl who has overcome and survived too much to roll over and give up now.

When I finally glance around the room, I realize I'm not alone. All four of the men around the table are also standing. Watching me, encouraging me, deferring to me.

I inhale and straighten my spine, setting my sights on the woman at the head of the table.

"I don't know where you got those pictures or why you felt compelled to put them in a *slideshow presentation*, considering you're propagating photos of a minor without consent."

Misty huffs and opens her mouth to defend herself, I assume, but Decker shuts her down before she can get a single word out.

"She's speaking," he growls with so much animosity Misty's mouth audibly snaps shut.

Good. I hope she chipped a veneer.

"I will not be shamed, manipulated, or coerced because of choices I made when I was a child. Or by footage that was used against me in a rape case. Because that's what that is." I tilt my chin toward the screen behind her as Misty pales to a ghostly white. "Those are pictures of a child."

I gulp past the sick threatening to rise up in my chest and push forward. I do it for the girl I used to be. I do it for the woman I am today.

"And that picture in the bottom right corner," I sneer, my voice shaking, "was taken moments before my unconscious body was taken into a garage and I was sexually assaulted."

Misty looks like she's going to be sick. I hope her dress is dry-clean only.

"If you were going for shock value, you lost. They already know. Every person in this room knows what happened to me when I was sixteen years old." I cock a brow. "And the pictures you shared from the game last week? And from the patio last night? Those were all taken after they knew the details about the girl I used to be."

I step back from the table, physically shaking. My voice quavers as I deliver my final request.

"Leave me out of this. All of it—any of it. I don't want to interfere with the guys' careers, but I also won't stand to be bullied and manipulated because you feel threatened."

The screen goes black as the last word leaves my mouth. It's then that I realize Kylian's no longer by my side.

He pulled the plug on the projector.

He skirts around Misty, mumbling "excuse me" and snatches her laptop off the table.

"Let's go," he whispers, grasping my elbow gently and encouraging me forward. Two steps later, Locke's hand connects with my low back.

Misty lets out a cry of protest, but Decker immediately shuts her down once again.

"You and I have some things to discuss," he snarls, crossing his arms over his chest.

He nods at Kendrick and mouths, "Go."

I deflate with relief when Kendrick's eyes meet mine. He doesn't focus anywhere but on me as he makes his way to join us.

As soon as we push through the dining room door, leaving Decker to deal with Misty, I slump against the wall.

Shit on a crumbly cracker.

Will I ever truly escape who I was or what happened?

This is all too much.

And yet—I'm still standing.

I'm still standing, with my guys by my side.

"Baby. You handled that beautifully. You did so good. You're okay now. We're here. What do you need?" Kylian implores, a pained expression screwing up his face.

I inhale and close my eyes, willing myself to keep it together.

Surprisingly, I'm *not* on the cusp of breaking down.

I'm spent, sure. Tired in a way that sleep won't rectify. But maybe there's something else that will.

"Fresh air," I answer as I force my eyes open and look to each of them. "Fresh air and sunshine. Maybe an afternoon at the beach? But I want to wait for Cap."

"You got it, Mama." Kendrick pulls me into his side and kisses my hair, then takes my hand to lead us out the back door.

Chapter 51

Josephine

As soon as we step out into the sun, I feel lighter. Brighter. Proud of myself for standing up to Misty. Hopeful that this feature coverage won't be a big deal and that any chatter about my relationship with the guys will blow over quickly. By the time I step fully into the light, I'm practically skipping down the steps that lead from the upper deck to the beach.

But then lightning strikes, sending a bolt of panic through me.

It's out of place. Illogical. Lightning should be impossible on such a cloudless, sunny morning.

But then there's another flash. Then two more in quick succession.

I blink back the tears I didn't invite and swallow past the panic clogging my throat.

The flashes, they're real. But they aren't lightning.

"The fuck?" Kendrick growls, spotting the photographers holding a massive reflector down by the lake. The group consists of two men with cameras, a woman who's waving her arms as though she's directing their movements, and a fourth person who's angling the reflector.

Shit on a crumbly cracker.

Light. Sunshine. Freedom. That's all I wanted.

Yet I walked out the door of one nightmare and stepped firmly into a fresh version of hell.

I need space. Shelter from the cameras. I'm desperate to put distance between us and the house.

"Can we go out on the boat?" I call back to the guys. Without waiting for a response, I dip around Kendrick and jog down the stairs ahead of them.

I'm okay.

I am here. This is now.

Once I get a little space, I can catch my breath. I can take a minute to make sense of this morning without the prying eyes and flashing lights of—

"Whoa!"

There's another flash, this one much closer. Black spots dance in my vision, but they don't block out the sight of a man who seemingly came out of nowhere and is now standing only feet from me.

He's holding a massive camera, not even looking through the viewfinder as he snaps away.

Picture after picture. Shot after shot.

The panic slams into me at full force. Because this asshole is taking pictures of *me*.

He's just one stair below me now, so I cut right, attempting to go around him.

But instead of moving out of the way like any decent human would, he steps directly into my path.

Not only that; he shifts so we're on the same stair, making it impossible for me to step around him without falling.

He's so close I rear back to avoid coming into contact with him, and in the process, I lose my balance. Throwing my arms out, I try to steady myself, but I'm too late.

I close my eyes, bracing for impact.

But I'm not falling after all.

Blunt nails dig into the tender skin on the underside of my upper arm. I yelp at the sharp pain and wince when the man's grip tightens.

"Josephine? Or is it Joey? Jo? Or maybe I should call you Jolene?" he sneers.

I step back, yanking my arm to shake him loose. But his grip just grows tighter the more I struggle.

"Let her fucking go!"

A blur whizzes into my field of vision, and a second later, the fingers digging into my arm disappear. Relief is instant.

Blinking, I home in on the commotion, taking in the scene before me. It's Locke.

It's Locke, on the ground below me, straddling the man who had his hand wrapped around my arm.

It's Locke, screaming "don't you fucking touch her! I saw you! I saw you, man! I saw you make her stumble. I saw the way you grabbed her!"

It's Locke, pounding into the face and chest of the asshole who had his hands on me, even as blood seeps from the man's nose.

It's Locke, being pulled off the offender by Kendrick and Kylian but fighting against their hold, lunging toward the man, hell-bent on continuing what he started.

It's Locke, being photographed by the people on the beach—the colleagues, I assume, of the jackass photographer—as they scramble to come to their friend's aid and document the altercation.

It's Locke, looking at me with the most heart-wrenching expression as we overhear one of the other photographers calling 911.

It's Locke, who finally wraps his arms around me, and whispers, "Baby, please don't cry."

In that moment, his words sound like a goodbye.

Chapter 52

Kendrick

Everyone's retreated to separate sides of the beach by the time the red and blue lights of a police vessel cut across the water.

I grew up on the lake, and being the son of the Lake Chapel sheriff means I've got more insight into what's coming than most. The clock is running out for all of us.

As soon as they dock, we're done.

Someone's life is about to take an unexpected turn for the worse.

It's like the two-minute warning, but with so much more at stake.

I survey my brothers, my girl. Kylian has one protective arm wrapped around Jojo, but his focus is cast down on his phone. I know without asking that he's working overtime to get rid of as much evidence as possible.

He knows how to play his part. Just like I know how to play mine.

Decker hasn't come outside, meaning Kylian updated him and he knows exactly what's going on. Keeping Misty out of this so we can handle it without her input is crucial.

We all have roles to play. Some are harder than others.

To her credit, our girl's keeping it together beautifully. She's rattled, but her focus is on Nicky. Her arms are wrapped tight around his waist, her chin nuzzling into his shoulder as she reassures him in soft, hushed tones.

I breathe through the emotion that tightens through my chest as I take him in.

He's so fucking wrecked right now. And not because of what he did.

Nicky's been flaring for weeks—has been since the fucking Sharks took her and we spent those three days desperately trying to get her back.

No one understands what he's dealing with better than me. Even at that, I don't have a good grasp on how the chronic, unrelenting inflammation from his rheumatoid arthritis eats away at him. I've been in remission for nearly two years. Even at its worst, I can look forward to the moment my lupus flare will recede and I'll get a fucking break.

Not Nicky.

His baseline pain is beyond what most people deal with on their worst day.

Throwing a punch and lashing out isn't who he is. He's a fucking philosophy major. A pacifist through and through. He's not well right now. Not himself. Operating from a place of desperation and pain.

There's absolutely no way he can sit on the cold, unyielding bench in a cell for even an hour without severely impacting his physical and mental health.

It can't stand.

I won't allow it.

Decidedly, I make my way over to them, zeroed in on Kylian.

"What sort of evidence are we dealing with?" I ask, tipping my chin toward his phone. I assume he's already knocked out the Wi-Fi and cut off the towers and satellites for all the major service providers. A benefit to living in the middle of the lake? We can control every outgoing message and attempted upload so long as the devices haven't left the isle.

"Blocked. Done. Even corrupted the one phone so there's no way to recover footage. It's still their word against ours, though. And I can't do much about the bloody nose or nasty bruises that fucker will be sporting in a few hours. Nicky's got a mean left hook."

"Kylian."

He meets my gaze, which takes concerted effort on his part. He can hear the trepidation in my tone, I'm sure of it, so he's pushing past the discomfort for my benefit. I need to level with him and make sure he understands what's about to happen so he can keep the others calm.

"I know what I'm doing." I lick my lips and steal a glance at Locke. "Make sure he ices and rests that hand. Don't let her panic. Keep Cap grounded. Keep her safe."

His light blue eyes narrow behind his glasses and scan my face, blinking quickly as he processes my words. After a breath, he gives me a quick bow of his head. It's all the confirmation I need.

I glance over my shoulder, gauging the distance between the police boat and the dock. I've got thirty or forty seconds until they dock, then maybe another minute before they reach us, depending on who's on that boat and just how much authority they feel like swinging around today.

"Jojo."

Her eyes snap to mine, and my stomach twists with dread. She looks so goddamn worried. Forlorn, distressed. I was off base with my assumption. I'm not the only one who knows exactly what state Nicky's in right now and what that jail cell will do, not only to his pain, but to his spirit.

She sees him. She sees us all. She's a beacon of hope to each and every one of us, lighting up our world when and how we need her.

"Come here."

She rushes me, somehow understanding the gravity of the situation before I've even made my intentions known.

I cradle the back of her head and bow low, breathing in the sweet, feminine scent and committing it to memory.

"That's my girl," I murmur into her hair, caressing her spine. With a quick dip, I can't resist giving her peachy ass a squeeze.

Fuck. Everything has changed between us so quickly. The depth of my desire for her, the lengths I'll go to make her happy, to keep her safe. It all happened too fast. But I have no regrets. I wouldn't change a damn thing.

"You hold us together, Jojo. You know that, right? Be good. Be strong for them. Don't let them fall apart."

"K—"

I cut her off with a bruising kiss, pushing my tongue into her mouth, desperate for this moment. Desperate to claim her, to make sure she goddamn knows I'm coming back for more.

She matches my energy, just like she always does. She kisses me like it's the first time and the last time. I pour everything I am and everything I want to be for her into our kiss.

It's a vow. A promise. It's everything I'm too chicken to say yet but desperate to make sure she feels.

Forcing myself to pull back, I nod to Kylian, and he springs into action. He wraps his arms around her from behind the second I let her go.

The red and blue lights reflect in the lenses of his glasses as we lock eyes.

He nods once.

It's time.

Behind us, the production folks and photographer are recounting the scene, growing increasingly agitated as they approach with officers by their side.

A cursory glance at the group confirms they sent Officer Rodriguez, plus a greenhorn I've never met. I've known Rodriguez since I was a kid, which makes this both easier and harder.

Locke's eyes are filled with dread, focused on the officers as they grow nearer.

"Don't fight it, Nicky," I advise, cupping the back of his neck as gently as I can manage but squeezing enough to get his attention.

His Adam's apple bobs beneath the ink covering his throat as he nods, though he doesn't look my way. He's too intent on what's unfolding twenty feet away.

I step in front of him and lean in close until our foreheads are touching, forcing him to meet my gaze.

"Don't fight it," I repeat. "It's for you. It's for her and for everything we're going to be. You got me?"

He doesn't have time to answer. Doesn't have time to process my words.

Officer Rodriguez is right behind me now, so I spin to intercept the play and cut her off at the pass.

"Nicholas Lockewood," she starts, glancing at me, then back at my brother, "you are under arr—"

"I did it."

Silence.

Silence so loud, I swear my eardrums might burst.

"I threw the punch," I admit, stepping in front of Locke and holding my hands out in front of me. The photographer opens his mouth to argue, so I lunge forward, moving too fast for anyone to stop me. I'm right up in his face before Rodriguez realizes what's going on.

"I'll fucking sack him again if he opens his mouth. And this time, I won't hold back."

The greenhorn springs into action.

I let him pull me back, clasping my arms behind my back so it's easier for him to cuff me.

Nicky's yelling in my direction.

Jojo's sob pierces through my heart.

Rodriguez watches me with calculated consideration, scanning over my friends—*my family*—before meeting my gaze once again.

Sighing, she knows I've got her.

I admitted to the crime.

There's no evidence to the contrary.

Given who I am, and my pops's position with the force, her hands are more than tied.

They're cuffed.

Just like mine are about to be.

"Kendrick Taylor, you are under arrest. You have a right to remain silent. Anything you say can be used against you in court. You have a right to talk to a lawyer and to have them present when the police interrogate you..."

I don't need to hear my rights.

All I need to know is that I did the right thing.

For him. For her. *For us.*

Afterword

The way this ending HURT to write. Ugh. I'm so, so sorry!!

If you're confused, frustrated, livid, and yeah, maybe still a little hot and bothered from what Mrs. Lansbury interrupted in the kitchen—I see you. I AM you. And I appreciate you! Thank you for going on this journey with me. This is your gentle reminder that this *is* a romance series!! Joey and her boys will get to happily ever after... eventually. It just might hurt a bit more before we get there.

If you loved this story, please consider leaving a review on Amazon or Goodreads to show your support. I would also highly recommend signing up for my email newsletter. I'll be sharing extended excerpts and lots of updates about the Boys of Lake Chapel in the coming months.

Acknowledgments

This book was made possible thanks to my infinitely supportive husband, my outstanding frienditors, several mental health professionals, and Baby Brightside finally sleeping through the night... sort of.

Special shoutouts to those who walked by my side on this journey:

David, AKA Mr. Abby, who just *gets* me and usually knows what I need before I do. How sweet it is to be seen and loved by you.

Mel, for providing infinite emotional support, wisdom, and empathy in support of this story. Thank you for traveling all the way to Ohio this summer, and holding my hand (and holding back judgement) as I flailed myself on the table of the AirBNB and tortured us about the trajectory of this series. I am so grateful for our friendship and our cosmic connection.

Beth, for letting me f*** up your calendar all year long, and for diligently updating my medical charts on a weekly (daily?) basis. Where would I be (who would I even be?!) without your friendship and support. I love and appreciate you so much!

Silver, for helping me create my dream covers and graphics for this series, and for embracing every project and challenge I dream up!

Alina, Ashley, Jen, Jessi, Kelly, and Krystal, for beta reading the only "closed door" romance I've ever written, and for forgiving me for sending you such an underwritten version of this story. Your feedback and encouragement was critical to craft this into the book it is today!

To the readers, reviewers, and influencers who embraced Joey and her boys, and who kept talking about them long after release week. You've been instrumental in blowing up this series and and making Stats Daddy a household name.

To my Personal ARC + Promo team members, many of whom have been with me for years at this point. Thank you for embracing every story I dream up, and for loving my characters so well. I love you more than Kylian loves extra sprinkles!

More From Abby Millsaps

presented in order of publication

When You're Home
While You're There
When You're Home for the Holidays
When You're Gone
Rowdy Boy
Mr. Brightside
Fourth Wheel
Full Out Fiend
Hampton Holiday Collective
Too Safe: Boys of Lake Chapel Book One
Too Fast: Boys of Lake Chapel Book Two

About The Author

Abby Millsaps is an author and storyteller who loves to unapologetically angsty romance. Her characters are relatable, lovable, and occasionally confused about the distinction between right and wrong. Her books are set in picturesque settings that feel like home.

Abby started writing romance in 7th grade. Then in 8th grade, she failed to qualify for the Power of the Pen State Championships because "all her submissions contained the same theme: young people falling in love." #LookAtHerNow

Abby met her husband at a house party the summer before her freshman year of college. He had a secret pizza stashed in the trunk of his car that he was saving for a midnight snack— how was she supposed to resist? When Abby isn't writing, she's reading, traveling, and raising three daughters.

Connect with Abby
Website: www.authorabbymillsaps.com
Instagram: @abbymillsaps
TikTok: @authorabbymillsaps
Email: authorabbymillsaps@gmail.com
Newsletter: https://geni.us/AuthorAbbyNewsletter
Facebook Reader Group: Abby's Full Out Fiends

Printed in Great Britain
by Amazon